Saying Yes To The Dress!

CARA COLTER

SORAYA LANE

DONNA ALWARD

MIX
Paper from
responsible sources

FSC
www.fsc.org
FSC C007454

This book is produced from independently certified FSC™
paper to ensure responsible forest management.

For more information visit: www.harpercollins.co.uk/green

Printed and bound in Spain
by CPI, Barcelona

MILLS & BOON

First Published in Great Britain 2018
by Mills & Boon, an imprint of HarperCollins*Publishers*
1 London Bridge Street, London, SE1 9GF

SAYING YES TO THE DRESS! © 2018 Harlequin Books S. A.

The Wedding Planner's Big Day © 2016 Cara Colter
Married For Their Miracle Baby © 2016 Soraya Lane
The Cowboy's Convenient Bride © 2016 Donna Alward

ISBN: 978-0-263-27462-2

1018

Cara ... bia,
Canad... ... nall
... ...rom
...rs, and you can learn more about her and contact her
... ...ugh Facebook.

... child, **Soraya Lane** dreamed of becoming an author. Fast
...ward a few years, and Soraya is now living her dream! She
...ribes being an author as 'the best job in the world'. She
... with her own real-life hero and two young sons on a
... farm in New Zealand, surrounded by animals, with an
... overlooking a field where their horses graze.

...ore information about Soraya, her books and her writing
...isit www.sorayalane.com.

...a Alward is a busy wife and mother of three (two
...ters and the family dog), and she believes hers is the best
... the world: a combination of stay-at-home mum and
... ...e novelist. An avid reader since childhood, Donna has
... made up her own stories. She completed her arts degree
... ...lish literature in 1994, but it wasn't until 2001 that she
... her first full-length novel and found herself hooked on
... ...g romance. In 2006, she sold her first manuscript, and
now ...rites warm, emotional stories for Mills & Boon.

... new home office in Nova Scotia, Donna loves being
... ...n the east coast of Canada after nearly twelve years in
Al... ...a, where her career began, writing about cowboys and
the ...est. Donna's debut romance, *Hired by the Cowboy*, was
a...d a Booksellers' Best Award in 2008 for Best
...ional Romance.

W... the Atlantic Ocean only minutes from her doorstep,
... ...a has found a fresh take on life and promises even more
... ...omances in the near future!

... loves to hear from readers. You can contact her through
... ...bsite, www.donnaalward.com, or follow@DonnaAlward
... ...witter.

THE WEDDING PLANNER'S BIG DAY

CARA COLTER

To all those readers who have made the last 30 years
such an incredible journey.

CHAPTER ONE

"No."

A paper fluttered down on her temporary desk, slowly floating past Becky English's sunburned nose. She looked up, and tried not to let her reaction to what she saw—or rather, whom she saw—show on her face.

The rich and utterly sexy timbre of the voice should have prepared her, but it hadn't. The man was gorgeous. Bristling with bad humor, but gorgeous, nonetheless.

He stood at least six feet tall, and his casual dress, a dark green sports shirt and pressed sand-colored shorts, showed off a beautifully made male body. He had the rugged look of a man who spent a great deal of time out of doors. There was no sunburn on his perfectly shaped nose!

He had a deep chest, a flat stomach and the narrow hips of a gunslinger. His limbs, relaxed, were sleekly muscled and hinted at easy strength.

The stranger's face was mesmerizing. His hair, dark brown and curling, touched the collar of his shirt. His eyes were as blue as the Caribbean Sea that Becky could just glimpse out the open patio door over the incredible broadness of his shoulder.

Unlike that sea, his eyes did not look warm and inviting. In fact, there was that hint of a gunslinger, again, something cool and formidable in his uncompromising gaze. The look in his eyes did not detract, not in the least, from the fact that his features were astoundingly perfect.

"And no," he said.

Another piece of paper drifted down onto her desk, this one landing on the keyboard of her laptop.

"And to this one?" he said. "Especially no."

And then a final sheet glided down, hit the lip of the desk, forcing her to grab it before it slid to the floor.

Becky stared at him, rather than the paper in her hand. A bead of sweat trickled down from his temple and followed the line of his face, slowly, slowly, slowly down to the slope of a perfect jaw, where he swiped at it impatiently.

It was hot here on the small, privately owned Caribbean island of Sainte Simone. Becky resisted a temptation to swipe at her own sweaty brow with the back of her arm.

She found her voice. "Excuse me? And you are?"

He raised an arrogant eyebrow at her, which made her rush to answer for him.

"You must be one of Allie's Hollywood friends," Becky decided.

It seemed to her that only people in Allie's field of work, acting on the big screen, achieved the physical beauty and perfection of the man in front of her. Only they seemed to be able to carry off that rather unsettling I-own-the-earth confidence that mere mortals had no hope of achieving. Besides, it was more than evident how the camera would love the gorgeous planes of his face, the line of his nose, the fullness of his lips…

"Are you?" she asked.

This was exactly why she had needed a guest list, but no, Allie had been adamant about that. She was looking after the guest list herself, and she did not want a single soul—up to and including her event planner, apparently—knowing the names of all the famous people who would be attending her wedding.

The man before Becky actually snorted in disgust, which was no kind of answer. Snorted. How could that possibly sound sexy?

"Of course, you are very early," Becky told him, trying for a stern note. Why was her heart beating like that, as if she had just run a sprint? "The wedding isn't for two weeks."

It was probably exactly what she should be expecting. People with too much money and too much time on their hands were just going to start showing up on Sainte Simone whenever they pleased.

"I'm Drew Jordan."

She must have looked as blank as she felt.

"The head carpenter for this circus."

Drew. Jordan. Of course! How could she not have registered that? She was actually expecting him. He was the brother of Joe, the groom.

Well, he might be the head carpenter, but she was the ringmaster, and she was going to have to establish that fact, and fast.

"Please do not refer to Allie Ambrosia's wedding as a circus," the ringmaster said sternly. Becky was under strict orders word of the wedding was not to get out. She was not even sure that was possible, with two hundred guests, but if it did get out, she did not want it being referred to as a circus by the hired help. The paparazzi would pounce on that little morsel of insider information just a little too gleefully.

There was that utterly sexy snort again.

"It is," she continued, just as sternly, "going to be the event of the century."

She was quoting the bride-to-be, Hollywood's latest "it" girl, Allie Ambrosia. She tried not to show that she, Becky English, small-town nobody, was just a little intimidated that she had been chosen to pull off that event of the century.

She now remembered Allie warning her about this very man who stood in front of her.

Allie had said, *My future brother-in-law is going to head up construction. He's a bit of a stick-in-the-mud. He's a few years older than Joe, but he acts, like, seventy-five. I find him quite cranky. He's the bear-with-the-sore-bottom type. Which explains why he isn't married.*

So, this was the future brother-in-law, standing in front of Becky, looking nothing at all like a stick-in-the-mud, or like a seventy-five-year-old. The bear-with-the-sore-bottom part was debatable.

With all those facts in hand, why was the one that stood out the fact that Drew Jordan was not married? And why would Becky care about that, at all?

Becky had learned there was an unexpected perk of being a wedding planner. She had named her company, with a touch of whimsy and a whole lot of wistfulness, Happily-Ever-After. However, her career choice had quickly killed what shreds of her romantic illusions had remained after the bitter end to her long engagement. She would be the first to admit she'd had far too many fairy-tale fantasies way back when she had been very young and hopelessly naive.

Flustered—here was a man who made a woman want to believe, all over again, in happy endings—but certainly not wanting to show it, Becky picked up the last paper Drew Jordan had cast down in front of her, the *especially no* one.

It was her own handiwork that had been cast so dismissively in front of her. Her careful, if somewhat rudimentary, drawing had a big black X right through the whole thing.

"But this is the pavilion!" she said. "Where are we supposed to seat two hundred guests for dinner?"

"The location is fine."

Was she supposed to thank him for that? Somehow words, even sarcastic ones, were lost to her. She sputtered ineffectually.

"You can still have dinner at the same place, on the front lawn in front of this monstrosity. Just no pavilion."

"This monstrosity is a castle," Becky said firmly. Okay, she, too, had thought when she had first stepped off the private plane that had whisked her here that the medieval stone structure looked strangely out of place amidst the palms and tropical flowers. But over the past few days, it had been growing on her. The thick walls kept it deliciously cool inside and every room she had peeked in had the luxurious feel of a five-star hotel.

Besides, the monstrosity was big enough to host two hundred guests for the weeklong extravaganza that Allie wanted for her wedding, and monstrosities like that were very hard, indeed, to find.

With the exception of an on-site carpenter, the island getaway came completely staffed with people who were accustomed to hosting remarkable events. The owner was record mogul Bart Lung, and many a musical extravaganza had been held here. The very famous fund-raising documentary *We Are the Globe*, with its huge cast of musical royalty, had been completely filmed and recorded here.

But apparently all those people had eaten in the very expansive castle dining room, which Allie had said with a sniff would not do. She had her heart set on alfresco for her wedding feast.

"Are you saying you can't build me a pavilion?" Becky tried for an intimidating, you-can-be-replaced tone of voice.

"Not can't. Won't. You have two weeks to get ready for the circus, not two years."

He was not the least intimidated by her, and she suspected it was not just because he was the groom's brother. She suspected it would take a great deal to intimidate Drew Jordan. He had that don't-mess-with-me look about his eyes, a set to his admittedly sexy mouth that said he was far more accustomed to giving orders than to taking them.

She debated asking him, again, not to call it a circus, but that went right along with not being able to intimidate him. Becky could tell by the stubborn set of his jaw that she might as well save her breath. She decided levelheaded reason would win the day.

"It's a temporary structure," she explained, the epitome of calm, "and it's imperative. What if we get inclement weather that day?"

Drew tilted his head at her and studied her for long enough that it was disconcerting.

"What?" she demanded.

"I'm trying to figure out if you're part of her Cinderella group or not."

Becky lifted her chin. Okay, so she wasn't Hollywood gorgeous like Allie was, and today—sweaty, casual and sporting a sunburned nose—might not be her best day ever, but why would it be debatable whether she was part of Allie's Cinderella group or not?

She didn't even know what that was. Why did she want to belong to it, or at least seem as if she could?

"What's a Cinderella group?" she asked.

"Total disconnect from reality," he said, nodding at the plan in her hand. "You can't build a pavilion that seats two hundred on an island where supplies have to be barged in. Not in two weeks, probably not even in two years."

"It's temporary," she protested. "It's creating an illusion, like a movie set."

"You're not one of her group," he decided firmly, even though Becky had just clearly demonstrated her expertise about movie sets.

"How do you know?"

"Imperative," he said. *"Inclement."* His lips twitched, and she was aware it was her use of the language that both amused him and told him she was not part of Allie's regular set. Really? She should not be relieved that it was vocabulary and not her looks that had set her apart from Allie's gang.

"Anyway, *inclement* weather—"

Was he making fun of her?

"—is highly unlikely. I Googled it."

She glanced at her laptop screen, which was already open on Google.

"This side of this island gets three days of rain per year," he told her. "In the last forty-two years of record-keeping, would you care to guess how often it has rained on the Big Day, June the third?"

The way he said *Big Day* was in no way preferable to *circus*.

Becky glared at him to make it look as if she was annoyed that he had beat her to the facts. She drew her computer to her, as if she had no intention of taking his word for it, as if she needed to check the details of the June third weather report herself.

Her fingers, acting entirely on their own volition, without any kind of approval from her mind, typed in D-r-e-w J-o-r-d-a-n.

CHAPTER TWO

DREW REGARDED BECKY ENGLISH thoughtfully. He had expected a high-powered and sophisticated West Coast event specialist. Instead, the woman before him, with her sunburned nose and pulled-back hair, barely looked as if she was legal age.

In fact, she looked like an athletic teenager getting ready to go to practice with the high school cheer squad. Since she so obviously was not the image of the professional woman he'd expected, his first impression had been that she must be a young Hollywood hanger-on, being rewarded for loyalty to Allie Ambrosia with a job she was probably not qualified to do.

But no, the woman in front of him had nothing of slick Hollywood about her. The vocabulary threw his initial assessment. The way she talked—with the earnestness of a student preparing for the Scripps National Spelling Bee—made him think that the bookworm geeky girl had been crossed with the high school cheerleader. Who would have expected that to be such an intriguing combination?

Becky's hair was a sandy shade of brown that looked virgin, as if it had never been touched by dye or blond highlights. It looked as if she had spent about thirty seconds on it this morning, scraping it back from her face and capturing it in an elastic band. It was a rather nondescript shade of brown, yet so glossy with good health, Drew felt a startling desire to touch it.

Her eyes were plain old brown, without a drop of makeup around them to make them appear larger, or wider, or darker, or greener. Her skin was pale, which would have been considered unfashionable in the land of endless summer that he came from. Even after only a few days in the tropics, most of which he suspected had been spent inside, the tip of her nose and her cheeks were glowing pink, and she was showing signs of freckling. There was a bit of a sunburn on her slender shoulders.

Her teeth were a touch crooked, one of the front ones ever so slightly overlapping the other one. It was oddly endearing. He couldn't help but notice, as men do, that she was as flat as a board.

Drew Jordan's developments were mostly in Los Angeles. People there—especially people who could afford to buy in his subdivisions—were about the furthest thing from *real* that he could think of.

The women he dealt with had the tiny noses and fat lips, the fake tans and the unwrinkled foreheads. They had every shade of blond hair and the astonishingly inflated breast lines. Their eyes were widened into a look of surgically induced perpetual surprise and their teeth were so white you needed sunglasses on to protect you from smiles.

Drew was not sure when he had become used to it all, but suddenly it seemed very evident to him why he had. There was something about all that fakeness that was *safe* to a dyed-in-the-wool bachelor such as himself.

The cheerleader bookworm girl behind the desk radiated something that was oddly threatening. In a world that seemed to celebrate phony everything, she seemed as if she was 100 percent real.

She was wearing a plain white tank top, and if he leaned forward just a little bit he could see cutoff shorts. Peeking out from under the desk was a pair of sneakers with startling pink laces in them.

"How did you get mixed up with Allie?" he asked. "You do not look the way I would expect a high-profile Hollywood event planner to look."

"How would you expect one to look?" she countered, insulted.

"Not, um, wholesome."

She frowned.

"Take it as a compliment," he suggested.

She looked uncertain about that, but marshaled herself.

"I've run a very successful event planning company for several years," she said with a proud toss of her head.

"In Los Angeles," he said with flat disbelief.

"Well, no, not exactly."

He waited.

She looked flustered, which he enjoyed way more than he should have. She glared at him. "My company serves Moose Run and the surrounding areas."

Was she kidding? It sounded like a name Hollywood would invent to conjure visions of a quaintly rural and charming America that hardly existed anymore. But, no, she had that cute and geeky earnestness about her.

Still, he had to ask. "Moose Run? Seriously?"

"Look it up on Google," she snapped.

"Where is it? The mountains of Appalachia?"

"I said look it up on Google."

But when he crossed his arms over his chest and raised an eyebrow at her, she caved.

"Michigan," she said tersely. "It's a farm community in Michigan. It has a population of about fourteen thousand. Of course, my company serves the surrounding areas, as well."

"Ah. Of course."

"Don't say *ah* like that!"

"Like what?" he said, genuinely baffled.

"Like *that explains everything.*"

"It does. It explains everything about you."

"It does not explain everything about me!" she said. "In fact, it says very little about me."

There were little pink spots appearing on her cheeks, above the sunburned spots.

"Okay," he said, and put up his hands in mock surrender. Really, he should have left it there. He should keep it all business, let her know what she could and couldn't do construction wise with severe time restraints, and that was it. His job done.

But Drew was enjoying flustering her, and the little pink spots on her cheeks.

"How old are you?" he asked.

She folded her arms over her own chest—battle stations—and squinted at him. "That is an inappropriate question. How old are you?" she snapped back.

"I'm thirty-one," he said easily. "I only asked because you look sixteen, but not even Allie would be ridiculous enough to hire a sixteen-year-old to put together this cir—event—would she?"

"I'm twenty-three and Allie is not ridiculous!"

"She isn't?"

His brother's future wife had managed to arrange her very busy schedule—she was shooting a movie in Spain—to grant Drew an audience, once, on a brief return to LA, shortly after Joe had phoned and told him with shy and breathless excitement he was getting married.

Drew had not been happy about the announcement. His brother was twenty-one. To date, Joe hadn't made many major decisions without consulting Drew, though Drew had been opposed to the movie-set building and Joe had gone ahead anyway.

And look where that had led. Because, in a hushed tone of complete reverence, Joe had told Drew *who* he was marrying.

Drew's unhappiness had deepened. He had shared it with Joe. His normally easygoing, amenable brother had yelled at him.

Quit trying to control me. Can't you just be happy for me?

And then Joe, who was usually happy-go-lucky and sunny in nature, had hung up on him. Their conversations since then had been brief and clipped.

Drew had agreed to meet Joe here and help with a few construction projects for the wedding, but he had a secret agenda. He needed to spend time with his brother. Face-to-face time. If he managed to talk some sense into him, all the better.

"I don't suppose Joe is here yet?" he asked Becky with elaborate casualness.

"No." She consulted a thick agenda book. "I have him arriving tomorrow morning, first thing. And Allie arriving the day of the wedding."

Perfect. If he could get Joe away from Allie's influence, his mission—to stop the wedding, or at least reschedule it until cooler heads prevailed—seemed to have a better chance of succeeding.

Drew liked to think he could read people—the woman in front of him being a case in point. But he had come away from his meeting with Allie Ambrosia feeling a disconcerting sense of not being able to read her at all.

Where's my brother? Drew had demanded.

Allie Ambrosia had blinked at him. *No need to make it sound like a kidnapping.*

Which, of course, was exactly what Drew had been feeling it was, and that Allie Ambrosia was solely responsible for the new Joe, who could hang up on his brother and then ignore all his attempts to get in touch with him.

"Allie Ambrosia is sensitive and brilliant and sweet."

Drew watched Becky with interest as the blaze of color deepened over her sunburn. She was going to rise to defend someone she perceived as the underdog, and that told him almost as much about her as the fact that she hailed from Moose Run, Michigan.

Drew was just not sure who would think of Allie Ambrosia as the underdog. He may have been frustrated about his inability to read his future sister-in-law, but neither *sensitive* nor *sweet* would have made his short list of descriptive adjectives. Though they probably would have for Becky, even after such a short acquaintance.

Allie? Brilliant, maybe. Though if she was it had not shown in her vocabulary. Still, he'd been aware of the possibility of great cunning. She had seemed to Drew to be able to play whatever role she wanted, the real person, whoever and whatever that was, hidden behind eyes so astonishingly emerald he'd wondered if she enhanced the color with contact lenses.

He'd come away from Allie frustrated. He had agreed to build some things for the damn wedding, hoping, he supposed, that this seeming capitulation to his brother's plans would open the door to communication between them and he could talk some sense into Joe.

He'd have his chance tomorrow. Today, he could unabashedly probe the secrets of the woman his brother had decided to marry.

"And you would know Allie is sensitive and brilliant and sweet, why?" he asked Becky, trying not to let on just how pleased he was to have found someone who actually seemed to know Allie.

"We went to school together."

Better still. Someone who knew Allie *before* she'd caught her big break playing Peggy in a sleeper of a movie called *Apple Mountain*.

"Allie Ambrosia grew up in Moose Run, Michigan?" He prodded her along. "That is not in the official biography."

He thought Becky was going to clam up, careful about saying anything about her boss and old school chum, but her need to defend won out.

"Her Moose Run memories may not be her fondest ones," Becky offered, a bit reluctantly.

"I must say Allie has come a long way from Moose Run," he said.

"How do you know? How well do you know Allie?"

"I admit I'm assuming, since I hardly know her at all," Drew said. "This is what I know. She's had a whirlwind relationship with my little brother, who is building a set on one of her movies. They've known each other weeks, not months. And suddenly they are getting married. It can't last, and this is an awful lot of money and time and trouble to go to for something that can't last."

"You're cynical," she said, as if that was a bad thing.

"We can't all come from Moose Run, Michigan."

She squinted at him, not rising to defend herself, but staying focused on him, which made him very uncomfortable. "You are really upset that they are getting married."

He wasn't sure he liked that amount of perception. He didn't say anything.

"Actually, I think you don't like weddings, period."

"What is this, a party trick? You can read my mind?" He intended it to sound funny, but he could hear a certain amount of defensiveness in his tone.

"So, it's true then."

"Big deal. Lots of men don't like weddings."

"Why is that?"

He frowned at her. He wanted to ferret out some facts about Allie, or talk about construction. He was comfortable talking about construction, even on an ill-conceived project like this. He was a problem solver. He was not comfortable discussing feelings, which an aversion to weddings came dangerously close to.

"They just don't like them," he said stubbornly. "Okay, I don't like them."

"I'm curious about who made you your brother's keeper," she said. "Shouldn't your parents be talking to him about this?"

"Our parents are dead."

When something softened in her face, he deliberately hardened himself against it.

"Oh," Becky said quietly, "I'm so sorry. So you, as older brother, are concerned, and at the same time have volunteered to help out. That's very sweet."

"Let's get something straight right now. There is nothing sweet about me."

"So why did you agree to help at all?"

He shrugged. "Brothers help each other."

Joe's really upset by your reaction to our wedding, Allie had told him. *If you agreed to head up the construction, he would see it was just an initial reaction of surprise and that of course you want what is best for your own brother.*

Oh, he wanted what was best for Joe, all right. Something must have flashed across Drew's face, because Becky's brow lowered.

"Are you going to try to stop the wedding?" she asked suspiciously.

Had he telegraphed his intention to Allie, as well? "Joe's all grown up, and capable of making up his own mind. But so am I. And it seems like a crazy, impulsive decision he's made."

"You didn't answer the question."

"You'd think he would have asked me what I thought," Drew offered grimly.

A certain measure of pain escaped in that statement, and so he frowned at Becky, daring her to give him sympathy.

Thankfully, she did not even try. "Is this why I can't have the pavilion? Are you trying to sabotage the whole thing?"

"No," he said curtly. "I'll do what I can to give my brother and his beloved a perfect day. If he comes to his senses before then—" He lifted a shoulder.

"If he changes his mind, that would be a great deal of time and money down the tubes," Becky said.

Drew lifted his shoulder again. "I'm sure you would still get paid."

"That's hardly the point!"

"It's the whole point of running a business." He glanced at her and sighed. "Please don't tell me you do it for love."

Love.

Except for what he felt for his brother, his world was comfortably devoid of that pesky emotion. He was sorry he'd even mentioned the word in front of Becky English.

CHAPTER THREE

"SINCE YOU BROUGHT it up," Becky said solemnly, "I got the impression from Allie that she and your brother are head over heels in love with one another."

"Humph." There was no question his brother was over the moon, way past the point where he could be counted on to make a rational decision. Allie was more difficult to interpret. Allie was an actress. She pretended for a living. It seemed to Drew his brother's odds of getting hurt were pretty good.

"Joe could have done worse," Becky said, quietly. "She's a beautiful, successful woman."

"Yeah, there's that."

"There's that cynicism again."

Cynical. Yes, that described Drew Jordan to an absolute T. And he liked being around people who were as hard-edged as him. Didn't he?

"Look, my brother is twenty-one years old. That's a little young to be making this kind of decision."

"You know, despite your barely contained scorn for Moose Run, Michigan, it's a traditional place where they love nothing more than a wedding. I've planned dozens of them."

Drew had to bite his tongue to keep from crushing her with a sarcastic *Dozens?*

"I've been around this for a while," she continued. "Take it from me. Age is no guarantee of whether a marriage is going to work out."

"He's known her about eight weeks, as far as I can tell!" He was confiding his doubts to a complete stranger, which was not like him. It was even more unlike him to be hoping this wet-behind-the-ears country girl from Moose Run, Michigan, might be able to shed some light on his brother's mysterious, flawed decision-making process. This was why he liked being around people as *not* sweet as himself. There was no probing of the secrets of life.

"That doesn't seem to reflect on how the marriage is going to work out, either."

"Well, what does then?"

"When I figure it out, I'm going to bottle it and sell it," she said. There was that earnestness again. "But I've planned the weddings of lots of young people who are still together. Young people have big dreams and lots of energy. You need that to buy your first house and have your first baby, and juggle three jobs and—"

"Baby?" Drew said, horrified. "Is she pregnant?" That would explain his brother's rush to the altar of love.

"I don't think so," Becky said.

"But you don't know for certain."

"It's none of my business. Or yours. But even if she is, lots of those kinds of marriages make it, too. I've planned weddings for people who have known each other for weeks, and weddings for people who have known each other for years. I planned one wedding for a couple who had lived together for sixteen years. They were getting a divorce six months later. But I've seen lots of marriages that work."

"And how long has your business been running?"

"Two years," she said.

For some reason, Drew was careful not to be quite as sarcastic as he wanted to be. "So, you've seen lots that work for two years. Two years is hardly a testament to a solid relationship."

"You can tell," she said stubbornly. "Some people are going to be in love forever."

Her tone sounded faintly wistful. Something uncomfortable shivered along his spine. He had a feeling he was looking at one of those forever kinds of girls. The kind who were not safe to be around at all.

Though it would take more than a sweet girl from Moose Run to penetrate the armor around his hard heart. He felt impatient with himself for the direction of his thoughts. Wasn't it proof that she was already penetrating something since they were having this discussion that had nothing to do with her unrealistic building plans?

Drew shook off the feeling and fixed Becky with a particularly hard look.

"Sheesh, maybe you are a member of the Cinderella club, after all."

"Despite the fact I run a company called Happily-Ever-After—"

He closed his eyes. "That's as bad as Moose Run."

"It is a great name for an event planning company."

"I think I'm getting a headache."

"But despite my company name, I have long since given up on fairy tales."

He opened his eyes and looked at her. "Uh-huh," he said, loading those two syllables with doubt.

"I have!"

"Lady, even before I heard the name of your company, I could tell that you have 'I'm waiting for my prince to come' written all over you."

"I do not."

"You've had a heartbreak."

"I haven't," she said. She was a terrible liar.

"Maybe it wasn't quite a heartbreak. A romantic disappointment."

"Now who is playing the mind reader?"

"Aha! I was right, then."

She glared at him.

"You'll get over it. And then you'll be in the prince market all over again."

"I won't."

"I'm not him, by the way."

"Not who?"

"Your prince."

"Of all the audacious, egotistical, ridiculous—"

"Just saying. I'm not anybody's prince."

"You know what? It is more than evident you could not be mistaken for Prince Charming even if you had a crown on your head and tights and golden slippers!"

Now that he'd established some boundaries, he felt he could tease her just a little. "Please tell me you don't like men who wear tights."

"What kind of man I like is none of your business!"

"Correct. It's just that we will be working in close proximity. My shirt has been known to come off. It has been known to make women swoon." He smiled.

He was enjoying this way more than he had a right

to, but it was having the desired effect, putting up a
nice big wall between them, and he hadn't even had to
barge in the construction material to do it.

"I'm not just *getting* a headache," she said. "I've had
one since you marched through my door."

"Oh, great," he said. "There's nothing I like as much
as a little competition. Let's see who can give who a
bigger headache."

"The only way I could give you a bigger headache
than the one you are giving me is if I smashed this lamp
over your head."

Her hand actually came to rest on a rather heavy-
looking brass lamp on the corner of her desk. It was
evident to him that she would have loved to do just that
if she wasn't such a prim-and-proper type.

"I'm bringing out the worst in you," he said with satisfaction. She looked at her hand, resting on the lamp,
and looked so appalled with herself that Drew did the
thing he least wanted to do. He laughed.

Becky snatched her hand back from the brass lamp,
annoyed with herself, miffed that she was providing
amusement for the very cocky Mr. Drew Jordan. She
was not the type who smashed people over the head
with lamps. Previously, she had not even been the type
who would have ever thought about such a thing. She
had dealt with some of the world's—or at least Michigan's—worst Bridezillas, and never once had she laid
hand to lamp. It was one of the things she prided herself in. She kept her cool.

But Drew Jordan had that look of a man who could
turn a girl inside out before she even knew what had
hit her. He could make a woman who trusted her cool

suddenly aware that fingers of heat were licking away inside her, begging for release. And it was disturbing that he knew it!

He was laughing at her. It was super annoying that instead of being properly indignant, steeling herself against attractions that he was as aware of as she was, she could not help but notice how cute he was when he laughed—that sternness stripped from his face, an almost boyish mischievousness lurking underneath.

She frowned at her computer screen, pretending she was getting down to business and that she had called up the weather to double-check his facts. Instead, she learned her head of construction was also the head of a multimillion-dollar Los Angeles development company.

The bride's future brother-in-law was not an out-of-work tradesman that Becky could threaten to fire. He ran a huge development company in California. No wonder he seemed to be impatient at being pressed into the service of his very famous soon-to-be sister-in-law.

No wonder he'd been professional enough to Google the weather. Becky wondered why she hadn't thought of doing that. It was nearly the first thing she did for every event.

It was probably because she was being snowed under by Allie's never-ending requests. Just now she was trying to find a way to honor Allie's casually thrown-out email, received that morning, which requested freshly planted lavender tulips—picture attached—to line the outdoor aisle she would walk down toward her husband-to-be.

Google, that knowledge reservoir of all things, told

Becky she could not have lavender tulips—or any kind of tulip for that matter—in the tropics in June.

What Google confirmed for her now was not the upcoming weather forecast or the impossibility of lavender tulips, but that Drew Jordan was used to million-dollar budgets.

Becky, on the other hand, had started shaking when she had opened the promised deposit check from Allie. Up until then, it had seemed to her that maybe she was being made the butt of a joke. But that check—made out to Happily-Ever-After—had been for more money than she had ever seen in her life.

With trembling fingers she had dialed the private cell number Allie had provided.

"Is this the budget?"

"No, silly, just the deposit."

"What exactly is your budget?" Becky had asked. Her voice had been shaking as badly as her fingers.

"Limitless," Allie had said casually. "And I fully intend to exceed it. You don't think I'm going to be outdone by Roland Strump's daughter, do you?"

"Allie, maybe you should hire whoever did the Strump wedding, I—"

"Nonsense. Have fun with it, for Pete's sake. Haven't you ever had fun? I hope you and Drew don't manage to bring down the mood of the whole wedding. Sourpusses."

Sourpuss? She was studious to be sure, but sour? Becky had put down the phone contemplating that. Had she ever had fun? Even at Happily-Ever-After, planning fun events for other people was very serious business, indeed.

Well, now she knew who Drew was. And Allie had

been right when it came to him. He could definitely be a sourpuss! It was more worrying that he planned to take off his shirt. She had to get back to business.

"Mr. Jordan—"

"Drew is fine. And what should I call you?"

Barnum. "Becky is fine. We can't just throw a bunch of tables out on the front lawn as if this were the church picnic."

"We're back to that headache." His lips twitched. "I'm afraid my experience with church picnics has been limited."

Yes, it was evident he was all devilish charm and dark seduction, while it was written all over her that that was what she came from: church picnics and 4-H clubs, a place where the Fourth of July fireworks were *the* event of the year.

She shifted her attention to the second *no.* "And we absolutely need some sort of dance floor. Have you ever tried to dance on grass? Or sand?"

"I'm afraid," Drew said, "that falls outside of the realm of my experience, too. And you?"

"Oh, you know," she said. "We like to dust up our heels after the church picnic."

He nodded, as if that was more than evident to him and he had missed her sarcasm completely.

She focused on his third veto. She looked at her clumsy drawing of a small gazebo on the beach. She had envisioned Allie and Joe saying their vows under it, while their guests sat in beautiful lightweight chairs looking at them and the sea beyond them.

"And what's your complaint with this one?"

"I'll forgive you this oversight because of where you are from."

"Oversight?"

"I wouldn't really expect a girl from Michigan to have foreseen this. The *wedding*—" he managed to fill that single word with a great deal of contempt "—according to my notes, is supposed to take place at 4:00 p.m. on June third."

"Correct."

"If you Google the tide chart for that day, you'll see that your gazebo would have water lapping up to the third stair. I'm not really given to omens, but I would probably see that as one."

She was feeling very tired of Google, except in the context of learning about him. It seemed to her he was the kind of man who brought out the weakness in a woman, even one who had been made as cynical as she had been. Because she felt she could ogle him all day long. And he knew it, she reminded herself.

"So," she said, a little more sharply than intended, "what do you suggest?"

"If we scratch the pavilion for two hundred—"

"I can get more people to help you."

He went on as if she hadn't spoken. "I can probably build you a rudimentary gazebo at a different location."

"What about the dance floor?"

"I'll think about it."

He said that as if he were the boss, not her. From what she had glimpsed about him on the internet he was very used to being in charge. And he obviously knew his stuff, and was good with details. He had spotted the weather and the tides, after all. Really, she should be grateful. What if her bride had marched down her tulip-lined aisle—or whatever the aisle ended up being lined with—to a wedding gazebo that was slowly being swallowed by water?

It bothered her to even think it, but Drew Jordan was right. That would have been a terrible omen.

Still, gratitude was not what Becky felt. Not at all.

"You are winning the headache contest by a country mile," she told him.

"I'm no kind of expert on the country," he said, without regret, "but I am competitive."

"What did Allie tell you? Are you in charge of construction?"

"Absolutely."

He said it too quickly and with that self-assured smile of a man way too used to having his own way, particularly with the opposite sex.

"I'm going to have to call Allie and see what that means," Becky said, steeling herself against that smile. "I'm happy to leave construction to you, but I think I should have the final word on what we are putting up and where."

"I'm okay with that. As long as it's reasonable."

"I'm sure we define that differently."

He flashed his teeth at her again. "I'm sure we do."

"Would it help you do your job if I brought more people on-site? Carpenters and such?"

"That's a great idea, but I don't work with strangers. Joe and I have worked together a lot. He'll be here tomorrow."

"That wouldn't be very romantic, him building the stuff for his own wedding."

"Or you could see it as him putting an investment and some effort into his own wedding."

She sighed. "You want him here so you can try to bully him out of getting married."

"I resent the implication I would bully him."

But Becky was stunned to see doubt flash across those self-confident features. "He isn't talking to you, is he?" Becky guessed softly.

She could tell Drew was not accustomed to this level of perception. He didn't like it one little bit.

"I have one of my teams arriving soon. And Joe. I'm here a day early to do some initial assessments. What I need is for you to pick the site for the exchange of vows so that I can put together a plan. We don't have as much time as you think."

Which was truly frightening, because she did not think they had any time at all. Becky looked at her desk: flowers to be ordered, ceremony details to be finalized, accommodations to be organized, boat schedules, food, not just for the wedding feast, but for the week to follow, and enough staff to pull off pampering two hundred people.

"And don't forget fireworks," she added.

"Excuse me?"

"Nothing," she muttered. She did not want to be thinking of fireworks around a man like Drew Jordan. Her eyes drifted to his lips. If she were ever to kiss someone like that, it would be the proverbial fireworks. And he knew it, too. That was why he was smiling evilly at her!

Suddenly, it felt like nothing in the world would be better than to get outside away from this desk—and from him—and see this beautiful island. So far, she had mostly experienced it by looking out her office window.

The sun would be going down soon. She could find a place to hold the wedding and watch the sun go down.

"Okay," she said. "I'll find a new site. I'll let you know as soon as I've got it."

"Let's do it together. That might save us some grief."

She was not sure that doing anything with him was going to save her some grief. She needed to get away from him…and the thoughts of fireworks he had caused.

CHAPTER FOUR

"I'D PREFER TO do it on my own," Becky said, even though it seemed ungracious to say so. She felt a need to establish who was running the cir—show.

"But here's the problem," Drew said with annoying and elaborate patience.

"Yes?"

"You'll pick a site on your own, and then I'll go look at it and say no, and so then you'll pick another site on your own, and I'll go look at it and say no."

She scowled at him. "You're being unnecessarily negative."

He shrugged. "I'm just making the point that we could, potentially, go on like that endlessly, and there is a bit of a time crunch here."

"I think you just like using the word *no*," she said grumpily.

"Yes," he said, deadpan, as if he was not being deliberately argumentative now.

She should argue that she was quite capable of picking the site by herself and that she had no doubt her next selection would be fine, but her first choice was not exactly proof of that. And besides, then who would be the argumentative one?

"It's too late today," Drew decided. "Joe's coming in on the first flight. Why don't we pick him up and the three of us will pick a site that works for the gazebo?"

"Yes, that would be fine," she said, aware her voice was snapping with ill grace. Really, it was an opportunity. Tomorrow morning she would not scrape her hair back into a careless ponytail. She would apply makeup to hide how her fair skin, fresh out of a Michigan winter, was already blotchy from the sun.

Should she wear her meet-the-potential-client suit, a cream-colored linen by a famous designer? That would certainly make a better impression than shorty-shorts and a sleeveless tank that could be mistaken for underwear!

But the following morning it was already hot, and there was no dry cleaner on the island to take a sweat-drenched dress to.

Aware she was putting way too much effort into her appearance, Becky donned white shorts and a sleeveless sun-yellow shirt. She put on makeup and left her hair down. And then she headed out of her room.

She met Drew on the staircase.

He looked unreasonably gorgeous!

"Good morning," she said. She was stupidly pleased by how his eyes trailed to her hair and her faintly glossed lips.

He returned her greeting gruffly and then went down the stairs in front of her, taking them two at a time. But he stopped and held open the main door for her. They were hit by a wall of heat.

"It's going to be even hotter in two weeks," Drew

told her, when he watched her pause and draw in her breath on the top stair of the castle.

"Must you be so negative?"

"Pragmatic," he insisted. "Plus…"

"Don't tell me. I already know. You looked it up. That's how you know it will be even hotter in two weeks."

He nodded, pleased with himself.

"Keep it up," she warned him, "and you'll have to present me with the prize. A king-size bottle of head-ache relief."

They stood at the main door to the castle, huge half circles of granite forming a staircase down to a spar-kling expanse of emerald lawn. The lawn was edged with a row of beautifully swaying palm trees, and be-yond that was a crescent of powdery white sand beach.

"That beach looks so much less magical now that I know it's going to be underwater at four o'clock on June the third."

Drew glanced at Becky. She looked older and more so-phisticated with her hair down and makeup on. She had gone from cute to attractive.

It occurred to Drew that Becky was the kind of woman who brought out things in a man that he would prefer to think he didn't have. Around a woman like this a man could find himself wanting to protect himself—and her—from disappointments. That's all he wanted for Joe, too, not to bully him but to protect him.

He'd hated that question, the one he hadn't answered. Had he bullied his brother? He hoped not. But the sad truth was Joe had been seven when Drew, seventeen, was appointed his guardian. Drew had floundered, in way over his head, and he'd resorted to doing whatever needed to be done to get his little brother through childhood.

No wonder his brother was so hungry for love that he'd marry the first beautiful woman who blinked sideways at him.

Unless he could talk some sense into him. He cocked his head. He was pretty sure he could hear the plane coming.

"How hot is it supposed to be on June third?" she asked. He could hear the reluctance to even ask in her voice.

"You know that expression? Hotter than Hades—"

"Never mind. I get it. All the more reason that we really need the pavilion," she said. "We'll need protection from the sun. I planned to have the tables running this way, so everyone could just turn their heads and see the ocean as the sun is going down. The head table could be there, at the bottom of the stairs. Imagine the bride and groom coming down that staircase to join their guests."

Her voice had become quite dreamy. Had she really tried to tell him she was not a romantic? He knew he'd pegged it. She'd had some kind of setback in the romance department, but inside her was still a giddy girl with unrealistic dreams about her prince coming. He had to make sure she knew that was not him.

"Well, I already told you, you can't have that," he said gruffly. He did not enjoy puncturing her dream as much as he wanted to. He did not enjoy being mean as much as he would have liked. He told himself it was for her own good.

He was good at doing things for other people's own

good. You could ask Joe, though his clumsy attempts at parenting were no doubt part of why his brother was running off half-cocked to get married.

"I'm sure we can figure out something," Becky said of her pavilion dream.

"We? No, *we* can't."

This was better. They were going to talk about practicalities, as dream-puncturing as those could be!

The plane was circling now, and they moved toward the airstrip.

He continued, "What you're talking about is an open, expansive structure with huge unsupported spans. You'd need an architect and an engineer."

"I have a tent company I use at home," Becky said sadly, "but they are booked nearly a year in advance. I've tried a few others. Same story. Plus, the planes that can land here aren't big enough to carry that much canvas, and you have to book the supply barge. There's only one with a flat enough bottom to dock here. An unlimited budget can't get you what you might think."

"Unlimited?" He heard the horror in his voice.

She ignored him. "Are you sure I'd need an architect and an engineer, even for something so temporary?"

He slid her a look. She looked quite deflated by all this.

"Especially for something so temporary," he told her. "I'm sure the last thing Allie wants is to be making the news for the collapse of her wedding pavilion. I can almost see the headlines now. 'Three dead, one hundred and eighty-seven injured, event planner and building contractor missing.'"

He heard her little gasp and glanced at her. She was blushing profusely.

"Not missing like *that*," he said.

"Like what?" she choked.

"Like whatever thought is making you blush like that."

"I'm not blushing. The sun has this effect on me."

"Sheesh," he said, as if she had not denied the blush at all. "It's not as if I said that while catastrophe unfolded all around them, the event planner and the contractor went missing *together*."

"I said I wasn't blushing! I never would have thought about us together in any way." Her blush deepened.

He watched her. "You aren't quite the actress that your employer is."

"I am not thinking of us together," she insisted. Her voice was just a little shrill. He realized he quite enjoyed teasing her.

"No?" he said, silkily. "You and I seeking shelter under a palm frond while disaster unfolds all around us?"

Her eyes moved skittishly to his lips and then away. He took advantage of her looking away to study her lips in profile. They were plump little plums, ripe for picking. He was almost sorry he had started this. Almost.

"You're right. You are not a prince. You are evil," she decided, looking back at him. There was a bit of reluctant laughter lurking in her eyes.

He twirled an imaginary moustache. "Yes, I am. Just waiting for an innocent from Moose Run, Michigan, to cross my path so that in the event of a tropical storm, and a building collapse, I will still be entertained."

A little smile tugged at the lips he had just noticed were quite luscious. He was playing a dangerous game.

"Seriously," she said, and he had a feeling she was

the type who did not indulge in lighthearted banter for long, "Allie doesn't want any of this making the news. I'm sure she told you the whole wedding is top secret. She does not want helicopters buzzing her special day."

Drew felt a bit cynical about that. Anyone who wanted a top secret wedding did not invite two hundred people to it. Still, he decided, now might not be the best time to tell Becky a helicopter buzzing might be the least of her worries. When he'd left the States yesterday, all the entertainment shows had been buzzing with the rumors of Allie's engagement.

Was the famous actress using his brother—and everyone else, including small-town Becky English—to ensure Allie Ambrosia was front and center in the news just as her new movie was coming out?

Even though it went somewhat against his blunt nature, the thought that Becky might be being played made Drew soften his bad news a bit. "This close to the equator it's fully dark by six o'clock. The chance of heatstroke for your two hundred guests should be minimized by that."

They took a path through some dense vegetation. On the other side was the airstrip.

"Great," she said testily, though she was obviously relieved they were going to discuss benign things like the weather. "Maybe I can create a kind of 'room' feeling if I circle the area with torches and dress up the tables with linens and candles and flowers and hope for the best."

"Um, about the torches? And candles?" He squinted at the plane touching down on the runway.

"What?"

"According to Google, the trade winds seem to pick

up in the late afternoon. And early evening. Without any kind of structure to protect from the wind, I think they'll just blow out. Or worse."

"So, first you tell me I can't have a structure, and then you tell me all the problems I can expect because I don't have a structure?"

He shrugged. "One thing does tend to lead to another."

"If the wind is strong enough to blow out the candles, we could have other problems with it, too."

"Oh, yeah, absolutely. Tablecloths flying off tables. Women's dresses blowing up over their heads. Napkins catching fire. Flower arrangements being smashed. There's really a whole lot of things people should think about before planning their wedding on a remote island in the tropics."

Becky glared at him. "You know what? I barely know you and I hate you already."

He nodded. "I have that effect on a lot of people."

He watched the plane taxi toward them and grind to a halt in front of them.

"I'm sure you do," she said snippily.

"Does this mean our date under the palm frond is off?"

"It was never on!"

"You should think about it—the building collapsed, the tablecloths on fire, women's dresses blowing over their heads as they run shrieking…"

"Please stop."

But he couldn't. He could tell he very nearly had her where he wanted her. Why did he feel so driven to make little Miss Becky English angry? But also to make her laugh?

"And you and me under a palm frond, licking wedding cake off each other's fingers."

At first she looked appalled. But then a smile tickled her lips. And then she giggled. And then she was laughing. In a split second, every single thing about her seemed transformed. She went from plain to pretty.

Very pretty.

This was exactly what he had wanted: to glimpse what the cool Miss English would look like if she let go of control.

It was more dangerous than Drew had anticipated. It made him want to take it a step further, to make her laugh harder or to take those little lips underneath his and…

He reminded himself she was not the type of girl he usually invited out to play. Despite the fact she was being relied on to put on a very sophisticated event, there didn't seem to be any sophistication about her.

He had already figured out there was a heartbreak in her past. That was the only reason a girl as apple pie as her claimed to be jaundiced about romance. He could tell it wasn't just dealing with people's wedding insanity that had made her want to be cynical, even as it was all too evident she was not. He had seen the truth in the dreamy look when she had started talking about how she wanted it all to go.

He could tell by looking at her exactly what she needed, and it wasn't a job putting together other people's fantasies.

It was a husband who adored her. And three children. And a little house where she could sew curtains for the windows and tuck bright annuals into the flower beds every year.

It was whatever the perfect life in Moose Run, Michigan, looked like.

Drew knew he could never give her those things. Never. He'd experienced too much loss and too much responsibility in his life.

Still, there was one thing a guy as jaundiced as him did not want or need. To be stuck on a deserted island with a female whose laughter could turn her from a plain old garden-variety girl next door into a goddess in the blink of an eye.

He turned from her quickly and watched as the door of the plane opened. The crew got off, opened the cargo hold and began unloading stuff beside the runway.

He frowned. No Joe.

He took his phone out of his pocket and stabbed in a text message. He pushed Send, but the island did not have great service in all places. The message to his brother did not go through.

Becky was searching his face, which he carefully schooled not to show his disappointment.

"I guess we'll have to find that spot ourselves. Joe will probably come on the afternoon flight. Let's see what we can find this way."

Instead of following the lawn to where it dropped down to the beach, he followed it north to a line of palm trees. A nice wide trail dipped into them, and he took it.

"It's like jungle in here," she said.

"Think of the possibilities. Joe could swing down from a vine. In a loincloth. Allie could be waiting for him in a tree house, right here."

"No, no and especially no," she said.

He glanced behind him. She had stopped to look at

a bright red hibiscus. She plucked it off and tucked it behind her ear.

"In the tropics," he told her, "when you wear a flower behind your ear like that, it means you are available. You wouldn't want the cook getting the wrong idea."

She glared at him, plucked the flower out and put it behind her other ear.

"Now it means you're married."

"There's no winning, is there?" she asked lightly.

No, there wasn't. The flower looked very exotic in her hair. It made him very aware, again, of the enchantment of tropical islands. He turned quickly from her and made his way down the path.

After about five minutes in the deep shade of the jungle, they came out to another beach. It was exposed to the wind, which played in the petals of the flower above her ear, lifted her bangs from her face and pressed her shirt to her.

"Oh," she called, "it's beautiful."

She had to shout because unlike the beach the castle overlooked, this one was not in a protected cove.

It was a beautiful beach. A surfer would probably love it, but it would have to be a good surfer. There were rocky outcrops stretching into the water that looked like they would be painful to hit and hard to avoid.

"It's too loud," he said over the crashing of the waves. "They'd be shouting their vows."

He turned and went back into the shaded jungle. For some reason, he thought she would just follow him, and it took him a few minutes to realize he was alone.

He turned and looked. The delectable Miss Becky English was nowhere to be seen. He went back along the path, annoyed. Hadn't he made it perfectly clear they had time constraints?

When he got back out to the beach, his heart went into his throat. She had climbed up onto one of the rocky outcrops. She was standing there, bright as the sun in that yellow shirt, as a wave smashed on the rock just beneath her. Her hands were held out and her face lifted to the spray of white foam it created. With the flower in her hair, she looked more like a goddess than ever, performing some ritual to the sea.

Did she know nothing of the ocean? Of course she didn't. They had already established that. That, coming from Moose Run, there were things she could not know about.

"Get down from there," he shouted. "Becky, get down right now."

He could see the second wave building, bigger than the first that had hit the rock. The waves would come in sets. And the last wave in the set would be the biggest.

The wind swallowed his voice, though she turned and looked at him. She smiled and waved. He could see the surf rising behind her alarmingly. The second wave hit the rock. She turned away from him, and hugged herself in delight as the spray fell like thick mist all around her.

"Get away from there," he shouted. She turned and gave him a puzzled look. He started to run.

Becky had her back to the third wave when it hit. It hit the backs of her legs. Drew saw her mouth form a surprised O, and then her arms were flailing as she tried to regain her balance. The wave began pulling back, with at least as much force as it had come in with. It yanked her off the rock as if she were a rag doll.

CHAPTER FIVE

BECKY FELT THE shocked helplessness as her feet were jerked out from under her and she was swept off the rock. The water closed over her head and filled her mouth and nose. She popped back up like a cork, but her swimming skills were rudimentary, and she was not sure they would have helped her against the fury of the sea. She was being pulled out into what seemed to be an endless abyss. She tried frantically to swim back in toward shore. In seconds she was as exhausted as she had ever been.

I'm going to drown, she thought, stunned, choking on water and fear. How had this happened? One moment life had seemed so pleasant and beautiful and then…it was over.

Her life was going to be over. She waited, helplessly, for it to flash before her eyes. Instead, she found herself thinking that Drew had been right. It hadn't been a heartbreak. It had been a romantic disappointment. Ridiculous to think that right now, but on the other hand, right now seemed as good a time as any to be acutely and sadly aware of things she had missed.

"Hey!" His voice carried over the crashing of the sea. "Hang on."

Becky caught a glimpse of the rock she had fallen off. Drew was up there. And then she went under the water again.

When she surfaced, Drew was in the water, slashing through the roll of the waves toward her. "Don't panic," he called over the roar of the water pounding the rock outcropping.

She wanted to tell him it was too late for that. She was already panicked.

"Tread," he yelled. "Don't try to swim. Not yet. Look at my face. Nowhere else. Look at me."

Her eyes fastened on his face. There was strength and calm in his features, as if he did this every day. He was close to her now.

"I'm going to come to you," he shouted, "but you have to be calm first. If you panic, you will kill us both."

It seemed his words, and the utter strength and determination in his face, poured a honey of calm over her, despite the fact she was still bobbing like a cork in a ravaged sea. He seemed to see or sense the moment she stopped panicking, and he moved in close.

She nearly sobbed with relief when Drew reached out and touched her, then folded his arms around her and pulled her in tight to him. He was strong in the water—she suspected, abstractly, he was strong everywhere in his life—and she rested into his embrace, surrendering to his warmth. She could feel the power of him in his arms and where she was pressed into the wet slickness of his chest.

"Just let it carry you," he said. "Don't fight it anymore"

It seemed as if he could be talking about way more than water. It could be a message about life.

It seemed the water carried them out forever, but eventually it dumped them in a calmer place, just beyond where the waves began to crest. Becky could feel the water lose its grip on her, even as he refused to.

She never took her eyes off his face. Her mind seemed to grow calmer and calmer, even amused. If this was the last thing she would see, it told her, that wasn't so bad.

"Okay," he said, "can you swim?"

"Dog paddle." The water was not cold, but her voice was shaking.

"That will do. Swim that way. Do your best. I've got you if you get tired." He released her.

That way was not directly to the shore. He was asking her to swim parallel to the shore instead of in. But she tried to do as he asked. She was soon floundering, so tired she could not lift her arms.

"Roll over on your back," he said, and she did so willingly. His hand cupped her chin and she was being pulled through the water. He was an enormously strong swimmer.

"Okay, this is a good spot." He released her again and she came upright and treaded water. "Go toward shore. I've got you, I'm right with you."

She was scared to go back into the waves. It was too much. She was exhausted. But she glanced at his face once more and found her own courage there.

"Get on your tummy, flat as a board, watch for the next wave and ride it in. Watch for those rocks on the side."

She did as she was told. She knew she had no choice. She had to trust him completely. She felt the wave lift her up and drive her toward the shore at a stunning speed. And then it spit her out. She was lying in shallow water, but she could already feel the wave pulling at her, trying to drag her back in. She used what little strength she had left to scramble to her knees and crawl through the sugar pebbles of the sand.

Drew came and scooped her out of the water, lifted her to his chest and struggled out of the surf.

On the beach, above the foaming line of the ocean, he set her down on her back in the sun-warmed sand. For a moment she looked at the clear and endless blue of the sky. It was the very same sky it had been twenty minutes ago, but everything felt changed, some awareness sharp as glass within her. She rolled over onto her stomach and rested her head on her forearms. He flung himself onto the sand beside her, breathing hard.

"Did you just save my life?" she whispered. Her voice was hoarse. Her throat hurt from swallowing salt water. She felt drowsy and extraordinarily peaceful.

"You'll want to make sure this beach is posted before guests start arriving," he finally said, when he spoke.

"You didn't answer the question," she said, taking a peek at him over her folded arm. "Is that a habit with you?"

Drew didn't answer. She looked at him, feeling as if she was drinking him in, as if she could never get enough of looking at him. It was probably natural to feel that way after someone had just saved your life, and she did not try to make herself stop.

She was in a state of altered awareness. She could see the water beading on his eyelashes, and the sun streaming through his wet hair. She could see through his soaked shirt where it was plastered to his body.

"Did you just save my life?" she asked again.

"I think you Michigan girls should stay away from the ocean."

"Do you ever just answer a question, Drew Jordan? Did you save my life?"

He was silent again.

"You did," she finally answered for him.

She could not believe the gratitude she felt. To be alive. It was as if the life force was zinging inside her, making her every cell quiver.

"You risked yourself for me. I'm nearly a complete stranger."

"No, you're not. Winning the headache competition, by the way."

"By a country mile?"

"Oh, yeah."

"That was incredibly heroic." She was not going let him brush it off, though he was determined to.

"Don't make it something it wasn't. I'm nobody's hero."

Just like he had insisted earlier he was nobody's prince.

"Well," she insisted, "you're mine."

He snorted, that sexy, cynical sound he made that was all his own and she found, right now, lying here in the sand, alive, so aware of herself and him, that she liked that sound very much, despite herself.

"I've been around the ocean my whole life," he told her grimly. "I grew up surfing some pretty rough water. I knew what I was doing. Unlike you. That was incredibly stupid."

In her altered state, she was aware that he thought he could break the bond that had been cementing itself into place between them since the moment he had entered the water to rescue her.

"Life can change in a blink," he said sternly. "It can be over in a blink."

He was lecturing her. She suddenly *needed* him to know she could not let him brush it off like that. She needed him to know that the life force was flowing through her. She had an incredible sense of being alive.

"You were right," she said, softly.

There was that snort again. "Of course I'm right. You don't go climbing up on rocks when the surf is that high."

"Not about that. I mean, okay, about that, too, but I wasn't talking about that."

"What were you talking about?"

"It wasn't a heartbreak," Becky said. "It was a romantic disappointment."

"Huh?"

"That's what I thought of when I went into the water. I thought my whole life would flash before my eyes, but instead I thought of Jerry."

"Look, you're obviously in shock and we need to—"

"He was my high school sweetheart. We'd been together since I was seventeen. I'd always assumed we were going to get married. Everybody in the whole town thought we would get married. They called us Salt and Pepper."

"You know what? This will keep. I have to—"

"It won't keep. It's important. I have to say it before I forget it. Before this moment passes."

"Oh, sheesh," he said, his tone indicating he wanted nothing more than for this moment to pass.

"I wanted that. I wanted to be Salt and Pepper, *for-*

ever. My parents had split up the year before. It was awful. My dad owned a hardware store. One of his clerks. And him."

"Look, Becky, you are obviously rattled. You don't have to tell me this."

She could no more have stopped herself from telling him than she could have stopped those waves from pounding on the shore.

"They had a baby together. Suddenly, they were the family we had always been. That we were supposed to be. It was horrible, seeing them all over town, looking at each other. Pushing a baby carriage. I wanted it back. I wanted that feeling of being part of something back. Of belonging."

"Aw, Becky," he said softly. "That sucks. Really it does, but—"

But she had to tell all of it, was compelled to. "Jerry went away to school. My mom didn't have the money for college, and it seemed my dad had new priorities.

"I could see what the community needed, so I started my event company."

"Happily-Ever-After," he said. "Even though you had plenty of evidence of the exact opposite."

"It was way more successful than I had thought it could be. It was way more successful than Jerry thought it could be, too. The more successful I became, the less he liked me."

"Okay. Well. Some guys are like that."

"He broke up with me."

"Yeah, sorry, but now is not the time—"

"This is the reason it's important for me to say it right now. I understand something I didn't understand before. I thought my heart was broken. It is a terrible thing to suffer the humiliation of being ditched in a small town. It was a double humiliation for me. First my dad, and then this. But out there in the water, I felt glad. I felt if I had married him, I would have missed something. Something essential."

"Okay, um—"

"A grand passion."

He said a word under his breath that they disapproved of in Moose Run, Michigan.

"Salt and pepper?" She did a pretty good imitation of his snort. "Why settle for boring old salt and pepper when the world is full of so many glorious flavors?"

"Look, I think you've had a pretty bad shake-up. I don't have a clue what you are talking about, so—"

She knew she was making Drew Jordan wildly uncomfortable, but she didn't care. She planned to make him more uncomfortable yet. She leaned toward him. He stopped talking and watched her warily.

She needed to know if the life force was as intense in him right now as it was in her. She needed to take advantage of this second chance to be alive, to really live.

She touched Drew's back through the wetness of his shirt, and felt the sinewy strength there. The strength that had saved her.

She leaned closer yet. She touched her forehead to his, as if she could make him *feel* what was going on inside her, since words could not express it. He had a chance to move away from her. He did not. He was as caught in what was unfolding as she had been in the wave.

And then, she touched her lips to his, delicately, *needing* the connection to intensify.

His lips tasted of salt and strength and something

more powerful and more timeless than the ocean. That desire that people had within them, not just to live, but to go on.

For a moment, Drew was clearly stunned to find her lips on his. But then, he seemed to get whatever she was trying to tell him, in this primal language that seemed the only thing that could express the celebration of all that lived within her.

His lips answered hers. His tongue chased the ridges of her teeth, and then probed, gently, ever so gently...

It was Becky's turn to be stunned. It was everything she had hoped for. It was everything she had missed.

No, it was *more* than what she had hoped for, and more than what she could have ever imagined. A kiss was not simply a brushing of lips. No! It was a journey, it was a ride on pure energy, it was a connection, it was a discovery, it was an intertwining of the deepest parts of two people, of their souls.

Drew stopped kissing her with such abruptness that she felt forlorn, like a blanket had been jerked from her on a freezing night. He said Moose Run's most disapproved-of word again.

She *liked* the way he said that word, all naughty and nasty.

He found his feet and leaped up, staring down at her. He raked a hand through his hair, and water droplets scattered off his crumpled hair, sparkling like diamonds in the tropical heat. His shirt, crusted in golden sand, was clinging to his chest.

"Geez," he said. "What was that about?"

"I don't know," she said honestly. *But I liked it.*

"A girl like you does not kiss a guy like me!"

She could ask what he meant by a girl like her, but

she already knew that he thought she was small town and naive and hopelessly out of her depth, and not just in the ocean, either. What she wanted to know was what the last half of that sentence meant.

"What do you mean a guy like you?" she asked. Her voice was husky from the salt and from something else. Desire. Desire was burning like a white-hot coal in her belly. It was brand-new, it was embarrassing and it was wonderful.

"Look, Becky, I'm the kind of guy your mother used to warn you about."

Woo-hoo, she thought, but she didn't dare say it. Instead, she said, "The kind who would jump in the water without a thought for his own safety to save someone else?"

"Not that kind!"

She could point out to him that he obviously *was* that kind, and that the facts spoke for themselves, but she probed the deeper part of what was going on.

"What kind of guy then?" she asked, gently curious.

"Self-centered. Commitment-phobic. Good-time Charlie. Confirmed bachelor. They write whole articles about guys like me in your bridal magazines. And not about how to catch me, either. How to give a guy like me a wide berth."

"Just in case you didn't listen to your mother's warnings," she clarified.

He glanced at her. She bit her lip and his gaze rested there, hot with memory, until he seemed to make himself look away.

"I wouldn't have pictured you as any kind of expert about the content of bridal magazines," she said.

"That is not the point!"

"It was just a kiss," she pointed out mildly, "not a posting of the banns."

"You're in shock," he said.

If she was, she hoped she could experience it again, and soon!

CHAPTER SIX

DREW LOOKED AT Becky English. Sprawled out, belly down in the sand, she looked like a drowned rat, her hair plastered to her head, her yellow shirt plastered to her lithe body, both her shirt and her white shorts transparent in their wetness. For a drowned rat, and for a girl from Moose Run, Michigan, she had on surprisingly sexy underwear.

She looked like a drowned rat, and she was a small-town girl, but she sure as hell did not kiss like either one of those things. There had been nothing sweet or shy about that kiss!

It had been hungry enough to devour him.

But, Drew told himself sternly, she was exceedingly vulnerable. She was obviously stunned from what had just happened to her out there at the mercy of the ocean. It was possible she had banged her head riding that final wave in. The blow might have removed the filter from her brain that let her know what was, and what wasn't, appropriate.

But good grief, that kiss. He had to make sure nothing like that ever happened again! How was he going to be able to look at her without recalling the sweet, salty taste of her mouth? Without recalling the sweet welcome? Without recalling the flash of passion, the pull of which was at least as powerful as those waves?

"Becky," he said sternly, "don't make me your hero. I've been cast in that role before, and I stunk at it."

Drew had been seventeen when he became a parent to his brother. He had a sense of having grown up too fast and with too heavy a load. He was not interested in getting himself back into a situation where he was responsible for someone else's happiness and well-being. He didn't feel the evidence showed he had been that good at it.

"It was just a kiss," she said again, a bit too dreamily.

It wasn't just a kiss. If it had been just a kiss he would feel nothing, the same as he always did when he had just a kiss. He wouldn't be feeling this need to set her straight.

"When were you cast in that role before? How come you stank at it?" she asked softly. He noticed that, impossibly, the flower had survived in her hair. Its bright red petals were drooping sadly, kissing the tender flesh of her temple.

"This is not the time or the place," he said curtly before, in this weakened moment, in this contrived atmosphere of closeness, he threw himself down beside her, and let her save him, the way he had just saved her.

"Are you hurt?" he asked, cold and clinical. "Any bumps or bruises? Did you hit your head?"

Thankfully, she was distracted, and considered his question with an almost comical furrowing of her brow.

"I don't think I hit my head, but my leg hurts," she decided. "I think I scraped it on a rock coming in."

She rolled onto her back and then struggled to sit up. He peered over her shoulder. There was six inches of scrapes on the inside of her thigh, one of the marks looked quite deep and there was blood clumping in the sand that clung to it.

What was wrong with him? The first thing he should have done was check for injuries.

He stripped off his wet shirt and got down beside her. This was what was wrong with him. He was way too aware of her. The scent of the sea was clinging to her body, a body he was way too familiar with after having dragged her from the ocean and then accepted the invitation of her lips.

Becky was right. There was something exhilarating about snatching life back out of the jaws of death. That's why he was so aware of her on every level, not thinking with his customary pragmatism.

He brushed the sand away from her wound. He should have known touching the inner thigh of a girl like Becky English was going to be nothing like a man might have expected.

"Ow," she said, and her fingers dug into his shoulder and then lingered there. "Oh, my," she breathed. "You did warn me what would happen if you took your shirt off."

"I was kidding," he said tersely.

"No, you weren't. You were warning me off."

"How's that working for you, Drew?" he muttered to himself. He cleaned the sand away from her wound as best he could, then wrapped it in his soaked shirt.

She sighed with satisfaction like the geeky girl who had just gotten all the words right at the spelling bee. "Women adore you."

"Not ones as smart as you," he said. "Can you stand? We have to find a first aid kit. I think that's just a superficial scrape, but it's bleeding quite a lot and we need to get it looked after."

He helped her to her feet, still way too aware, steeling himself against the silky resilience of her skin. She swayed against him. Her wet curves were pressed into him, and her chin was pressed sharply into his chest as she looked up at him with huge, unblinking eyes.

Had he thought, just an hour ago, her eyes were ordinary brown? They weren't. They were like melted milk chocolate, deep and rich and inviting.

"You were right." She giggled. "I'm swooning."

"Let's hope it's not from blood loss. Can you walk?"

"Of course."

She didn't move.

He sighed and scooped her up, cradling her to his chest, one arm under her knees, the other across her back. She was lighter than he could have believed, and her softness pressed into him was making him way more vulnerable than the embraces of women he'd known who had far more in the curvy department.

"You're very masterful," she said, snuggling into him.

"In this day and age how can that be a good thing?"

"It's a secret longing."

He did not want to hear about her secret longings!

"If you don't believe me, read—"

"Stop it," he said grimly.

"I owe you my life."

"I said stop it."

"You are not the boss over me."

"That's what I was afraid of."

He carried her back along the path. She was small and light and it took no effort at all. At the castle, he found the kitchen, an enormous room that looked like the kind of well-appointed facility one would expect to find in a five-star hotel.

"Have you got a first aid attendant here?" Drew asked one of the kitchen staff, who went and fetched the chef.

The chef showed him through to an office adjoining the kitchen, and Drew settled Becky in a chair. The chef sent in a young man with a first aid kit. He was slender and golden-skinned with dark, dark hair and almond-shaped eyes that matched.

"I am Tandu," he said. "I am the medical man." His accent made it sound as if he had said *medicine man*.

Relived that he could back off from more physical contact with the delectable Miss Becky, Drew motioned to where she sat.

Tandu set down his first aid kit and crouched down in front of her. He carefully unwrapped Drew's wet shirt from her leg. He stared at Becky's injury for a moment, scrambled to his feet, picked up the first aid kit and thrust it at Drew.

"I do not do blood."

"What kind of first aid attendant doesn't—?"

But Tandu had already fled.

Drew, even more aware of her now that he had nearly escaped, went and found a pan of warm water, and then cleaned and dressed her wound, steeling himself to be as professional as possible.

Becky stared down at the dark head of the man kneeling at her feet. He pressed a warm, wet cloth against the tender skin of her inner thigh, and she gasped at the sensation that jolted through her like an electric shock.

He glanced up at her, then looked back to his task quickly. "Sorry," he muttered. "I will try to make this as painless as possible."

Despite the fact his touch was incredibly tender—or maybe because of it—it was one of the most deliciously painful experiences of Becky's life. He carefully cleaned the scrapes, dabbed an ointment on them and then wound clean gauze around her leg.

She could feel a quiver within her building. There was going to be an earthquake if he didn't finish soon! She longed to reach out and touch his hair, to brush the salt and sand from it. She reached out.

A pan dropped in the kitchen, and she felt reality crashing back in around her. She snatched her hand back, just as Drew glanced up.

"Are you okay?"

"Sure," she said shakily, but she really wasn't. What she felt like was a girl who had been very drunk, and who had done all kinds of uninhibited and crazy things, and was now coming to her senses.

She had kissed Drew Jordan shamelessly. She had shared all her secrets with him. She had blabbered that he was masterful, as if she enjoyed such a thing! Now she had nearly touched his hair, as if they were lovers instead of near strangers!

Okay, his hand upon her thigh was obviously creating confusion in the more primal cortexes of her brain, but she had to pull herself together.

"There," he said, rocking back on his heels and studying the bandage around her thigh, "I think—"

She didn't let him finish. She shot to her feet, gazed down at her bandaged thigh instead of at him. "Yes, yes, perfect," she said. She sounded like a German engineer approving a mechanical drawing. Her thigh was tingling unmercifully, and she was pretty sure it was from his touch and not from the injury.

"I have to get to work," she said in a strangled voice.

He stood up. "You aren't going to work. You're going to rest for the afternoon."

"But I can't. I—"

"I'm telling you, you need to rest."

She thought, again, of telling him he was masterful. Good grief, she could feel the blush rising up her cheeks. She had probably created a monster.

In him and in herself.

"Go to bed," he said. Drew's voice was as caressing as his hand had been, and just as seductive. "Just for what is left of the afternoon. You'll be glad you did."

You did not discuss bed with a man like this! And especially not after he had just performed intimate rituals on your thigh! Particularly not after you had noticed his voice was seduction itself, all deep and warm and caressing.

You did not discuss bed with a man like this once you had come to your senses. She opened her mouth to tell him she would decide for herself what needed to be done. It would not involve the word *bed*. But before she could speak, he did.

"I'll go scout a spot for the wedding. Joe will be here in a while. By the time you wake up, we'll have it all taken care of."

All her resolve to take back the reins of her own life dissolved, instantly, like sugar into hot tea.

It felt as if she was going to start crying. When was the last time anything had been taken care of for her? After her father had left, her poor shattered mother had absconded on parenting. It felt as if Becky had been the one who looked after everything. Jerry had seemed to like her devoting herself to organizing his life. Even her career took advantage of the fact that Becky English was the one who looked after things, who tried valiantly to fix all and to achieve perfection. She took it all on… until the weight of it nearly crushed her.

Where had that thought come from? She *loved* her job. Putting together joyous and memorable occasions for others had soothed the pain of her father's abandonment, and had, thankfully, been enough to fill her world ever since the defection of Jerry from her personal landscape.

Or had been enough until less than twenty-four hours ago, when Drew Jordan had showed up in her life and showed her there was still such a thing as a hero.

She turned and fled before she did something really foolish. Like kissing him again.

Becky found that as much as she would have liked to rebel against his advice, she had no choice but to take it. Clear of the kitchen, her limbs felt like jelly, heavy and nearly shaking with exhaustion and delayed reaction to all the unexpected adventures of the day. It took every bit of remaining energy she had to climb the stone staircase that led to the wing of the castle with her room in it.

She went into its cool sanctuary and peeled off her wet clothes. It felt like too much effort to even find something else to put on. She left the clothes in a heap and crept under the cool sheets of the welcoming bed. Within seconds she was fast asleep.

She dreamed that someone was knocking on her door, and when she went to answer it, Drew Jordan was on the other side of it, a smile of pure welcome on his face. He reached for her, he pulled her close, his mouth dropped over hers...

Becky started awake. She was not sure what time it was, though the light suggested early evening, which meant she had frittered away a whole precious afternoon sleeping.

She wanted to leap from bed, but her body would not let her. She felt, again, like the girl who had had too much to drink. She tested each of her limbs. It was official. Her whole body hurt. Her head hurt. Her mouth and throat felt raw and dry. But mostly, she felt deeply ashamed. She had lost control, and she hated that.

Her door squeaked open.

"How you doing?"

She shot up in bed, pulled the sheet more tightly around herself. "What are you doing here?"

"I knocked. When there was no answer, I thought I'd better check on you. You slept a long time."

Drew Jordan looked just as he had in the dream— gorgeous. Though in real life there was no expression of tender welcome on his face. It did not look like he was thinking about sweeping her into his big strong arms.

In fact, he slipped into the room, but rested himself against the far wall—as far away from her as possible— those big, strong arms folded firmly across his chest. He was wearing a snowy-white T-shirt that showed off the sun-bronzed color of his arms, and khaki shorts that showed off the long, hard muscle of equally sun-bronzed legs.

"A long time?" She found her cell phone on the bedside table. "It's only five. That's not so bad."

"Um, maybe you should have a look at the date on there."

She frowned down at her phone. Her mouth fell open. "What? I slept an entire day? But I couldn't have! That's impossible."

She started to throw back the covers, then remembered she had slipped in between the sheets naked. She yanked them up around her chin.

"It was probably the best thing you could do. Your body knows what it needs."

She looked up at him. Her body, treacherous thing, did indeed know what it needed! And all of it involved him.

"If you would excuse me," she said, "I really need—"

Now her brain, treacherous thing, silently screamed *you*.

"Are you okay?"

No! It simply was not okay to be this aware of him, to yearn for his touch and his taste.

"I'm fine. Did your brother come?" she asked, desperate to distract him from her discomfort, and from the possibility of him discerning what was causing it.

"Nope. I can't seem to reach him on my phone, either."

"Oh, Drew," she said softly.

Her tone seemed to annoy him. "You don't really look fine," he decided.

"Okay, I'm not fine. I don't have time to sleep away a whole day. Despite all that rest, I feel as if I've been through the spin cycle of a giant washing machine. I hurt everywhere, worse than the worst hangover ever."

"You've had a hangover?" He said this with insulting incredulousness.

"Of course I have. Living in Moose Run isn't like taking vows to become a nun, you know."

"You would be wasted as a nun," he said, and his gaze went to her lips before he looked sharply away.

"Let's talk about that," she said.

"About you being wasted as a nun?" he asked, looking back at her, surprised.

"About the fact you think you would know such a thing about me. I don't normally act like that. I would never, under ordinary circumstances, kiss a person the way I kissed you. Naturally, I'm mortified."

He lifted an eyebrow.

"There was no need to throw myself at you, no matter how grateful and discombobulated I was."

His lips twitched.

"It's not funny," she told him sternly. "It's embarrassing."

"It's not your wanton and very un-nun-like behavior I was smiling about."

"Wanton?" she squeaked.

"It was the fact you used *discombobulated* in a sentence. I can't say as I've ever heard that before."

"Wanton?" she squeaked again.

"Sorry. Wanton is probably overstating it."

"Probably?"

"We don't all have your gift for picking exactly the right word," he said. He lifted a shoulder. "People do weird things when they are in shock. Let's move past it, okay?"

Actually, she would have preferred to find out exactly what he meant by wanton—it had been a little kiss really, it didn't even merit the humiliation she was feeling about it—but she didn't want to look like she was unwilling to move past it.

"Okay," she said grudgingly. "Though just for the

record, I want you to know I don't like masterful men. At all."

"No secret longing?"

He was teasing her! There was a residue of weakness in her, because she liked it, but it would be a mistake to let him know her weaknesses.

"As you have pointed out," Becky said coolly, "I was in shock. I said and did things that were completely alien to my nature. Now, let's move past it."

Something smoky happened to his eyes. His gaze stopped on her lips. She had the feeling he would dearly like to prove to her that some things were not as alien to her nature as she wanted them both to believe.

But he fended off the temptation, with apparent ease, pushing himself away from the wall and heading back for the door. "You have one less thing to worry about. I think I have the pavilion figured out."

"Really?" She would have leaped up and gave him a hug, except she was naked underneath the sheet, he already thought she was wanton enough, and she was not exposing anything to him, least of all not her longing to let other people look after things for a change. And to feel his embrace once more, his hard, hot muscles against her naked flesh.

"You do?" she squeaked, trying to find a place to put her gaze, anywhere but his hard, hot muscles.

"I thought about what you said, about creating an illusion. I started thinking about driving some posts, and suspending fabric from them. Something like a canopy bed."

She squinted at him. That urge to hold him, to feel him, to touch him, was there again, stronger. It was because he was looking after things, taking on a part of the burden without being asked. It was because he had listened to her.

Becky English, lying there in her bed, naked, with her sheet pulled up around her chin, studied her ceiling, so awfully aware that a woman could fall for a guy like him before she even knew what had happened to her.

CHAPTER SEVEN

THANKFULLY FOR BECKY, Drew Jordan had already warned her about guys like him.

"What does a confirmed bachelor know about canopy beds?" she said, keeping her gaze on the ceiling and her tone deliberately light. "No, never mind. I don't want to know. I think I'm still slightly discombobulated."

"Admit it."

She glanced over at him just as he grinned. His teeth were white and straight. He looked way too handsome. She returned her gaze to the ceiling. "I just did. I'm still slightly discombobulated."

"Not that! Admit it's brilliant."

She couldn't help but smile. And look at him again. "It is. It's brilliant. It will create that illusion of a room, and possibly provide some protection from the sun if we use fabric as a kind of ceiling. It has the potential to be exceedingly romantic, too. Which is why I'm surprised you came up with it."

"Hey, nobody is more surprised than me. Sadly, after traipsing all over the island this afternoon, I still haven't found a good site for the ceremony. But you might as well come see what's going on with the pavilion."

She should not appear too eager. But really? Pretending just felt like way too much effort. She would have to chalk it up to her near drowning and the other rattling events of the day. "Absolutely. Give me five minutes."

"Sure. I'll meet you on the front stairs."

Of course, it took Becky longer than five minutes. She had to shower off the remains of her adventure. She had sand in places she did not know sand could go. Her hair was destroyed. Her leg was a mess and she had to rewrap it after she was done. She had faint bruising appearing in the most unlikely places all over her body.

She put on her only pair of long pants—as uninspiring as they were in a lightweight grey tweed—and a long-sleeved shirt in a shade of hot pink that matched some of the flowers that bloomed in such abundance on this island. Her outfit covered the worst of the damage to her poor battered body, but there was nothing she could do about the emotional battering she was receiving. And it wasn't his fault. Drew Jordan was completely oblivious to the effect he was having on her.

Or accustomed to it!

Becky dabbed on a bit of makeup to try to hide the crescent moons from under her eyes. She looked exhausted. How was that possible after nearly twenty-four hours of sleep? At the last minute, she just touched a bit of gloss to her lips. It wasn't wrong to want him to look at them, but she hoped she would not be discombobulated enough to offer them to him again anytime in the near future.

"Or any future!" she told herself firmly.

She had pictured Drew waiting impatiently for her, but when she arrived at the front step, he had out a can of spray paint and was marking big X's on the grassy lawn in front of the castle.

Just when she was trying not to think of kisses anymore. What was this clumsy artwork on the lawn all about? An invitation? A declaration of love? A late Valentine?

"Marking where the posts should go," he told her, glancing toward her and then looking back at what he was doing. "Can you come stand right here and hold the tape measure?"

So much for a declaration of love! Good grief. She had always harbored this secret and very unrealistic side. She thought Jerry had cured her of her more fantastic romantic notions, but no, some were like little seeds inside her, waiting for the first hint of water and sun to sprout into full-fledged fairy tales. Being rescued from certain death by a very good-looking and extremely competent man who had so willingly put his own life on the line for her had obviously triggered her most fanciful longings.

She just needed to swat herself up the side of the head with the facts. She and Drew Jordan barely knew one another, and before she was swept off the rock they had been destined to butt heads.

She had to amend that: she barely knew Drew Jordan, but he knew her better than he should because she had blurted out her whole life story in a moment of terrible weakness. It was just more evidence that she must have hit her head somewhere in that debacle. Except for the fact she was useful for holding the tape measure, he hardly seemed aware that she was there.

Finally, he rolled up the tape measure. "What do you think?"

His X's formed a large rectangle. She could picture it already with a silken canopy and the posts swathed in fabric. She could picture the tables and the candles, and music and a beautiful bride and groom.

"I think it's going to be perfect," she breathed. And for the first time since she had taken on this job, she felt like maybe it would be.

How much of that had to do with the man who was, however reluctantly, helping her make it happen?

"Don't get your hopes up too high," he said. "Perfection is harder to achieve than you think. And we still have the evening tropical breezes to contend with. And I haven't found a ceremony site. It could go sideways yet."

"Especially if you talk to your brother?"

He rolled his shoulders. "There doesn't seem to be much chance of that happening. But there are a lot of things that could go sideways before the big day."

Yes, she had seen in recent history how quickly things could go sideways. In fact, when she looked at him, she was pretty sure Drew Jordan was the kind of man who could make your whole life go sideways with no effort on his part at all.

"Let's go see if we can find a place for the ceremony."

She *had* to go with him. It was her job. But tropical breezes seemed to be the least of her problems at the moment.

"I should be getting danger pay," she muttered to herself.

"Don't worry, I won't be letting you anywhere near any rocks."

No sense clarifying with him that was not where the danger she was worried about was coming from. Not at all.

They were almost at the edge of the lawn when a voice stopped them.

"Miss Becky. Mr. Drew."

They turned to see Tandu struggling across the lawn with a huge wicker basket. "So sorry, no good with blood. Take you to place for wedding vow now."

"Oh, did you tell him we were looking for a new ceremony site?" Becky asked. "That was smart."

"Naturally, I would like to take credit for being smart, but I didn't tell him. They must do weddings here all the time. He's used to this."

"Follow, follow," Tandu ordered.

They fell into step behind him, leaving the lawn and entering the deep, vibrant green of the jungle forest. Birds chattered and the breeze lifting huge leaves made a sound, too.

"Actually, the owner of the island told me they had hosted some huge events here, but never a wedding," Becky told Drew. "He's the music mogul, Bart Lung. He's a friend of Allie's. He's away on business but he'll be back for the wedding. He's very excited about it."

"Are you excited about meeting him?"

"I guess I hadn't really thought about it. We better catch up to Tandu, he's way ahead of us."

Drew contemplated what had just happened with a trace of self-loathing.

Are you excited about meeting him? As bad as asking the question was how much he had liked her answer. She genuinely seemed not to have given a thought to meeting Bart Lung.

But what had motivated Drew to ask such a question? Surely he hadn't been feeling a bit threatened about

Becky meeting the famously single and fabulously wealthy record broker? He couldn't possibly have felt the faintest little prickle of…jealousy.

He never felt jealous. He'd had women he had dated who had tried to make him jealous, and he'd been annoyed by how juvenile that felt. But at the heart of it, he knew they had wanted him to show what he couldn't: that he cared.

But he'd known from the moment she had instigated that kiss that Becky English was different from what his brother liked to call the rotating door of women in his life. The chemistry between them had been unexpected, but Drew had had chemistry before. He wasn't sure exactly what it was about the cheerleader-turned-event-planner that intrigued him, but he knew he had to get away from it.

Which was exactly why he had marched up to her room. He had two reasons, and two reasons only, to interact with her: the pavilion and the ceremony site. He'd promised his brother and Becky his help, and once the planning for his assigned tasks was solidly in place, he could minimize his interactions with her. He was about to get very busy with construction. That would leave much less time for contemplating the lovely Miss English.

"I hate to say it," he told Becky, looking at Tandu's back disappearing down a twisting path in front of them, "but I've already been over this stretch of the island. There is no—"

"This way, please." Tandu had stopped and was holding back thick jungle fronds. "Path overgrown a bit. I will tell gardening staff. Important for all to be ready for big day, eh?"

It was just a short walk, and the path opened onto a beautiful crescent of beach. Drew studied it from a construction point of view. He could see the high tide line, and it would be perfect for building a small pavilion and setting up chairs for the two hundred guests. Three large palms grew out of the center of the beach, their huge leathery leaves shading almost the entire area.

Becky, he could see, was looking at it from a far less practical standpoint than he was. She turned to look at him. Her eyes were shiny with delight, and those little plump lips were curved upward in the nicest smile.

Task completed! Drew told himself sternly. Pavilion, check. Wedding location, check. Missing brother...well, that had nothing to do with her. He had to get away from her—and her plump little lips—and *stay* away from her.

"It's perfect," he said. "Do you agree?"

She turned those shining eyes to him. "Agree?" she said softly. "Have you ever seen such a magical place in your whole life?"

He looked around with magic in mind rather than construction. He was not much of a magic kind of person, but he supposed he had not seen a place quite like this before. The whole beach was ringed with thick shrubs with dark green foliage. Tucked in amongst the foliage was an abundance of pale yellow and white flowers the size of cantaloupes. The flowers seemed to be emitting a perfume that was sweet and spicy at the same time. Unfortunately, that made him think of her lips again.

He glared at the sand, which was pure white and finer than sugar. They were in a cove of a small bay, and the water was striped in aqua shades of turquoise, all the way out to a reef, where the water turned dark navy blue, and the waves broke, white-capped, over rocks.

"Well," he said, "I'll just head back."

"Do you ever just answer a question?"

"Sit, sit," Tandu said from behind them.

Drew swung around to look at him. While he had been looking out toward the sea, Tandu had emptied the wicker basket he carried. There was a blanket set up in the sand, and laid out on it was a bottle of wine, beaded with sweat, two wineglasses and two plates. There was a platter of blackened chicken, fresh fruit and golden, steaming croissants.

"What the hell?" Drew asked.

"Sit, sit—amens…amens."

"I'm not following," Drew said. He saw that Becky had had no trouble whatsoever plopping herself down on the blanket. Had she forgotten she'd lost a whole day? She had to be seriously behind schedule.

"I make amens," Tandu said quietly, "for not doing first aid."

"Oh, *amends*," Drew said uncomfortably. "Really, it's not necessary at all. I have a ton of stuff to do. I'm not very hungry." This was a complete lie, though he had not realized quite how hungry he was until the food had *magically* appeared.

Tandu looked dejected that his offer was being refused.

"You very irritated with me," Tandu said sadly.

Becky caught his eye, lifted her shoulder—*come on, be a sport*—and patted the blanket. With a resigned shake of his head, Drew lowered himself onto the blanket. He bet if he ate one bite of this food that had been set out the spell would be complete.

"Look, I wasn't exactly irritated." This was as much a lie as the one about how he wasn't hungry, and he had a feeling Tandu was not easily fooled. "I was just a little surprised by a first aid man who doesn't like blood."

"Oh, yes," Tandu said happily. "Sit, sit, I fix."

"I am sitting. There's to nothing to fix." Except that Sainte Simone needed a new first aid attendant—before two hundred people descended on it would be good—but Drew found he did not have the heart to tell Tandu that.

Maybe the place was as magical as it looked, because he found himself unable to resist sitting beside Becky on the picnic blanket, though he told himself he had complied only because he did not want to disappoint Tandu, who had obviously misinterpreted his level of annoyance.

"I am not a first aid man," Tandu said. "Uh, how you say, medicine man? My family are healers. We see things."

"See things?" Drew asked. "I'm not following."

"Like a seer or a shaman?" Becky asked. She sounded thrilled.

Drew shot her a look. *Don't encourage him.* She ignored him. "Like what kind of things? Like the future?"

Drew groaned.

"Well, how did he know we needed a wedding site?" she challenged him.

"Because two hundred people are descending on this little piece of paradise for a marriage?"

She actually stuck one of her pointy little elbows in his ribs as if it was rude of him to point out the obvious.

"Yes, yes, like future," Tandu said, very pleased,

missing or ignoring Drew's skepticism and not seeing Becky's dig in his ribs. "See things."

"So what do you see for the wedding?" Becky asked eagerly, leaning forward, as if she was going to put a great deal of stock in the answer.

Tandu looked off into the distance. He suddenly did not look like a smiling servant in a white shirt. Not at all. His expression was intense, and when he turned his gaze back to them, his liquid brown eyes did not seem soft or merry anymore.

"Unexpected things," he said softly. "Lots of surprises. Very happy, very happy wedding. Everybody happy. Babies. Many, many babies in the future."

Becky clapped her hands with delight. "Drew, you're going to be an uncle."

"How very terrifying," he said drily. "Since you can see things, Tandu, when is my brother arriving?"

"Not when you expect," Tandu said, without hesitation.

"Thanks. Tell me something I don't know."

Tandu appeared to take that as a challenge. He gazed off into the distance again. Finally he spoke.

"Broken hearts mended," Tandu said with satisfaction.

"Whose broken hearts?" Becky asked, her eyes wide. "The bride? The groom?"

"For Pete's sake," Drew snapped.

Tandu did not look at him, but gazed steadily and silently at Becky.

"Oh," Becky said, embarrassed. "I don't have a broken heart."

Tandu cocked his head, considering. Drew found himself listening with uncomfortable intentness.

"You left your brokenness in the water," Tandu told Becky. "What you thought was true never was."

She gasped softly, then turned faintly accusing eyes to Drew. "Did you tell him what I said about Jerry?"

He was amazed how much it stung that she thought he would break her confidence. That accusing look in her eyes should be a good thing—it might cool the sparks that had leaped up between them.

But he couldn't leave well enough alone. "Of course not," he said.

"Well, then how did he know?"

"He's a seer," Drew reminded her with a certain amount of satisfaction.

Tandu seemed to have not heard one word of this conversation.

"But you need to swim," he told Becky. "Not be afraid of water. Water here very, very good swimming. Safe. Best swimming beach right here."

"Oh, that's a good idea," she said, turning her head to look at the inviting water, "but I'm not prepared."

"Prepared?" Tandu said, surprised. "What to prepare?"

"I don't have a swimming suit," Becky told him.

"At all?" Drew asked, despite himself. "Who comes to the Caribbean without a swimming suit?"

"I'm not here to play," she said with a stern toss of her head.

"God forbid," he said, but he could not help but feel she was a woman who seemed to take life way too seriously. Which, of course, was not his problem.

"I don't actually own a swimming suit," she said. "The nearest pool is a long way from Moose Run. We aren't close to a lake."

"Ha. Born with swimming suit," Tandu told her seriously. "Skin waterproof."

Drew watched with deep pleasure as the crimson crept up her neck to her cheeks. "Ha-ha," he said in an undertone, "that's what you get for encouraging him."

"You swim," Tandu told her. "Eat first, then swim. Mr. Drew help you."

"Naked swimming," Drew said. "Happy to help when I can. Tandu, do you see skinny-dipping in my future?"

There was that pointy little elbow in his ribs again, quite a bit harder than it had been the last time.

But before he could enjoy Becky's discomfort too much, suddenly Drew found himself pinned in Tandu's intense gaze. "The heart that is broken is yours, Mr. Drew?"

CHAPTER EIGHT

DREW JORDAN ORDERED himself to say no. No to magic. No to the light in Becky's eyes. And especially no to Tandu's highly invasive question. But instead of saying no, he found he couldn't speak at all, as if his throat was closing and his tongue was stuck to the roof of his mouth.

"They say a man is not given more than he can take, eh?" Tandu said.

If there was an expression on the face of the earth that Drew hated with his whole heart and soul it was that one, but he still found he could say nothing.

"But you were," Tandu said softly. "You were given more than you could take. You are a strong man. But not that strong, eh, Mr. Drew?"

His chest felt heavy. His throat felt as if it was closing. There was a weird stinging behind his eyes, as if he was allergic to the overwhelming scent of those flowers.

Without warning, he was back there.

He was seventeen years old. He was standing at the door of his house. It was the middle of the night. His feet and chest were bare and he had on pajama bottoms. He was blinking away sleep, trying to comprehend the stranger at the door of his house. The policeman said, "I'm sorry, son." And then Drew found out he wasn't anyone's son, not anymore.

Drew shook his head and looked at Tandu, fiercely.

"You heal now," Tandu said, not intimidated, as if it was an order. "You heal." And then suddenly Tandu was himself again, the easygoing grin on his face, his teeth impossibly perfect and white against the golden brown of his skin. His eyes were gentle and warm. "Eat, eat. Then swim. Then sunset."

And then he was gone.

"What was that about?" Becky asked him.

"I don't have a clue," he said. His voice sounded strange to him, choked and hoarse. "Creepy weirdness."

Becky was watching him as if she knew it was a lie. When had he become such a liar? He'd better give it up, he was terrible at it. He poured two glasses of wine, handed her one and tossed back the other. He set down the glass carefully.

"There. I've toasted the wedding spot. I'm going to go now." He didn't move.

"Have you?" she asked.

"Have I what? Toasted the wedding spot?"

"Had a heartbreak?" she asked softly, with concern.

And he felt, suddenly, as alone with his burdens as he had ever felt. He felt as if he could lay it all at her feet. He looked at the warmth and loveliness of her brushed-suede eyes. *You heal now.*

He reeled back from the invitation in her eyes. He was the most pragmatic of men. He was not under the enchantment of this beach, or Tandu's words, or her.

Not yet, an inner voice informed him cheerfully.

Not ever, he informed the inner voice with no cheer

at all. He was not touching that food with its potential to weaken him even further. And no more wine.

"People like me," he said, forcing a cavalier ease into his voice.

She leaned toward him.

"We don't have hearts to break. I'm leaving now." Still, he did not move.

She looked as if she wanted to argue with that, but she took one look at his face and very wisely turned her attention to the chicken. "Is this burned?" she asked, poking one of the pieces gingerly with her fingertip.

"I think it's jerked, a very famous way of cooking on these islands." It felt like a relief to focus on the chicken instead of what was going on inside himself.

She took a piece and nibbled it. Her expression changed to one of complete awe. "You have to try it," she insisted. "You have to try it and tell me if it isn't the best thing you have ever tasted. Just one bite before you go."

Despite knowing this food probably had a spell woven right into it, he threw caution to the wind, picked up a leg of chicken and chomped into it. Just a few hours ago it definitely would have been the best thing he had ever tasted. But now that he was under a spell, he saw things differently.

Because the blackened jerk chicken quite possibly might have been the best thing he'd ever tasted, if he hadn't very foolishly sampled her lips when she had offered them yesterday afternoon.

"You might as well stay and eat," she said. She reached over and refilled his empty wineglass. "It would be a shame to let it go to waste."

He was not staying here, eating enchanted food in

an enchanted cove with a woman who was clearly putting a spell on him. On the other hand, she was right. It would be a shame to let the food go to waste.

There was no such thing as spells, anyway. He picked up his second piece of chicken. He watched her delicately lick her fingertips.

"We don't have this kind of food in Moose Run," she said. "More's the pity."

"What kind of food do you have?" He was just being polite, he told himself, before he left her. He frowned. That second glass of wine could not be gone.

"We have two restaurants. We have the Main Street Diner which specializes in half-pound hamburgers and claims to have the best chocolate milk shake in all of Michigan."

"Claims?"

"I haven't tried all the chocolate milk shakes in Michigan," she said. "But believe me, I'm working on it."

He felt something relax within him. He should not be relaxing. He needed to keep his guard up. Still, he laughed at her earnest expression.

"And then we have Mr. Wang's All-You-Can-Eat Spectacular Smorgasbord."

"So, two restaurants. What else do you do for fun?"

She looked uncomfortable. It was none of his business, he told himself firmly. Why did he care if it was just as he'd suspected? She did not have nearly enough fun going on in her life. Not that it was any concern of his.

"Is there a movie theater?" he coaxed her.

"Yes. And don't forget the church picnic."

"And dancing on the grass," he supplied.

"I'm not much for the church socials, actually. I don't really like dancing."

"So what do you like?"

She hesitated, and then met his eyes. "I'm sure you are going to think I am the world's most boring person, but you know what I really do for fun?"

He felt as if he was holding his breath for some reason. Crazy to hope the answer was going to involve kissing. Not that anyone would consider that boring, would they? Was his wineglass full again? He took a sip.

"I read," she said, in a hushed whisper, as if she was in a confessional. She sighed. "I love to read."

What a relief! Reading, not kissing! It should have seemed faintly pathetic, but somehow, just like the rest of her, it seemed real. In an amusement park world where everyone was demanding to be entertained constantly, by bigger things and better amusements and wilder rides and greater spectacles, by things that stretched the bounds of what humans were intended to do, it seemed lovely that Becky had her own way of being in the world, and that something so simple as opening a book could make someone contented.

She was bracing herself, as if she expected him to be scornful. It made him wonder if the ex-beau had been one of those put-down kind of guys.

"I can actually picture you out in a hammock on a sunny afternoon," he said. "It sounds surprisingly nice."

"At this time of year, it's a favorite chair. On my front porch. We still have front porches in Moose Run."

He could picture a deeply shaded porch, and a sleepy street, and hear the sound of birds. This, too, struck him as deliciously simple in a complicated world. "What's your favorite book?" he asked.

"I have to pick one?" she asked with mock horror.

"Let me put it differently. If you had to recommend a book to someone who hardly ever reads, which one would it be?"

And somehow it was that easy. The food was disappearing and so was the wine, and she was telling him about her favorite books and authors, and he was telling her about surfing the big waves and riding his motorbike on the Pacific Coast Highway between LA and San Francisco.

The fight seemed to ease out of him, and the wariness. The urgent need to be somewhere else seemed silly. Drew felt himself relaxing. Why not enjoy it? It was no big deal. Tomorrow his crew would be here. He would immerse himself in his work. He could enjoy this last evening with Becky before that happened, couldn't he?

Who would have ever guessed it would be so easy to be with a man like this? Becky thought. The conversation was comfortable between them. There was so much work that needed to be done on Allie's wedding, and she had already lost a precious day. Still, she had never felt less inclined to do work.

But as comfortable as it all was, she could feel a little nudge of disappointment. How could they go from that electrifying kiss, to this?

Not that she wanted the danger of that kiss again, but she certainly didn't want him to think she was a dull small-town girl whose idea of an exciting evening was sitting out on her front porch reading until the fireflies came out.

Dinner was done. The wine bottle was lying on its

side, empty. All that was left of the chicken was bones, and all that was left of the croissants were a few golden crumbs. As she watched, Drew picked one of those up on his fingertip and popped it in his mouth.

How could such a small thing be so darned sexy?

In her long pants and long-sleeved shirt, Becky was suddenly aware of feeling way too warm. And over-dressed. She was aware of being caught in the enchantment of Sainte Simone and this beautiful beach. She longed to be free of encumbrances.

Like clothing? she asked herself, appalled, but not appalled enough to stop the next words that came out of her mouth.

"Let's go for that swim after all," she said. She tried to sound casual, but her heart felt as if she had just finished running a marathon.

"I really need to go." He said it without any kind of conviction. "Are you going to swim in nature's bathing suit?"

"Don't be a pervert!"

"I'm not. Tandu suggested it. One-hundred-percent waterproof."

"Don't look," she said.

"Sure. I'll stop breathing while I'm at it."

What was she doing? she asked herself.

For once in her life, she was acting on a whim, that's what she was doing. For once in her life she was being bold, that's what she was doing. For once in her life, she was throwing convention to the wind, she was doing what she wanted to do. She was not leaving him with the impression she was a dull small-town girl who had spent her whole life with her nose buried in a book. Even if she had been!

She didn't want that to be the whole truth about her anymore, and not just because of him, either. Because the incident in the water yesterday, that moment when she had looked her own death in the face and somehow been spared, had left her with a longing for second chances.

She stood up and turned her back to him. Becky took a deep breath and peeled her shirt over her head, then unbuckled her slacks and stepped out of them. She had on her luxurious Rembrandt's Drawing brand underwear. The underwear was a matching set, a deep shade of turquoise not that different from the water. It was as fashionable as most bathing suits, and certainly more expensive.

She glanced over her shoulder, and his expression—stunned, appreciative, approving—made her run for the water. She splashed in up to her knees, and then threw herself in. The water closed over her head, and unlike yesterday afternoon, it felt wonderful in the heat of the early evening, cool and silky as a caress on her nearly naked skin.

She surfaced, then paddled out and found her footing when she was up to her neck in water, her underwear hidden from him. She turned to look at where he was still sitting on the blanket. Even from here, she could see the heat in his eyes.

Oh, girlfriend, she thought, *you do not know what you are playing with.* But the thing about letting a bolder side out was that it was very hard to stuff it back in, like trying to get a jack-in-the-box back in its container.

"Come in," she called. "It's glorious."

He stood up slowly and peeled his shirt off. She held

her breath. It was her turn to be stunned, appreciative and approving.

She had seen him without his shirt already when he had sacrificed it to doctor her leg. But this was different. She wasn't in shock, or in pain, or bleeding all over the place.

Becky was aware, as she had been when she had first laid eyes on him, that he was the most beautifully made of men. Broad shouldered and deep chested, muscular without being muscle-bound. He could be an actor or a model, because he had that mysterious something that made her—and probably every other woman on earth— feel as if she could look at him endlessly, drink in his masculine perfection as if he was a long, cool drink of water and she was dying of thirst.

Was he going to take off his shorts? She was aware she was holding her breath. But no, he kicked off his shoes and, with the khaki shorts safely in place, ran toward the water. Like she had done, he ran in up to about his thighs and then she watched as he dived beneath the surface.

"I didn't peg you for shy," she told him when he surfaced close to her.

He lifted an eyebrow at her.

"I've seen men's underwear before. I'm from Moose Run, not the convent."

"You've mentioned you weren't a nun once before," he said. "What's with the fascination with nuns?"

"You just seem to think because I'm small town I'm prim and proper. You didn't have to get your shorts all wet to save my sensibilities."

"I don't wear underwear."

Her mouth fell open. She could feel herself turning crimson. He laughed, delighted at her discomfort.

"How are your sensibilities doing now?" he asked her.

"Fine," she squeaked. But they both knew it was a lie, and he laughed.

"Come on," he said, shaking the droplets of water from his hair. "I'll race you to those rocks."

"That's ridiculous. I don't have a hope of winning."

"I know," he said fiendishly.

"I get a head start."

"All right."

"A big one."

"Okay, you tell me when I can go."

She paddled her way toward the rocks. When it seemed there was no chance he could catch her, she called, "Okay, go."

She could hear him coming up behind her. She paddled harder. He grabbed her foot!

"Hey!" She went under the water. He let go of her foot, and when she surfaced, he had surged by her and was touching the rock.

"You cheater," she said indignantly.

"You're the cheater. What kind of head start was that?"

"Watch who you are calling a cheater." She reached back her arm and splashed him, hard. He splashed her back. The war was on.

Tandu had been so right. She needed to leave whatever fear she had remaining in the water.

And looking at Drew's face, she realized, her fear was not about drowning. It was about caring for someone else, as if pain was an inherent ingredient to that.

Becky could see that if she had not let go enough in

life, neither had he. Seeing him like this, playful, his face alight with laugher and mischief, she realized he did carry some burden, like a weight, just as Tandu had suggested. Drew had put down his burden for a bit, out here in the water, and she was glad she had encouraged him to come swim with her.

She wondered what his terrible burden was. Could he really have been given more than he thought he could handle? He seemed so unbelievably strong. But then again, wasn't that what made strength, being challenged to your outer limits? She wondered if he would ever confide in her, but then he splashed her in the face and took off away from her, and she took chase, and the serious thoughts were gone.

A half hour later, exhausted, they dragged themselves up on the beach. Just as he had promised, the trades came up, and it was surprisingly chilly on her wet skin and underwear. She tried to pull her clothes over her wet underwear, but it was more difficult than she thought. Finally, with her clothes clinging to her uncomfortably, she turned to him.

He had pulled his shirt back on over his wet chest and was putting the picnic things back in the basket.

"We have to go," she said. "I feel guilty."

"Tut-tut," he said. "There's that nun thing again. But I have to go, too. My crew is arriving first thing in the morning. I'd like to have things set up so we can get right to work. You're a terrible influence on me, Sister English."

"Sister Simone, to you."

He didn't appear to be leaving, and neither did she.

"I am so far behind in what I need to get done," Becky said. "I didn't expect to be here this long. If I go to work right now, I can still make a few phone calls. What time do you think it is in New York?"

"Look what I just found."

Did he ever just answer the question?

He had been rummaging in the picnic basket and he held up two small mason jars that looked as if they were filled with whipped cream and strawberries.

"What is that?" Knowing the time in New York suddenly didn't seem important at all.

"I think it's dessert."

She licked her lips. He stared at them, before looking away.

"I guess a little dessert wouldn't hurt," she said. Her voice sounded funny, low and seductive, as if she had said something faintly naughty.

"Just sit in the sand," he suggested. "We'll wrap the picnic blanket over our shoulders. We might as well eat dessert and watch the sun go down. What's another half hour now?"

They were going to sit shoulder to shoulder under a blanket eating dessert and watching the sun go down? It was better than any book she had ever read! The time in New York—and all her other responsibilities—did a slow fade-out, as if it was the end of a movie.

CHAPTER NINE

BECKY PLUNKED HERSELF down like a dog at obedience class who was eager for a treat. Drew picked up the blanket and placed it carefully over her shoulders, then sat down in the sand beside her and pulled part of the blanket over his own shoulders. His shoulder felt warm and strong where her skin was touching it. The chill left her almost instantly.

He pried the lid off one of the jars and handed it to her with a spoon.

"Have you ever been to Hawaii?" He took the lid off the other jar.

"No, I'm sorry to say I haven't been. Have you?"

"I've done jobs there. It's very much like this, the climate, the foliage, the breathtaking beauty. Everything stops at sunset. Even if you're still working against an impossible deadline, you just stop and face the sun. It's like every single person stops and every single thing stops. This stillness comes over everything. It's like the deepest form of gratitude I've ever experienced. It's this thank-you to life."

"I feel that right now," she said, with soft reverence. "Maybe because I nearly drowned, I feel so intensely alive and so intensely grateful."

No need to mention sharing this evening with him might have something to do with feeling so intensely alive.

"Me, too," he said softly.

Was it because of her he felt this way? She could feel the heat of his shoulder where it was touching hers. She desperately wanted to kiss him again. She gobbled up strawberries and cream instead. It just made her long, even more intensely, for the sweetness of his lips.

"I am going to hell in a handbasket," she muttered, but still she snuggled under the blanket and looked at where the sun, now a huge orb of gold, was hovering over the ocean.

He shot her a look. "Why would you say that?"

Because she was enjoying him so much, when she, of all people, was so well versed in all the dangers of romance.

"Because I am sitting here watching the sun go down when I should be getting to work," she clarified with a half-truth. "I knew Allie's faith in me was misplaced."

"Why would you say that?"

"I'm just an unlikely choice for such a huge undertaking."

"So, why did she pick you, then?"

"I hadn't seen her, or even had a note from her, since she moved away from Moose Run." Becky sighed and pulled the blanket tighter around her shoulders. "Everyone in Moose Run claims to have been friends with Allison Anderson *before* she became Allie Ambrosia the movie star, but really they weren't. Allison was lonely and different, and many of those people who now claim to have been friends with her were actually exceptionally intolerant of her eccentricities.

"Her mom must have been one of the first internet daters. She came to Moose Run and moved in with Pierce Clemens, which anybody could have told her was a bad bet. Allie, with her body piercings and colorful hair and hippie skirts, was just way too exotic for Moose Run. She only lived there for two years, and she and I only had a nodding acquaintance for most of that time. We were in the same grade, but I was in advanced classes."

"That's a surprise," he teased drily.

"You could have knocked me over with a feather when I got an out-of-the-blue phone call from her a couple of weeks ago and she outlined her ambitious plans. She told me she was putting together a guest list of two hundred people and that she wanted it to be so much more than a wedding. She wants her guests to have an *experience*. The island was hers for an entire week after the wedding, and she wanted all the guests to stay and have fun, either relaxing or joining in on organized activities.

"You know what she suggested for activities? Volleyball tournaments and wienie roasts around a campfire at night, maybe fireworks! You're from there. Does that strike you as Hollywood?"

"No," he said. "Not at all. Hollywood would be Jet Skis during the day and designer dresses at night. It would be entertainment by Cirque and Shania and wine tasting and spa treatments on the beach."

"That's what I thought. But she was adamant about what she wanted. I couldn't help but think that Allie's ideas of fun, despite this exotic island setting, are those of a girl who had been largely excluded from the teen cliques who went together to the Fourth of July activities. She seems, talking to her, to be more in sync with the small-town tastes of Moose Run than with lifestyles of the rich and famous."

"It actually makes me like her more," he said reluctantly.

"I asked her if what she wanted was like summer camp for adults, to make sure I was getting it right. She said—" Becky imitated the famous actress's voice "—'Exactly! I knew I could count on you to get it right.'"

Drew chuckled at Becky's imitation of Allie, which encouraged her to be even more foolish. She did both voices, as if she was reading for several parts in a play.

"Allie, I'm not sure I'm up to this. My event company has become the go-to company for local weddings and anniversaries, but— 'Of course you are up to it, do you think I don't do my homework? You did that great party for the lawyer's kid. Ponies!'

"She said *ponies* with the same enthusiasm she said *fireworks* with," Becky told Drew ruefully. "I think she actually wanted ponies. So I said, 'Um...it would be hard to get ponies to an island—and how did you know that? About the party for Mr. Williams's son?' And she said, 'I do my research. I'm not quite as flaky as the roles I get might make you think.' Of course, I told her I never thought she was flaky, but she cut me off and told me she was sending a deposit. I tried to talk her out of it. I said a six-week timeline was way too short to throw together a wedding for two hundred people. I told her I would have to delegate all my current contracts to take it on. She just insisted. She said she would make it worth my while. I told her I just wasn't sure, and she said she was, and that I was perfect for the job."

"You were trying to get out of the opportunity of a lifetime?" Drew weighed in, amused.

"Was I ever. But then her lighthearted delivery kind of changed and she said I was the only reason she survived Moose Run at all. She asked me if I remembered the day we became friends."

"Did you?"

"Pretty hard to forget. A nasty group of boys had her backed into the corner in that horrid place at the high school where we used to all go to smoke.

"I mean, I didn't go there to smoke. I was Moose Run High's official Goody Two-shoes."

"No kidding," he said drily. "Do not elbow my ribs again. They are seriously bruised."

They sat there in companionable silence for a few minutes. The sun demanded their stillness and their silence. The sunset was at its most glorious now, painting the sky around it in shades of orange and pink that were reflecting on a band on the ocean, that seemed to lead a pathway of light right to them. Then the sun was gone, leaving only an amazing pastel palette staining the sky.

"Go on," he said.

Becky thought she was talking too much. Had they really drunk that whole bottle of wine between the two of them? Still, it felt nice to have someone to talk to, someone to listen.

"I was taking a shortcut to the library—"

"Naturally," he said with dry amusement.

"And I came across Bram Butler and his gang tormenting poor Allie. I told them to cut it out.

"Allie remembers me really giving it to them. She told me that for a long time she has always thought of me as having the spirit of a gladiator."

"I'll attest to that," he said. "I have the bruises on my ribs to prove it." And then his tone grew more serious. "And you never gave up in the water yesterday, either."

"That was because of you. Believe me, I am the little bookworm I told you I was earlier. I do not have the spirit of a gladiator."

Though she did have some kind of unexpected spirit of boldness that had made her, very uncharacteristically, rip off her clothes and go into the water.

"How many guys were there?"

"Hmm, it was years ago, but I think maybe four. No, five."

"What were they doing?"

"They kind of had her backed up against a wall. She was quite frightened. I think that stupid Bram was trying to kiss her. He's always been a jerk. He's my second cousin."

"And you just waded right in there, with five high school guys being jerks? That seems brave."

She could not allow herself to bask in his admiration, particularly since it was undeserved.

"I didn't exactly wade right in there. I used the Moose Run magic words."

"Which were?"

"Bram Butler, you stop it right now or I'll tell your mother."

He burst out laughing, and then so did she. She noticed that it had gotten quite dark. The wind had died. Already stars were rising in the sky.

"Allie and I hung out a bit after that," she said. "She was really interesting. At that time, she wanted to be a clothing designer. We used to hole up in my room and draw dresses."

"What kind of dresses?"

"Oh, you know. Prom. Evening. That kind of thing. Allie and her mom moved away shortly after that. She said we would keep in touch—that she would send me her new address and phone number—but she never did."

"You and Allie drew wedding dresses, didn't you?"

"What would make you say that?" Becky could feel a blush rising, but why should she have to apologize for her younger self?

"I'm trying to figure out if she has some kind of wedding fantasy that my brother just happened into."

"Lots of young women have romantic fantasies. And then someone comes along to disillusion them."

"Like your Jerry," he said. "Tell me about that."

"So little to tell," she said wryly. "We lived down the street from one another, we started the first grade together. When we were seventeen he asked me to go to the Fourth of July celebrations with him. He held my hand. We kissed. And there you have it, my whole future mapped out for me. We were just together after that. I wanted exactly what I grew up with, until my dad left. Up until then my family had been one of those solid, dull families that makes the world feel so, so safe.

"An illusion," she said sadly. "It all ended up being such an illusion, but I felt determined to prove it could be real. Jerry went away to college and I started my own business, and it just unraveled, bit by bit. It's quite humiliating to have a major breakup in a small town."

"I bet."

"When I think about it, the humiliation actually might have been a lot harder to handle than the fact that I was not going to share my life with Jerry. It was like a second blow. I had just barely gotten over being on the receiving end of the pitying looks over my dad's scandal."

"Are you okay with your dad's relationship now?"

"I wish I was. But they still live in Moose Run, and I have an adorable little sister who I am pathetically jealous of. They seem so happy. My mom is still a mess. Aside from working in the hardware store, she'd never even had a job."

"And you rushed in to become the family breadwinner," he said.

"It's not a bad thing, is it?"

"An admirable thing. And kind of sad."

His hand found hers and he gave it a squeeze. He didn't let go again.

"Were you thinking of Jerry when you were drawing those dresses?" he finally asked softly.

"No," she said slowly, "I don't think I was."

She suddenly remembered one dress in particular that Allie had drawn. *This is your wedding dress*, she had proclaimed, giving it to Becky.

It had been a confection, sweetheart neckline, fitted bodice, layers and layers and layers of filmy fabric flowing out in that full skirt with an impossible train. The dress had been the epitome of her every romantic notion. Becky had been able to picture herself in that dress, swirling in front of a mirror, giggling. But she had never, not even once, pictured herself in that dress walking down an aisle toward Jerry.

When Jerry had broken it to her that her "business was changing her"—in other words, he could not handle her success—and he wanted his ring back, she had never taken that drawing from where it was tucked in the back of one of her dresser drawers.

"I've talked too much," she said. "It must have been the wine."

"I don't think you talked too much."

"I usually don't confide in people so readily." She suddenly felt embarrassed. "Your name should be a clue."

"To?"

"You *drew* my secrets right out of me."

"Ah."

"We have to go now," she said.

"Yes, we do," he said.

"Before something happens," she said softly.

"Especially before that," he agreed just as softly.

Her hand was still in his. Their shoulders were touching. The breeze was lifting the leathery fronds of the palm trees and they were whispering songs without words. The sky was now almost completely black, and finding their way back was not going to be easy.

"Really," Becky said. "We need to go."

"Really," he agreed. "We do.

Neither of them moved.

CHAPTER TEN

DREW ORDERED HIMSELF to get up and leave this beach. But it was one of those completely irresistible moments: the stars winking on in the sky, their shoulders touching, the taste of strawberries and cream on his lips, the gentle lap of the waves against the shore, her small hand resting within the sanctuary of his larger one.

He turned slightly to look at her. She was turning to look at him.

It seemed like the most natural thing in the world to drop his head over hers, to taste her lips again.

Her arms came up and twined around his neck. Her lips were soft and pliant and welcoming.

He could taste everything she was in that kiss. She was bookish. And she was bold. She was simple, and she was complex. She was, above all else, a forever kind of girl.

It was that knowledge that made him untangle her hands from around his neck, to force his lips away from the soft promise of hers.

You heal now.

He swore under his breath, scrambled to his feet. "I'm sorry," he said.

"Are you?"

Well, not really. "Look, Becky, we have known each other for a shockingly short period of time. Obviously circumstances have made us feel things about each other a little too quickly."

She looked unconvinced.

"I mean, in Moose Run, you probably have a date or two before you kiss like that."

"What about in LA?"

He thought about how fast things could go in Los Angeles and how superficial that was, and how he was probably never going to be satisfied with it again. Less than forty-eight hours, and Becky English, bookworm, was changing everything in his world.

What was his world going to look like in two weeks if this kept up?

The answer was obvious. This could not keep up.

"Look, Becky, I obviously like you. And find you extremely attractive."

Did she look pleased? He did not want her to look pleased!

"There is obviously some kind of chemistry going on between us."

She looked even more pleased.

"But both of us have jobs to do. We have very little time to do those jobs in. We can't afford a, um, complication like this."

She stared at him, uncomprehending.

"It's not professional, Becky," he said gruffly. "Kissing on the job is not professional."

She looked as if he had slapped her. And then she just looked crushed.

"Oh," she stammered. "Of course, you're right."

He felt a terrible kind of self-loathing that she was taking it on, as if it were her fault.

She pulled herself together and jumped up, doing what he suspected she always did. Trying to fix the whole world. Her clothes were still wet. Her pink blouse looked as though red roses were blooming on it where it was clinging to that delectable set of underwear that he should never have seen, and was probably never going to be able to get out of his mind.

"I don't know what's gotten into me. It must still be the aftereffects of this afternoon. And the wine. I want you to know I don't usually rip my clothes off around men. In fact, that's extremely uncharacteristic. And I'm usually not such a blabbermouth. Not at all."

Her voice was wobbling terribly.

"No, it's not you," he rushed to tell her. "It's not. It's me, I—"

"I've given you the impression I'm—what did you call it earlier—wanton!"

"I told you at the time I was overstating it. I told you that was the wrong word."

She held up her hand, stopping him. "No, I take responsibility. You don't know how sorry I am."

And then she rushed by him, found the path through the darkened jungle and disappeared.

Perfect, he thought. He'd gotten rid of her before things got dangerously out of control. But it didn't feel perfect. He felt like a bigger jerk than the chicken they had eaten for supper.

She had fled up that path—away from him—with extreme haste, probably hoping to keep the truth from him. That she was crying.

But that's what I am, Drew told himself. He was a

jerk. Just ask his brother, who not only wasn't arriving on the island, but who also was not taking his phone calls.

The truth was, Drew Jordan sucked at relationships. It was good Becky had run off like that, for her own protection, and his. It would have been better if he could have thought of a way to make her believe it was his fault instead of hers, though.

Sitting there, alone, in the sand, nearly choking on his own self-loathing, Drew thought of his mother. He could picture her: the smile, the way she had made him feel, that way she had of cocking her head and listening so intently when he was telling her something. He realized the scent he had detected earlier had reminded him of her perfume.

The truth was, he was shocked to be thinking of her. Since that day he had become both parents to his younger brother, he had tried not to think of his mom and dad. It was just too painful. Losing them—everything, really, his whole world—was what life had given him that was too much to bear.

But the tears in Becky's eyes that she had been holding back so valiantly, and the scent in the air, made him think of his mother. Only in his mind, his mother wasn't cocking her head, listening intently to him with that soft look of wonder that only a mother can have for her offspring.

No, it felt as if his mother was somehow near him, but that her hands were on her hips and she was looking at him with total exasperation.

His mother, he knew, would never have approved of the fact he had made that decent, wholesome young woman from Moose Run, Michigan, cry. She would be really angry with him if he excused his behavior by saying, *But it was for her own good.* His mother, if she was here, would remind him of all the hurt that Becky had already suffered at the hands of men.

She would show him Becky, trying to keep her head up as her father pushed a stroller down the main street of Moose Run, as news got out that the wedding planner's own wedding was a bust.

Sitting there in the sand with the stars coming out over him, Drew felt he was facing some hard truths about himself. Would his mother even approve of the man he had become? Work-obsessed, so emotionally unavailable he had driven his brother right out of his life and into the first pair of soft arms that offered comfort. His mother wouldn't like it one bit that not only was he failing to protect his brother from certain disaster, his brother would not even talk to him.

"So," he asked out loud, "what would you have me do?"

Be a better man.

It wasn't her voice. It was just the gentle breeze stirring the palm fronds. It was just the waves lapping onshore. It was just the call of the night birds.

But is that what her voice had become? Everything? Was his mother's grace and goodness now in everything? Including him?

Drew scrambled out of the sand. He picked up the picnic basket and the blanket and began to run.

"Becky! Becky!"

When he caught up with her, he was breathless. She was walking fast, her head down.

"Becky," he said, and then softly, "Please."

She spun around. She stuck her chin up in the air.

But she could not hide the fact that he was right. She had been crying.

"I didn't mean to hurt your feelings," he said. "I'm the one in the wrong here, not you."

"Thank you," she said icily. "That is very chivalrous of you. However the facts speak for themselves."

Chivalrous. Who used that in a sentence? And why did it make him feel as if he wanted to set down the picnic basket, gather her in his arms and hold her hard?

"Facts?"

"Yes, facts," she said in that clipped tone of voice. "They speak for themselves."

"They do?"

She nodded earnestly. "It seems to me I've just dragged you along with my *wanton* behavior, kissing you, tearing off my clothes. You were correct. It is not professional. And it won't be happening again."

He knew that it not happening again was a good thing, so why did he feel such a sense of loss?

"Becky, I handled that badly."

"There's a good way to handle 'keep your lips off me'?"

He had made her feel rejected. He had done to her what every other man in her life had done to her: given her the message that somehow she didn't measure up, she wasn't good enough.

He rushed to try to repair the damage.

"It's not that I don't want your lips on me," he said. "I do. I mean I don't. I mean we can't. I mean I won't."

She cocked her head, and looked askance at him.

"Do I sound like an idiot?" he said.

"Yes," she said, unforgivingly.

"What I'm trying to say, Becky, is I'm not used to women like you."

"What kind of women are you used to?"

"Guess," he said in a low voice.

She did not appear to want to guess.

He raked his hand through his hair, trying desperately to think of a way to make her get it that would somehow erase those tearstains from her cheeks.

"I'm scared I'll hurt you," he said, his voice gravelly in his own ears. "I don't think it's a good idea to move this fast. Let's back up a step or two. Let's just be friends. First."

He had no idea where that *first* had come from. It implied there would be something following the friendship. But really, that was impossible. And he just had to get through what remained of two weeks without hurting her any more than he already had. He could play at being the better man for eleven damn days. He was almost sure of it.

"Do you ever answer a question?" she asked. "What kind of women are you used to?"

"Ones who are as shallow as me," he said.

"You aren't shallow!"

"You don't know that about me."

"I do," she said firmly.

He sucked in his breath and tried again. Why was she insisting on seeing him as a better man when he did not deserve that? "Ones who don't expect happily-ever-after."

"Oh."

"You see, Becky, my parents died when I was seventeen." *Shut up*, he ordered himself. *Stop it.* "It broke something in me. The sense of loss was just as Tandu said this afternoon. It was too great to bear. When I've had relationships, and it's true, I have, they have been deliberately superficial."

Becky went very still. Her eyes looked wide and beautiful in the starlight that filtered through the thick leaves of the jungle. She took a step toward him. And she reached up and laid the palm of her hand on his cheek.

Her touch was extraordinary. He had to shut his eyes against his reaction to the tenderness in it. In some ways it was more intimate than the kisses they had shared.

"Because you cannot handle one more loss," she guessed softly.

Drew opened his eyes and stared at Becky. It felt as if she could see his soul and was not the least frightened by what she saw there.

This was going sideways! He was not going to answer that. He could not. If he answered that, he would want to lay his head on her shoulder and feel her hand in his hair. He would want to suck up her tenderness like a dry sponge sucking up moisture. If he answered that he would become weak, instead of what he needed to be most.

He needed to be strong. Since he'd been seventeen years old, he had needed to be strong. And it wasn't until just this minute he was seeing that as a burden he wanted to lay down.

"I agree," she said softly, dropping her hand away from his cheek. "We just need to be friends."

His relief was abject. She got it. He was too damaged to be any good for a girl like her.

Only then she went and spoiled his relief by standing on her tiptoes and kissing him on the cheek where her hand had lay with such tender healing. She whispered something in his ear.

And he was pretty sure it was the word *first*.

And then she turned and scampered across the moon-lit lawn to the castle door and disappeared inside it.

And he had to struggle not to touch his cheek, where the tenderness of her kiss lingered like a promise.

You heal now.

But he couldn't. He knew that. He could do his best to honor the man his mother had raised him to be, to not cause Becky any more harm, but he knew that his own salvation was beyond what he could hope for.

Because really in the end, for a man like him, wasn't hope the most dangerous thing of all?

CHAPTER ELEVEN

BECKY LISTENED TO the sound of hammers, the steady *ratta-tat-tat* riding the breeze through the open window of her office. When had that sound become like music to her?

She told herself, sternly, she could not give in to the temptation, but it was useless. It was as if a cord circled her waist and tugged her toward the window.

This morning, Drew's crew had arrived, but not his brother. They had arrived ready to work, and in hours the wedding pavilion was taking shape on the emerald green expanse of the front lawn. They'd dug holes and poured the cement they had mixed by hand out of bags. Then they had set the posts—which had arrived by helicopter—into those holes.

She had heard helicopters delivering supplies all morning. It sounded like a MASH unit around here.

Now she peeped out the window. In all that activity, her eyes sought him. Her heart went to her throat. Drew, facing the ocean, was straddling a beam. He had to be fifteen feet off the ground, his legs hanging into nothingness. He had a baseball cap on backward and his shirt off.

His skin was sun-kissed and perfect, his back broad

and powerful. He was a picture of male strength and confidence.

She could barely breathe he was so amazing to look at. It was also wonderful to be able to look at him without his being aware of it! She could study the sleek lines of his naked back at her leisure.

"You have work to do," she told herself. Drew, as if he sensed someone watching, turned and glanced over his shoulder, directly at her window. She drew back into the shadows, embarrassed, and pleased, too. Was he looking to glimpse her? Did it fill him with this same sense of delight? Anticipation? Longing?

Reluctantly, she turned her back to the scene, but only long enough to try to drag her desk over to the window. She could multitask. The desk was very heavy. She grunted with exertion.

"Miss Becky?" Tandu was standing in the doorway with a tray. "Why you miss lunch?"

"Oh, I—" For some reason she had felt shy about lunch, knowing that Drew and his crew would be eating in the dining room. Despite their agreement last night to be friends, her heart raced out of control when she thought of his rescue of her, and eating dinner with him on the picnic blanket last night, and swimming with him. But mostly, she thought of how their lips had met. Twice.

How was she going to choke down a sandwich around him? How was she going to behave appropriately with his crew looking on? Anybody with a heartbeat would take one look at her—them—and know that something primal was sizzling in the air between them.

This was what she had missed by being with Jerry

for so long. She had missed all the years when she should have been learning the delicate nuances of how to conduct a relationship with a member of the opposite sex.

Not that it was going to be a relationship. A friendship. She thought of Drew's lips. She wondered how a friendship was going to be possible.

There must be a happy medium between wanton and so shy she couldn't even eat lunch with him!

"What you doing?" Tandu asked, looking at the desk she had managed to move about three feet across the room.

"The breeze!" she said, too emphatically. "I thought I might get a better breeze if I moved the desk."

Tandu set down the lunch tray. With his help it was easier to wrestle the big piece of furniture into its new location.

He looked out the window. "Nice view," he said with wicked amusement. "Eat lunch, enjoy the view. Then you are needed at helicopter pad. Cargo arriving. Many, many boxes."

"I have a checklist. I'll be down shortly. And Tandu, could you think of a few places for wedding photographs? I mean, the beaches are lovely, but if I could preview a few places for the photographer, that would be wonderful."

"Know exactly the place," he said delightedly. "Waterfall."

"Yes!" she said.

"I'll draw you a map."

"Thank you. A waterfall!"

"Now eat. Enjoy the view."

She did eat, and she did enjoy the view. It was actually much easier to get to work when she could just glance up and watch Drew, rather than making a special trip away from her desk and to the window.

Later that afternoon, she headed down to the helicopter loading dock with her checklist and began sorting through the boxes and muttering to herself.

"Candles? Check. Centerpieces? Check."

"Hi there." She swung around.

Drew was watching her, a little smile playing across his handsome features.

"Hello." Oh, God, did she have to sound so formal and geeky?

"Do you always catch your tongue between your teeth like that when you are lost in thought?"

She hadn't been aware she was doing it, and pulled her tongue back into her mouth. He laughed. She blushed.

"The pavilion is looking great," she said, trying to think of something—anything—to say. She was as tongue-tied as if she were a teenager meeting her secret crush unexpectedly at the supermarket!

"Yeah, my guys are pretty amazing, aren't they?"

She had not really spared a glance to any of the other guys. "Amazing," she agreed.

"I just thought I'd check and see if the fabric for draping the pavilion has arrived. I need to come up with a method for hanging it."

"I'll look."

But he was already sorting through boxes, tossing them with easy strength. "This might be it. It's from a fabric store. There's quite a few boxes here." He took a box cutter out of his shirt pocket and slit open one of the boxes. "Come see."

She sidled over to him. She could feel the heat radiating off him as they stood side by side.

"Yes, that's it."

He hefted up one of the boxes onto his shoulder. "I'll send one of the guys over for the rest."

She stood there. That was going to be the whole encounter. *Very professional*, she congratulated herself.

"You want to come weigh in on how to put it up?" he called over his shoulder.

And she threw professionalism to the wind and scampered after him like a puppy who had been given a second chance at affection.

"Hey, guys," he called. "Team meeting. Fabric's here."

His guys, four of them, gathered around.

"Becky, Jared, Jason, Josh and Jimmy."

"The J series," one of them announced. "Brothers. I'm the good-looking one, Josh." He gave a little bow.

"But I'm the strong one," Jimmy announced.

"And I'm the smart one."

"I'm the romantic," Jared said, and stepped forward, picked up her hand and kissed it, to groans from his brothers. "You are a beauty, me lady. Do you happen to be available? I see no rings, so—"

"That's enough," Drew said.

His tone had no snap to it, at all, only firmness, but Becky did not miss how quickly Jared stepped back from her, or the surprised looks exchanged between the brothers.

She liked seeing Drew in this environment. It was obvious his crew of brothers didn't just respect him, they adored him. She soon saw why.

"Let's see what we have here," Drew said. He opened

a box and yards and yards of filmy white material spilled out onto the ground.

He was a natural leader, listening to all the brothers' suggestions about how to attach and drape the fabric to the pavilion poles they had worked all morning installing.

"How about you, Becky?" Drew asked her.

She was flattered that her opinion mattered, too. "I think you should put some kind of bar on those side beams. Long bars, like towel bars, and then thread the fabric through them."

"We have a winner," one of the guys shouted, and they all clapped and went back to work.

"I'll hang the first piece and you can see if it works," Drew said.

With amazing ingenuity he had fabricated a bar in no time. And then he shinnied up a ladder that was leaning on a post and attached the first bar to the beam. And then he did the same on the other side.

"The moment of truth," he called from up on the wall.

She opened the box and he leaned way down to take the fabric from her outstretched hand. Once he had it, he threaded it through the first bar, then came down from the ladder, trailing a line of wide fabric behind him. He went up the ladder on the other side of what would soon look like a pavilion, and threaded the fabric through there. The panel was about three feet wide and dozens of feet long. He came down to the ground and passed her the fabric end.

"You do it," he said.

She tugged on it until the fabric lifted toward the sky, and then began to tighten. Finally, the first panel was in place. The light, filmy, pure-white fabric formed a dreamy roof above them, floating walls on either side of them. Only it was better than walls and a roof because of the way the light was diffused through it, and the way it moved like a living thing in the most gentle of breezes.

"Just like a canopy bed," he told her with satisfaction.

"You know way too much about that," she teased him.

"Actually," he said, frowning at the fabric, "come to think of it, it doesn't really look like a canopy bed. It looks like—"

He snatched up the hem of fabric and draped it over his shoulder. "It looks like a toga."

She burst out laughing.

He struck a pose. "'To be or not to be…'" he said.

"I don't want to be a geek…" she began.

"Oh, go ahead—be a geek. It comes naturally to you."

That stung, but even with it stinging, she couldn't let *To be or not to be* go unchallenged. "'To be or not to be' is Shakespeare," she told him. "Not Nero."

"Well, hell," he said, "that's what makes it really hard for a dumb carpenter to go out with a smart girl."

She stared at him. "Are we going out?" she whispered.

"No! I just was pointing out more evidence of our incompatibility."

That stung even worse than being called a geek. "At least you got part of it right," she told him.

"Which part? The geek part?"

"I am not a geek!"

He shook his head sadly.

"That line? 'To be or not to be.' It's from a soliloquy in the play *Hamlet*. It's from a scene in the nunnery."

"The nunnery?" he said with satisfaction. "Don't *you* have a fascination?"

"No! You *think* I have a fascination. You are incorrect, just as you are incorrect about me being a geek."

"Yes, and being able to quote Shakespeare, chapter and verse, certainly made that point."

She giggled, and unraveled the fabric from around him.

"Hey! Give me back my toga. I already told you I don't wear underwear!

But it was her turn to play with the gauzy fabric. She inserted herself in the middle of it and twirled until she had made it into a long dress. Then she swathed some around her head, until only her eyes showed. Throwing inhibition to the wind, she swiveled her hips and did some things with her hands.

"Guess who I am?" she purred.

He frowned at her. "A bride?"

The thing he liked least!

"No, I'm not a bride," she snapped.

"A hula girl!"

"No."

"I give up. Stop doing that."

"I'm Mata Hari."

"Who? I asked you to stop."

"Why?"

"It's a little too sexy for the job site."

"A perfect imitation of Mata Hari, then," she said with glee. And she did not stop doing it. She was rather enjoying the look on his face.

"Who?"

"She was a spy. And a dancer."

He burst out laughing as if that was the most improbable thing he had ever heard. "How well versed was she in her Shakespeare?"

"She didn't have to be." Becky began to do a slow writhe with her hips. He didn't seem to think it was funny anymore.

In fact, the ease they had been enjoying—that sense of being a team and working together—evaporated.

He stepped back from her, as if he thought she was going to try kissing him again. She blushed.

"I have so much to do," she squeaked, suddenly feeling silly, and at the very same time, not silly at all.

"Me, too," he said.

But neither of them moved.

"Uh, boss, is this a bad time?"

Mata Hari dropped her veil with a little shriek of embarrassment.

"The guys were thinking maybe we could have a break? It's f—"

Drew stopped his worker with a look.

"It's flipping hot out here. We thought maybe we could go swimming and start again when it's not so hot out."

"Great idea," Drew said. "We all need cooling off, particularly Mata Hari here. You coming swimming, Becky?"

She knew she should say no. She had to say no. She didn't even have a proper bathing suit. Instead she unraveled herself from the yards of fabric, called, "Race you," ran down to the water and flung herself in completely clothed.

Drew's crew crashed into the water around her,

following her lead and just jumping in in shorts and T-shirts. They played a raucous game of tag in the water, and she was fully included, though she was very aware of Drew sending out a silent warning that no lines were to be crossed. And none were. It was like having five brothers.

And wouldn't that be the safest thing? Wasn't that what she and Drew had vowed they were going to do? Hadn't they both agreed they were going to retreat into a platonic relationship after the crazy-making sensation of those shared kisses?

What had she been thinking, playing Mata Hari? What kind of craziness was it that she wanted him to not see her exactly as she was: not a spy and dancer who could coax secrets out of unsuspecting men, but a book-loving girl from a small town in America?

After that frolic in the water, the J brothers included her as one of them. Over the next few days, whenever they broke from work to go swimming, one of them came and pounded on her office door and invited her to come.

Today, Josh knocked on the door.

"Swim time," he said.

"I just can't. I have to tie bows on two hundred chairs. And find a cool place to store three thousand potted lavender plants. And—"

Without a word, Josh came in, picked her up and tossed her over his shoulder like a sack of potatoes.

"Stop it. This is my good dress!" She pounded on his back, but of course, with her laughing so hard, he did not take her seriously. She was carried, kicking and screaming and pounding on his back, to the water, where she was unceremoniously dumped in.

"Hey, what the hell are you doing?" Drew demanded, arriving at the water's edge and fishing her out.

The fact that she was screaming with laughter had softened the protective look on his face.

Josh had lifted a big shoulder. "Boss, you said don't take no for an answer."

"No means no, boss," she inserted, barely able to breathe she was laughing so hard.

Drew gave them both an exasperated look, and turned away. Then he turned back, picked her up, raced out into the surf and dumped her again!

She rose from the water sputtering, still holding on to his neck, both their bodies sleek with salt water, her good dress completely ruined.

Gazing into the mischief-filled face of Drew Jordan, Becky was not certain she had ever felt so completely happy.

CHAPTER TWELVE

AFTER THAT BECKY was "in." She and the J's and Drew became a family. They took their meals together and they played together. Becky soon discovered this crew worked hard, and they played harder.

At every break and after work, the football came out. Or the Frisbee. Both games were played with rough-and-tumble delight at the water's edge. She wasn't sure how they could have any energy left, but they did.

The first few times she played, the brothers howled hysterically at both her efforts to throw and catch balls and Frisbees. They good-naturedly nicknamed her Barnside.

"Barnside?" she protested. "That's awful. I demand a new nickname. That is not flattering!"

"You have to earn a new nickname," Jimmy informed her seriously.

"Time to go back to work," Drew told them, after one coffee-break Frisbee session when poor Josh had to climb a palm tree to retrieve a Frisbee she'd thrown. He caught her arm as she turned to leave. "Not you."

"What?" she said.

"Have you heard anything from Allie recently?" he asked.

"The last I heard from her was a few days ago, when she okayed potted lavender instead of tulips." She scanned his face. "You still haven't heard from Joe?"

He shrugged. "It's no big deal."

But she could tell it was. "I'm sorry."

He obviously did not want to talk about his distress over his brother. Becky was aware that she felt disappointed. He was okay with their relationship—with being "friends" on a very light level.

Did he not trust her with his deeper issues?

Apparently not. Drew said, "It's time you learned how to throw a Frisbee. I consider it an essential life skill."

"How could I have missed that?" she asked drily. As much as she wanted to talk to him about his brother, having fun with him was just too tempting. Besides, maybe the lighthearted friendship growing between them would develop some depth, and some trust on his part, if she just gave it time.

"I'm not sure how you could have missed this important life skill," he said, "but it's time to lose 'Barnside.' They are calling you that because you could not hit the side of a barn with a Frisbee at twenty feet."

"At twenty feet? I could!"

"No," Drew informed her with a sad shake of his head, "you couldn't. You've now tossed two Frisbees out to sea, and Josh risked his life to rescue the other one out of the palm tree today. We can't be running out of Frisbees."

"That would be a crisis," she agreed, deadpan.

"I'm glad you understand the seriousness of it. Now, come here."

He placed her in front of him. He gave her a Frisbee. "Don't throw it. Not yet."

He wrapped his arms around her from behind, drawing her back into the powerful support of his chest. He laid his arm along her arm. "It's in the wrist, not the arm. Flick it, don't pitch it." He guided her throw.

Becky actually cackled with delight when it flew true, instead of her normal flub. Soon, he released her to try on her own, and then set up targets for her to throw at. The troubled look that had been on his face since he mentioned his brother evaporated.

Finally, he high-fived her, gave her a little kiss on the nose and headed back to his crew. She watched him go and then looked at the Frisbee in her hand.

How could such a small thing make it feel as if a whole new world was opening up to her? Of course, it wasn't the Frisbee, it was him.

It was being with him and being with his crew.

It occurred to Becky she felt the sense of belonging she had craved since the disintegration of her own family. They were all becoming a team. Drew and his crew were a building machine. The pavilion went up, and they designed and began to build the dance floor. And Becky loved the moments when she and Drew found themselves alone. It was so easy to talk to each other.

The conversation flowed between them so easily. And the laughter.

The hands-off policy had been a good one, even if it was making the tension build almost unbearably between them. It was like going on a diet that had an end date. Not that they had named an end date, but some kind of anticipation was building between them.

And meanwhile, her admiration for him did nothing but grow. He was a natural leader. He was funny. He was smart. She found herself making all kinds of excuses to be around him. She was pretty sure he was doing the same thing to be around her.

The days flew by until there were only three days until the wedding. The details were falling into place seamlessly, not just for the wedding but for the week following. The pagoda and dance floor were done, the wedding gazebo was almost completed, though it still had to be painted.

Usually when she did an event, as the day grew closer her excitement grew, too. But this time she had mixed feelings. In a way, Becky wished the wedding would never come. She had never loved her life as much as she did right now.

Today she was at the helipad looking at the latest shipment of goods. Again, there was a sense of things falling into place: candles in a large box, glass vases for the centerpieces made up of single white roses. She made a note as she instructed the staff member who had been assigned to help her where to put the boxes. Candles would need to be unwrapped and put in candle holders, glass vases cleaned to sparkling. The flowers—accompanied by their own florist—would arrive the evening before the wedding to guarantee freshness.

Then one large, rectangular box with a designer name on it caught her eye. It was the wedding dress. She had not been expecting it. She had assumed it would arrive with Allie.

And yet it made sense that it would need to be hung.

Becky plucked it from all the other boxes and, with some last-minute instructions, walked back to the castle with it. She brought it up to the suite that Allie would inhabit by herself the day before the wedding, and with her new husband after that.

The suite was amazing, so softly romantic it took
Becky's breath away. She had a checklist for this room,
too. It would be fully supplied with very expensive toi-
letries, plus fresh flowers would abound. She had chosen the linens from the castle supply room herself.

Becky set the box on the bed. A sticker in red caught
her eye. They were instructions stating that the dress
should be unpacked, taken out of its plastic protective
bag and hung immediately upon arrival. And so Becky
opened the box and lifted it out. She unzipped the bag,
and carefully lifted the dress out.

Her hands gathered up a sea of white foam. The
fabric was silk, so sensuous under her fingertips that
Becky could feel the enchantment sewn right into the
dress. There was a tall coatrack next to the mirror, and
Becky hung the silk-wrapped hanger on a peg and stood
back from it.

She could not believe what she was seeing. That
long-ago dress that Allie had drawn and given to her,
that drawing still living in the back of Becky's dresser
drawer, had been brought to life.

The moment was enough to make a girl who had
given up on magic believe in it all over again.

Except that's not what it did. Looking at the dress
made Becky feel as though she was being stabbed with
the shards of her own broken dreams. The dress shim-
mered with a future she had been robbed of. In every
winking pearl, there seemed to be a promise: of someone to share life with, of laughter, of companionship,
of passion, of "many babies," fat babies chortling and
clapping their hands with glee.

Becky shook herself, as if she was trying to break
free of the spell the dress was weaving around her. She

wanted to tell herself that she was wrong. That this was not the dress that Allie had drawn on that afternoon of girlish delight all those years ago, not the drawing she had handed to her and said, *This is your wedding dress.*

But she still had that drawing. She had studied it too often now not to know every line of that breathtakingly romantic dress. She had dreamed of herself walking down the aisle in that dress one too many times. There was simply no mistaking which dress it was. Surely, Allie was not being deliberately cruel?

No, Allie had not kept a drawing of the dress. She had given the only existing drawing to Becky. Allie must have remembered it at a subliminal level. Why wouldn't she? The dress was exactly what every single girl dreamed of having one day.

But Becky still felt the tiniest niggle of doubt. What if Drew's cynicism was not misplaced? What if his brother was making a mistake? What if this whole wedding was some kind of publicity stunt orchestrated by Allie? The timing was perfect: Allie was just finishing filming one movie, and another was going to be released in theaters within weeks.

With trembling hands, Becky touched the fabric of the dress one more time. Then she turned and scurried from the room. She felt as if she was going to burst into tears, as if her every secret hope and dream had been shoved into her face and mocked. And then she bumped right into Drew and did what she least wanted to do. She burst into tears.

"Hey!" Drew eased Becky away from him. She was crying! If there was something worse than her laughing and being joyful and carefree, it was this. "What's the matter?"

"Nothing," she said. "I'm just tired. There's so much to do and—"

But he could tell she wasn't just tired. And from working with her for the past week, he could tell there was hardly anything she liked more than having a lot to do. Her strength was organizing, putting her formidable mind to problems that needed to be solved. No, something had upset her. How had he come to be able to read Becky English so accurately?

She was swiping at those tears, lifting her chin to him with fierce pride, backing away from a shoulder to cry on.

The wisest thing would be to let her. Let her go her own way and have a good cry about whatever, and not involve himself any more than he already had.

Who was he kidding? Just himself. He'd noticed his crew sending him sideways looks every time she was around. He'd noticed Tandu putting them together. He was already involved. Spending the past days with her had cemented that.

"You want to be upset together?" he asked her.

"I told you I'm not upset."

"Uh-huh."

"What are you upset about?"

He lifted a shoulder. "You're not telling, I'm not telling."

"Fine."

"Tandu asked me to give you this."

"How could Tandu have possibly known you were going to bump into me?" Becky asked, taking the paper from him.

"I don't know. The man's spooky. He seems to know things."

Becky squinted at the paper. "Sheesh."

"What?"

"It's a map. He promised it to me over a week ago. Apparently there's a waterfall that would make a great backdrop for wedding pictures. Can you figure out this drawing?"

She handed the map back to him. It looked like a child's map for a pirate's treasure. Drew looked at a big arrow, and the words, *Be careful this rock. Do not fall in water, please.*

"I'll come with you," he decided.

"Thank you," she said. "That's unnecessary." She snatched the map back and looked at it. "Which way is north?"

"I'll come."

The fight went out of her. "Do you ever get tired of being the big brother?"

He thought of how tired he was of leaving Joe messages to call him. He looked at her lips. He thought of how tired he was getting of this friendship between them.

"Suck it up, buttercup," he muttered to himself.

She sighed heavily. "If you have a fault, do you know what it is?"

"Please don't break it to me that I have a fault. Not right now."

"What happened?"

"I said I'm not talking about it, if you're not talking about it."

"Your fault is that you don't answer questions."

"Your fault is—" What was he going to say? Her

fault was that she made him think the kind of thoughts he had vowed he was never going to think? "Never mind. Let's go find that waterfall."

"I don't know," Becky said dubiously, after they had been walking twenty minutes. "This seems like kind of a tough walk at any time. I'm in a T-shirt and shorts and I'm overheating. What would it be like in a wedding dress?"

Drew glanced at her. Had she flinched when she said *wedding dress*?

"Maybe her royal highness, the princess Allie is expecting to be delivered to her photo op on a litter carried by two manservants," Drew grumbled. "I hope I'm not going to be one of them."

Becky laughed and took the hand he held back to her to help her scramble over a large boulder.

"Technically, that would be a sedan chair," she said, puffing.

"Huh?"

"A seat that two manservants can carry is sedan chair. Anything bigger is a litter."

He contemplated her. "How do you know this stuff?" he asked.

"That's what a lifetime of reading gets you, a brain teeming with useless information." She contemplated the rock. "Maybe we should just stop here. There's no way Allie can scramble over this rock in a wedding dress."

He contemplated the map. "I think it's only a few more steps. I'm pretty sure I can hear the falls. We might as well see it, even if Allie never will."

And he was right. Only a few steps more and they

pushed their way through a gateway of heavy leaves, as big and as wrinkled as elephant ears, and stood in an enchanted grotto.

"Oh, my," Becky breathed.

A frothing fountain of water poured over a twenty-foot cliff and dropped into a pool of pure green water. The pond was surrounded on all sides by lush green ferns and flowers. A large flat rock jutted out into the middle of it, like a platform.

"Perfect for pictures," she thought out loud. "But how are we going to get them here?"

"Wow," Drew said, apparently not the least bit interested in pictures. In a blink, he had stripped off his shirt and dived into the pond. He surfaced and shook his head. Diamonds of water flew. "It's wonderful," he called over the roar of the falls. "Get in."

Once again, there was the small problem of not having bathing attire.

And once again, she was caught in the spell of the island. She didn't care that she didn't have a bathing suit. She wanted to be unencumbered, not just by clothing, but by every single thought that had ever held her prisoner.

CHAPTER THIRTEEN

So AWARE OF the look on Drew's face as he watched her, Becky undid the buttons of her blouse, shrugged it off and then stepped out of her skirt.

When she saw the look on Drew's face, she congratulated herself on her investment in the ultra-sexy and exclusive Rembrandt's Drawing brand underwear. Today, her matching bra and panties were white with tiny red hearts all over them.

And then she stepped into the water. She wanted to dive like him, but because she was not that great a swimmer, she waded in up to her ankles first. The rocks were slipperier than she had expected. Her arms began to windmill.

And she fell, with a wonderful splash, into where he was waiting to catch her.

"The water is fantastic," Becky said, blinking up at him.

"Yes, it is."

She knew neither of them were talking about the water. He set her, it seemed with just a bit of reluctance, on her feet. She splashed him.

"Is that any way to thank me for rescuing you?"

"That is to let you know I did not need to be rescued!"

"Oh," he said. "You planned to fall in the water."

She giggled. "Yes, I did."

"Don't take up poker."

She splashed him again. He got a look on his face. She giggled and bolted away. He was after her in a flash. Soon the grotto was filled with the magic of their splashing and laughter. The days of playing with him—of feeling that sense of belonging—all seemed to have been leading to this. Becky had never felt so free, so wondrous, so aware as she did then.

Finally, exhausted, they hauled themselves out onto the warmth of the large, flat rock, and lay there on their stomachs, side-by-side, panting to catch their breaths.

"I'm indecent," she decided, without a touch of remorse.

"I prefer to think of it as wanton."

She laughed. The sun was coming through the greenery, dappled on his face. His eyelashes were tangled with water. She laid her hand—wantonly—on the firmness of his naked back. She could feel the warmth of him seeping into her hand. He closed his eyes, as if her touch had soothed something in him. His breathing slowed and deepened.

And then so did hers.

When she awoke, her hand was still on his back. He stirred and opened his eyes, looked at her and smiled.

She shivered with a longing so primal it shook her to the core. Drew's smile disappeared, and he found his feet in one catlike motion. As she sat up and hugged herself, chilled now, he retrieved his T-shirt. He came back and slid it over her head. Then he sat behind her, pulled her between the wedge of his legs and wrapped his arms around her until she stopped shivering.

The light was changing in the grotto and the magic deepened all around them.

"What were you upset about earlier?" he asked softly.

She sighed. "I unpacked Allie's wedding dress."

He sucked in his breath. "And what? You wished it was yours?"

"It was mine," she whispered. "It was the dress she drew for me one of those afternoons all those years ago."

"What? The very same dress? Maybe you're just remembering it wrong."

Was there any way to tell him she had kept that picture without seeming hopelessly pathetic?

"No," she said firmly. "It was that dress."

"Representing all your hopes and dreams," he said. "No wonder you were crying."

She felt a surge of tenderness for him that there was no mockery in his tone, but instead, a lovely empathy.

"It was just a shock. I am hoping it is just a weird coincidence. But I'm worried. I didn't know Allie that well when we were teenagers. I don't know her at all now. What if it's all some gigantic game? What if she's playing with everyone?"

"Exactly the same thing I was upset about," Drew confessed to her. "My brother was supposed to be here. He's not. I've called him twice a day, every day, since I got here to find out why. He won't return my calls. That isn't like him."

"Tell me what *is* like him," Becky said gently.

And suddenly he just wanted to unburden himself. He felt as if he had carried it all alone for so long, and he was not sure he could go one more step with the weight of it all. It felt as if it was crushing him.

He was not sure he had ever felt this relaxed or this at ease with another person. Drew had a deep sense of being able to trust this woman in front of him. It felt as if every day before this one—all those laughter-filled days of getting to know one another, of splashing and playing, and throwing Frisbees—had been leading to this.

He needed to think about that: that this wholesome woman, with her girl-next-door look, was really a Mata Hari, a temptress who could pull secrets from an unwilling man. But he didn't heed the warning that was flashing in the back of his brain like a red light telling of a train coming.

Drew just started to talk, and it felt as if a rock had been removed from a dam that had held back tons of water for years. Now it was all flowing toward that opening, trying to get out.

"When my parents died, I was seventeen. I wasn't even a mature seventeen. I was a superficial surfer dude, riding a wave through life."

Something happened to Becky's face. A softness came to it that was so real it almost stole the breath out of his chest. It was so different than the puffy-lipped coos of sympathy that he had received from women in the past when he'd made the mistake of sharing even small parts of his story.

This felt as if he could go lay his head on Becky's slender, naked shoulder, and rest there for a long, long time.

"I'm so sorry," she said quietly, "about the death of your parents. Both of them died at the same time?"

"It was a car accident." He could stop right there, but no, he just kept going. All those words he had never spoken felt as if they were now rushing to escape a building on fire, jostling with each other in their eagerness to be out.

"They had gone out to celebrate the anniversary of some friends. They never came home. A policeman arrived at the door and told me what had happened. Not their fault at all, a drunk driver…"

"Drew," she breathed softly. Somehow her hand found his, and the dam within him was even more compromised.

"You have never met a person more totally unqualified for the job of raising a seven-year-old brother than the seventeen-year-old me."

She squeezed his hand, as if she believed in the younger him, making him want to go on, to somehow dissuade this faith in him.

He cleared his throat. "It was me or foster care, so—" He rolled his shoulders.

"I think that's the bravest thing I ever heard," she said.

"No, it wasn't," he said fiercely. "Brave is when you have a choice. I didn't have any choice."

"You did," she insisted, as fierce as him. "You did have a choice and you chose love."

That word inserted into any conversation between them should have stopped it cold. But it didn't. In fact, it felt as if more of the wall around everything he held inside crumbled, as if her words were a wrecking ball seeking the weakest point in that dam.

"I love my brother," he said. "I just don't know if he knows how much I do."

"He can't be that big a fool," Becky said.

"I managed to finish out my year in high school and

then I found a job on a construction crew. I was tired all the time. And I never seemed to be able to make enough money. Joe sure wasn't wearing the designer clothes the rest of the kids had. I got mad if he asked. That's why he probably doesn't have a clue how I feel about him."

Becky's hand was squeezing his with unbelievable strength. It was as if her strength—who could have ever guessed this tiny woman beside him held so much strength?—was passing between them, right through the skin of her hand into his, entering his bloodstream.

"I put one foot in front of the other," Drew told her. "I did my best to raise my brother. But I was so scared of messing up that I think I was way too strict with him. I thought if I let him know how much I cared about him he would perceive it as weakness and I would lose control. Of him. Of life.

"I'd already seen what happened when I was not in control."

"Did you feel responsible for the death of your parents?" she asked. He could hear that she was startled by the question.

"I guess I asked myself, over and over, what I could have done. And the answer seemed to be, 'Never let anyone you love out of your sight. Never let go.' Most days, I felt as if I was hanging on by a thread.

"When he was a teen? I was not affectionate. I was like Genghis Khan, riding roughshod over the troops. The default answer to almost everything he wanted to do was *no*. When I did loosen the reins a bit, he had to check in with me. He had a curfew. I sucked, and he let me know it."

"Sucked?" she said, indignant.

"Yeah, we both agreed on that. Not that I let him know I agreed with him in the you-suck department."

"Then you were both wrong. What you did was noble," she said quietly. "The fact that you think you did it imperfectly does not make it less noble."

"Noble!" he snapped, wanting to show only annoyance and not vulnerability. "There's nothing noble about acting on necessity."

But she was having none of it. "It's even noble that you saw it as a necessity, not a choice."

"Whatever," he said. He suddenly disliked himself. He felt as if he was a small dog yapping and yapping and yapping at the postman. He sat up. She sat up, too. He folded his arms over his chest, a shield.

"Given that early struggle, you seem to have done well for yourself."

"A man I worked for gave me a break," Drew admitted, even though he had ordered himself to stop talking. "He was a developer. He told me I could have a lot in one of his subdivisions and put up a house on spec. I didn't have to pay for the lot until the house sold. It was the beginning of an amazing journey, but looking back, I think my drive to succeed also made me emotionally unavailable to my brother."

"You feel totally responsible for him, still."

Drew sighed, dragged a hand through his sun-dried hair. "I'm sure it's because of how I raised him that we are in this predicament we're in now, him marrying a girl I know nothing about, who may be using him. And you. And all of us."

"I don't see that as your fault."

"If I worked my ass off, I could feed him," he heard himself volunteering. "I could keep the roof over his head. I could get his books for school. I even managed to get him through college. But—"

"But what?"

"I could not teach him about finding a good relationship." Drew's voice dropped to a hoarse whisper. It felt as if every single word he had said had been circling around this essential truth.

"I missed them so much, my mom and dad. They could have showed him what he should be looking for. They were so stable. My mom was a teacher, my dad was a postal worker. Ordinary people, and yet they elevated the ordinary.

"I didn't know what I had when I had it. I didn't know what it was to wake up to my dad downstairs, making coffee for my mom, delivering it to her every morning. He sang a song while he delivered it. An old Irish folk song. They were always laughing and teasing each other. We were never rich but our house was full. The smell of cookies, the sound of them arguing good-naturedly about where to put the Christmas tree, my mom reading stories. I loved those stories way after I was too old for them. I used to find some excuse to hang out when she was reading to Joe at night. How could I hope to give any of that kind of love to my poor orphaned baby brother? When even thinking about all we had lost felt as if it would undermine the little bit of control that I was holding over my world? Instead, the environment I raised Joe in was so devoid of affection that he's gotten involved with Allie out of his sheer desperation to be loved."

"Maybe he longs for your family as much as you do."

"It's not that I didn't love him," Drew admitted gruffly. "I just didn't know how to say that to him."

"Maybe that's the area where he's going to teach you," she said softly.

Something shivered up and down Drew's spine, a tingle of pure warning, like a man might feel seconds before the cougar pounced from behind, or the plane began to lose altitude, or the earth began to shake. The remainder of the dam wall felt as if it tumbled down inside him.

"You can say that, even after finding the dress? When neither of us is sure about Allie or what her true motives are?"

"I'm going to make a decision to believe love is going to win. No matter what."

He stared at her. There should have been a choice involved here. There should have been a choice to get up and run.

But if there was that choice? He was helpless to make it.

Instead he went into her open arms like a warrior who had fought too many battles, like a warrior who had thought he would never see the lights of familiar fires again. He laid his head upon her breast and felt her hand, tender, on the nape of his neck.

He sighed against her, like a warrior who unexpectedly found himself in the place he had given up on. That place was home.

"You did your best," she said softly. "You can forgive yourself if you weren't perfect."

She began to hum softly. And then she began to sing. Her voice was clear and beautiful and it raised the hair on the back of his neck. It was as if it affirmed that love was the greatest force of all, and that it survived everything, even death.

Because of the millions of songs in the world, how was it possible Becky was gently singing this one, in her soft, true voice?

It was the same song his father had sung to his mother, every day as he brought her coffee.

Drew's surrender was complete. He had thought his story spilling out of him, like water out of a dam that had been compromised, would make him feel weak, and as though he had lost control.

Instead, he felt connected to Becky in a way he had not allowed himself to feel connected to another human being in a long, long time.

Instead, he realized how alone he had been in the world, and how good it felt not to be alone.

Instead, listening to her voice soar above the roar of the waterfall and feeling it tingle along his spine, it felt as though the ice was melting from around his heart. He felt the way he had felt diving into the water to save her all those days ago. He felt brave. Only this time, he felt as if he might be saving himself.

Drew realized he felt as brave as he ever had. He contemplated the irony that a complete surrender would make him feel the depth of his own courage.

You heal now.

And impossibly, beautifully, he was.

CHAPTER FOURTEEN

NIGHT HAD FALLEN by the time they left the waterfall and found their way back to the castle grounds. He left her with his T-shirt and walked beside her bare-chested, happy to give her the small protection of his clothing. He walked her to her bedroom door, and they stood there, looking at each other, drinking each other in like people who had been dying of thirst and had found a spring.

He touched the plumpness of her lip with his thumb, and her tongue darted out and tasted him.

She sighed her surrender, and he made a guttural, groaning sound of pure need. He did what he had been wanting to do all this time.

He planted his hands, tenderly, on either side of her head, and dropped his lips over hers. He kissed her thoroughly, exploring the tenderness of her lips with his own lips, and his tongue, probing the cool grotto of her mouth.

He had thought Becky, his little bookworm, would be shy, but she had always had that surprising side, and she surprised him now.

That gentle kiss of recognition, of welcome, that sigh of surrender, deepened quickly into something else.

It was need and it was desire. It was passion and it

was hunger. It was nature singing its ancient song of wanting life to have victory over the cycle of death.

That was what was in this kiss: everything it was to be human. Instinct and intuition, power and surrender, pleasure that bordered on pain it was so intense. He dragged his lips from hers and anointed her earlobes and her eyelids, her cheeks and the tip of her nose. He kissed the hollow of her throat, and then she pulled him back to her lips.

Her hands were all over him, touching, exploring, celebrating the hard strength in the muscles that gloried at the touch of her questing fingertips.

Finally, rational thought pushed through his primal reaction to her, calling a stern *no*. But it took every ounce of Drew's substantial strength to peel back from her. She stood there, quivering with need, panting, her eyes wide on his face.

His rational mind was gaining a foothold now that he had managed to step back from her. She had never looked more beautiful, even though her hair was a mess, and any makeup she had been wearing had washed off long ago. She had never looked more beautiful, even though she was standing there in a T-shirt that was way too large for her.

But nothing could hide the light shining from her. It was the purity of that light that reminded Drew that Becky was not the kind of girl you tangled with lightly. She required his intentions to be very clear.

In the past few days, he had felt his mother's spirit around him in a way he had not experienced since her death. It was the kind of idea he might have scoffed at two short weeks ago.

And yet this island, with its magic, and Becky with

her own enchantment, made things that had seemed impossible before feel entirely possible now.

Drew knew his mother would be expecting him to be a decent man, expecting him to rise to what she would have wanted him to be if she had lived.

She knew what he had forgotten about himself: that he was a man of courage and decency. Drew took another step back from Becky. He saw the sense of loss and confusion in her face.

"I have to go," he said, his voice hoarse.

"Please, don't."

Her voice was hoarse, too, and she stepped toward him. She took the waistband of his shorts and pulled her to him with surprising strength.

"Don't go," she said fiercely.

"You don't know what you're asking."

"Yes, I do."

For a moment he was so torn, but then his need to be decent won out. If things were going to go places with this girl—and he knew they were—it would require him to be a better man than he had been with women in the past.

It would require him to do the honorable thing.

"I have to make a phone call tonight, before it's too late." It was a poor excuse, but it was the only one he could think of. With great reluctance, he untangled her hands from where they held him, and once again stepped back from her.

If she asked again, he was not going to be able to refuse. A man's strengths had limits, after all.

But she accepted his decision. She raked a hand through her hair and looked disgruntled, but pulled herself together and tilted her chin at him.

"I have a phone call to make, too," she said. She was, just like that, his little bookworm spelling-bee contestant again, prim and sensible, and pulling back from the wild side she had just shown him.

She took a step back from him.

Go, he ordered himself. But he didn't. He stepped back toward her. He kissed her again, quickly, and then he tore himself away from her and went to his own quarters.

Rattled by what he was feeling, he took a deep breath. He wandered to the window and looked at the moon, and listened to the lap of the water on the beach. He felt as alive as he had ever felt.

He glanced at the time, swore softly, took out his cell phone and stabbed in Joe's number.

There was, predictably, no answer. He needed to tell Joe what he had learned of love tonight. It might save Joe from imminent disaster. But, of course, there was no answer, and you could hardly leave a message saying somehow you had stumbled on the secret of life and you needed to share that *right now*.

Joe would think his coolheaded, hard-hearted brother had lost his mind. So, that conversation would have to wait until tomorrow.

According to the information Becky had, Joe and Allie were supposed to arrive only on the morning of the wedding day. This was apparently to slip under the radar of the press.

Tomorrow, the guests would begin arriving, in a co-ordinated effort that involved planes and boats landing on Sainte Simone all day.

Two hundred people. It was going to be controlled chaos. And then Joe and Allie would arrive the next

day, just hours before the wedding. How was he going
to get Joe alone? Drew was aware that he *had* to get his
brother alone, that he *had* to figure out what the hell
was really going on between him and Allie.

And he was aware that he absolutely *had* to protect Becky. He thought of her tears over that dress that
Allie had had specially made, and he felt fury building
in him. In fact, all the fury of his powerlessness over
Joe's situation seemed to be coming to a head.

"Look, Joe," he said, after that annoying beep that
made him want to pick up the chair beside his bed and
throw it against the wall, "I don't know what your fiancée is up to, but you give her a message from me. You
tell your betrothed if she does anything to hurt Becky
English—anything—I will not rest until I've tracked
her to the ends of the earth and dealt with it. You know
me well enough to know I mean it. I'm done begging
you to call me. But I don't think you have a clue what
you're getting mixed up in."

Drew disconnected the call, annoyed with himself.
He had lost control, and probably reduced his chances
of getting his brother to meet with him alone.

Becky went to her room and shut the door, leaning
against it. Her knees felt wobbly. She felt breathless.
She touched her lips, as if she could still feel the warmth
of his fire claiming her. She hugged herself. She could
not believe she had invited Drew Jordan into her room.
She was not that kind of girl!

Thank goodness his good sense had prevailed, but
what did that mean? That he was not feeling things quite
as intensely as she was?

She sank down on her bed. It was as if the world had

gone completely silent, and into that silence flowed a frightening truth.

She had fallen for Drew Jordan. She loved him. She had never felt anything like what she was feeling right now: tingling with aliveness, excited about the future, aware that life had the potential to hold the most miraculous surprises. She, Becky English, who had sworn off it, had still fallen under its spell. She was in love. It wasn't just the seduction of this wildly romantic setting. It wasn't.

She loved him so much.

It didn't make any sense. It was too quick, wasn't it?

But, in retrospect, her relationship with Jerry had made perfect sense, and had unfolded with respectable slowness.

And there had been nothing real about it. She had been chasing security. She had settled for safety. Salt and pepper. Good grief, she had almost made herself a prisoner of a dull and ordinary life.

But now she knew how life was supposed to feel. And she felt so alive and grateful and on fire with all the potential the days ahead held. They didn't feel safe at all. They felt like they were loaded with unpredictable forces and choices. It felt as if she was plunging into the great unknown, and she was astonished to find she *loved* how the great adventure that was life and love was making her feel.

And following on the heels of her awareness of how much she loved Drew, and how much that love was going to make her life change, Becky felt a sudden fury with his brother. How could he treat Drew like this? Surely Joe was not so stupid that he could not see his brother had sacrificed everything for him?

Drew's whole life had become about making a life for his brother, about holding everything together. He had tried so hard and done so much, and now Joe would not even return his phone calls?

It was wrong. It was just plain old wrong.

Becky's fingers were shaking when she dialed Allie's number. She didn't care that it was late in Spain. She didn't care at all. Of course, after six rings she got Allie's voice commanding her to leave a message.

"Allie, it's Becky English. I need you to get an urgent message to Joe. He needs to call his brother. He needs to call Drew right now. Tomorrow morning at the latest." There, that was good enough. But her voice went on, shaking with emotion. "It's unconscionable that he would be ignoring Drew's attempts to call him after all Drew has done for him. I know you will both be arriving here early on the morning of the wedding, but he needs to talk to Drew before that. As soon as you get this message he needs to call."

There. She didn't need to say one other thing. And yet somehow she was still talking.

"You tell him if he doesn't call his brother immediately he'll be…" She thought and then said, "Dealing with me!"

She disconnected her phone. Then snickered. She had just used a terrible, demanding tone of voice on the most prosperous client she had ever had. She didn't care. What was so funny was her saying Drew's brother would be dealing with her, as if that was any kind of threat.

And yet she felt more powerful right now than she had ever felt in her entire life. It did feel as if she could whip that disrespectful young pup into shape!

That's what love did, she supposed. It didn't take away power, it gave it.

Becky allowed herself to feel the shock of that. She had somehow, someway, fallen in love with Drew Jordan. And not just a little bit in love: irrevocably, crazily, impossibly, feverishly in love.

It was nothing at all like what she had thought was love with Jerry. Nothing. That had felt safe and solid and secure, even though it had turned out to be none of those things. This was the most exciting thing that she had ever felt. It felt as if she was on the very crest of the world's highest roller coaster, waiting for that stomach-dropping swoop downward, her heart in her throat, both terrified and exhilarated by the pathway ahead. And just like that roller coaster, it felt as if somehow she had fully committed before she knew exactly where it was all leading. It felt like now she had no choice but to hang on tight and enjoy the wildest ride of her life.

In a trance of delight at the unexpected turn in her life, Becky pulled off Drew's T-shirt and put on her pajamas. And then she rolled up the T-shirt, and even though it was still slightly damp, she used it as her pillow and drifted off to sleep with the scent of him lulling her like a boat rocking on gentle waves.

She awoke the next morning to the steady *wop-wop-wop* of helicopter blades slicing the air. At first, she lay in bed, hugging Drew's T-shirt, listening and feeling content. Waking up to the sound of helicopters was not unusual on Sainte Simone. It was the primary way that supplies were delivered, and with the wedding just one day away, all kinds of things would be arriving today. Fresh flowers. The cake. The photographer.

Two hundred people would also be arriving over

the course of the day, on boats and by small commercial jets.

There was no time for lollygagging, Becky told herself sternly. She cast back the covers, gave the T-shirt one final hug before putting it under her pillow and then got up and went to the window.

One day, she thought, looking at the helicopters buzzing above her. She had to focus. She had to shake off this dazed, delicious feeling that she was in love and that was all that mattered.

And then it slowly penetrated her bliss that something was amiss. Her mouth fell open. She should have realized from the noise levels that something was dreadfully wrong, but she had not.

There was not one helicopter in the skies above Sainte Simone. From her place at the window, she could count half a dozen. It looked like an invasion force, but with none of the helicopters even attempting to land. They were hovering and dipping and swooping.

She could see a cameraman leaning precariously out one open door! There were so many helicopters in the tiny patch of sky above the island that it was amazing they were managing not to crash into each other.

As she watched, one of the aircraft swooped down over the pavilion. The beautiful white gauze panels began to whip around as though they had been caught in a hurricane. One ripped away, and was swept on air currents out to the ocean, where it floated down in the water, looking for all the world like a bridal veil.

A man—Josh, she thought—raced out into the surf and grabbed the fabric, then shook his fist at the helicopter. The helicopter swooped toward him, the cameraman leaning way out to get that shot.

Becky turned from the window, got dressed quickly and hurried down the stairs and out the main door onto the lawn. The staff were all out there—even the chef in his tall hat—staring in amazement at the frenzied sky dance above them.

Josh came and thrust the wet ball of fabric at her.

"Sorry," he muttered. Tandu turned and looked at her sadly. "It's on the news this morning. That the wedding is here, tomorrow. I have satellite. It's on every single channel."

She felt Drew's presence before she saw him. She felt him walk up beside her and she turned to him, and scanned his familiar face, wanting him to show her how to handle this and what to do.

He put his hand on her shoulder, and she nestled into the weight of it. This is what it meant to not be alone. Life could throw things at you, but you didn't have to handle it all by yourself. The weight of the catastrophe could be divided between them.

Couldn't it? She turned to him. "What are we going to do?"

He looked at her blankly, and she realized he was trying to read her lips. There was no way he could have heard her. She repeated her question, louder.

"I don't know," he said.

He didn't know? She felt a faint shiver of disappointment.

"How could we hold a wedding under these circumstances?" she shouted. "No one will be able to hear anything. The fabric is already tearing away from the pavilion. What about Allie's dress? And veil? What about dinner and candles and…" Her voice fell away.

"I don't think there's going to be a wedding," he said.

Her sense of her whole world shifting intensified. He could not save the day. Believing that he could would only lead to disillusionment. Believing in another person could only lead to heartache.

How on earth had she been so swept away that she had forgotten that?

She shot him a look. He sounded sorry, but was there something else in his voice? She studied Drew more carefully. He had his handsome head tilted to look at the helicopters, his arms folded over his chest.

Did he look grimly satisfied that there was a very good possibility that there was going to be no wedding?

CHAPTER FIFTEEN

BECKY FELT HER heart plummet, and it was not totally because the wedding she had worked so hard on now seemed to be in serious danger of being canceled.

Who, more than any other person on the face of the earth, did not want this wedding to happen?

Drew took his eyes from the sky and looked at her. He frowned. "Why are you looking at me like that?"

"I was just wondering about that phone call you were all fired up to make last night," she said. She could hear the stiffness in her own voice, and she saw that her tone registered with him.

"I recall being all fired up," he said, "but not about a phone call."

How dare he throw that in her face right now? That she had invited him in. He saw it as being all fired up. She saw, foolishly, that she had put her absolute trust in him.

"Is this why you didn't come in?" she said, trying to keep her tone low and be heard above the helicopters at the same time.

"Say what?"

"You didn't give in to my wanton invitation because you already knew you were planning this, didn't you?"

"Planning this?" he echoed, his brow furrowing. "Planning what, exactly?"

Becky sucked in a deep breath. "You let it out, didn't you?"

"What?"

"Don't play the innocent with me! You let it out on purpose, to stop the wedding. To stop your brother and Allie from getting married, to buy yourself a little more time to convince him not to do it."

He didn't deny it. Something glittered in his eyes, hard and cold, that she had never seen before. She reminded herself, bitterly, that there were many things about him she had never seen before. She had only known him two weeks. How could she, who of all people should be well versed in the treachery of the human heart, have let her guard down?

"That's why you had to rush to the phone last night," she decided. "Maybe you even thought you were protecting me. I should have never told you about the wedding dress."

"There are a lot of things we should have never told each other," he bit out.

She stared at him and realized the awful truth. It had all happened too fast between them. It was a reminder to her that they didn't know each other at all. She had been susceptible to the whole notion of love. Because the island was so romantic, because of that dress, because of those crazy moments when she had wanted to feel unencumbered, she had thrown herself on the altar of love with reckless abandon.

She'd been unencumbered all right! Every ounce of good sense she'd possessed had fled her!

But really, hadn't she known this all along? That love

was that roller coaster ride, thrilling and dangerous? And that every now and then it went right off the tracks?

She shot him an accusing look. He met her gaze unflinchingly.

A plane circled overhead and began to prepare to land through the minefield of helicopters. Over his shoulder, she could see a passenger barge plowing through seas made rough by the wind coming off those blades.

"Guess what?" she said wearily. "That will be the first of the guests arriving. All those people are expecting a wedding."

He lifted a shoulder negligently. What all those people were expecting didn't matter one iota to him. And neither did all her hard work. Or what this disaster could mean to her career. He didn't care about her at all.

But if he thought she was going to take this lying down, he was mistaken.

"I'm going to call Allie's publicity people," she said, with fierce determination. "Maybe they can make this disaster stop. Maybe they can call off the hounds if they are offered something in exchange."

"Good luck with that," Drew said coolly. "My experience with hounds, limited as it might be, is once they've caught the scent, there is no calling them off."

"I'm sure if Allie offers to do a photo shoot just for them, after the wedding, they will stop this. I'm sure of it!"

Of course, she was no such thing.

He gazed at her. "Forever hopeful," he said. She heard the coldness in his tone, as if being hopeful was a bad thing.

And it was! She had allowed herself to hope she could love this man. And now she saw it was impossible. Now, when it was too late. When she could have none of the glory and all of the pain.

Drew could not let Becky see how her words hit him, like a sword cleaving him in two. Last night he had taken the biggest chance he had ever taken. He had trusted her with everything. He had been wide-open.

Love.

Sheesh. He, of all people, should know better than that. Joe had not called him back. That's what love really was. Leaving yourself wide-open, all right, wide-open to pain. And rejection. Leaving yourself open to the fact that the people you loved most of all could misinterpret everything you did, run it through their own filter and come to their own conclusions, as wrong as those might be. He, of all people, should know that better than anyone else.

How could she think that he would do this to her? How could she trust him so little? He felt furious with her, and fury felt safe. Because when his fury with Becky died down, he knew what would remain. What always remained when love was gone. Pain. An emptiness so vast it felt as though it could swallow a man whole.

And he, knowing that truth as intimately as any man could know it, had still left himself wide-open to revisiting that pain. What did that mean?

"That I'm stupid," he told himself nastily. "Just plain old garden-variety stupid."

Becky felt as if she was in a trance. Numb. But it didn't matter what she was feeling. She'd agreed to do a job, and right now her job was welcoming the first of the wedding guests to the island and trying to hide it from them all that the wedding of the century was quickly turning into the fiasco of the century.

She stood with a smile fixed on her face as the door of the plane opened and the first passenger stepped down onto the steps.

In a large purple hat, and a larger purple dress, was Mrs. Barchkin, her now retired high school social sciences teacher.

"Why, Becky English!" Mrs. Barchkin said cheerily. "What on earth are you doing here?"

Her orders had been to keep the wedding secret. She had not told one person in her small town she was coming here.

Her smile clenched in place, she said, "No, what on earth are you doing here?"

Mrs. Barchkin was clutching a rumpled card in a sweaty hand. She passed it to Becky. Despite the fact people were piling up behind Mrs. Barchkin, Becky smoothed out the card and read, "In appreciation of your kindness, I ask you to be my guest at a celebration of love." There were all the details promising a limousine pickup and the adventure of a lifetime.

"Pack for a week and plan to have fun!" And all this was followed with Allie Ambrosia's flowing signature, both the small *i*'s dotted with hearts.

"Isn't this all too exciting?" Mrs. Barchkin said.

"Too exciting," Becky agreed woodenly. "If you just go over there, that golf cart will take you to your accommodations. Don't worry about your luggage."

Don't worry. Such good advice. But Becky's sense of worry grew as she greeted the rest of the guests coming down the steps of the plane. There was a poor-looking young woman in a cheaply made dress, holding a baby who looked ill. There was a man and a wife and their three kids chattering about the excitement of their first plane ride. There was a minister. At least he *might* be here to conduct the ceremony.

Not a single passenger who got off that plane was what you would expect of Hollywood's A-list. And neither, Becky realized an hour later, was anyone who got off the passenger barge. In fact, most everyone seemed to be the most ordinary of people, people who would have fit right in on Main Street in Moose Run.

They were all awed by the island and the unexpected delight of an invitation to the wedding of one of the most famous people in the world. But none of them—not a single person of the dozens that were now descending on the island—actually seem to know Allie Ambrosia or Joe Jordan.

Becky had a deepening conviction that somehow they were all pawns in Allie's big game. Maybe, just maybe, Drew had not been so wrong in doing everything he could to stop the wedding.

But why had he played with her? Why had he made it seem as if he was going along with getting a wedding ready if he was going to sabotage it? Probably, this— the never-ending storm of helicopters hovering overhead—had been a last-ditch effort to stop things when his every effort to reach his brother had been frustrated.

Still, the fact was she had trusted him. She was not going to make excuses for him! She was determined to not even think about him.

As each boat and plane delivered its guests and departed, Becky's unease grew. Her increasingly frantic texts and messages to Allie and members of Allie's staff were not being answered. In fact, Allie's voice mailbox was now full.

Becky crawled into bed that night, exhausted. The wedding was less than twenty-four hours away. If they were going to cancel it, they needed to do that now.

Though one good thing about all the excitement was that she had not had time to give a thought to Drew. But now she did.

And lying there in her bed, staring at the ceiling, she burst into tears. And the next morning she was thankful she had used up every one of her tears, because a private jet landed at precisely 7:00 a.m.

The door opened.

And absolutely nothing happened. Eventually, the crew got off. A steward told her, cheerfully, they were going to layover here. He showed her the same invitation she had seen at least a dozen times. The one that read, "In appreciation of your kindness, I ask you to be my guest at a celebration of love."

Becky had to resist the impulse to tear that invitation from his hands and rip it into a million pieces. Because now she knew the plane was empty. And Allie and Joe had not gotten off it.

Of course, it could be part of the elaborate subterfuge that was necessary to avoid the paparazzi, but the helicopters overhead were plenty of evidence they had already failed at that.

How could she, Becky asked herself with a shake of her head, still hope? How could she still hope they were coming, and still hope that love really was worth celebrating?

She quit resisting the impulse. She took the invitation from the crew member, tore it into a dozen pieces and threw them to the wind. Despite the surprised looks she received, it felt amazingly good to do that!

She turned and walked away. No more hoping. No more trying to fill in the blanks with optimistic fiction. She was going to have to find Tandu and cancel everything. She was going to have to figure out the logistics of how to get all those disappointed people back out of here.

Her head hurt thinking about it.

So Drew had won the headache competition after all. And by a country mile at that.

CHAPTER SIXTEEN

DREW PULLED HIMSELF from the ocean and flung himself onto the beach. His crew had just finished the gazebo and had departed, sending him looks that let him know he'd been way too hard on them. He'd had them up at dawn, putting the final touches of paint on the gazebo, making sure the dance floor was ready.

What did they expect? There was supposed to be a wedding here in a few hours. Of course he had been hard on them.

Maybe a little too hard, since it now seemed almost everyone on the island, except maybe the happy guests, had figured out the bride and groom were missing.

Drew knew his foul mood had nothing to do with the missing bride and groom, or the possibility, growing more real by the second, that there wasn't going to be a wedding. He had driven his crew to perfection anyway, unreasonably.

He had tried to swim it off, but now, lying in the sand, he was aware he had not. The helicopter that buzzed him to see if he was anyone interesting did not help his extremely foul mood.

How could Becky possibly think he had called the

press? After all they had shared together, how could she not know who he really was?

It penetrated his morose that his phone, lying underneath his shirt, up the beach, was ringing. And then he froze. The ring tone was the one he had assigned for Joe!

He got up and sprinted across the sand.

"Hello?"

"Hi, bro."

It felt like a shock to hear his brother's voice. Even in those two small syllables, Drew was sure he detected something. Sheepishness?

"How are you, Drew?"

"Cut the crap."

Silence. He thought Joe might have hung up on him, but he heard him breathing.

"Where the hell have you been? Why haven't you been answering my calls? Are you on your way here?"

"Drew, I have something to tell you."

Drew was aware he was holding his breath.

"Allie and I got married an hour ago."

"What?"

"The whole island thing was just a ruse. Allie leaked it to the press yesterday morning that we were going to get married there to divert them away from where we really are."

"You lied to me?" He could hear the disbelief and disappointment in his own voice.

"I feel terrible about that. I'm sorry."

"But why?"

Inside he was thinking, *How could you get married without me to stand beside you? I might have made mistakes, but I'm the one who has your back. Who has always had your back.*

"It's complicated," Joe said.

"Let me get this straight. You aren't coming here at all?"

"No."

Poor Allie, Drew thought.

"We got married an hour ago, just Allie and me and a justice of the peace. We're in Topeka, Kansas. Who would ever think to look there, huh?"

"Topeka, Kansas," he repeated dully.

His brother took it as a question. "You don't have to be a resident of the state to get married here. There's a three-day waiting period for the license, but I went down and applied for it a month ago."

"You've been planning this for a month?" Drew felt the pain of it. He had been excluded from one of the most important events of his brother's life. And it was his own fault.

"I'm sorry," he said.

"For what?" Joe sounded astounded.

"That I could never tell you what you needed to hear."

"I'm not following."

"That I loved you and cared about you and would have fought alligators for you."

"Drew! You think I don't know that?"

"I guess if you know it, I don't understand any of this."

"It's kind of all part of a larger plan. I'll fill you in soon. I promise. Meanwhile, Allie's got her people on it right now. In a few hours the press will know we aren't there, and whatever's going on there will die down. They'll leave you guys alone."

"Leave us alone? You think I'm going to stay here?"

"Why not? It's a party. That's all the invitations ever said. That it was a party to celebrate love."

"Who are all these people arriving here?"

And when Joe told him, Drew could feel himself, ever so reluctantly, letting go of the anger.

Even his anger at Becky felt as if it was dissipating. He understood, suddenly, exactly why she had jumped at the first opportunity to see him in a bad light. That girl was terrified of love. She'd been betrayed by it at too many turns. She was terrified of what she was feeling for him.

"Joe? Tell Allie not to call Becky about the wedding not happening. I'll look after it. I'll tell her myself."

There was a long silence. And then Joe said softly, "All part of a larger plan."

"Yeah, whatever." He wanted to tell his brother congratulations, but somehow he couldn't. Who was this woman that Joe had married? It seemed as if she was just playing with all their strings as if they were her puppets.

Drew threw on his shirt and took the now familiar path back toward the castle. What remained of his anger at Becky for not trusting him was completely gone.

All he wanted to do was protect her from one more devastating betrayal. He understood, suddenly, what love was. With startling clarity he saw that it was the ability to see that it was not all about him. To be able to put her needs ahead of his own and not be a baby because his feelings had been hurt.

As he got closer to the castle, he could see there were awestruck people everywhere prowling the grounds. He spotted Tandu in the crowd, talking to a tall, distinguished-looking man in a casual white suit and bare feet.

"Mr. Drew Jordan, have you met Mr. Lung?" Tandu asked him.

"Pleasure," Drew said absently. "Tandu, can I talk to you for a minute?"

Tandu stepped to the side with him. "Have you seen Becky?" he asked, with some urgency.

"A few minutes ago. She told me to cancel everything."

So, she already knew, or thought she did. She was carrying the burden of it by herself.

"Impossible to cancel," Tandu said. "The wedding must go on!"

"Tandu, there is not going to be a wedding. I just spoke to my brother."

"Ah," he said. "Oh, well, we celebrate love anyway, hmm?" And then he gave Drew a look that was particularly piercing, and disappeared into the crowd.

"How are you enjoying my island?" Bart Lung was on his elbow.

"It's a beautiful place," Drew said, scanning the crowd for Becky. "Uh, look, Mr. Lung—"

"Bart, please."

"Bart, I think you need to have a qualified first aid person on the island to host this many guests."

"I have an excellent first aid attendant. That was him who just introduced us. Don't be fooled by the tray of canapés."

"Look, Tandu is a nice guy. Stellar. I just don't think being afraid of blood is a great trait for a first aid attendant."

"Tandu? Afraid of blood? Who told you that?"

Before Drew could answer that Tandu himself had told him that, Bart went on.

"Tandu is from this island, but don't be fooled by that island boy accent or the white shirt or the tray of canapés. He's a medical student at Oxford. He comes back in the summers to help out." Bart chortled. "Afraid of blood! I saw him once when he was the first responder to a shark attack. I have never seen so much blood and I have never seen such cool under pressure."

Drew felt a shiver run up and down the whole length of his spine.

And then he saw Becky. She was talking to someone who was obviously a member of the flight crew, and she was waving her arms around expressively.

"Excuse me. I have an urgent matter I need to take care of."

"Of course."

"Becky!"

She turned and looked at him, and for a moment, everything she felt was naked in her face.

And everything she was.

Drew realized fully that her lack of trust was a legacy from her past, and that to be the man she needed, the man worthy of her love, he needed to not hurt her more, but to understand her fears and vulnerabilities and to help her heal them.

Just as she had, without even knowing that was what she was doing, helped him heal his own fears and vulnerabilities.

"We need to talk," he said. "In private."

She looked at him, and then looked away. "Now? I don't see that there is any way they are coming. I was just asking about the chances of getting some flight schedules changed."

Despite the fact she *knew* Allie and Joe weren't coming, despite the fact that she had asked Tandu about canceling, despite the fact that she was trying to figure out how to get rid of all these people, he saw it, just for a second, wink behind her bright eyes.

Hope.

Against all odds, his beautiful, funny, bookish, spunky Becky was still hoping for a happy ending.

"We need to talk," Drew told her.

She hesitated, scanned the sky for an incoming jet and then sighed. "Yes, all right," she said.

He led her away from the crowded front lawn and front terrace.

"I just talked to Joe," he said in a low voice.

"And? Is everything okay? Between you?"

This was who she really was: despite it all, despite thinking that he had betrayed her trust, she was worried about him and his troubled relationship with his brother, first. And the wedding second.

"I guess time will tell."

"You didn't patch things up," she said sadly.

"He didn't phone to patch things up. Becky, he gave me some bad news."

"Is he all right?" There it was again, a boundless compassion for others. "What?" she whispered.

"There isn't going to be a wedding."

It was then that he knew she had been holding her breath, waiting for a miracle, because the air whooshed out of her and her shoulders sagged.

"Because of the press finding out?" she said.

"No, Becky, there was never going to be a wedding."

She looked at him with disbelief.

"Apparently this whole thing—" he swept his arm to indicate the whole thing "—was just a giant ruse planned out in every detail by Allie. She sent the press here, yesterday morning, on a wild-goose chase."

"It wasn't you," she whispered. Her skin turned so pale he wondered if she was going to faint.

"Of course it wasn't me."

She began to tremble. "But how are you ever going to forgive me for thinking it was you?"

"I don't believe," he said softly, "that you ever did believe that. Not in your heart."

"Why did she do that?" Becky wailed.

"So that she and my brother could sneak away and get married in peace. Which they did. An hour ago. In Topeka, Kansas, of all places."

Her hand was on his arm. She was looking at him searchingly. "Your brother got married without you?"

He lifted a shoulder.

"Oh! That is absolutely unforgivable!"

"It's not your problem."

"Oh, my God! Here I am saying what is unforgivable in other people, and what I did was unforgivable. I accused you of alerting the press!"

"Is it possible," he asked her softly, "that you wanted to be mad at me? Is it possible it was just one last-ditch effort to protect yourself from falling in love with me?"

She was doing now what she had not done when he told her there would be no wedding. She was crying.

"I'm so sorry," she said.

"Is it true then? Are you in love with me?"

"Yes, I'm afraid it is. It's true."

"It's true for me, too. I'm in love with you, Becky. I am so in love with you. And I'm as terrified as you are. I'm afraid of loving. I'm afraid of loss. I'm afraid I can't be the man you need me to be. I'm afraid…"

She stopped him with her lips. She stopped him by twining her hands around his neck and pulling him close to her.

And when she did that, he wasn't afraid of anything anymore.

CHAPTER SEVENTEEN

"WHY DID SHE do all this?" Becky asked.

"Joe told me that she never told any of these people they were coming to a wedding."

"She didn't! That's true. She told them in appreciation for their kindness they were being invited to a celebration of love. I saw some of the invitations today. It doesn't really answer *why* she did all this, does it? All this tremendous expense for a ruse? There are a million things that would have been easier and cheaper to send the press in the wrong direction so they could get married in private."

"Joe told me why she did it."

"And?"

"Joe told me that people would look at her humble beginnings and share personal stories about themselves. And so she sent invitations to the ones with the most compelling personal stories, a comeback from cancer, a bankruptcy, surviving the death of a child.

"Joe says she has thought of nothing else for months—that she did her homework. That she chose the ones who rose above their personal circumstances and still gave back to others.

"He said those are the ones they want to celebrate

love with them. He said Allie wants her story to bring
hope to lives where too many bad things had occurred.
He says she's determined to make miracles happen."

"Wow," Becky said softly. "It almost makes me not
want to be mad at her."

"Regretfully, me, too."

They laughed softly together.

"It's quite beautiful, isn't it?" Becky said quietly.

He wanted to harrumph it. He wanted to say it was
impossibly naive and downright dumb. He wanted to
say his future sister-in-law—no, make that his current
sister-in-law—was showing signs of being extraordinarily clever about manipulating others.

He wanted to say all that, but somehow he couldn't.

Because here he was, the beneficiary of one of the
miracles that Allie Ambrosia had been so determined
to make happen.

You heal now, Tandu had said to him. And somehow
his poor wounded heart had healed, just enough to let
this woman beside him past his defenses. Now, he found
himself hoping they would have the rest of their lives
to heal each other, to get better and better.

"You know, Becky, all those people are expecting
a wedding. Tandu said it's impossible to put a hold on
the food now."

"It's harder to reschedule those exit flights than you
might think."

"The minister is already here. And so is the photographer."

"What of it?"

"I think any wedding that is a true expression of love
will honor why we are all here."

"What are you suggesting?"

"I don't think she ever had that dress made to hurt you."

"Oh, my God." Becky's fist flew to her mouth, and tears shone behind her eyes.

"And I've been thinking about this. There is no way my brother would ever get married without me. Not unless he thought it was for my own good."

"They put us together deliberately!"

"I'm afraid that's what I'm thinking."

"It's maddening."

"Yes."

"It's a terrible manipulation."

"Yes."

"It's like a blind date on steroids."

"Yes."

"Are you angry?"

"No."

"Me, neither."

"Because it worked. If they would have just introduced us over dinner somewhere, it would have never worked out like this."

"I know. You would have seen me as a girl from Moose Run, one breath away from becoming a nun."

"You would have seen me as superficial and arrogant and easily bored."

"You would have never given me a second chance."

"You wouldn't have wanted one."

They were silent for a long time, contemplating how things could have gone, and how they did.

"What time is the wedding?" he asked her.

"It's supposed to be at three."

"That means you have one hour and fifteen minutes to make up your mind."

"I've made up my mind," Becky whispered.

"You should put on that dress and we should go to that gazebo I built, and in the incredible energy of two hundred people who have been hand-chosen for the bigness of their hearts, we should get married."

"It won't be real," she whispered. "I mean, not legal. It will be like we're playing roles."

"Well, I won't be playing a role, and I don't think you're capable of it. We'll go to Kansas when it's all over. In three days we'll have a license."

"Are you asking me to marry you? For real? Not as part of Allie's amazing pretend world?"

"Absolutely, 100 percent for real."

She stared at him. She began to laugh, and then cry. She threw her arms around his neck. "Yes! Yes! Yes!" she said.

All the helicopters had gone away. The world was perfect and silent and sacred.

Despite the fact they were using up a great deal of that one hour and fifteen minutes, they talked. They talked about children. And where they would live. And what they would do. They talked about how Tandu seemed as if he was a bit of a matchmaker, too, leaving Drew to doctor Becky's leg when he had been more than capable of doing it himself, of delivering them to the best and most romantic places on the island, of "seeing" the future.

Finally, as the clock ticked down, they parted ways with a kiss.

Tandu was waiting for her when she arrived back at the castle. He took in her radiant face with satisfaction.

"You need my help to be best bride ever?"

"How do you know these things?" she asked him.

"I see."

"I know you're a medical student at Oxford."

He chuckled happily. "That is when *seeing* is the most helpful."

Tandu accompanied her up the stairs, but when she went to go to her room, Tandu nudged her in a different direction. "Take the bridal suite."

Becky stared at him suspiciously. "Have you been in on this all along?"

He smiled. "Allie has been to Sainte Simone before. I count her as my friend. I will go let the guests know there has been a slight change in plan and arrange some helpers. I will look after everything."

She could not argue with him. All her life she had never been able to accept good things happening to her, but she was willing to change. She was willing to embrace each gift as it was delivered.

Had she not been delivered a husband out of a storybook? Why not believe? She went to the bridal suite, and stood before the dress that she had hung up days before. She touched it, and it felt not unlike she had been a princess sleeping, who was now waking up.

Tandu had assembled some lovely women helpers and she was treated like a princess. Given that the time until the wedding was so brief, Becky was pampered shamelessly. Her hair was done, her makeup was applied.

And then the beautiful dress was delivered to her. She closed her eyes. Becky let her old self drop away with each stich of her clothing. The dress, and every dream that had been sewn right into the incredible fabric, skimmed over her naked skin. She heard the zipper whisper up.

"Look now," one of her shy helpers instructed.

Becky opened her eyes. Her mouth fell open. The most beautiful princess stood in front of her, her hair piled up on top of her head, with little tendrils kissing the sides of her face. Her eyes, expertly made-up, looked wide and gorgeous. Her cheekbones looked unbeliev-able. Her lips, pink glossed and slightly turned up in an almost secretive smile, looked sensual.

Her eyes strayed down the elegant curve of her neck to the full enchantment of the dress. The vision in the mirror wobbled like a mirage as her eyes filled with tears.

The dress was a confection, with its sweetheart neck-line and fitted bodice, and layers and layers and layers of filmy fabric flowing out in that full skirt with an im-possible train. It made her waist look as if a man could span it with his two hands.

Shoes were brought to her, and they looked, fantas-tically, like the glass slippers in fairy tales.

All those years ago this dress had been the epitome of her every romantic notion. Becky had been able to picture herself in it, but she had never been able to pic-ture it being Jerry that she walked toward.

Because she had never felt like she felt in this mo-ment.

She was so aware that the bride's beauty was not created by the dress. The dress only accentuated what was going on inside, that bubbling fountain of life that love had built within her.

"No crying! You'll ruin your makeup."

But everyone else in the room was crying, all of them feeling the absolute sanctity of this moment, when someone who has been a girl realizes she is ready to be a woman. When someone who has never known the reality of love steps fully into its light.

A beautiful bouquet of island flowers was placed in her hands.

"This way."

Still in a dream, she moved down the castle stairs and out the door. The grounds that had been such a beehive of activity were strangely deserted. A golf cart waited for her and it whisked her silently down the wide path, through the lushness of the tropical growth, to the beach.

She walked down that narrow green-shaded trail to where it opened at the beach. The chairs were all full. If anyone was disappointed that it was not Allie who appeared at the edge of the jungle, it did not show on a single face.

If she had to choose one word to explain the spirit she walked in and toward it would be *joy*.

Bart Lung bowed to her and offered her his arm. She kicked off the glass slippers and felt her feet sink into the sand. She was so aware that she felt as if she could feel every single grain squish up between her toes.

A four-piece ensemble began to play the traditional wedding march.

She dared to look at the gazebo. If this weren't true, this was the part where she would wake up. In her nightmares the gazebo would be empty.

But it was not empty. The minister that she had welcomed on the first plane stood there in purple cleric's robes, beaming at her.

And then Drew turned around.

Becky's breath caught in her throat. She faltered, but the light that burned in his eyes picked her up and made her strong. She moved across the space between them unerringly, her eyes never leaving his, her sense of wonder making it hard to breathe.

She was marrying this man. She was marrying this strong, funny, thrillingly handsome man who would protect those he loved with his life. She was the luckiest woman in the world and she knew it.

Bart let go of her arm at the bottom of the stairs, and Becky went to Drew like an arrow aimed straight for his heart.

She went to him like someone who had been lost in the wilderness catching sight of the way home.

She went to him with his children already being born inside her.

She repeated the vows, those age-old vows, feeling as if each word had a deep meaning she had missed before.

And then came these words:

"I now pronounce you husband and wife."

And before the minister could say anything more, Becky turned and cast her beautiful bouquet at the gathering and went into his arms and claimed his lips.

And then he picked her up and carried her down the steps and out into the ocean, and with the crowd cheering madly, he kissed her again, before he wrapped his arms tightly around her and they both collapsed into the embrace of a turquoise sea.

When they came up for air, they were laughing and sputtering, her perfect hair was ruined, her makeup was running down her face and her dress was clinging to her in wet ribbons.

"This has been the best day of my entire life," she told him. "There will never be another day as good as this one."

And Drew said to her, "No, that's not quite right. This day is just the beginning of the best days of our lives."

And he kissed her again, and the crowd went wild, but her world felt like a grotto of silence and peace, a place cut out of a busy world, just for them. A place created by love.

EPILOGUE

"Who agreed to this insanity?" Drew demanded of his wife.

"You did," Becky told him. She handed him a crying baby and scooped the other one out of the car seat that had been deposited on their living room floor.

Drew frowned at the baby and held it at arm's length. "Does he stink?"

"Probably. I don't think that's he. I think it's she. Pink ribbon in hair."

Drew squinted at the pink ribbon. It would not be beyond his brother to put the ribbon in Sam's hair instead of Sally's.

"I've changed my mind," Drew declared over the howling of the smelly baby. "I am not ready for this. I am not even close to being ready for this."

"Well, it's too late. Your brother and Allie are gone to Sainte Simone. They never had a honeymoon, and if ever a couple needed one, they do."

"I'm not responsible for their choices," he groused, but he was aware it was good-naturedly. His sister-in-law, Allie, was exasperating. And flaky. She was completely out of touch with reality, and her career choice of pretending to be other people had made that quality even more aggravating in her. She believed, with a childlike enthusiasm, in the fairy tales she acted out, and was a huge proponent of happily-ever-after.

And yet…and yet, could you ask for anyone more genuinely good-hearted than her? Or generous? Or kind? Or devoted to her family in general, and his brother in particular?

There was no arguing that Joe, his sweet, shy brother, had blossomed into a confident and happy man under the influence of his choice of a life partner.

In that Hollywood world where a marriage could be gone up in smoke in weeks, Allie and Joe seemed imminently solid. They had found what they both longed for most: that place called home. And they were not throwing it away.

"Mommy gone? Daddy gone?"

Drew juggled the baby, and stared down at one more little face looking up at him. It occurred to him now would be a bad time to let his panic show.

"Yes, Andrew," he said quietly, "You're staying with Uncle Drew and Aunt Becky for a few days."

"Don't want to," Andrew announced.

That makes two of us.

Joe and Allie had adopted Andrew from an orphanage in Brazil not six months after they had married. The fact that the little boy was missing a leg only seemed to make them love him more. He'd only been home with them for about a month when they had found out they were pregnant. The fact that they had been pregnant with twins had been a surprise until just a few weeks before Sam and Sally had been born.

But the young couple had handled it with aplomb. Drew could see what he had never seen before: that

Joe longed for that sense of family they had both lost even more than he himself had. Joe had chosen Allie, out of some instinct that Drew did not completely understand, as the woman who could give him what he longed for.

So, Joe and Allie were celebrating their second anniversary with a honeymoon away from their three children.

And Drew and Becky would celebrate their second anniversary, one day behind Joe and Allie, with a pack of children, because Allie had announced they were the only people she would trust with her precious offspring.

"I wish I had considered the smell when I agreed to this," he said. "How are we going to have a romantic anniversary now?"

"Ah, we'll think of something," Becky said with that little wink of hers that could turn his blood to liquid lava. "They have to sleep sometime."

"Are you sure?"

"It will be good practice for us," she said. She said it very casually. Too casually. She shot him a look over the tousled dandelion-fluff hair of the baby she was holding.

He went very still. He moved the baby from the crook of one arm to the crook of the other. He stared at his wife, and took in the radiant smile on her face as she looked away from him and gazed at the baby in her arms.

"Good practice for us?"

Andrew punched him in the leg. "I hate you," he decided. "Where's my daddy?"

Becky threw back her head and laughed.

And he saw it then. He wondered how he had missed

it, he who thought he knew every single nuance of his wife's looks and personality and moods.

He saw that she was different. Becky was absolutely glowing, softly and beautifully radiant.

"Yes," she said softly. "Good practice for us."

Andrew kicked him again. Drew looked down at him. Soon, sooner than he could ever have prepared for, he was going to have a little boy like this. A boy who would miss him terribly when he went somewhere. Who would look to him for guidance and direction. Who would think he got up early in the morning and put out the sun for him.

Or maybe he would have a little girl like the one in his arms, howling and stinky, and so, so precious it could steal a man's breath away. A little girl who would need him to show her how to throw a baseball so that the boys wouldn't make her think less of herself. And who would one day, God forbid, need him to sort through all the boys who wanted to date her to find one that might be suitable.

How could a man be ready for that?

He looked again into his wife's face. She was watching him with a soft, knowing smile playing across the fullness of her lips.

That's how he could be ready.

Because love made a man what he could never hope to be on his own. Once, because of the loss of those he had loved the most, he'd thought it was the force that could take a man's strength completely.

Now he saw that all love wove itself into the person a man eventually became. His parents were with him. Becky's love shaped him every day.

And made him ready for whatever was going to happen next.

Andrew punched him again. Juggling the baby, he bent down and scooped Andrew up in his other arm.

"I know," he said. "I know you miss your daddy."

Andrew wailed his assent and buried his head in Drew's neck. The stinky baby started to cry. Becky laughed again. He leaned over and kissed her nose.

And it felt as if in a life full of perfect moments, none had been more perfect than this one.

Daddy. He was going to be a daddy.

It was just as he had said to her the day they had gotten married. It wasn't the best day of their lives. All that was best was still in front of him, in a future that shone bright in the light of love. That love flowed over him from the look in her eyes. It flowed over him and drenched him and all of those days that were yet to come in its shimmering light.

* * * * *

MARRIED FOR THEIR MIRACLE BABY

SORAYA LANE

For my mother, Maureen. Thank you for everything.

CHAPTER ONE

BLAKE GOLDSMITH TOOK a slow sip of whiskey, enjoying the burn of the straight liquor as he swallowed. He wasn't a big drinker, but he'd fast developed a taste for whiskey on the rocks to help get him through the torturous task of attending cocktail parties and gala events. He gazed down at the ice sitting forlorn in the glass. *Darn.* He either had to go without or brave the crowd mingling near the bar again. Neither option appealed to him right now.

Instead he decided to stretch his legs and head outside. If anyone stopped him, he could blame his departure on needing some fresh air. As soon as the auction was over, he was heading home anyway. He craved the solitude of flying, the closeness of being with his unit when he was serving. If he had half the chance, he'd be hightailing it to wherever they were stationed and not coming back. *If only that were an option.*

"Excuse me," he muttered, touching a woman's elbow as he passed, eyes downcast so he didn't have to engage.

After a while, everyone started to look the same—

a sea of black tuxedos and white shirts mixed with elegant women in sparkly dresses. He should have been used to it by now, but playing the black sheep turned good wasn't a part he'd ever wanted, and neither was being part of glittering society parties.

Wow. Blake squared his shoulders, stood a little straighter as he stared across the room. She was standing alone, back to the large windows that overlooked a twinkling New York City below. Her dark red hair was loose and falling over her shoulders, lipstick bright in contrast to her pale skin. She was like a perfectly formed doll, her posture perfect, one hand holding a full glass of champagne, the other clasping a tiny purse. In a room where all the women were starting to look scarily similar with their perfectly coiffed updos and black dresses, she was like the breath of fresh air he'd been so desperately craving only moments before.

Blake didn't waste time. She was alone, which meant she was either waiting for her date to return or actually solo. Either way, he wanted to get to her before anyone else did. He might be avoiding the pressure to settle down, but introducing himself to a beautiful woman would make the night a whole lot more interesting.

He excused himself past a few more people, striding across the room, eyes locked on her. *So much for a boring night out to buy some art and make the company look good.* His evening was looking better by the second. Blake cleared his throat and smiled when dark brown eyes met his.

"I'd ask if you want another drink, but it doesn't look

like you've even touched this one," he said. "Unless you don't like champagne."

The redhead laughed, tipping back a little so her hair tumbled over her shoulders, the unblemished skin of her neck on show. "I love champagne. I'm just…"

Blake laughed. "Bored?"

She grimaced, and it only made him like her more. "Yeah," she said softly. "You could say that."

"I'm Blake," he said, holding out a hand. "Blake Goldsmith."

She reached hers out and he shook it, her skin warm against his. "Saffron Wells."

"So what's a girl like you doing here alone?"

"A bored girl?" she asked.

Blake raised an eyebrow. "No, a beautiful one."

Her smile was sweet. "I promised a friend I'd come, but it's not really my thing." Saffron shrugged. "She's an artist—one of her pieces is being auctioned tonight, so I couldn't really say no. Besides, I don't get out much."

She might feel out of place, but she sure looked the part, as if it was exactly her scene. Blake glanced down when she looked away, eyes traveling over her blue satin dress, admiring her legs. It was short and strapless, and it took every inch of his willpower to stop staring. She was a knockout.

"So what do you do?" he asked.

"I'm having some time out right now," she replied, her smile fading. "I'm just making coffee and…"

Blake cringed, wishing he'd asked something less invasive. He hadn't wanted to put her on the spot or make her uncomfortable. "I love coffee. The barista at my local café is my favorite person in the world."

"How about you?" she asked.

Now Blake was really regretting his line of questioning. He'd walked straight into that one. "Family business. I'm here tonight because no one else would take my place."

"Poor you."

"Yeah, something like that." Blake hated talking about himself, and he liked the fact that this beautiful woman seemed to have no idea who he was. If he read another tabloid or blog article about his most-eligible-bachelor status, he'd lose it. And the lies surrounding his dad's death were driving him to drink. So to chat with a woman like Saffron and not deal with any of that was refreshing to say the least.

A waiter passed and Blake held up a hand, beckoning him over. He smiled and placed his empty whiskey glass on the tray, taking a champagne and putting it into Saffron's hand. He removed her other one, ignoring the look of protest on her face, and then he took another glass for himself.

"I was perfectly happy nursing that," she said.

"Nothing worse than warm champagne," Blake told her. "Want to get some fresh air?"

Saffron's smile was small, but it was there. "Sure. Any excuse to get out of here."

Blake grinned back and touched the small of her back as she turned, guiding her to the only exit he could see. There was a large balcony, which was probably full of smokers, but the room was stifling and he didn't care.

"Excuse me." A loud voice boomed through the speakers, making him turn. "May I have your attention please?"

Blake groaned. Just as he'd been about to escape... "Want to make a run for it?" he murmured, leaning down to whisper into Saffron's ear. Her hair smelled like perfume, and it was soft against his cheek when she tipped her head back.

"I think we need to stay," she whispered in reply, dark brown eyes locked on his for a second. "As much as I'd love to disappear."

Blake shrugged. He would have happily disappeared and made a phone bid, but he wasn't about to leave the most interesting woman he'd seen all evening. Her dark red hair stood out in a sea of bright blondes and raven-haired heads, the color subtle but stunning. And in a room full of slim woman, she seemed even smaller, but not in a skinny way. Blake had noticed the way she was standing when he'd first seen her, her posture perfect, limbs long yet muscled, her body even more sculptured up close than it had appeared from afar. He was intrigued.

"Thank you all for being here tonight to raise funds for underprivileged children right here in New York City," the host said. Blake was tall, so even from the back of the room he could see what was going on, but he doubted Saffron would be able to see a thing. She was almost a head shorter than him. "Funds raised to-night will help to provide a winter assistance package for under-twelve-year-old children who don't have the basics to help them through our harsh colder months.

They will receive a warm coat, shoes, hat, pajamas and other things so many of us take for granted."

Blake glanced down at Saffron. He watched her raise the slender glass to her mouth, taking a sip. He did the same, even though champagne wasn't his usual drink of choice.

"This is my friend's piece," Saffron said, meeting his gaze for a moment. "She's been working on this on and off all year, as part of her latest collection."

Blake pulled the brochure from his inside jacket pocket and stared at the first painting on the crumpled paper. He wasn't the type to get superexcited over art—all he cared about was making a sizable donation to a worthy cause—but he didn't dislike it. The bright swirls of multicolored paint looked interesting enough, and a quick scan over the bio told him the emerging artist could be one to watch. If he got a worthwhile, long-term investment for his donation, he'd be happy.

"We'll open the bidding at five hundred dollars," the auctioneer said, taking over from the host.

Blake raised his hand just high enough for the spotter to see. The bidding quickly moved up to five thousand dollars, and Blake stayed with it, nodding each time now that he was being watched. He didn't like drawing attention to himself, and from the look on Saffron's face when the bidding stopped at just over ten thousand, even she had no idea it was him pushing the price up. He was buying on behalf of the company, so to him it was small change, but he was certain it would be exciting for an emerging artist trying to make a name for herself.

"She'll be thrilled!" Saffron said, eyes bright as she

connected with him. "All the other artists are so well-known, and…" She narrowed her gaze and he laughed.

"What?"

"Why are you smiling like that?" she asked.

Blake grinned. "I bought it," he said simply. "Hopefully she'll be superfamous one day, and I'll have a good story to tell and a decent investment on the wall of my office."

Saffron raised her glass and clinked it to his. "You're crazy."

"No, just in a generous mood." Blake had done his good deed, and now he was ready to go. The auctioneer started all over again, and he placed a hand to the small of Saffron's back. "Meet me outside? I just need to sign for the painting." He'd intended on buying two pieces, but he decided to make a donation with his purchase instead.

He watched as she nodded. "Sure."

Blake paused, hoping she wasn't about to walk out on him, then decided it was a risk he was just going to have to take.

"You never did tell me which café you work at."

She just smiled at him. "No, I don't believe I did."

When she didn't elaborate, Blake walked backward a few steps, not taking his eyes off her before finally moving away. He was used to women throwing themselves at him, wanting his money, being so obvious with their intentions. Saffron was different, and he liked it. There was no desperation in her eyes, no look as though she wanted to dig her claws in and catch him, and it only made him want to get to know her all the more. If she genuinely didn't know who he was right now, then he could be himself, and that was a role he hadn't been able to play in a very long time.

Saffron watched Blake from across the room. She'd been dreading coming out, not looking forward to making small talk and having people ask about her injury, but so far no one had really bothered her. Until Blake. She had no idea who he was or if she was supposed to know who he was, but he'd purchased Claire's painting as if it were no big deal, so he either had money or worked for a company that had told him to spend up. Either way she didn't care, but she was definitely curious.

The night air was cool when she moved out, but the large balcony was virtually empty. There was a couple kissing in the corner, obscured by the shadows, so Saffy walked closer to the edge, admiring the view. She'd never tire of New York. The vibrant atmosphere, the twinkling lights, the fact the city never seemed to sleep. It had a vibe about it that she'd never known anywhere else in the world, and for the first time in her life she felt as if she belonged, as though she was where she was supposed to be.

"Am I interrupting?"

The deep rumble of a voice behind her pulled her from her thoughts and made her turn. Blake was standing a few feet away, his champagne glass hanging from one hand and almost empty, his bow tie no longer perfectly placed against his shirt. The black satin tie was messed up, his top button undone and his jacket open.

Saffy thought he looked sexy and so much more interesting than the rest of the suits she'd seen inside.

"Not at all. I was just admiring the city."

"You're not from here, are you?" he asked, moving
closer and standing beside her, gazing down at the city
as she glanced at him.

"Is my accent still that obvious?" Saffron frowned.
She'd lived in New York for almost ten years now, since
she was sixteen, and to her own ears she sounded more
like a local than a girl from a small town in Kentucky.

"It's just a little twang every now and again. I can't
quite put my finger on it, but…" Blake laughed. "Small
town?"

Saffy gave him a stare she hoped looked evil before
bursting out laughing. "A little place called Maysville,
in Kentucky. But I haven't even been back in—" she
sighed "—forever. You can take the girl out of the small
town, but not the town out of the girl, right?"

Blake leaned against the railing and stared at her,
his smile slow and steady as it spread across his face.
She should have shrunk away from his stare, from his
attention, but instead she bravely faced him. All the
years she'd focused on her career, dancing from her
childhood through her teens and then through almost
all her twenties, she hadn't had time for boyfriends.
But flirting with Blake felt good, and it wasn't as if she
had anywhere else she needed to be or anything else
she should be doing.

"So what's a girl from Maysville doing in New
York?" he asked.

Saffy raised her glass and took a sip, wondering how much or little to tell him. "It's a long story."

His grin was infectious, the way it lit up his dark eyes and made a crease form at each side of his mouth. The man was gorgeous, textbook handsome with his dark hair and even darker features, his golden skin sexy against the white of his shirt.

"It just so happens," he said in his deep, raspy voice, "that I have all night."

"I'd rather hear about you," Saffy said, clearing her throat and trying not to become lost in his stare, hypnotized by his gold-flecked dark eyes.

"I'm guessing you want to open up about yourself about as much as I like talking about *myself*," Blake said with a chuckle.

Saffron raised her glass again, realizing she was drinking way more than usual. She was usually too busy training to drink or socialize. Unless it had been with other dancers, she'd hardly seen anyone else, and she'd had to be so careful with her calorie count and her energy levels to waste on alcohol. She felt good tonight, though—alive and buzzing, even if it was due to the champagne and the smooth talker charming her.

"How about we agree to no personal questions then? I don't want to talk about work or my life," she admitted. She'd lived her work all her life as a ballerina, but every night she flexed her leg, only to be rewarded by ongoing shoots of pain, and she was reminded of what had happened. How little time she had left in the city she loved, and how quickly her dream had ended.

"It just so happens that I don't want to talk about

work, either," Blake said. "Want to go somewhere less…" His voice trailed off.

"Dull?" she suggested.

"Yeah, dull," he agreed, knocking back the rest of his champagne. "I hate these kinds of parties."

"I always thought it would be incredible to be asked to amazing parties, rubbing shoulders with the city's elite," Saffron admitted. "But I quickly realized that the part I liked was getting all dressed up. The parties weren't exactly as amazing as they looked from the outside once I'd attended a few."

"So you'd rather be somewhere more fun?" he asked with a chuckle.

"Ah, yes. I guess you could say that."

Saffron passed Blake her glass, not bothering to drink any more. She liked to stay in control, and if she was going somewhere with a man she hardly knew, she wasn't going to get drunk. Blake took it, turning his back for a moment as he found somewhere to leave them. She quickly pulled out her phone to text Claire.

Hey, you did great tonight. I'm heading out with the guy who bought your painting! If you haven't heard from me in the morning…

Saffy grinned as she hit Send. Claire would flip out, or maybe she'd just cheer her on. Her friend was always telling her to have more fun and stop taking life so seriously, but she wasn't the one in danger of having to pack her bags and go back to Maysville if she didn't get her job back. Saffron was serious because her job had demanded it, and she'd been happy to make it her life.

Her phone pinged back almost instantly.

Have fun. I'll track him down if I need to. xoxo

"Shall we go?"

Saffron put her phone back into her purse. "Sure thing."

Blake held out his arm and she slipped her hand through, laughing to herself about how absurd the evening had turned out. She wasn't the girl who went on dates with strangers or disappeared with men and left her friends at a party. But nothing about the past month had gone according to plan, so she had nothing to lose.

"Do you like dancing?" Blake asked as they walked around the back of the crowd. He was leading her around the room, and she could feel eyes on them. Either because they were leaving too early or because of who he was. Or maybe she was just being overly sensitive and imagining it.

Dancing. When in her life hadn't she loved dancing? "Sometimes." If her leg didn't hurt like hell when she tried to dance, she'd love to.

"I was hoping you were going to say no."

Saffron laughed. This guy was hilarious. "It's a no. For tonight, anyway."

"Then why don't we go back to my place?" He must have seen the hesitation written all over her face, because he stopped walking and stared down at her. "Sorry, that came out all wrong."

"It's not that I don't want to…" Saffron actually didn't know what she thought, but she wasn't about to jump into bed with him. Maybe that's what he was used to? She hoped she hadn't read the situation wrong.

"I just meant that if we don't want to dance and we're bored here, it might be nice to just chill with a drink. Or we could find a nice quiet bar somewhere. It wasn't supposed to sound like that."

Saffy looked deep into his dark eyes, didn't see a flicker of anything that alarmed her. "Why should I trust you?" she asked.

He cleared his throat. "United States Army Officer Blake Goldsmith," Blake said, giving her a quick salute. "One of the only things I'm good at in life is keeping people safe, and that's about the only good reason I can give you."

She was more shocked that he was an officer than the fact he'd asked her back to his place so fast. "You're in the army?"

"Was." Blake grimaced. "So much for not talking about my work life, huh? But yeah, you can trust me."

Saffron knew that just because he was a former officer didn't make him trustworthy on its own, but she wasn't actually worried about Blake. She felt as though she could take him at face value. What worried her was how he was making her feel, how desperate she suddenly was to know what it was like to meet a man and go home with him. Not that she could actually go through with a one-night stand, but the thought was making her tingle all over.

"So what do you say?" Blake asked. "I have a car

waiting, so we can either jump in and head to my place or duck into a nearby bar."

Saffron passed a number over and collected her coat, snuggling into it before they stepped out into the chilly night air. On the balcony she'd been so busy admiring the view that she'd hardly noticed it, but now she was feeling the cold.

"Yours," she finally said. "It had better be warm, though."

Blake was holding a black scarf, and he tucked it around her neck, his hand falling to her back as they walked. "I promise."

She walked until he pointed out a black town car, and within seconds he was opening the door for her and ushering her inside.

"Tell me—how does a former soldier end up at a glitzy charity gala with a plush town car at his beck and call?" she asked, curious.

"Goldsmith Air," Blake said, pulling the door shut as he slid in beside her, his thigh hard to hers. "Family business, one I tried to steer clear of but somehow ended up right in the thick of."

Saffron knew what that felt like. "Sorry, I know we promised no work questions."

They only seemed to travel for a few blocks before they were outside a pretty brick building that looked old but had been renovated and kept immaculate. A huge glass frontage showed off a contemporary-looking café inside, the lights still on but the signs pulled in. She guessed he lived upstairs.

"So this is your local coffee place?" Saffron asked.

"I wake up to the smell of their coffee brewing, and by eight I've usually ordered my second cup for the day."

"They deliver to you?"

Blake gave her a guilty look before pushing the door open. "One of the perks of being landlord."

She didn't show her surprise. He was definitely not your average US Army veteran! Saffron stepped out and followed Blake as he signaled his driver to leave before taking her in through a locked security door that required him to punch a code in. They went in, and it locked behind them before he was punching in another code and ushering her into an elevator. Saffy admired the old-fashioned metal doors he pulled across, and within moments they were on the second floor.

"Wow." They stepped out into one of the hugest loft-style apartments Saffron had ever seen. Interior brickwork was paired with high-gloss timber floors, a stainless steel industrial-type kitchen taking center stage. She had to fight to stop her jaw from hitting the floor.

"So this is home?" she asked.

Blake shrugged. "For now."

He closed the door behind them and touched her shoulders, slipping her coat off and throwing it over the arm of a huge L-shaped sofa. Saffy spun around to ask him something and ended up almost against him. He must have moved forward, his arms instantly circling her, steadying her. She stared up at him, touched his arm, her fingers clasping over his tuxedo jacket as she became hypnotized by his stare.

Blake was handsome and strong and intriguing... all of the things that sparked her interest and made her want to run in the opposite direction but at the same time want to throw herself hard up against him.

"Are you okay?" he asked, the deep timbre of his voice sending a shiver down her spine.

Saffron nodded. "Uh-huh," she managed, still not pulling away, not letting go.

Blake watched her back, his eyes never leaving hers, and just when she thought she was going to step back, his face suddenly moved closer to her, *dangerously close*. Saffron's breath halted in her throat; her heart started to race. What was she even doing? In this man's apartment? In his arms? She barely even knew his name!

"Can I kiss you?" he murmured, his whisper barely audible, his mouth so near.

Saffy felt herself nodding even though she knew she shouldn't. But he clearly wasn't going to ask her twice. Blake's lips connected with hers, just a gentle, soft caress at first, his mouth warm to hers, unbearably gentle. She lifted her arms and tucked them around his neck as Blake deepened their kiss, his lips moving back and forth across hers as his hands skimmed down her back.

"I think we should get that drink," he muttered, barely pulling his lips from hers.

"Me, too," she whispered back. But her body had other ideas, pressed tight to him as he cupped her even tighter against him. Saffron had never been with a man she didn't know, her only experience from the one relationship she'd had with a dancer she'd performed alongside. But right now she wanted Blake, and no amount of willpower was going to let her move away.

Blake's groan was deep as he scooped her up, lifting her heels clean off the ground and walking her backward to the closest sofa. She only had a second to gaze up at him, a bare moment to wonder what the heck she was doing as he ripped off his tie and discarded it, staring down at her, his big body looming above.

And then he was covering her, his body over hers. Saffy lifted her mouth up to his, met his lips and hungrily kissed him back. She knew it was all types of wrong, but tonight she was going to be bad. If this was one of her last weekends in New York, then she was going to make the most of it. Her career might be over, but it didn't mean her life had to be.

CHAPTER TWO

SAFFRON OPENED HER eyes and quickly closed them. She groaned and pulled the covers over her head. She'd never had firsthand experience with what to do the morning after, and nothing clever was springing to mind. What had she been thinking?

"Morning."

She took a deep breath and slowly slipped the covers down, clutching them tight to her chest as she sat up. Blake was standing in the doorway, looking just as chiseled and sexy and gorgeous as he had the night before. No wonder she'd ended up in his bed. He crossed the room and sat on the bed beside her.

"Ah, morning," she finally stammered, clearing her throat and trying to pull herself together. She didn't usually lack in confidence, but then again she didn't usually have to deal with handsome men so early in the morning. Saffron ran her tongue over her teeth, wishing she could have had ten minutes in the bathroom before having to face Blake.

"So I need to show you something," he said, eyebrows drawn together as he leaned closer.

It was only then she realized he was holding an iPad. Curious, she reached for it.

"What is it?"

"You know how we didn't want to talk about our personal lives or our work?"

Saffy nodded. She didn't understand what he was trying to tell her. Until she looked at the screen.

"Oh," she blurted.

"I think we probably *should* have had that conversation," Blake muttered. "Maybe we could have taken a back exit and made sure no one saw us."

Saffy kept hold of the covers with one hand and swiped through the photos with the other. There was Blake with his hand to her back, Blake laughing, her laughing with her head tipped back and her eyes locked on his, and there was them getting into his town car. Paired with headlines screaming that Blake was one of the city's most eligible bachelors and naming her as one of ballet's finest forgotten stars. The description stung.

She swallowed away the emotion in her throat, the familiar burn behind her eyes that always hit when she thought about her career. When she passed the iPad back and glanced up at Blake, she wished she hadn't.

"Hey, it's not so bad," he said, discarding the iPad and leaning over. He reached for her hand and lifted it, kissing the soft skin on the inside of her arm.

Saffy smiled. *This* was how she'd ended up in his bed! He was so smooth yet seemed so genuine at the same time, although hearing that he was such a prized bachelor only made her wonder if he'd expertly played her to get her into bed.

"You're really upset about it, aren't you? I was hoping you wouldn't think it was that big a deal being papped."

She shrugged. "I don't care about being seen with you, or the photos. It's the headlines that sting," Saffy admitted.

Blake looked confused. "I'm not sure I'm following. You do realize that the whole bachelor thing has been completely blown out of proportion, right? It's rubbish."

Saffy shook her head. "It hurts to read that I'm a washed-up former ballerina. Sometimes the truth stings more than we realize."

Blake kept hold of her hand, staring into her eyes. "You look far too young to be washed up, surely."

"I'll give you points for being kind, but I'm not too young, not in the ballet world. My body broke down on me, so I'm out."

He chuckled. "By out, you mean injured, right? Taking some time out? From what I've read this morning, you're pretty incredible."

Now it was Saffy chuckling. "You've been googling me?"

He shrugged. "Yeah. I'm an early riser. I saw this, and I've been reading up about you ever since."

She liked that he was at least honest. He could have lied and not admitted to it, but he was obviously curious about who he'd spent the night with. And if she was honest, she was starting to get pretty intrigued about him, too.

"What did it say?" Saffy wasn't clutching the sheet quite so tightly now, not as concerned as she had been about him seeing her.

"From what I've read, you came to New York as a teenager, wowed all the right people and eventually landed your dream role as lead in *Swan Lake* last year."

Saffron smiled. "Sounds about right." She wasn't sure she wanted to talk about it, not anymore. For years ballet had been her life, since she was a little girl in love with the idea of being a pretty dancer to a determined teenager and a dedicated adult. She'd lived and breathed her dream all her life, which was why she was at such a loss now. How did anyone move on if they'd lost the one thing that meant more to them than anything else?

Blake surprised her by stroking her face, his thumb caressing her cheek as he stared into her eyes. "I know the feeling."

She smiled, but it was forced. There was no way he knew how she was feeling. "You don't happen to have coffee, do you?" she asked, hoping he'd say *yes* then go and make her a cup so she had a little privacy.

"Sure do." Blake pulled back then rose, and the moment was over. He looked down at her, his height imposing. He was already dressed, barefoot but wearing dark jeans and a plain white tee.

Saffy waited for him to go then quickly scanned for her clothes. She hardly even remembered how they'd gotten to the bedroom. From what she could recall, her dress was in the living room wherever he'd thrown it, but her underwear was somewhere in the bedroom. She jumped up, taking the sheet with her. It wasn't until she had her underwear back on that she relaxed. Saffy looked around the room but he didn't have any clothes scattered, so she opened his closet and grabbed a sweat-shirt. It was fleecy on the inside with a zipper, and given the size on her, she had to zip it all the way just to cover her body. Then she dashed into his bathroom, splashed some water on her face and ran her fingers through her hair to tame it. Given the fact she'd just woken and didn't have all her usual things with her, she didn't think she looked too terrible.

"So I—" Blake's deep voice cut off. "You look cute in my hoodie."

"Sorry." Saffron spun around, feeling guilty. "I should have asked first, but I didn't want to walk out half-naked."

Blake's laugh made her smile. He waved her toward him and turned, and she followed him out to the living area. He had music playing softly, just audible, and she tried not to gape at the apartment all over again. It was incredible, and it oozed money. He pointed to the coffee machine.

"I can make an okay black coffee, but if you want something fancy, I'll call downstairs."

Saffron shook her head. "I don't need fancy café coffee. Just give it to me however it comes, with a heaped teaspoon of sugar."

"Not what I expected from a ballerina. I thought all dancers would think of sugar as the devil and have eating disorders." Blake turned straight around then, his face full of apology. "Sorry, that was in bad taste. I didn't mean it."

She was used to it. "It's fine, and it's kind of true. There are plenty of dancers with problems."

"Yeah, still. Bad form. Want to tell me what happened?" he asked, pushing a big mug of steaming coffee across the counter and shoving his hands into his jean pockets as he stood watching her on the other side. "Sounds to me like you've had a rough year."

"Yeah, you could say that again," Saffy muttered.

"I have waffles and bacon on their way up, so you can tell me over breakfast."

She groaned. "Do I have to?"

His laugh made her smile. "Yeah, you kind of do."

Saffron hated talking about what had happened, didn't want to have to explain what she'd been through and what it meant for her, but breakfast did sound good and she wasn't about to run out. Especially not if there were paparazzi waiting outside to see if she'd spent the night.

"We could talk about what happened last night instead," he suggested, giving her a smile that made her want to slap him.

"Um, how about no?" she quipped straight back, heart racing.

"So let me guess," Blake started, walking away from her when a buzz rang out. She tracked him with her eyes, admired how tall and built he was. His hair was thick and dark, a full mop of it, and whereas last night it had been styled, this morning it was all mussed up. She liked him even better less groomed, although he had looked pretty hot in a suit the night before.

The next thing he was pressing a button. "Just give me a sec," Blake called over his shoulder before disappearing from the apartment.

Saffy let out a breath she hadn't even known she was

holding. She reached for her coffee and took a slow, long sip. It was hot, but the burn felt nice down her throat, helped her to calm down somehow.

She could run. It wouldn't be her stupidest idea, and she could just grab her dress and bolt for it. Make up an excuse and dash past him. Get out of Dodge and never have to see him again or talk about what happened. She could even mail him back his hoodie, forget what she'd done. Only she wasn't sure she wanted to. The last few months, after the worst of her pain had passed, she'd been bored and miserable. She was working on autopilot, making coffee and serving people food, seeing her dreams disappear. It hadn't mattered what she'd done or how hard she'd tried, her leg hadn't healed fast enough, the ligaments badly torn, and with arthritis on top of it making the pain debilitating at best.

Blake had reminded her she was alive. If she hadn't met him, she'd have stayed another hour at the party, chatted with her friend, then gone home alone. Almost all her friends were dancers, and she wasn't in that world anymore.

So she stayed put, only leaving her seat on one of Blake's leather bar stools to retrieve her purse. It was tiny so she didn't have a lot in there, but she did have her foundation stick and some lip gloss, and she was keen to use both to make herself look half-decent. Plus she needed to text Claire.

She laughed. Her friend had already sent her three text messages, first wondering where she was, then asking how fab her night had been after seeing the article on some lame website. Then asking if she needed to send out a search party. Trust Claire to be scanning those types of pages as she ate her breakfast in the morning.

She sent her a quick message back.

I'm fine. He's gorgeous. Do you know anything about him?

The door clicked then, and she shoved her phone back in her purse. She hadn't had time to google him, and not being a native New Yorker, she didn't know the company name he'd mentioned the night before. He didn't strike her as a spoiled rich kid—more like a man who'd made his own money or his own way in the world, and she wanted to know more. Especially how he'd come to be listed as an eligible bachelor worthy of paparazzi.

"Breakfast is served," he announced.

Saffron stood and made her way back to the bar stool. "Mmm, smells delicious." Now she had clothes and some makeup on, she was a lot less self-conscious.

"Waffles with whipped caramel cream and fresh fruit. I went with sweet." His grin was naughty and she laughed at him.

"Can I just set the record straight about last night," she said, cringing at the way the words had come out.

"Sure. But you don't have to explain anything, if that's what you're worried about."

She sighed, taking the plate he held out to her. It did look delicious, the waffles thick and square, with pineapple and blueberries piled beside a swirl of the cream. "I just don't want you to think I do this sort of thing all the time."

He joined her around the other side of the counter, sitting down and passing her a knife and fork. "I kind of got that impression when you were peeking out at me from beneath the covers this morning with a horrified look on your face."

"Really?" She had to give it to him—he hadn't turned out to be a jerk the morning after.

Blake leaned over, smiling before dropping his mouth to hers, not giving her a second to hesitate. His lips were warm and tasted of coffee, his hand soft as he cupped the back of her head. He kissed the breath from her then pulled back, lips hovering as he stared down at her. Saffy felt the burn of heat as it spread up her neck, every inch of her body tingling from the unexpected kiss.

"You're too cute," he said with a grin, digging into breakfast like he hadn't just kissed her as if it was their last kiss on earth.

"And you're too suave for your own good," she muttered, stabbing her waffle with the fork, irate that he'd had such a visceral effect on her. "I'm guessing most of the women you bed are happy to drag you into bed the moment they lock eyes on you."

She had no idea why she was so mad with him when all he'd done was kiss her, but something about his attitude had gotten under her skin.

"Hey," he said, setting down his fork and turning to face her. "I meant it as a compliment, not to get you all fired up."

She went back to her breakfast, ignoring him.

"And I haven't exactly had the chance to meet a whole lot of ladies since I've been back. First I moved back home, then when I finally took over this place, I was spending more hours in the office than anywhere else. I haven't had time for socializing, other than when I've had to for work."

"You mentioned you were in the army," she said, calmed down and not so ready to jump down his throat. She'd seriously overreacted before.

"In another lifetime, yeah," he said, but he looked away as if he wasn't at all interested in talking about that other life. "Anyway, we're supposed to be talking about you. Tell me what happened. Why aren't you dancing now?"

Blake was intrigued. He'd bedded her already, and most of the time that was when his interest stopped, but she was something else. Even before he'd seen the blog post about them leaving the benefit together, which his sister had been so kind as to forward to him with a message that this one sounded a whole lot more promising than the airheads he'd been photographed with other times.

Blake kept eating his waffles, not wanting to stare at her and make her uncomfortable. He believed her that this wasn't her usual scene—she'd looked like a deer in headlights when he'd come back into the bedroom after hearing that she'd woken. His first instinct had been to dive straight back under the covers, until he'd seen her face and changed his mind. He still wanted her—he just wasn't going to be so forward.

Having a late breakfast with her and relaxing for once was making it clear he'd been way too focused on work the last few months. He'd become so determined not to buckle under the pressure and settle down, just because it would be good for business, but he was starting to realize he'd been missing out.

Saffron's red hair looked darker in the morning. Maybe it was the lack of bright lights, but it still looked incredible. The richest color against skin the lightest, barely there shade of gold, and dark brown eyes that just kept on drawing him in. He cleared his throat and set down his fork.

"Come on, what happened? Maybe I can help?" He doubted it, but he wanted to hear the story, and if she needed help finding work or someone to assist her with whatever injury she had, he did have helpful contacts.

His phone buzzed and he quickly glanced at it, not wanting to be rude by picking it up. He could read just enough of the text to see it was from his assistant and that the investor he'd been trying to impress had seen the paparazzi story. *Great.* Just when he'd been making some headway, now he was going to be labeled the rich playboy again.

"Nobody can help me," she said in a low voice. "Most dancers get injured and that's it, they're injured. Me, I'm out. Which means my career is over, because soon I'll have to go home with my tail between my legs, the washed-up former ballerina. I don't have enough money to stay here without working, and my physical therapy and specialist bills are crazy."

Blake frowned, forgetting the text and focusing on Saffron. "There's no other way for you to stay here?"

Saffron picked at her food, taking a mouthful that he was sure was a delaying tactic. When she finally looked up at him, her eyes were swimming. Big brown pools of hurt, bathed in unshed tears.

"I had a dream of dancing with the best ballet companies in the world, right from when I was a kid. I used to practice so hard, train my heart out and eventually it paid off." He listened as she blew out a big breath, sending a few tendrils of shorter hair around her face up into the air. "My hours of practicing got me noticed at the Lexington Ballet School in Kentucky, and eventually it turned into a dance scholarship with the New York Ballet Company. I started training there, danced my heart out and eventually went on to be an apprentice by the time I was eighteen."

"Wait, you moved to New York on your own *before* you were even eighteen? How old were you when you got the scholarship?" He knew plenty of models and other creative types started their careers early, but he'd never really thought about teenagers making such a big leap on their own. "Your parents didn't come, too?"

She shook her head. "Nope. Just me. I stayed with a relative for the first few months, then I moved into an apartment with some other dancers. I was only seventeen when I officially went out on my own, but I was so determined and focused on what I was doing that my parents didn't have any other choice. I would have resented them for the rest of my life if they hadn't let me come."

He got that. They'd let her follow her dream, and he admired any parent who encouraged their kids. "And then what? You make it sound like your career has already ended, like there isn't any hope." Blake hated hearing her talk as if it was over. She was doing what she wanted to be doing, and nobody was trying to hold her back, stifle her dreams.

"I tore three ligaments in my leg one night when I was dancing *Swan Lake*. I was finally in the role I wanted, as the lead, and I didn't even dance for an entire season at the top before my accident." She was looking away now, couldn't seem to meet his gaze. Blake wanted to reach for her, but he didn't, *couldn't*. The pain of what he'd lost and left behind was too raw for him, and he was barely coping with it on his own without having to help someone else.

"You could recover from that," he said gently, careful to choose the right words.

"No, I won't. I have a form of arthritis that I've battled for years. It first showed when I was stressed over a big performance, and in the past my doctors have been able to manage it. But from what I've been told, we're past that point now. That's why I'm out, why they wouldn't just let me stay on leave due to injury. They don't ever expect me to make a full recovery."

Blake steeled his jaw, hating that someone had had the nerve to put a damper on her dreams. On anyone's dreams. As far as he was concerned, the fight was worth it until the very last.

"You need to see more specialists, research more treatment, get your body strong again," he told her, wishing his voice didn't sound so raspy and harsh. "You can't take no for an answer when you're so close to living that dream."

Her eyes were angry, glaring when she met his gaze. "Don't you think I've done everything? As much as I could?"

He held up both his hands. "Sorry, I didn't mean to jump down your throat like that. I just…"

"I don't need to be told what to do," she said angrily, still holding his stare. "The only thing that will save me now is winning the lottery or a miracle. Money is the only way I can stay a part of this world, to keep searching for help, trying to keep training. Either money or a new treatment to help me get back on stage." She slumped forward, looked defeated. "Instead I'll be back in Hicksville, the girl who had so much potential and still ended up a nobody."

Blake bunched his fists, wished there was something he could do. He didn't know why her situation made him so angry, but it did.

Just then his phone buzzed and he glanced at it quickly. He read the screen, cursed his sister for wanting to be so involved in his love life.

So? Spill! Is she really a ballerina? She looked gorgeous. Keep this one!

Blake didn't bother replying, not about to engage with his younger sister over anything personal. And then he looked up and found Saffron watching him, her full lips parted, dark eyes trained on his.

She needed a way to stay in New York. He needed a wife.

He pushed his sister from his mind and pulled his bar stool closer to Saffron's, thinking that she was the most intriguing, beautiful woman he'd met in a long time. He didn't want to be married to anyone, but the truth was, he needed to be. That text just before was a slap-in-the-face kind of reminder. He was at the helm of a family business that was worth tens of millions of dollars, and he needed to maintain the right image. They were negotiating for a huge contract, one worth millions over the next two years alone, not to mention the investors he was trying to bring on board to grow the business. But his biggest potential investor had made it beyond clear that he was worried about Blake's playboy status, didn't like the fact that he wasn't settled down and married. They were rich men with strong family values, the kind his own father had always managed to impress. Being married could be the key to finalizing those deals, and no matter how much he'd tried to pretend otherwise, it was true, which meant he had some serious damage control to do.

He reached for his coffee and drained it. Real marriage wasn't something he wanted, hadn't been on his agenda since the day his first love had walked away from him as though what they'd had meant nothing. He could still feel the cool sting of betrayal as if it was yesterday. But if he could package a marriage of convenience into something that could work for both him and Saffron? Now that was something he'd be willing to do.

CHAPTER THREE

BLAKE CONTINUED TO sip his coffee, watching Saffron. She was beautiful. She was talented and accomplished. She was interesting. If he had to pick a wife on paper, she was it.

"So come on, spill," she said, setting her knife and fork down, surprising him by the fact she'd actually finished her entire breakfast. "The more you tell me you don't want to talk about yourself, the more I want to know."

He shook his head. "No."

Saffron's laughter made him smile. "What do I have to do then? To make you tell me?"

Now it was Blake's laughter filling the space between them. "Marry me."

Her smile died faster than it had ignited, falling from her mouth. She stared back at him, eyebrows drawing slightly closer together. "I think I misheard you."

Blake smiled, knew he had to tell her his plan carefully, to sell the idea to her instead of having her run for the door and get a restraining order against him. She was probably thinking he was a nut job, some kind of stalker who was obsessed with her after one night together.

"Look," he said, spreading his hands wide as he watched her. "If you married someone like me, you would have access to the best medical treatments, and you could stay in New York without any worries."

She did a slow nod. "Funnily enough, I've been joking about that with my friends for weeks—that I need to find a wealthy husband. But I'm used to having a successful career and standing on my own two feet."

Blake shrugged. "What if we did it? If we got married so you could stay in New York and get back on your feet, so to speak? I could pay for any specialist treatment you need to get you dancing again."

Her gaze was uncertain, maybe even cool. He couldn't figure out exactly what she thought now that her smile had disappeared. "I know why it would be good for me, I just don't get why you'd want to do it. What's in it for you? Why would you want to help me?"

"Marriage to a beautiful ballerina?" he suggested.

"Blake, I'm serious. Why would you marry me unless there's something in it for you? A hidden catch?"

"Look, plenty of people marry for convenience. Gay men marry women all the time to hide their sexuality if they think it's going to help their career or please their family."

She sighed. "Well, I know you're not gay. Unless you put on the performance of your life last night, that is. And anyway, I know plenty of gay people, and it hasn't hurt their careers at all, to be honest."

"Well, you're a dancer. Corporate America isn't always so accepting, even if they pretend to be."

"Back to you," Saffron said, studying him intensely, her eyes roving over his face. "Tell me now, or I'm walking out that door."

Blake wasn't about to call her bluff. Just because she needed a boost in finances didn't mean she was automatically going to say yes to marrying a stranger.

"Running my father's company was never part of my plan," he told her. "Now I'm CEO of a company that I'm proud of, but not a natural fit for. It's not the role I want to be in, but there's also no way I'm about to let that company fall into the wrong hands. I need to keep growing it, and I'm working on two of the biggest deals in the company's history."

"I hear you, and I'm sorry you don't like what you do, but it doesn't explain why you need a wife. Why you need to marry *me*?"

Blake didn't want to tell her everything, didn't like talking about his past and what he'd lost to anyone, why he didn't want a real wife, to open himself up to someone again. Eventually he'd have to tell her, otherwise she'd end up blindsided and their marriage would be uncovered as a sham, but not right now. Not until he knew he could trust her.

"I'm sick of the whole tabloid thing, the paps following me because some stupid magazine announced that I was one of New York's most eligible men." They'd called him the Billion Dollar Bachelor, the headlines had screamed out that women should be fighting over the former soldier back in the city as a corporate CEO and he hated it. Hated the attention and being known for his family's money after doing everything in his power to prove his own worth, make his own way in the world. But most of all he hated that people he most needed to impress right now read the rubbish being written, viewed him as a playboy, were unsettled by the fact that he *wasn't* settled.

"My dad built up the company as a family business, and our clients like that, especially a large-scale investor I've been working on for months. I don't want them to start thinking the company isn't going to continue to succeed because some loser rich-kid playboy is at the helm, and if I can set the right image now, it won't matter if I'm not married in a few years' time because the deals will be done."

Saffron didn't say anything when he paused, just stared at him.

Blake laughed. "Plus I'd like to get my mother and two sisters off my back. They're driving me crazy, trying to set me up all the time." He stood, pushing his hands into his pockets, watching, waiting for a reaction. He probably shouldn't have added the joke about getting them off his back. "So what do you think?"

"What do I think?" she muttered. "I think you're crazy!"

"We can talk through the details later, but please just think about it."

"Wow," Saffron said, holding up her hand. "I need time to think, to process how absurd this is."

"It's not that absurd," he disagreed.

"This is only-in-the-movies absurd," she fired back. "I'm not saying no, but I can't say yes right now, either."

Blake nodded. "I need to head in to the office. Why don't you stay here a bit, take your time and meet me back here tonight if you decide to say yes. I can get the paperwork and everything sorted out pretty quick, and we can go choose a ring together tomorrow."

Saffron shook her head, smiling then bursting into laughter. "I can't believe you're actually serious, that I'm not just being punked right now."

"Sweetheart, I'm deadly serious."

Blake took a few steps forward, touched her chin gently and tipped her face up, his thumb against her smooth skin. He slowly lowered his head and dropped his lips over hers, plucking softly at her lips.

"So we'd actually be married?" she asked, breathless, when she pulled back, mouth still parted as if she was waiting for more.

"Yes," he said, thinking how cute she looked in his hoodie. "You can set the boundaries, but we need it to look real."

He bent and kissed her again, softly.

Saffron could hardly breathe. She'd been outside for at least ten minutes, but her lungs still felt as though they couldn't pull in enough air. Marry him? How could he have asked her to marry him? They'd spent one night together—but marriage? Did she need rescuing that bad?

She pushed through a crowd of people passing on the street to reach a bench seat, dropping the second she found one. Could she actually marry a man she didn't even know, just to stay in New York? Just to get her career back on track, if that was even possible? She wished she could laugh it off and tell him there was no way she'd accept his proposal, but the truth was that it was the perfect solution for her. If it was the only way to give her recovery one last, real shot… Saffron gulped and turned her attention to the people walking past. Tried to lift her thoughts from Blake and failed.

What she needed was a piece of paper and her laptop. She would do what she always did—make a list of all the pros and cons, just like when she'd been offered the scholarship to dance with the New York Ballet in the first place. When she was sixteen, the list had been heavy on the pros and low on the cons, the only drawbacks coming from her parents, who wanted her to stay and didn't understand how desperately she wanted it. This time her list might be more balanced.

Marriage had always seemed so sacred to her, so special, but… She held her breath then slowly blew it out. Dancing was all she had. It was her life. If getting that back, having the one thing in the world back that meant so much to her, meant having to get married, then she had to consider it. Dancing had been her salvation. Could Blake really help her get that back?

Her phone buzzed and she picked it up, seeing it was Claire. She'd been out of touch with most of her dancing friends for the past couple of months, finding it too hard to hear about ballet and what they were training, the pain like a knife to her heart. But Claire had been there for her, been different and she'd enjoyed being part of her arty world.

"Hey," Saffy said when she answered.

"You're not still there, are you?" Claire giggled. "I still can't believe you did it. You're usually such a prude!"

Saffy laughed. "I am not a prude! Just because you have loose morals."

Now it was Claire in fits of laughter. "I'm not loose, I just don't see the point in saying no to a good time. Obviously my amazing personality has rubbed off on you."

Saffron felt better already after talking to Claire. "He…" Saffy changed her mind, not wanting to tell her. Claire was pretty open-minded, but even she might think it was crazy to consider the proposal.

"What? Tell me what you were going to say! He was amazing, wasn't he? Tell me more!" her friend begged.

Saffy sighed, the weight of her decision hanging heavy. "He was amazing, incredible, but…" Her voice trailed off again. "He wants to meet again tonight."

"Awesome! He's seriously hot stuff. Not to mention he paid up big-time for my painting. I've already had phone calls from buyers asking about my commissions and existing work."

If there hadn't been the whole marriage thing to consider, she would have been more excited. Giddy over being with a man like Blake, a man who'd made her pulse race and her mind forget all about what she'd lost while she'd been with him. She'd have liked the idea of getting to know him better, *dating* him, not marrying him.

"Good, you deserve it. And he was lovely. I'm just not sure about everything."

Silence stretched out between them, just long enough for it to be noticeable. "You're thinking about having to go back home?"

"Yeah." Saffy wasn't lying; she just wasn't telling her everything. Besides, Claire would be the one person to know the truth if it did happen, that she'd only met Blake the night before. She trusted her not to say anything, to keep her secret, but she just wasn't ready to open up about it yet, not when she was still trying to process it herself.

"Do you have any more doctors to see? Any other specialists you could visit or anything?" Claire asked. "Can you afford to keep going for a bit longer?"

Saffy shook her head, even though she knew Claire couldn't see her. This was why she was considering the marriage—this was why she *had* to. "No," she murmured. "I've done everything. There's no one left to see, or at least no one I can afford now, and I'm like damaged goods on the dance scene. If I dance again, there's only one company I want to be with, and that's a firm no right now."

"Fight till the bitter end, Saffy. Don't go quitting until you have no other options left."

Saffron had no intention of giving up until the last; it had been her attitude all her life. But even she had to admit that when it was over, it was over.

"There's one last thing I have to consider," she told Claire. "One last option."

"Give it a go—you owe it to yourself."

"I'm going to go, I have a few jobs to get done," Saffy said, wanting to end the call so she could think some more. She started to walk, the familiar twinge in her knee bearable at a walk when she was wearing heels. Barefoot it was almost unnoticeable. It was when she tried to push herself harder or dance that it really hurt. "Enjoy the weekend."

"You, too. Give me a call tomorrow so I can hear all the juicy details from tonight."

Saffy said goodbye and kept walking, suddenly realizing how terrible she must look. She was wearing her blue satin dress, her hair was tangled, and her heels weren't exactly daytime wear. Thank goodness there had been no cameras flashing when she'd exited out the back of Blake's building, through the café. Her career being over was bad enough—the last thing she needed was for the public to see pictures of her looking like she was right now.

Marriage. No matter how hard she tried to clear her head, Blake's proposal was the only thing on her mind. And she was pretty certain that, like it or not, she was going to have to say yes.

Blake sat in his office, staring out the huge windows that bordered two sides. It was a stunning corner office—luxurious and extravagant—but it didn't feel like his. For two decades it had been his father's office, and he'd been in it numerous times, often when his father was trying to convince him that the company was where he should be. That it should be his dream, as if he should grow up to be a carbon copy of the man who'd raised him. But Blake had never wanted to be his father, had had dreams of his own, dreams that were still with him that he'd been forced to leave behind.

He stood and walked to the window, restless being inside and having to stare at paperwork and sign contracts. The city was alive below him, people milling everywhere, and he wished he could just disappear in the crowd and leave his responsibilities behind. But he'd made the decision to come back, and he wasn't a quitter.

"This is your life, son. You're my eldest, and I expect you to take over the business. To look after your family."

The words had echoed in his mind long before his father had died, but now they were never ending. Every time he wanted to walk away, they haunted him, kept him awake at night. He was the eldest, and he'd always had a sense of responsibility that his younger brother and sisters had never had. But it hadn't stopped his brother from wanting to run the company, to absorb everything their father had to share and teach.

Everything had been going to plan—Blake was doing what he loved, and his brother was shadowing their dad, learning the ropes, prepared to take over the company one day. Until everything had gone horribly wrong.

Blake clenched his teeth together and crossed the room, reaching for the whiskey his father had always kept in the office, filling one of the crystal tumblers he'd seen his father drink from so many times. He poured a small amount into the glass and downed it, liking the burn. *Needing* the burn.

The chill he'd felt when they'd died, when his mother

had phoned him and he'd heard the choke in her voice, knowing the helicopter had gone down. He'd gotten there as fast as he could, been with the rescue team on the ground, seen the wreckage with his own eyes. At that moment, he'd known he had no other choice—he had to step up and take over the business just like his father had always wanted him to do. He'd lost so many good people in his life, but losing his father had never been something he'd thought about until it had happened.

Blake set the glass down again and went back to his desk. There were things he couldn't change, memories that would be with him forever, but the only thing that mattered right now was doing the best, given what life had served him. And Saffron would go a long way to helping make his life easier, making sure he secured the deals and the financial backing he needed to take the company to the next level. He needed a wife at his side, and she was the perfect match to him, could be the perfect, capable woman at his side…because they could enter into the relationship with a contract that gave them both exactly what they wanted.

He checked his phone. He'd half expected her to text or phone him after thinking about it, but then he'd also seen the determined look in her eyes, known that she was a fighter from the moment he'd heard about how she'd risen to the top. A ballerina who'd defied all odds and risen through the ranks to become one of New York's most respected dancers. It wasn't an easy path, and he doubted she would like having to do something she didn't want to do.

It was easy for him because it was a win-win situation. He would have a wife, a beautiful woman by his side who intrigued him, and they'd be divorced within the year. He didn't want a family, didn't want children, and he certainly didn't want an *actual* wife. They were things he'd dreamed of a decade ago, before the only person in his life he'd ever completely opened up to and been himself with had ripped out his heart and torn it to shreds. He wasn't ever going to put himself in that position again, just like he would never deceive a woman into marrying him without clearly setting out his terms.

Blake smiled and sat back down in the plush leather chair. Usually Saturdays were his favorite day to work, when the office was quiet and no one was around to bother him. But today his mind was wandering, and it was a stunning redhead on his mind that he couldn't stop thinking about. Whoever said he couldn't mix a little pleasure with business?

Saffron stared at the list she'd made, chewing on the end of her pen. It was a pretty short list. She leaned back into the sofa. There was no other way. Blake had just given her the perfect way to stay in the city, but being at the beck and call of a man like him was…scary. She shut her eyes, smiled when she thought about the night they'd shared.

She was going to do it. Saffy laughed out loud, feeling kind of crazy. Maybe she'd drunk too much the night before and it was still in her system, or maybe she was actually crazy, but she had to do it. She stood and flexed, grimaced when she tried to push up onto her toes and flex her muscles. The pain was tolerable, barely there compared to the excruciating pain she'd experienced at the time, but it still told her that things weren't right. That without some kind of miracle, she wouldn't be dancing anytime soon. But it didn't mean she couldn't keep her body strong and exercise.

She pulled on her trainers and laced them up, carefully stretching out her muscles just like her physical therapist had showed her. Her body was everything to her, and she had always taken care to stretch and warm up slowly, but now she had to treat it with even more care than ever before. Saffron rose up onto her toes, watched herself in the full-length mirror she had propped against a door. She held her arms out, tucked one leg up, bit down hard on her bottom lip as she flexed, forced herself to take the weight on first her good leg and then her bad.

No more. She released her lip from her teeth, expecting to taste blood she'd been biting so hard. The pain was there, was just as bad, and that meant she had to stop even though she would have loved to have tried to push through it.

Instead she grabbed her iPhone and stuck her earbuds in, planning on walking for an hour. She'd rather be running or dancing, but right now it was either walking and swimming or nothing at all. If she pushed herself too hard before she was ready, she wouldn't have the chance to make the same mistake again.

She checked the time before pulling the door shut behind her. She could walk for an hour or so, grab a coffee, then shower and head to Blake's house. Money was tight, which was another pro on her list, because if she married him then she'd be living with him. If she didn't, it would look like the sham it was, and she knew he wanted to keep it real. Besides, he'd told her as much—that she wouldn't have to worry about finances.

Right away she could cut almost all of her expenses, and her back account was already screaming out in the red after the cash she'd spent on all sorts of alternative therapies in conjunction with the specialist's advice.

Saffron Goldsmith. It sure had a ring to it. She glanced at her finger. Tomorrow there could be a diamond sparkling there, a real ring, a ring that would tell everyone that she was engaged. She hadn't exactly been the type to dream of a wedding when she was a girl—she'd been too focused on her career—but it still seemed weird.

She breathed in the fresh air once she was outside and started walking, slow at first. In a few hours' time she was going to be saying yes to a man she hardly knew, which meant this could very well be her last little glimpse of freedom before she had another human being to answer to.

CHAPTER FOUR

SAFFRON SHUFFLED HER bag from hand to hand, hating that her palms were so sweaty. She usually got nervous only before a performance, and even then it always passed as soon as she stepped on stage. This was a weird kind of nervousness that she hadn't felt before.

She took a big breath and squared her shoulders before pushing the button to Blake's apartment. He didn't say anything through the intercom, but the door clicked and she opened it and let herself in, going up in the elevator. When the metal doors opened, she found him leaning on the doorjamb, eyes searching hers out.

"I see you've brought a bag," he said, not taking his eyes from hers.

She kept her chin up, didn't want to appear weak. She felt like a prey animal having to stand up to a predator, standing her ground and being brave even when all she really wanted to do was cower.

"I have," she said back.

"Well, then, come on in. *Fiancée.*"

Saffy gulped and stepped forward, walking straight past Blake and into the apartment. The apartment she lived in was like a shoe box in comparison, small enough to fit inside his five times over. The sprawling spaces reminded her more of places back home, where space wasn't at a premium.

"We need to establish some ground rules," she said, deciding to start how she wanted things to be, not wanting him to think he could boss her around.

"I'm all ears." His smile made him even more handsome, eyes twinkling as he watched her.

She wasn't going to let him rattle her with his gorgeous face. Or his gorgeous body. Although the way his arms were folded across his chest as he stared at her made his shirt strain across his biceps. Even worse was how chilled out he seemed about the whole thing.

"I want everything in writing," she began, setting down her bag and taking a seat on the same bar stool she'd been perched on earlier in the day. "I need to give up the lease on my place and know that I can live here while we're married, for at least a year. I'll continue to pay for my own personal things, but you need to cover all my medical expenses, including any new specialists I find. I'm doing this only because I think there's a chance I could find someone to help me if I have the funds."

He raised an eyebrow, one side of his mouth kicked up at the sides. "Is that all? Or do you have a full list of ransom details?"

Saffy cracked a smile. "That's it."

He walked toward her, and a shiver ran down her spine. She had the distinct feeling that he was the one in charge, even though he'd just agreed to her terms.

"I agree," he said simply. "In fact, I already have a contract for you to sign."

She laughed. "Your lawyer did up an agreement for you on a Saturday?"

His shrug told her this wasn't out of the ordinary. "We have him on a pretty good retainer."

"So just like that, you agree?" she asked. Once again, it seemed too good to be true. For her, anyway. "To funding me and promising that this will go on for at least a year?"

"Sure. I'll even let you keep the diamond ring as a separation gift when we part ways." He didn't look worried about anything. "I need this *marriage* to exist for at least a year, too, to make sure my investors sign on the dotted line and to ensure it doesn't look like a sham. Once I have everything in place, it won't matter whether I'm married or not."

His smile was wolfish now, and she wasn't sure if he was joking or not. "You actually mean it about the diamond?"

"Yes. We can pick something tomorrow." She watched as he picked up a thick envelope from the coffee table. "This is some light reading for you—sign when you're ready."

She nodded. "Okay."

"I'm going to leave you to read it, give you a bit of space. Maybe a couple of hours for you to look over the paper, sign, and take a walk around the apartment without me being here. Feel free to consult with your own attorney if you want to, but you'll find that there's nothing in there not spelled out in plain English."

"Sure." It all seemed so weird, so formal, but she'd made up her mind and she was going to do it. There was no backing out now, not unless he had something sneaky in the contract that took her by surprise.

"We'll head out to dinner to celebrate," he said, passing her the envelope and reaching for her face, touching a stray tendril of hair and then running his thumb down her cheek.

She stared into his dark eyes, wishing she knew more about the mysterious man she was about to marry.

"My mother is going to love you," he said with a chuckle before stepping backward.

If only he loved her. She quickly pushed the thought away, checked herself. Blake was virtually a stranger— the last thing he'd feel was love for her! Maybe she was suffering from some sort of Cinderella complex, because it felt as if Blake was saving her, had ridden to her rescue and was offering her everything.

The everything part was true, but he was no Prince Charming. She was kidding herself if she saw him as anything other than a man who needed something and was prepared to do whatever he had to in order to make that happen.

"Your mother'd better love me," she finally managed in reply.

"Did I mention I also have two interfering sisters?" he asked as he shrugged into a jacket.

Saffy groaned. "Don't say anything else, or you might find the envelope unopened and me long gone." If only she had the power to do that, wasn't trapped in a corner with no other options. She'd still be interested in getting to know him better, but she sure wouldn't be jumping headfirst into marriage.

Blake just grinned and held up a hand. "See you soon. Anything you don't eat?"

She shook her head. "Not really."

"Good, I'll make us a reservation for seven. See you later on."

She watched him go, sat silently, until he had his hand on the door.

"Wait!" she called.

Blake turned, eyebrows raised in question.

"Why don't you stay? Then we can just talk through the whole thing." She didn't actually want to be left alone, didn't want to sit in silence trying to figure out legal jargon on her own.

Blake's smile made her heart skip a beat. "I thought you'd never ask." He shrugged off his jacket as fast as he'd put it on only moments earlier, dropping down onto the sofa, eyes still on hers. "You read, I'll answer questions."

She slowly ripped the envelope open, scanned a little of the first page before leaning on the bar and looking at Blake.

"So obviously there's a prenup," she said.

"Yep," he said. "Standard terms, including that if there were any children born during our marriage the child would be cared for." He laughed. "Obviously that's not in either of our plans, though, right?"

Saffy laughed straight back. "Have you ever seen a pregnant ballerina?" She definitely wouldn't be getting a penny from Blake, because there was no way she was getting pregnant, no way she *could* get pregnant.

"Which leads to the next clause, to ensure that every precaution is made to ensure no children *can* be conceived, something about blah-blah it not being part of either of our plans."

"Phew. Glad we got that sorted out," she said with a giggle, liking that she made Blake laugh again. His smile lit up his face, and it made her feel more relaxed. "Please tell me you have it in writing that I get to keep whatever rock you put on my finger?"

"Why, yes. The bride may keep the ring after separation or divorce. It'll be all yours once you've done your duty."

"Uh-huh," she said, scanning through a few more pages, seeing that everything he was saying was listed. And then she reached the part about the marriage being real, blushed as she looked up to find Blake watching her.

"We must live as a real husband and wife," she forced herself to say out loud.

"You're so cute when your face goes all pink," he said, rising and crossing the room.

She looked down, hating that she was so reactive when it came to him.

"It only stipulates that we have to live together at all times…that we remain faithful and don't speak to the media." He brushed past her, moving into the kitchen. "Beyond that, it's up to you. I just don't want anyone, from colleagues to housekeepers, not to believe that our marriage is real."

"So there's nothing in here you're trying to hide from me? Everything's as you say?" she asked, scanning though the pages again, pleased it wasn't a long document.

"I'm not trying to deceive you. It goes on to say that all your medical costs, including elective consultations and treatments, are covered. You have my word."

Saffy knew she needed to just sign it, that it was the best thing for her right now. So long as she didn't let herself get emotionally involved. She signed at the end, taking a pen from the kitchen counter that she could reach. Then there was a single document, just one page that fluttered out from beneath. From what she could see it was a separate contract.

This one was stamped confidential. She scanned it, realizing that this was the divorce contract. It was crazy—on the one hand she was signing a prenup, and on the other she was confirming a divorce was to take place when they both agreed it should, but in no longer than three years. She was to file for divorce, stating irreconcilable differences. Saffron hesitated, thinking of how long her own parents had been happily married, but she quickly pushed those thoughts away. This wasn't a real marriage. It was a convenient relationship for both of them, and they were both adults. There were no children involved, which meant that the only people that could be harmed by what they were doing were the two of them. The only thing she would have to be embarrassed about would be lying to her parents, because it wasn't exactly something she could keep from them. She'd never deceived them before about anything, had never lied to anyone she cared for, but this was her one chance to dance again and when it was all over she'd tell them the truth.

Saffy signed the second document, looking up and realizing how silent Blake had been.

"All done."

He exhaled loudly. "Guess it's my turn then." He leaned over her, his musky cologne making her wish she'd held her breath instead of inhaling. And then it was done.

"Take a look around. I'll make us a drink," he said with a wink.

"Mind if I take a shower?" She was dying to stand under hot water, needing some time to think.

"It's your home now. You can do whatever you like."

Saffron gulped and left him in the kitchen, going first into Blake's bedroom, taking a look around the very masculine space. The bed was made—a dove-gray cover paired with white pillows and a smattering of gray cushions against a black leather headboard. She'd already looked in his closet that morning and seen the bathroom, so instead of looking around more, she decided to just jump in the shower. Wash her hair and luxuriate in a bathroom that was bigger than her former bedroom, the floor-to-ceiling tiles reminding her of some of the lovely hotels she'd been fortunate to stay in when she'd been touring a few times. She went back out and got her suitcase, pleased to see that Blake was on the phone so she could just slip straight past him, putting her luggage in the middle of the bedroom.

Saffron stripped down, leaving her clothes in a puddle on the bathroom floor and turning the faucet on. The water was warm almost instantly, but she quickly walked out, naked, to retrieve her cosmetic bag that had her shampoo and conditioner in it. The shower was so good, the nozzle spraying so much water out and the steam feeling so good around her that she didn't want to get out. Instead she just shut her eyes and stood there, wishing she could stay there all day. Her hair was washed, the citrusy smell of her shampoo wafted around her, and all she had to do now was soap up her body...

"You need anything?"

Her eyes popped open and water blurred her gaze. Saffy quickly soaped herself and rinsed. Had he just walked in?

"Saffy? Do you still want that drink?" Blake's deep voice sent shivers down her spine, made her self-conscious with no clothes on.

"Just a sec!" she called back, hoping he'd stay in the bedroom and not actually walk on in.

Saffy turned the faucet off and jumped out, hurriedly reaching for a towel and rubbing it down her body then back up again. She was just about to dry her hair when his voice sounded out a whole lot closer.

"Hey. I wasn't sure if you'd heard me."

She wrapped the towel around herself and flung her hair back. Blake was standing in the doorway, looking straight in at her in the bathroom. Granted, she hadn't closed the door properly, but she hadn't expected him to walk in on her!

"Um, I just..." She stammered, knowing it was stupid being so body conscious, given the fact he'd seen her stripped bare less than twenty-four hours earlier, but she couldn't help it.

"Sorry, I didn't think you'd…" Blake was talking to her, but his eyes weren't on hers. They kept drifting down, and she held the towel a little tighter. "I can see this wasn't a good idea. I'll make you that drink."

"Uh, yeah, sure."

Blake was still watching her, but his eyes were trained on her face now. "This is weird, huh?"

She tucked the towel in at her breasts. "Um, yeah. Very weird."

Blake backed up. "I'll give you a minute to get, ah, dressed."

Saffy slipped to the floor in a puddle when he disappeared, her back against the glass of the shower. This was ridiculous! She was craving him, wanted him against her so she could kiss him all night, but at the same time she was a bundle of nerves about him even seeing her bare skin.

Maybe it was just because there was so much at stake now. Or maybe she just didn't want to admit that after being bored for so long after she'd had to quit dancing, she was finally feeling alive again and it scared her.

She picked herself up, dashed into the bedroom to get some clean underwear, and slipped on a big thick white terry cloth robe that she'd seen earlier in Blake's closet. She tied it around herself, liking how snuggly it was. It also covered up her body, which she thought might be a good idea in case Blake came back in. Saffy towel dried her hair, deciding to put on her makeup first and rub some moisturizer into her legs since she wanted to wear a dress out for dinner.

They weren't even married yet, and already she felt as if she'd lost control.

Blake sat on the sofa then jumped up and paced back toward the kitchen. He wasn't used to being so...rattled. Seeing Saffron in his bathroom, knowing exactly what was under the towel she'd had clasped to her slick wet body... He groaned. Maybe the marriage contract had been a bad idea. *A very bad idea.* She was supposed to make his life easier, and instead she was stopping him from thinking about anything else.

He glanced at the paperwork on the counter and then looked back toward his bedroom. It was all signed, which meant all that was left was for him to actually go down on bended knee for real so they had a story to tell everyone about their engagement.

Blake opened a bottle of wine, needing to take his mind off Saffron. There was something easy about what they'd agreed to, but for a man who'd sworn off marriage and family years ago, it was unsettling, too. He'd lived alone all his life unless he'd been working, when he'd been bunked down with his unit, and until Saffy he hadn't even brought a woman back to his apartment. And now he'd gone and broken all his rules, let someone get close to him, even though this time around he was in control of the situation. He was never going to be made a fool of again, never wanted to voluntarily feel hurt like he'd felt in the past, but so long as they both stuck to the rules...

"Dollar for them?"

Blake looked up, pulled from his thoughts. She was standing forlorn in the middle of the room, staring at him. Her hair was still damp, hanging loose and tumbling down over her shoulders, and she was wrapped in his robe. A robe he hardly ever wore, but his nonetheless. It was the second time he'd seen her in his clothes, and he was starting to more than like it.

"Nothing," he said, turning his body to face her. "Nothing important, anyway."

He watched as she shifted, looked uncomfortable. Blake had a feeling he wasn't going to like what she had to say.

"Is everything okay?"

She sighed loud enough for him to hear. "I don't know about you, but this whole thing just seems…"

"Unusual?" he suggested.

"Kind of uncomfortable," she said. "I don't know, I just don't know how to act around you. Last night I was me, or at least a version of me. But now…"

Saffron didn't seem to be able to finish her sentences, as though she was overly nervous. He stood but decided not to walk over to her, to keep some space between them instead of pushing her. The last thing he wanted to do was scare her off now.

"How about you finish getting ready for dinner," Blake said gently, trying his hardest to say the right thing. He had two sisters, so being around women and knowing what to say should be second nature to him, only for some reason it wasn't helping him right now. "Maybe we can take a step back, forget about the contract for a bit. We can pretend this is real if we like. Just actually date and try to ignore the marriage part to make it easier."

He had to fight a grin when her saw her lips kick up into a small smile.

"You really think we can go back? Trick ourselves that this is real?"

Not for a minute, because the only way he would ever propose to a woman was in a situation like this. "Sure we can," he said, trying to sound optimistic. "And if we can't do that, then there's no reason we can't be friends, enjoy the next year or so together." He knew that was a lie, too. Because there were plenty of ways they could enjoy being together, but strictly as friends wasn't what he had in mind right now or probably ever would with her.

Saffron turned and disappeared back into the bedroom, and within minutes he heard her hair dryer going. The beautiful ballerina would no doubt emerge a knockout, just like she'd looked last night.

He could be plenty of things to Saffron without having to open up, though. He had no interest in baring his soul to another human being, or reliving any of his past and opening up about anything. If he was in a real relationship, those things would be nonnegotiable, but with Saffron he could choose how much to divulge, how much of his true self to give. Because no matter what they pretended to the contrary, what they had was a contract. He'd fallen in love before, had his heart broken by someone he'd trusted more than anyone else. Fool him once, but never twice…

Blake took a sip of his wine and stared at the documents sitting in front of him.

It was done. He was officially about to become a married man.

Blake pulled his phone from his pocket and dialed his mother. He wanted to get it over and done with now, and he only had to phone one of the women in his family, because news spread like wildfire between his mom and sisters.

"Hello, darling."

"Mom," he said, clearing his throat. He could still hear Saffron's hair dryer, so he launched into what he had to say. "I know you've seen the pictures from this morning."

"Of course I've seen them. I'm just disappointed you've kept such an interesting woman hidden away from us."

If Saffron was really his fiancée-to-be, he would definitely be keeping her hidden from his family! "Mom, I should have told you, but we've just been lying low, getting to know each other without…"

"You don't have to explain yourself, sweetheart. I'm just happy that you're seeing such a fantastic young woman!"

"The girls have been googling her and showing you the results, haven't they." Blake had no doubt that they'd be all over the internet. There was no way his mother was that tuned in on her own; he'd bet they'd all been gossiping and flicking through web pages together.

"Of course!"

"Mom, I hope you're sitting down, because I have news."

"Blake! What is it?"

"I've asked Saffron to marry me."

"Girls!" His mother's screech forced him to pull the phone from his ear.

"I have to go, Mom. We're going out to dinner to celebrate, and I wanted to share the good news with you before anyone else found out."

"Could we join you? Meet this woman who's going to be my daughter-in-law?"

Blake could hear the excitement in his mother's voice, felt a pang of guilt for deceiving her. His mother got on his nerves at the best of times when it came to his personal life, and his sisters drove him crazy sometimes, but he loved them as fiercely as was humanly possible and lying to them made him feel worse than he'd expected.

"Let me take Saffron out tonight, just the two of us. I promised her something special to celebrate," Blake said. "But we'll see you soon, okay? I won't keep her hidden away forever."

He wondered if his mother would even take the bait, if she'd be instantly suspicious, but then she was used to him keeping his personal life private. And as far as he knew, she'd been shielded from what his dad had done, had never been exposed to the truth of the only serious relationship he'd ever had before. Never known how much pain her eldest son had been in.

When he finally got her off the phone and managed to end the call, he glanced up to see that Saffron was sitting on the sofa. He'd been so engrossed in talking with his mom, staring out the window as day became night, that he hadn't even heard the hair dryer switch off.

"You heard all that?" he asked.

Saffron shrugged, still flipping through a magazine. "Mmm, some of it." She looked up. "Do you feel kind of guilty?"

He nodded. "Yes, but it's for the best."

"I'm going to have to put on the performance of my life for your mother, aren't I?"

Blake didn't want to scare her. "Look, she'll be so excited to meet you that she'll probably do all the talking. The real performance will be when I have you by my side at business functions. That's why I'm marrying you."

She didn't look worried about it.

Blake unbuttoned his shirt and stretched out. "Give me a minute to take a shower."

He could feel her eyes on him as he walked, knew she was watching him. His problem was that he didn't know how to behave, how to act. He wanted to forget everything and just... He steeled his jaw. Sex should be the last thing on his mind. He wasn't doing this for sex—he could get that without being married—but looking at Saffron made him think of one thing and one thing only.

He left her on the sofa and stripped, showering then tucking his towel around his waist when he was finished. He went back into the bedroom adjoining the bath and pulled out a fresh shirt. He dressed quickly, ran his fingers through his hair and put some product in.

When he went back out, Saffron was still sitting on the sofa where he'd left her.

"Ready?" he asked, voice sounding gruff to his own ears.

She stood. "Yep, ready."

He walked ahead, opened the door and stood back for her to follow. Her dress was short, cute and covered in sequins. It showed off her toned, slim legs, and there was plenty of skin for him to admire up top, too. Her top was loose but with a low front, hair flowing down her back. It was the hair that got him more than the skin, though. Because when he'd first woken after their night together, it had been her hair touching his skin, falling over his chest. Her hair that he'd stroked.

"Where are we going?" she asked.

Blake cleared his throat. He was lucky she wasn't a mind reader. "Somewhere close. We can walk."

She shrugged her leather jacket on and they walked side by side, lights twinkling and showing the way along the road.

"I booked us in for Japanese. I'm thinking sushi, sashimi and teppanyaki."

Her smile was so innocent he wanted to reach for her and tug her closer. Maybe that was why he'd been drawn to her in the first place, not just because she was beautiful, but because there was something vulnerable about her. Something so unlike most of the women he met, a fragility that was tempered by how successful she'd been in her career.

"Are we sitting at the teppan table?" Saffron asked, her grin infectious. She was more excited child than grown seductress for a moment.

"We sure are. I thought you might like watching the food cooked in front of us."

She laughed. "You mean you thought it would be a good distraction when we ran out of things to talk about."

Blake held up his hands. "Guilty."

They walked in silence a bit longer.

"This is the weirdest one-night stand I've ever had," Blake confessed. "It's kind of awkward, in a we-wouldn't-usually-see-each-other-again kind of way. It's like extending the morning-after part."

Her laughter was gone but her eyes were still twinkling with humor. "I wasn't lying when I said I hadn't had a one-night stand before. So the whole awkward-morning-after thing is all new to me."

"Well, let me tell you it's normally over really fast and then you forget about it." He chuckled. "Although if I'm honest, you might have taken a little longer to forget about."

"So no serious girlfriends? No ex-wives I should know about?"

The last thing Blake wanted to do was talk about his ex. With anyone. "Let's just say that my mother never thought I'd settle down. I've always made that pretty clear."

"Right," she said as he guided her into a restaurant. It was only a few blocks away, so the walk had been brief. "So you've preferred to be the party bachelor boy all your life?"

He kept his anger in check. The last thing he wanted was for her to think the same way about him that everyone else seemed to in this city. "I was too busy with my career to be the party boy, even though everyone seems to forget how long I was away serving."

Saffron seemed confused when she looked up at him. "I'm getting the feeling that there's someone who broke your heart. Someone you really don't want to talk about."

"So let's not talk about it," Blake ground out. It wasn't as if he had a problem talking about the dates he'd had or the women he'd been with—it was just one particular woman who still made him want to slam his fist into a wall. It wasn't because he still had feelings for her; it was the way she'd hurt him, the way his father had been able to hurt him so easily through her. "I'm starving. You?"

He listened to Saffron sigh, knew the sound and that it meant the conversation wasn't over. His sisters made the same noise all the time. But to her credit she didn't bring it up again.

Saffron stayed silent as they were taken to their table, sitting down and starting to toy with the menu. Blake couldn't stand it.

"Look, I didn't mean to shut you down like that, but there are just some things I don't want to talk about."

"Me, too, but we kind of need to know everything about each other."

"What do you want me to say?" he muttered, keeping his voice low so they weren't overheard. "That I was in love once and she ripped my heart out and tore it to pieces?"

Saffron blinked at him, but the expression on her face hardly changed. "You know what? I think this whole thing was a bad idea."

She stood and pushed back her chair, reaching for her purse.

"Saffron, wait." He jumped up and reached for her, one hand over her arm. "I'm sorry." What was he doing flying off the handle like that?

Her eyes were swimming with what he guessed was hurt or maybe just frustration. "This is crazy. I can't be this desperate," she murmured.

"I'm an idiot, and this isn't crazy. It's…" He shrugged. "Convenient. And it's going to work out just fine for both of us."

She looked unsure still, and he ran his hand down her arm until he could stroke her palm and then link fingers with her. He seriously needed to work on his bedside manner.

"Please. Just give me a chance. I promise I'll be better behaved."

Saffron slowly sat down again. Blake would bet there were eyes watching them, but he didn't care. He quickly ordered them champagne, then turned his full attention to Saffron. He sucked back a breath and forced himself to say the words.

"I was in love once, you were right. With a woman I wanted to spend the rest of my life with," he admitted, knowing that if he didn't do something, he was going to end up losing the woman he needed right now. Talking about his past wasn't something Blake made a habit of, and for ten years he hadn't shared what had happened with another soul. He cleared his throat. "Her name was Bianca, and we'd been together for three years. We met in school, and we were joined at the hip from that day on. I thought it was true love, or as true love as it can be when you're barely eighteen and haven't had a load of experience. I would have done anything for her, she was the love of my life."

Saffron's eyes were wide as she listened. "What happened to her?"

"Well," Blake said, nodding his thanks when their champagne arrived and reaching for the glass stem to worry between his forefinger and thumb, "we were off to college and planning our future, and I proposed to her. She said yes, we had crazy good sex, like we always did, and barely three weeks later she disappeared."

"What do you mean, disappeared?"

Blake held up his glass to clink against hers, taking a long sip. He wasn't big on bubbles, but they were supposed to be celebrating their engagement, and Saffron had seemed to enjoy the Veuve Clicquot the night before.

"She broke my heart," he said simply, still feeling the sting of betrayal. Not so much from her as from his father. "I searched for her. My father looked on, and eventually he admitted that he'd offered her money to leave. To not go through with the engagement."

"Your dad did that to you? You must have hated her for taking it!"

"I hated them both," Blake said honestly. "I already disliked my father, knew the moment I confronted him that it had been his doing. He never thought she was good enough for me—her family was not highly regarded or wealthy enough. But she was my girlfriend, the most important person in my life, the one person I was myself with and loved unconditionally." Blake leaned back. "My dad told me he'd known all along she was using me for our money, and he said all he'd done was prove he was right, that he hadn't actually done anything wrong. His theory was that she'd be knocked up within months just to make sure she had me trapped, well and good." He grunted. "Turns out the old man was right after all, although it didn't make me hate him any less. It was a lesson in love for me, and right then and there I decided it was going to be my last."

Saffron stroked his hand, her arm covering the space between them as she touched him. "Do you still love her?"

Blake laughed, but even to him it sounded cruel, dark. "No, sweetheart, I don't still love her. It was a decade ago now, and all it did was show me that the only person in life I could trust was myself."

"Do you still believe that?" she asked, leaving her hand on his as she sipped her champagne. "After all this time?"

He shifted so their connection was lost, disturbed by how easy their touch was. "I trusted my men when

I was serving and the pilot sitting to my left, but I've never trusted another woman since."

She nodded, as if she understood, but he doubted she could. "I've only had one proper relationship."

"Hard to believe," he joked. "I could imagine you having suitors lined up for you backstage."

Her smile was cute, almost bashful. "It wasn't for lack of interest, but I just haven't had time. Work meant everything to me, right from when I was at high school, so it just never happened. Until I met Raf, a dancer I was paired with…"

Blake lifted his glass and she did the same. He waited for her to continue, not wanting to push. He knew how hard opening up was; he was still wondering what he'd just done by telling her about his past. But if they were going to make this work, make the next twelve months bearable, it had to be done.

"I fell hard for him, thought what we had was special. But he was sleeping with every other dancer behind my back. I felt stupid and ashamed, and when I ended it, he made me feel like I was the problem, not him." She shrugged, but the casual action didn't match the emotion he could see on her face, in her eyes. "I decided then and there I was better on my own, and I haven't let myself even come close to being hurt ever since."

"Here's to keeping our hearts safe," Blake said, holding up his glass.

"I'll drink to that," she agreed.

"You see, we're both proof that what we're doing is for the best."

"Yeah, maybe," Saffron muttered.

Blake wasn't sure he liked the fact he'd been so open, but he'd told her now and it wasn't as if he could take it back.

"Let's order, and no more talking about exes," Saffron said.

Blake couldn't have put it better if he'd tried.

CHAPTER FIVE

"So here we are again."

Saffy shivered, even though the apartment was perfectly warm. She'd already discarded her leather jacket, so her arms were bare, but she felt exposed, as if she was naked. Blake's words were having an effect on her all over again; the only difference was that tonight she'd only had one glass of champagne, so she couldn't even blame the alcohol.

"Blake, can I ask you something?"

She watched as he threw his jacket down over the sofa and crossed the room, reaching for a bottle of whiskey.

"Did you know who I was when we met last night?"

He was frowning when he looked up. "No. I was bored, and you were the most interesting person in the room."

She had no other choice but to believe him. Saffy was about to say something else when he turned with two tumblers and moved toward her. "I want to make it very clear that you deserve someone amazing one day, a man who'll love you like every decent woman deserves to be loved. I'm not that guy to any woman, but I will treat you well while we're under contract."

Even though she'd known exactly what she'd signed up for, had her eyes wide-open, the truth of their agreement still stung when he said it like that. It hurt that she was good enough for sex but not a real relationship, even though she understood his reasons. She was being sensitive, but knowing that didn't make it any easier to deal with.

She took the glass he passed her. "So is this to celebrate our twenty-four-hour anniversary?" she asked.

Blake's smile made his already perfect face appear even more handsome. It softened his features, made her yearn to touch him and be in his arms again.

"Here's to us," he said, voice silky smooth. "I never break a contract, and I never back down on what I say. So I'll put good money on it that you'll be up and dancing again once you've had access to the best specialists money can buy."

She wished she could be as optimistic, but she knew firsthand that no matter how much money she had behind her, it wouldn't be easy. It gave her a better chance, but it didn't guarantee anything.

"And all I have to do is be the model wife, right?" She was only half joking, although she had no intention of giving a Stepford wife a run for her money.

"Don't lie to me, play the part when I need you to and we can coexist happily."

They stood facing each other, and Saffron held up her glass, clinking it to his and sipping when he did. The liquor was like silk in her mouth and fire in her throat, and when she swallowed her eyes burned. She blinked the tears away, not liking how amused Blake looked.

He laughed. "*More* than happily."

"I won't lie to you," she said honestly. "All I want to do is dance, and if you can give me that back, then I'll owe you everything." It was the pure, raw truth. There wasn't much she wouldn't do to get her dream back, and even though she was so close to losing hope, she would not stop fighting until the bitter end.

"Come here," he said gently.

Saffy hesitated, waited, wasn't sure if she wanted to give in to the way she was feeling just yet. Until Blake reached for her. His fingers closed over her arm, then worked their way up, each movement sending shivers through her body that she couldn't control. Her mouth parted as he slid his body forward, moved into her space, his body just grazing hers.

"I don't want to presume anything. I mean, anything we do for real has to be your choice."

Saffy stared up at him, eventually nodded. "Uh-huh," she whispered back. She liked that he wasn't pushing her, that the ball was in her court.

"It's your choice," Blake said softly, his eyes full of concern. "I have a perfectly nice spare bedroom with its own bathroom that I haven't even showed you yet, or you could just move into my room with me. We'd need to keep most of your things in my room, though, because I don't want my housekeeper being suspicious, or anyone else who might come over."

Saffron gulped, her eyes fixed on his mouth, carefully pressing her lips to his when he kissed her again, slipping her free arm around his neck to draw him even closer. He was magnetic and handsome and sexy…and technically he was hers. And she did want to be in his room. Besides, her excuse could be that she didn't think the housekeeper would buy their marriage as real if the sheets in the spare room were always rumpled.

When Blake finally pulled back it was to down the rest of his whiskey and discard his glass, placing it on the coffee table and turning back to her with a smile that made her think of only one thing. For a girl who was always so focused and made the right decisions, she was ready to make a bad one all over again very quickly.

"What do you say, fiancée?" he asked.

Saffron bravely sipped her drink, the burn just as bad this time as the first. "I say I haven't had much to make me smile these last few months. Why not?"

Blake took her hand and led her to his room. They stopped only for him to flick off the lights, bathing the apartment in darkness. The only light was from the bedside lamps in his room.

What she was doing was so out of character, but for some crazy reason it felt all kinds of right. Thankfully the awkwardness of earlier had faded a little.

When they reached the bedroom, Blake stood in front of her, kissing her again before gently slipping the strap on her dress down and covering her bare shoulder with his mouth.

If only it was real. She couldn't help her thoughts, even as she tried to push them away. Part of it was real, surely, but the other part…he might not want to date her, or marry her, but his hands on her body and the look in his eyes told her that his desire for her was definitely real.

"Blake, I…" Saffron groaned, not wanting to ruin the moment but needing to.

"What is it?"

"I just, I need you to know why I said yes."

"Right now?" he asked, eyebrows raised.

She nodded, reaching for his hand. Suddenly she needed to tell him, had to get it off her chest so he understood who she was.

"Talk to me," Blake said, pulling her over to sit beside him.

Saffy sighed. "When I was younger, I had an operation for cervical cancer. I've known since I was nineteen that I couldn't have children, so I want you to know that's something you don't need to worry about with me." It wasn't something she usually shared, except with other women to encourage them to have regular checkups, but she wanted Blake to know. She knew how lucky she was to be alive, and it had been the only other time in her life that she'd had a break from dancing. Although that had been a very short one, and it hadn't had any impact on her career, as she'd simply been declared injured for a month.

"I'd always imagined my future with kids in it, once I'd fulfilled my career ambitions, but since that happened I've focused on dancing being my future. I need to dance, because it's the only part of my future I feel I can have any control over."

"I get it," he said. "I'm sorry for what you went through."

"Thanks," she whispered, dropping her head to his shoulder.

"So you can't ever get pregnant, or it's unlikely?"

"Can't ever," she said. "So you've got no worries with me. Besides, I couldn't ever dance the hours I need to and be a mom, so it's not that big a deal to me anymore." Saffron could joke about it now, but at the time she'd mourned the children she would never have, and even joking about it still stung deep down. She'd been too young at the time to want to be a mother then and there, but when the possibility was taken away it had still cut deep, because it had changed the future she'd imagined for herself. But then she'd simply thrown herself back into ballet and tried never to think about it again.

"Come here," Blake murmured in a low tone that sent a delicious shiver down her spine. He pulled her closer, facing her now.

She loved the gruff way he spoke to her, tugging her hard against him.

"Kiss me again," Saffron whispered, forcing herself to be bolder, to ask for what she wanted. She wanted to forget about everything she'd just told him now she'd gotten it off her chest.

Blake didn't disappoint. His lips crushed her, hands skimming her body as she looped her arms around his neck. As far as forgetting all her troubles, this was exactly what she needed. Short-term, fun, mind-blowing… the perfect interlude while she focused on her body and got back her strength.

As she used her toes to push herself forward, climb

up closer to him, she couldn't help the grin that took over her mouth.

"What?" Blake muttered.

"It didn't hurt," she whispered back, flexing her toes and her legs again.

"What? My kissing you?"

"My leg, stupid." Saffy didn't want to talk about it, but her lack of pain when she'd put that kind of pressure on her pointed toes had sent another kind of thrill through her.

Saffron woke and reached out in the bed. She didn't connect with anything. She sat up and searched in the dark for Blake, but the only thing she saw was a sliver of light coming through the door from the living room.

She stretched and got up, still tired but feeling restless. It was weird waking up in Blake's apartment, feeling like a visitor yet knowing she was here to stay. She pulled on the shirt he'd discarded earlier, wrapping it around herself and padding across the thick carpet. The light that she'd seen was a lamp in the far corner of the living room. The light was bathing part of the apartment in a soft light, and she could see the back of Blake's head. She guessed he might be working, unable to sleep and putting his time to good use, but when she reached him, bending down to run her hands down his bare chest from behind, she saw he was staring at a photograph.

"Oh," she stammered.

Blake jumped, dropping the photo.

"I'm sorry. I thought you'd be working, or reading a book or something. I just…"

Saffy didn't know what to say. She looked away as he brushed his knuckles against his eyes, knew that she'd been right in thinking she'd seen tears glinting there. She'd interrupted what was definitely supposed to be a private moment.

"Are you okay?" she asked.

"No," he ground out, sitting deeper into the buttoned leather armchair again and wearing only his boxers.

"Was that…?" She had been about to ask if it was his dad before his blank look silenced her.

"Go back to bed," he said.

Saffron watched him for a moment, thought about pushing the point, then did as he said. He might appear carefree, as though he was in control of everything in his life, but Blake had demons. She'd just seen them firsthand, sitting there in the dark alone, and she knew there was more to her husband-to-be than met the eye. He was acting the part of the happy bachelor, but she didn't believe it for a second.

And he wasn't alone. Tears pricked her eyes as she closed the bedroom door behind her and flopped back onto the bed, pulling the covers up and wishing it were her room and she wouldn't have to face him again. There was so much she had locked away, hidden so deep within herself that she would never open up to anyone. Only she was better at hiding it than Blake, because she'd just glimpsed his soul and his hurt looked a lot closer to the surface than she would ever let hers be.

She pulled a pillow closer, hugged it tight and buried her face into it. If only she could dance again, then everything would be okay. And she wouldn't have to stay here if things turned weird and she wanted out.

Blake felt terrible. He wanted to roar like a lion, yell about the injustices in the world and smash something. Slam his fist into a wall. But instead he stayed silent, lived with the guilt that was weighing on him like a ton of bricks, pushing down so hard on him that he could hardly breathe. He wasn't the angry type, which was why he was beating himself up so much right now.

It always happened at night. He'd go to sleep, fall into a deep slumber, then wake in the darkness, a tangle of sheets and sweat. If it wasn't his father, the helicopter wreckage, doubling over when he saw his brother's mangled body, it was the carnage he'd seen when serving. And that's why it affected him so badly. When he'd been away, he'd been able to compartmentalize the horrors, put his memories into a little box that he'd mostly managed to keep a lid on. But seeing his father and brother dead, like casualties of war among the pieces of metal covering the grass and strewn through trees, had changed everything. Because now images of war, memories he'd once buried, were merging with fresher ones, morphing into visions that often took hours to push away, if he could at all.

Blake steeled his jaw, glanced over at the whiskey bottle but refused to get up and reach for it. He'd gone to sleep with a beautiful woman in his arms, felt at peace, but when he'd woken, his demons had returned stronger than ever.

He shouldn't have shut her down like that, but then he shouldn't have done a lot of things. Maybe everything was just catching up with him. Maybe he should have found new investors, cashed in the business. He could have left his family in a great financial position, provided more for his mother and sisters than they'd ever need, but he was too loyal, too proud or maybe just too stubborn to give up what his family had built.

He shut his eyes, leaned back. His father had finally managed to turn him into the puppet he'd always wanted him to be, controlling him from the grave. All the years he'd fought with him, hated him, stood up to him, and now he just wished he was back. Then everything could go back to normal. That he could have his brother alive and kicking again. Because that was his biggest regret, falling out with the one person who'd have had his back no matter what, but whom he'd been too pigheaded to apologize to. Just another thing he'd never forgive himself for.

Blake doubted he'd find it easy to get back to sleep, and he also doubted Saffron would want him crawling in beside her. And what would he say to her? How could he even start to explain the way he felt? The things that haunted him were not things he wanted to burden anyone else with. Besides, they'd known each other less than two entire days. He wasn't about to crack his heart open and pour out all his feelings to her. Or to any woman. He'd already told her enough when he'd confessed about his ex.

Trouble was, he liked Saffron. And he hated the way he'd spoken to her. Because behaving like that only made him like his father, and he'd rather jump off a bridge than turn into even a shadow of his dad.

He picked up the photo of his father and brother he'd been holding, stared into his brother's eyes one last time, remembering his smile, how passionate he'd been about helicopters and taking over their dad's corner office one day. How good he'd been at schmoozing clients and smoothing over problems. Problems that peeved Blake, first world issues that drove him nuts. After what he'd seen, the things he'd had to do to protect his country, to serve, they weren't real problems in his eyes. Their clients, who were worth millions, hired and leased Goldsmith's helicopters and private planes. They'd made his family a whole lot of money, and his father had been well-known among New York's elite—*America's* elite. But that man, that smiling face that everyone else saw, wasn't the true man. Which might have been half the reason Blake had never been able to smile himself unless he truly meant it.

He tucked the photo into a book and switched off the lamp, staring out the window for a while. New York was the city that never slept, and he was starting to be the guy who never slept. The fatigue was killing him, but somehow a few strong coffees always seemed to give him enough energy to get through the following day. *Just.*

Saffron had a sick feeling in her stomach when she woke. She kept her eyes shut, this time hoping that Blake wouldn't be there when she slowly slid her fingers across the sheets. She peeked out, breathing a sigh of relief when she found she was alone. Again.

She got up, walked into the bathroom and retrieved the robe she'd left in there, tucking herself up in it. Then she summoned all the bravery she could and walked out, expecting to find Blake asleep on the sofa. Instead, she discovered him standing in the kitchen, bare chested and staring intently at something.

"Morning," she called out, surprised by how normal her voice sounded when she was a bundle of nerves.

Blake was frowning when he looked up, but his face quickly transformed into a smile when he saw her. "Morning."

She wasn't sure what else to say, whether they were just going to pretend nothing had happened or whether she should bring it up.

"I'm trying to make you breakfast," he said. "And for a guy who's used to ordering in, it's not as easy as it sounds."

She relaxed a little. "What are you making over there?"

His smile encouraged her to go a little closer. "Waffles again. I was given this fancy maker and I've never used it, so here goes."

Saffron laughed. "First of all, you don't need to keep feeding me. I'll never be a ballerina again if I keep eating with you." She was going to lean over the counter but decided to go around instead. "Second, you just whisk up the batter and pour it in. It ain't rocket science."

"You've making me feel like an idiot," he said with a chuckle. "I can fly a helicopter, but I can't use a whisk."

"You can?"

He gave her a quick sideways glance. "Yeah. It's what I've been doing most of my life."

Saffron tried to hide her surprise. Instead she leaned over and checked out the batter. "You're doing okay, just keep whisking until the lumps are out and give it a go."

Blake turned his attention to her, and she found it hard to read his expression.

"I'm not good at apologies, but I shouldn't have been such an idiot last night."

She appreciated he was trying to say he was sorry. "It's fine. I didn't mean to sneak up on you. I had no idea…"

He shook his head. "Let's just forget it. Okay?"

She nodded. "Okay."

There was something so magnetic about him, a feeling that pooled in her belly whenever she was with him. And seeing him standing in his jeans, bare chested with all his sinewy muscles on display, only reminded her all over again of how much fun she'd had in his bed. Even if she was still cautious after the way he'd reacted.

It was as though they were playing some silly cat-and-mouse game, only she didn't quite have a grasp of the rules yet.

She decided to make coffee instead of ogling his gorgeous body. "Coffee?" she asked, realizing she had no idea how he liked it.

"Love one. Black with one sugar."

Saffy busied herself, keeping her back turned even though she was still crazy aware of him. She got that he had issues, and she'd been so hurt last night, but they hardly knew each other and they were suddenly living together. It was never going to be easy.

"Here we go," she said, spinning around and just about slamming into him. She hadn't been expecting him to be just standing there.

"Thanks." He held out a hand to steady her, smiled down at her with his dreamy dark eyes. She really needed to get back to work! It wasn't like her to be so taken with a man, and she was blaming it on not having anything else to think about.

Blake didn't pull away immediately, and she held her breath, gazing back at him. She was also starting to blame not getting this sort of thing out of her system on when she was younger. The excitement of what they were doing felt forbidden because it was so different from her usual behavior.

She smelled something that didn't seem quite right. "I think your waffle is burning."

Blake spun around, sloshing his coffee and making her laugh. "All I had to do was wait for the green light to come on. Who could burn a freaking waffle?"

Saffy perched on the bar stool so she could watch him. "Just throw it out. The next one will be perfect."

He muttered something and did what she'd suggested. Her stomach rumbled as he poured more batter in.

"So what would a normal Sunday look like for you?" she asked.

"Honestly?" he said, hands flat on the counter as he leaned forward. "I'd probably be eating breakfast that

I'd ordered from downstairs, then I'd be heading in to the office for a bit. Maybe going to the gym. You?"

She watched as he removed the first waffle and put it on a plate. He pushed it along the counter and passed her the maple syrup.

"If I was dancing, I'd be there around ten. My breakfast would probably be a protein shake instead of something like this, because I'd be being a lot more careful with my weight!"

"So you always worked on a Sunday?" he asked.

She cut into the waffle, slicing the first heart-shaped piece apart. "We only had Mondays off, and even then I'd be doing something work related. Although I always tried to get a massage in the afternoon." A wave of nostalgia hit her, just like it always did when she talked about dancing. "Every other day of the week I'd be in the studio by ten, and I'd be dancing or doing dancing-related things until around seven each night, unless we were performing, and then it'd be closer to eleven."

Blake whistled. "I had no idea the hours were so long."

She grimaced. "It's a killer, especially when you first start, but I love it. I would do it until I was sixty if I could."

"So tell me what happened," he said, voice suddenly a whole lot gentler. "I can see how much it hurts for you to talk about."

"I want to talk about that as much as you want to open up to me," Saffy said honestly.

Blake flipped out another waffle, stayed silent, although it wasn't awkward this time. She ate a few mouthfuls of her waffle, loving the drizzle of maple syrup.

"This is great," she praised him.

He smiled and passed her another, even though she stuck her hand out to protest.

"No more!" she managed when she'd finished her mouthful.

Blake just grinned and kept cooking.

"We were performing *Swan Lake*, and I was the lead. It had been amazing, night after night of great reviews," Saffron told him, suddenly needing to get it all out, to just tell him and get it over with instead of keeping it all bottled up inside. "I've had a lot of problems with a form of arthritis since I was young, and I was probably pushing myself too hard. That night I ripped three ligaments in my leg, which was bad enough without the crippling arthritis in my knee."

Blake looked up at her but didn't say anything, and she didn't want him to. There was nothing he could say that would make it any better.

"When I was in the army, I flew helicopters every day, doing what I loved," he said in a quiet voice, not making eye contact, just staring at the waffle machine. "I'd butted heads with my dad for years, but I wasn't going to back down on doing what I was passionate about. I wanted to make a difference, and I wanted to do something that made me feel great. The types of helicopters I was flying, dropping Navy SEALs into remote locations, being part of the most incredible teams..." He paused. "It was the best job in the world."

Saffron forced herself to keep eating, knowing how

hard it was to share when every word felt so raw. Maybe that was why she was so drawn to Blake, because even though they were so different, they'd both lost what they loved. It wasn't a person they'd lost, but the pain was so real, so true, that Saffy felt every day as if her heart had been ripped out. She got it.

"Last night, you saw me looking at a photo of my dad." She listened to him take a deep, shaky breath. "And my brother."

"You lost them, didn't you?" she asked quietly.

He nodded. "Yeah, I did. And as much as I miss my brother, so bad, I feel like it was just one more way for my dad to force me into what he always wanted me to do. Another way for him to control me. I know it sounds stupid, but in the middle of the night that's all I can think about."

Saffron wanted to reach for him, but she didn't know if it was the right thing to do or not. When he joined her at the counter and poured syrup over his waffles, she turned to face him, coffee cup in hand.

"We just have to cope as best we can, right?" she said. "It's so hard to make a career from doing what you love, and when that gets taken away..."

"It's heartbreaking," he muttered. "But yeah, you've just got to grit your teeth and keep on going. What other choice do we have?"

They sat side by side and finished their breakfast, and Saffron rose to rinse the plates and put them in a dishwasher.

"What do you say we go ring shopping?" Blake asked, taking her by surprise.

She tried to hide her grin. Ring shopping sounded like a lot more fun than her usual Sunday afternoon, and she liked the idea of getting out of the apartment. "Give me an hour. A girl's got to look good for that kind of outing."

"You always look good."

Saffy paused, heard what Blake had muttered. She was going to say something, but her brain was blank. Instead she closed the dishwasher door and headed for the bathroom. When she got there, she did what she always did in the mornings, lifting her right leg high and placing it on the edge of the bathroom cabinetry to stretch out her muscles. The granite in Blake's bathroom was cold against her skin, but it felt nice and she let her body fall down, the burn of her muscles making her feel alive. She lifted up then down again before repeating the stretch on the other side, the movement as natural to her as brushing her teeth.

Once she was finished she stared back at her reflection, checked her posture. She would always be a dancer. Every fiber in her body told her it wasn't over yet, and this morning her determination to listen to that feeling was back tenfold.

CHAPTER SIX

"WHAT DO YOU THINK?" Blake asked as they walked through the door of the antique jeweler his mother had always favored.

Saffron's eyes seemed to twinkle when she looked up at him, holding his hand. He'd linked their fingers as they'd headed through the door, conscious of how they appeared together, and somehow it felt right. He was oddly comfortable around Saffron most of the time, more himself than he probably was around even his family. Maybe because he'd laid it all out on the line with her, been honest from the get-go because of the kind of relationship they were in.

"I was expecting Tiffany's," she said.

"We can go there if you want."

"No," she said, letting go of his hand to peer into a display cabinet. "I didn't say I didn't like it—it's amazing. Besides, beggars can't be choosers, right?"

He laughed and watched as she wandered around, smiling to the assistant when she came over.

"Can I help you?"

"Yes," Blake said. "I'm looking for something for my fiancée here. Something elegant."

They started to look, with the assistant showing them a few engagement rings.

"Sir, is there any price range I need to be mindful of?" she asked in a hushed tone.

Blake smiled, reaching out for Saffron. "No. Whatever she wants."

Saffron shot him a look, and he just raised an eyebrow and smiled back at her. He was enjoying the charade more than he'd expected to.

"How about this one?" Saffron asked, pointing to a solitaire diamond surrounded by smaller ones, with baguette diamonds on each side forming the band.

The ring was beautiful and no doubt expensive, but he admired the fact she hadn't just chosen the largest, since he'd already told her she could keep it when their charade was over.

"Try it on," he instructed.

When the assistant passed it over, he quickly grabbed it, changing his mind. "Let me," he said.

Saffron turned to face him, and he smiled as he dropped to one knee in the store. "Saffron, will you marry me?" he asked, wanting to see her smile, knowing it would make her happy even though they weren't marrying for real.

They had talked about marriage, about what they were doing, but he hadn't actually proposed to her. Until now.

She held out her hand, letting him slip the ring on. "Yes," she whispered, laughing at him.

The shop assistant clapped as Blake rose and dropped a gentle kiss to her lips, liking how soft and warm her mouth was against his. It wasn't as though kissing her was a hardship.

"We'll take it," he said when he finally pulled away, reminding himself that it wasn't real, no matter how good Saffron felt against him.

The lines between fact and fiction were blurring between them, or maybe they'd always been blurred. The attraction between them was real; he just had to remember that it couldn't become—*wouldn't* become—anything more. It wasn't part of his plan, the future he imagined for himself, and there was no way he'd ever want a wife or a family. The example his father had set for him was testament to that. Besides, there would never be a woman he could trust enough with his heart or his money, and if he couldn't truly be himself without trying to protect himself and his family's fortune, then he'd never marry for real.

Once they'd paid for the ring, they left the shop with it on her finger.

"Well, that wasn't too hard," he said as they walked hand in hand down the sidewalk.

"It's beautiful," she said.

"And it's yours," he replied.

Saffron laughed as she leaned into him, still holding his hand. "It feels weird. I'm so girly and excited over the bling, but then this whole thing isn't real. I feel like I'm living someone else's life."

"Ditto," he said. Only he'd felt like that well before Saffron had come along. Every day he felt as if he was playing a role, one that had been destined for his brother, and he hated it. Every single day, he hated it.

"When we get back, I'll give you my planner to take a flick through. Anything marked social you'll need to attend with me, and I'll let you know in advance of any client dinners if I want you to join me."

Saffron looked up from admiring her ring. "Good. And I'll let you know how I do searching for specialists and treatments. There's an acupuncturist who works with celebrities I'd love to get in with, so I might need you to make the appointment!"

"I'll issue you a credit card tomorrow," Blake said, unworried, thinking through the logistics of everything. "That way you can pay for any medical expenses. Sound okay?"

She grasped his hand even tighter, but Blake didn't mind. "You've given me hope again, Blake. Just keep me in New York and I'll be the best wife you could have wished for."

He didn't doubt it.

"Oh, did I mention I want you to quit your job?" He'd forgotten all about telling her, but the last thing he wanted was for her to go back to pouring coffee. She could be a resting ballerina, holed up in his apartment or doing whatever she wanted, but he didn't want her tied to a job that she didn't even care about. If she was his wife, he would keep her and make sure she was available whenever he needed her. Besides, no one would believe in their marriage if he let Saffron work for minimum wage.

"You're serious?" Saffron asked, giving him a look that made him realize she actually thought he was joking.

"Deadly," he replied. "No one would believe you were my wife if I let you slave away nine to five."

He saw a hesitant look pass over her face that made him wonder if she didn't like the idea of him keeping her. "Okay," she said. "I guess if you were my husband that's what you'd want."

Blake nodded, but her words jolted him. It was weird hearing her say the *husband* word, especially when in his mind he could still see his mother sobbing over something his father had done when he was only a child. They weren't blurry memories like so many of his childhood recollections, but a perfect snapshot of his mom crying that the man she'd married didn't deserve to be called her *husband*, the man who slammed the door and left her to cry.

He pushed the thoughts away and smiled down at the gorgeous redhead at his side. All the more reason to have a contract, to be clear up front about what he wanted.

Blake wasn't fit to be a real husband, didn't want that life. But he did want to be the one to step his family business into the future, wanted to make his family proud. Because if he wasn't so honorable, he'd have left and never looked back after the funeral, returning to the life he loved. Selfishly leaving everything behind to pursue his dreams, away from his family name and far away from New York. But that was the past now, and it wasn't something he could get back. *Ever.*

Oddly, he felt happier with Saffron at his side than he had for a long while. Or maybe it was just the promise

of having her in his bed every night, and the fact he'd
been honest with her about who he truly was.

"So this is the woman who got you all tied up in knots?"
An elegant older woman with her hair pulled off her
face stepped forward to collect Saffron's hand. Her palm
was warm, and even though she screamed old New York
money, her smile was genuine.

"Mom, I'd like you to meet Saffron," Blake said,
coming to her rescue and slinging an arm around her
so he could pull her back.

"It's great to meet you," Saffron said, training a
smile. "I've heard so much about you."

His mother's smile was wry, and it reminded Saffron of Blake. "I can't say the same about you. My son
has been very tight-lipped about the beautiful woman
he's all set to marry."

"Nothing fancy," Blake cautioned, taking Saffy's
hand and pulling her toward him. She sat down on the
sofa beside him, careful to curl up close, keeping a hand
on his thigh. "Just a simple wedding."

He glanced down at her, and she retreated with her
hand. The heat in his gaze was making her uncomfortable. This might be fake, but their chemistry wasn't,
which was why she wasn't finding it that hard to pretend.

"When you say nothing fancy…?" his mother asked.

"I mean we're heading down to the registry office
and signing the paperwork. No big ceremony, no fuss.
You can wait until the girls get married for a big wedding, because I want this completely under the radar."

His mother pursed her lips, but Saffron could see she didn't want to argue with him, or maybe she knew from experience that there was just no point.

"Saffron, I don't want to offend you, but I must bring up the delicate subject of a prenuptial agreement."

Blake laughed and Saffron leaned into him. She'd been prepared for this, would have thought it odd if any mother with their kind of fortune hadn't raised an eyebrow at how quickly they were getting married.

"Please, Mrs. Goldsmith, that's not something you have to worry about. I have no intention of taking anything from your son or your family, and we've already organized the paperwork." Saffron chuckled. "But don't think for a moment I'm going to let your son run my life. I intend on having my career back on track very quickly. As soon as I've given my body a chance to rest and recover, I'll be back with the New York Ballet Company."

His mother smiled and looked to Blake. "I like her."

Blake dropped a kiss into her hair. It was just a casual, sweet gesture, but the gentleness of his touch took her by surprise.

"She's the one."

Saffron felt guilty sitting there, smiling away and pretending to dote on this woman's son. She seemed like a nice person, and lying wasn't something that came naturally to her, even if she was putting on a good show of doing exactly that right now. She wondered what it would be like if this were real, if she were actually being welcomed into the family. Saffron could see that she'd enjoy Blake's mother's company, which only made her guilt pangs stronger.

"You do realize the tabloids will stop hounding you. Not to mention it'll be good for business," his mother mused, shrugging into her coat and collecting her purse as they watched. "We should hold an engagement party for our clients, let them see what a family man you're becoming. What do you think?"

Blake stood, and she kept hold of him as she rose, too. "I think that sounds like a great idea. How about you organize it?"

His mother's smile was wide. "Excellent."

"Actually, maybe we should just start an annual party for our guests, and we can announce our marriage at this inaugural one to keep it low-key." He knew whom he wanted to impress, but it wouldn't do any harm to invite all their important clients.

Saffron nodded, listening and playing the part of attentive fiancée. She was used to playing a role as a dancer, to being in character, which was probably why this seemed easy. Or maybe Blake was just easy to be around. If she'd had to pick the kind of man she'd want to marry one day, it could have been him. *Maybe*. Although from what he'd said, he had no intention of ever marrying for real, never wanted to settle down.

And that was fine by her. Once she was dancing again, she'd have no time for a husband anyway. Blake would be a distant memory, and hopefully a pleasant one.

"Please tell me you'll invite me to the ceremony," his mother said as they walked out her door.

"Maybe," Blake answered. "Let's see if Saffron survives meeting my sisters first. She might run for the hills before I get her to sign on the dotted line."

Blake laughed and she forced a chuckle. If only his mother knew that she'd already well and truly signed on the dotted line. She was bound to marry Blake, which meant they were as good as husband and wife already. Besides, they'd already decided that they were going to get married in secret as soon as the license came through.

CHAPTER SEVEN

SAFFRON WAS SMILING, and even though her happiness wasn't forced, she wasn't finding it easy to look happy. What was she doing? Blake was treating her like his actual wife, and aside from when he woke up in hot sweats during the night and didn't want to talk about it, everything seemed…good. *Real.* Not that she was under any illusions, but still, it was weird.

"Come on, let's go," Blake said, kissing her on the lips and holding their joined hands in the air. "You were great tonight."

"You sound like my choreographer," she said with a laugh, still smiling as the crowd watched them. She was well used to being the center of attention, and far from feeling unusual having her every move watched just because she was on a man's arm, she was getting a kick out of it. Usually she basked in the attention, full of pride that so many people were enjoying her creative outlet, a performance she'd put hours of her time, not to mention sweat and sometimes blood, into. This time she felt like an actress, and for some reason it didn't feel any less satisfying. "Or maybe my cheerleader."

"You're brilliant, has anyone ever told you that?"

Blake swept her into his arms and out of the room. She was starting to get the feeling that he was enjoying the performance as much as she'd enjoyed putting it on.

Saffron didn't want their conversation to turn around to her dancing, so she let it go and didn't answer. They headed straight outside and into the waiting town car.

"I think they bought it," she said.

Blake leaned over and kissed her, his lips familiar to her now yet still making her body tingle. It would have been a much easier arrangement if they hadn't started out by being intimate, although given the way her body reacted to him, she was starting to wonder if they could ever have been platonic.

"I have some key accounts that have always referred to my dad every time we met, gone on about the roots of the company being a family business and questioning my commitment, or at least that's what it's seemed like," Blake said, settling back into the leather seat. "I don't know if a rival was trying to get to them and spinning rubbish, or if it was just the reputation they thought I had, but things felt fragile there for a little while. Marrying you has made all that go away, and after tonight, man. You seriously wowed my big investor. I definitely believe you can be my little star for the next while."

"So it's been worth it for you already?" Saffron asked.

He grinned. "Yes. You?"

"You've given me access to medical professionals I'd never have been able to afford to consult with," she said honestly. "And I'm still here. I still have a shot.

So yeah." Saffron laughed. "Marrying you hasn't been half-bad!"

The car ride was only short, and soon they were heading up to their apartment. It already felt like home for Saffron after two short weeks, or as home as anything ever felt to her. She wasn't used to spending a lot of time wherever she lived, and she'd been living out of a suitcase on and off for years. But she had some photos up, Blake had given up half his wardrobe space to her and her perfume lingered when she walked into their room.

"I'm just going to respond to some work emails. I'll be in bed soon."

Saffy undressed and put on a nightie, then padded into the bathroom to take her makeup off. She never took the luxurious space for granted, with its floor-to-ceiling tiles and beautiful fittings, and the oversize fluffy towels were her idea of heaven. Especially since he had the housekeeper come in twice a week, so she didn't even have to lift a finger to keep them that way.

The apartment was silent except for the low hum of the television—she was used to Blake having it on whenever he sat up and worked late, which was most nights. She lowered herself to the ground, relaxed into the splits and dropped her body down low, covering first one leg and then the other. Once she was done stretching, she stood and raised up, on tiptoe, smiling to herself as she leaned to each side, reached up high, before doing a little turn. The acupuncture had definitely helped, and even though she could have kept going until she collapsed, she was going to follow her new specialist's orders and only stretch her muscles like that for five minutes each evening and morning.

Still smiling, she curled up beneath the covers and flicked through a magazine before turning off the bedside lamp and closing her eyes. She was going to wait up for him, but they'd had late night after late night and…

Saffron woke up with a fright, sitting bolt upright, heart racing.

"No!"

She blinked in the darkness, eyes slowly adjusting, realizing that it was Blake who'd woken her. She instinctively pulled back, putting some space between them.

"Blake," she said, loudly, forcing her voice. "Blake!"

He groaned but didn't wake, pulled the sheets tighter around himself, thrashing out.

"Blake!"

His eyes opened, a flash of brightness that scared her for a moment until they locked on her. He sat up, disheveled and disoriented looking.

"Saffy?" His voice was hoarse as he pushed the covers down.

"You were dreaming. Are you okay?" she asked, hesitant. She didn't want to push him—they had a good thing going, and that didn't involve asking too many personal questions, going too deep, unless they had to.

"Same thing every time." Blake sighed. "Every single time."

Saffron tucked her knees up to her chin. "Your dad?" she asked.

Blake flicked his bedside lamp on. "Yeah. Always

him. Always a weird, I don't know, collage of memories, I guess. Just a jumble of things all mashed together."

"Do you still wish you were serving?" she asked. It was a question that had been on her lips all week, wanting to ask but not knowing if he'd want to talk to her. "That you could go back, even though you have these dreams?"

"Yeah," he said, running his fingers through his hair, shutting his eyes as he leaned back into the headboard. "Or maybe I don't. I don't know. All I know is that I miss flying, miss having my own identity that isn't tied to my family. As hard as it was, I still miss it, want it."

"I'm not sure what would be harder—having a dream and never turning it into reality, or the feeling of having that dream snatched away when you've already tasted the reality of it." Saffron reached for Blake, her fingers crawling the space between them until they connected with his. At least they knew what it felt like, understood what the other had been through on a level that no one else could.

"Having it taken away," he replied, squeezing her fingers back. "Definitely having it taken away."

"Or maybe we wouldn't have the same fire burning in us if we hadn't tasted that reality, that dream," she whispered. "Maybe we're still the lucky ones, we just can't see it."

"Maybe." He groaned, and she wasn't sure if it was from pain or the subject matter.

"Tell me what it was like, what you loved about it," she asked, suddenly wide-awake, not wanting to go back to sleep if he wanted to open up to her, to talk.

"One day," he said. "One day I'll tell you all about it. About the kick I got every time I put a Black Hawk up in the air or took a unit to safety in a Chinook. But not right now. I need some rest."

She knew he had issues, that whatever was troubling him needed to be dealt with, but as he kept reminding her, it wasn't her problem. She wasn't his real wife. She was more like a live-in mistress with extra benefits.

His problems were his. Her problems were hers. A year or two of fun. A year or two of great sex and parties. One year or maybe more to get her career back on track and have fun while she tried to find her way back to the top. It sure beat going home to serve coffee for the rest of her life at a diner and wishing for what she didn't have. At least this way, what she'd lost still felt as if it was within arm's reach. What she craved so badly was still a possibility instead of simply a memory of what could have been.

CHAPTER EIGHT

Three months later

SAFFRON SMILED UP at Blake, expertly running her fingers down his dinner jacket–clad arm. It wasn't hard to pretend she adored him, but the weird thing was reminding herself all the time that it wasn't *real*. They slept in the same bed, they went to parties and functions, and they put on a perfect show of being a real couple. Which they kind of were. Pity he was so darn irresistible.

A waiter passed and she took a glass of champagne. She held it for a while, listening to Blake talk business, before raising the glass to her lips. She went to sip but then recoiled as the bubbles hit her tongue.

"Excuse me," she said, stepping away from Blake quickly and scanning for the restroom. Bile rose in her throat, and she forced it down.

"Are you okay?" Blake's dark brown eyes met hers, concern etched on his face. So far she'd never let him down once, but this time she needed to bolt. Fast.

Saffy just nodded and hurried as fast as her high

heels would let her. Thankfully her leg was feeling great and she hadn't had any problems with her knee, so she was able to move fast. Otherwise she'd have been vomiting in the nearest corner!

She left her glass on a ledge in the bathroom and only just made it to a stall, holding her hair back as she threw up into the toilet. Her body felt burning hot then chilled, sweat beading across her forehead before her skin turned cold. What on earth had she eaten? Or had she caught the stomach flu?

"You okay in there, sweetheart?" A kind voice sounded out.

Saffron hadn't even noticed anyone else. She'd been so desperate not to be sick out in the open that she'd just hurried straight on through. "Um, I think so," she managed to say back, trying to hold down everything else in her stomach, if there was even anything else left.

"You don't sound drunk, and you didn't look drunk, so either you've eaten something bad or you've got a little one on the way. Am I right?"

Saffron laughed. "Has to be bad food." Another wave of nausea hit, and she leaned forward again, trying hard to hold it down and failing.

The woman sounded closer this time when she spoke. "You're sure it's not a baby?"

Saffron sighed and leaned against the wall of the stall. Usually she was grossed out by any kind of public toilet, but the cool felt nice against her body when she pushed back, and it was a pretty posh tiled bathroom with fancy lights and wallpaper. She hoped it was clean. Besides, she didn't have any other choice.

"Can't be a baby," she replied with a sigh. "Not for me." Saffron finally opened the door and came face to a face with a nice-looking lady dressed in a beautiful taffeta gown. Her gray hair was pulled up into an elegant do.

"I was sick as a dog when I had my boys. Thin as a whippet so nobody knew I was pregnant, and I threw up for months."

Saffron appreciated her concern, and it was nice to have someone to take her mind off how ill she felt. The nausea had passed now, only returning when she thought about the champagne she'd almost drunk. She usually had a cast-iron stomach, so it seemed strange.

"Saffy, you in here?" Blake's deep voice boomed through the restroom.

She cleared her throat. "Just a sec."

"I'll tell your man you're not well. You take your time."

Saffy pulled herself together, taking a mint from her purse and then walking over to the mirrors to check her face. She looked pale and gaunt, but the sick feeling had passed. After washing her hands, she went to find Blake.

"What's wrong?"

His eyes were searching her face, and she had to look away. The hardest part about being with Blake was trying not to fall in love with the man. They'd felt like a real team when she'd been at his side, meeting his new investor and his wife; when Blake had secured the investment, she'd fist pumped and squealed as if it was her deal that had come together!

"I started feeling all weird, sweats and nausea. I think I ate something bad."

He frowned and put his arm around her as they walked back out. "Let's head home."

"No, you stay," she insisted, looking away when a waiter passed. She couldn't stand the thought of alcohol or food. "Schmooze your clients, do your work and let me go. You don't need me here—they've already seen you're a doting husband if that's what you're worried about."

She'd meant to sound positive, but instead it had come out all wrong.

"Just because this isn't, ah—" he cleared his throat, frowning again "—doesn't mean I don't care about you."

Saffy squeezed his hand. "I know. I just meant that I've already fulfilled my purpose." She felt sick again and held his hand tight, waiting for it to pass. "I really have to go."

Blake let go of her hand and pulled out his phone. "Make your way out. I'll call the driver now and have him waiting for you."

Saffron smiled her thanks and hurried through the throng of people toward the exit. She kept her head down, not wanting to make eye contact and have to talk to anyone. She just wanted to undress and crawl into bed.

As promised the car was there within minutes of her walking outside, although she would have been happy to stand and gulp in the cold air for longer. She got in the vehicle and slumped on the backseat. As they headed for home she stared out the window, her hand resting on her stomach in an effort to calm it. It wasn't working, but she kept it there anyway.

Pregnant. She smiled despite how shaky she felt. There was no way she could be pregnant. The specialist had made it so clear to her, and she'd looked into freezing her eggs before having it done, but the success rates of thawing those frozen eggs hadn't seemed worth it to her, not when she'd been so short of money.

Pregnant. Was there even a slim chance? She'd only been with Blake that one time without protection, and if her chances of getting pregnant were statistically zero, surely it couldn't have happened…

"Pull over, please!" she cried as they passed a convenience store.

The driver did as she asked, pulling over farther up the block when it was safe and there was space to park.

"I'll only be a minute," she said, jumping out and rushing back. She entered the store and found the section with women's things, reaching for the first pregnancy test she could find. There were two types, so she grabbed the other one as well, hands shaking so hard she had to concentrate on getting her card out to pay.

"Thanks," she mumbled as she took her things and raced back to the car. It was only a short drive, but it seemed to take forever. When they pulled up outside she raced in, forgetting how ill she'd been. Saffy headed for the bathroom, not bothering to turn any lights on except the one she needed to. The rest of the apartment was dark, except for a couple of lamps, but she didn't care. All she wanted was to do the test so she could be sure that there was absolutely no chance of her being pregnant.

Saffy hovered above the toilet and held the stick out, counting to three before retrieving it. She put the cap back on it and placed it on the counter, staring at the tiny screen that would show one line if she wasn't pregnant. That line showed, strongly, and as she held her breath another faint line appeared, slowly but surely. *Two blue lines.* Nausea washed over her again, but this time she was sure it was from nerves. She couldn't be pregnant!

She paced around the bathroom for a few minutes then ripped open the wrapper on the other test. This one was more expensive, so she was sure it would be more accurate.

She'd only just been, but she forced herself to go again, to do just enough so that the test would work. And then she played the waiting game again, staring at the slightly bigger screen.

Pregnant. Just one word. One simple word.

And it changed everything.

CHAPTER NINE

SAFFRON CLUTCHED HER bag tight and walked back out onto the street. The day was warm and the sun was hot on her bare arms, but she hardly noticed. She just wanted to get to the studio where she'd been training.

Pregnant. She'd known the two home tests the night before couldn't be wrong, but still. After so many years of believing she could never be a mom, it was almost impossible to comprehend. And what was she going to tell Blake? Saffy groaned and held her bag tighter, scared of what was happening inside her, how much everything was changing.

She felt a vibration against her and realized it was her phone. She pulled it out, glancing at the screen and expecting it to be Blake, not ready to talk to him yet. But it was a number she didn't recognize.

She inhaled and stopped walking. "Hello, Saffron speaking."

"Saffron, it's Benjamin. From NYC Ballet."

Her heart just about stopped beating. "Oh, hi," she stammered.

"I wanted to know how you are. Whether you've had any success with your recovery?"

Saffy flexed her foot, something she always did whenever she thought about her injury or someone asked her about it. She couldn't help but smile when she did it without pain. "I'm doing really well. I've seen some great physical therapists, an acupuncturist and a specialist doctor, and I think I'm ready to ease back into dancing again."

It was a half lie, because the amazing people she'd been seeing had all told her to simply start exercising more, to slowly start dancing ten or so minutes a day after running through a series of stretches and strapping her leg. To try taking a few dance classes but not specifically ballet, and they'd been making her consume all types of natural wonder products in conjunction with the medicines the doctor had prescribed. The specialist had been incredibly helpful, referring her to the almost-impossible-to-get-in-with therapist in the first place. She'd already enrolled in modern dance, just to start using her muscles, but only ballet was going to fill the void she felt every day.

"That's fabulous news, darling," Benjamin said. "We all thought you might have gotten married and forgotten about us."

"Never," Saffron murmured. "Dance will always be the most important thing in my life."

He laughed. "Just don't let your new husband hear you talk like that!"

Saffron felt as though she was walking on ice, just teetering and waiting. Why had he phoned her? She was too scared to ask. There had to be a reason for a call to just come out of the blue after so long with no contact.

"Darling, the purpose of my call is to see if we can book you. It's not for another four months, but it's you we need." He cleared his throat. "Can you be ready by then? Are you planning on making a comeback?"

Saffy went burning hot then freezing cold, as if her body was going into shock. Four months? Her hand went instinctively to her stomach. In four months she was going to have a bump. A *very* big bump. If she had this baby, there was no way she'd be able to dance then, no matter how well her leg was holding out.

"Why me?" she asked.

"It's for Pierre. He's retiring from the company, and he's requested you as the dancer for his final show. It's just a one-off performance for him, to thank him for all the years he's put into our choreography, but it's you and only you he wants."

Saffron gulped. Pierre was the reason she'd been the lead in *Swan Lake*. Pierre had given her that big break, had believed in her and what her future could hold. Pierre was the key to her getting back on stage, because only he would request her and not take no for an answer.

"Can I have some time to think about it?" Saffron said, stalling, not ready to say no when she didn't even know what she was going to do, what the next few months of her life would even look like. "I'll need to talk to my physical therapist and specialist, make sure they don't think it's too soon. I don't want to risk injury again." She shook her head, wondering where the words were coming from. She wasn't even over her old injury yet!

"We love you here, Saffron," he said. "Take the week

to think about it and let me know. If you do this, you'll be officially invited back to join the company. You were one of Pierre's best principal dancers, darling. We want you back home where you belong, and I just don't believe you're done yet."

Tears welled in Saffy's eyes. It was the phone call she'd been dreaming of, her big chance. But even without the baby, she had no idea whether she'd ever be strong enough to be a principal again, not until she started training and saw firsthand if her leg tolerated the punishing hours.

"I'd do anything to be back. Trust me," she said, voice as shaky as her hands as she gripped her phone.

When she hung up, all she felt was emptiness. What she'd wanted was so close she could almost taste it, almost within her grasp. But then once upon a time, being a mother had seemed important, when the idea of being a parent had been taken from her. She'd been horrified at the time that she would never have children, something she'd slowly forgotten about the more she'd progressed in her career. But now... She slid her hand back down over her belly, the action seemingly normal now. She was suddenly protective of the little being growing inside her, even though she wasn't sure how she felt about the whole thing. *She was pregnant.*

She reached the studio and entered, pleased there was only one other dancer there running through a routine. She stripped down to her leotard and tights, carefully putting on her ballet shoes and looking down at her legs. She warmed up by stretching out slowly, trying not to think, trying to just focus on what she was about to do, on dance. She lifted a leg carefully into the air, stretched up, rose up then down, using the barre, feeling her muscles as they pulled then released. When she had both feet back on the ground, she stretched some more before leaving the barre to dance a quick routine, to cross the room once, dancing like she used to, dancing in a way that used to come as naturally as breathing to her.

And it still did. Breathless but not in pain, Saffy stopped, knew she had to. If she had it her way she would dance all day, but she wasn't ready. Not physically.

After warming down, stretching some more, she slipped her yoga pants back on and then her sweater, collecting her bag and heading back out the door. Saffy set off at a walk, heading for the apartment, needing to face reality. Either she told Blake and he would deal with it, let her make her own decision about what to do, or she never let him find out. He didn't want to be a dad—he'd made that clear when they'd signed the marriage contract—and she'd told him outright that her getting pregnant was impossible. He'd just think she was a liar, that she'd purposely deceived him, set out to fool him. This didn't have to be his problem; it was something she could deal with on her own. If she wanted this baby, she could do it. Trouble was, she'd signed a marriage contract, and she knew Blake only had one of the deals together that he'd needed her for, and she doubted he'd want to let her out of the contract so easily. Not until he had what he needed from their arrangement.

She let herself in and went straight for the kitchen,

pouring a big glass of water and drinking it down. Then she peeled a banana and sat in silence, eating.

"Saffy?"

She jumped, choking on her mouthful. What was Blake doing home?

"Blake?" Saffy walked toward the bedroom. "Where are you?"

"In bed. I'm sick," he said.

She peeked in. "I had no idea you were here."

"I think I've got the stomach flu that you had," Blake said, groaning. "Where have you been?"

It was an innocent question, but it felt like an interrogation all of a sudden. Because for once she'd been somewhere she shouldn't have. "Um, just the doctor," she told him, going closer and sitting down on the bed beside him, reaching for his hand. It was warm, his skin comforting against hers. "I've been thinking about going back to the studio some more, actually pushing my leg a little to see how I do, see if I'm ready to go back."

His smile was kind, and he let go of her hand to prop himself up on the pillows. They'd developed a relationship that went way beyond a simple contract, an easiness that she would miss. Blake was complicated yet beautiful, a man who was straight up about what he wanted, but one who was hiding a power load of pain. He'd shared so little with her about how he truly felt, had just scratched the surface and told her the bare bones of his past, but she knew how much he hurt, how hard it was for him to trust. And now she had to figure out how to tell him what had happened, make him believe that she hadn't deceived him.

"What happened?" he asked, staring into her eyes like he always did and making her feel as if she was the only person in the room, as though what they had was genuine. As real as it felt sometimes.

Heat started to rise up her body, flooding her cheeks. This time she had to lie. "I had a phone call. An opportunity."

"To dance again?" he asked.

Saffy nodded. "Yes. In four months' time, if I'm up to it."

"That's great news," Blake said with a smile. "I'd offer to celebrate with you, but…"

She held up her hand and rose. "I'll let you rest."

Saffron was relieved to walk away and not have to talk more, because she had a lot of thinking to do. More than that, she needed to make a decision. The doctor had been very diplomatic in explaining all her options, but the thought of anything other than protecting the growing baby inside her made her want to be physically sick. But what if this was her one and only chance to dance again? What if this was the last time in her life she'd be offered an opportunity like this? What if…

Saffy bit down hard on her lip. *Be a mother.* She collapsed onto the sofa, finding it hard to breathe. *Or be a dancer.*

She dug her nails into the cushion beside her. *Run away from Blake and never look back.*

Right now, it was sounding like the best option. Or maybe it was feeling like her only option. She couldn't give up this baby, which meant she couldn't be a dancer, not now, maybe not ever, because Pierre would be gone and then she'd have to try to impress a new chore-ographer who didn't know or love her. Besides, the two didn't go hand in hand, not with the hours she'd have to dedicate to dancing again *if* her body ever let her. And there was no way she could dance that punishing rou-tine at all during pregnancy, not a chance.

Blake checked his watch and frowned at the time. It was unusual for Saffron to be so late. He was going to wait another five minutes but changed his mind, leaving a tip on the table and simply walking out. He wasn't that hun-gry anyway, and he wanted to make sure she was okay.

He dialed her number and it went straight to voice mail. Again.

Blake left a message this time. "Hey Saffy, it's me. We had a dinner reservation at seven—did you forget? I'm on the way home now. We can always order some-thing in. Call me."

It didn't take him long to make it back, and when he let himself in, something felt wrong.

"Saffy?" he called. When she didn't answer he headed straight for the bedroom. Maybe she was in the shower. "Saffron?"

And then he stopped. There was no five-book-high pile on her bedside table, no perfume bottles or jew-elry scattered on the buffet beneath the big mirror. He walked faster into the bathroom. No makeup, no hair-spray, no deliciously citrus smell.

Blake stopped dead in front of the closet, not hesitating to yank the doors open and stare inside. The empty space hit him like a fist to his gut. What was going on?

Saffy was gone. She was gone as though she'd never existed in the first place, as if she'd been a figment of his imagination.

Just like Bianca. Just like the day he'd found their little apartment empty all those years ago.

He walked backward until his legs touched the bed, and he dropped down on to it, not noticing the cream envelope until he was sitting. He slipped his finger beneath the seal and plucked out the single piece of paper inside, unfolding it and instantly recognizing Saffron's handwriting.

Blake,

I left like this because I didn't want to look you in the eye and tell you the truth myself. The last few months might have been an arrangement, but I feel closer to you than I ever really have to any other person before. And that's why I didn't want to see the distrust in your eyes when you found out that I was pregnant. You deserved to know, but you don't owe me anything. This baby suddenly means the world to me, and I'll do everything I can to make this little person be loved. I'm sorry I left when I was supposed to stay with you as your wife for longer, but staying would have only made things more complicated. You made it clear that you never wanted a family, or a real wife, and the last thing I want to do is trap you into something else you don't want.

I've kept the ring only because you told me it
was mine, and it'll help tide me over until I can
work again.

I'm sorry things had to end this way, and I want
you to know that you'll always hold a special place
in my heart. Don't try to find me, just let me go.
Saffron

What the... Blake screwed up the letter into a tight
ball and threw it across the room. She was *pregnant*?

He rose and stormed into the kitchen, wrapping
his hand around a bottle of whiskey and pouring a big
splash into a glass. He knocked it straight back.

Pregnant? How? They'd always used protection. Besides, she'd told him she couldn't have children, that it
wasn't possible, that...*one night*. There had been that
one night, months ago. Before the contract. Before he'd
proposed. Before they'd gotten married.

Maybe this had been her plan all along, to lure him
in and have a child, just like countless women had done
to rich men in the past. Maybe she'd played him right
from that first night. Maybe she was no better than the
first woman who'd scorned him.

Damn it! They'd had an agreement, a contract, and
he'd be darned if he was going to let her walk out on
that and have a baby. A baby that he'd have no choice
but to support, to see, to know. A baby he didn't want.
A baby that shouldn't even exist. The one thing in life
he'd been certain about for the past decade was that he
didn't want a woman in his life and he didn't want a
family. Ever. The one and only time he'd slipped up,

put his trust in someone else… Blake poured himself another nip, swallowing it down fast before pushing the glass away. He'd had enough, needed to keep his head, to stay in control.

Saffron might be able to run, but he wasn't going to let her hide. Not with his baby on board. Not now, and not ever.

He sat in silence, in the dark. She was supposed to be dancing again, or had that been a lie? She was supposed to be in contention for a role that she'd seemed excited about. Or was that just a ruse to throw him off track, not make him suspicious?

Blake picked up his phone and scrolled through some numbers until he found the contact from the art auction. It was late but he didn't care—he'd make a donation large enough to make it count. If he found her friend Claire, he'd find Saffron. And if that didn't work, then he'd start at NYC Ballet. He'd contact the airlines, stop her from flying, do whatever it took. She wasn't leaving him—not with his baby.

CHAPTER TEN

SAFFRON HAD NEVER felt so guilty in her life. The pain
was shooting through her chest, making it hard to
breathe. But the problem was that guilt wasn't the only
thing she was feeling.

Her heart was broken. Saffy gripped her water glass
tighter, staring at the slice of lemon floating as she sat
at the bar in the hotel. Just like every time she started
to doubt herself, she touched her stomach, ran her palm
lightly across it, just enough so that she hoped the baby
could feel.

She checked the time and stood up, ready to take
her taxi to Newark airport. It had been a long night,
lying awake, wondering if she was doing the right
thing, but she'd made up her mind and it was time to
go. Maysville, Kentucky, wasn't New York, but it was
an amazing place to raise a child and she had her family
there. She could start a dance studio one day, nurture
young talent, incorporate what she loved with being a
mother. Or at least that was what she was telling herself to deal with the move.

"You're my little blessing," she murmured as she

walked, one hand carrying her bag, the other on her belly still.

She wasn't supposed to have a baby, and the fact that she'd gotten pregnant was a miracle. A miracle that she had no intention of turning her back on. Dancing had been her everything, until her body let her down. Now her body was doing what it was never supposed to do. It might have been a shock, but she could sure see the irony of it.

Saffron spoke to the concierge as she passed through the lobby and was directed to her taxi, getting in and letting them take care of her luggage. She didn't have a lot, just two suitcases. It seemed ironic that after so many years living in New York, she had so little to take home with her. But her mom would be there to welcome her with open arms, even though they hadn't seen each other in a long time. They were like that—could just pick up where they'd left off. Same with her dad. They knew she loved them and vice versa; she'd just spent so many years doing her own thing that they weren't the best at staying in touch.

She rested her head against the window, the cool glass refreshing against her hot skin. The city whizzed past once they'd gotten through the worst of the traffic, and when they finally reached the airport, she almost couldn't open her door. Leaving New York had never been part of her ten-year plan.

"Ma'am," the driver said, looking back over his shoulder.

Saffy smiled and forced a shaky hand up, opened the door and got out. He was nice enough to help her out with her bags, and she paid him the fare plus a decent tip. Then she went in, checked in for her flight and kept only her carry-on bag in her hand. She knew there would be a long wait ahead of her to get through security, so she went to get a coffee first. When she was finally in line, her hands began to shake, and she clutched the takeout cup tighter even though it was starting to burn her palm.

The line moved slowly, and the anxiety she'd started to feel in the taxi compounded so fast she could hardly breathe. What was she doing? How could she leave New York? She should be dancing for Pierre, she should be back as a principal, her leg was better... Saffy took a slow, steady sip of coffee in an attempt to calm herself.

She was having a baby, and that was the most important thing in the world. She was going to be a mother. She was going to have a gorgeous little child to hold in her arms and love. She could go back to ballet.

Couldn't she?

"Saffron!"

Saffy almost dropped the cup. What the...was she hearing things?

"Saffron!"

Saffy turned slowly, sure she was imagining the deep, commanding voice calling out her name above the din of the airport, the noise and bustle of the busy terminal. She was going crazy, actually crazy.

Blake? *Oh my god*, it *was* Blake! Her heart started to pound. Should she push to the front of the line? Get through security and away from him, beg to be let through? She knew that was stupid—Blake was worth a small fortune, and he'd just buy a ticket no matter what the price so he could follow her.

Saffron held her head high, not losing her place in the line as she defiantly met his gaze despite wanting to cower as he glared. She'd done her best to run away and not have to deal with him, to face a confrontation, but he'd found her and she couldn't back down. It had been cowardly of her to leave him a note, but it had seemed like the only way to break free from him.

"You're not getting on that plane."

Saffy gulped. She guessed they weren't exchanging pleasantries. "I'm going home, Blake, and you can't stop me."

His gaze was cool. Unrecognizable. "Oh, yes, I can. You're not abducting my child, Saffron. Not now, not ever."

She didn't know what to say. It was his child, but she'd expected him to want her to abort, to…maybe he still did, and he was just trying to take charge any way he could.

"I'm keeping this baby, Blake," she said, hand to her stomach, not caring who heard.

"You're coming with me. Now," Blake said, reaching for her, hand closing around her arm and holding tight.

"My luggage is already checked and my flight leaves in two hours."

"Saffron, you're not getting on that plane." Blake might have been angry before, but now he was furious.

"Let go of me," she hissed, tears welling in her eyes, her resolve fading fast, no longer feeling brave. "You can't just make me."

He didn't look like a man about to take no for an answer. "Sweetheart, we're leaving this airport together whether you like it or not."

She gasped when he pulled her, not letting go. She thought about screaming for security, yelling for help, but the people waiting behind her just looked away, not caring for someone else's problems. Saffron let herself be pulled, wished she was stronger or more determined, but the fight was gone. Extinguished as if it had never existed. Blake would have found her no matter where she was—she'd been kidding herself to think she could run and that he'd forget all about her.

"You can let go of me now," she huffed, pulling back and forcing him to slow down. Blake was impatient, but he did slow, his fingers not gripping her quite so tightly. "And in case you care, you're hurting me."

Blake let go completely then, his hand falling to her back instead, pointing her toward the exit. "Just come with me."

"What about my things?"

"I don't care about your things right now!"

She stopped walking, glared at him. "We're getting my luggage or you can go to hell."

He stared at her for a long moment before marching her back over toward a counter, keeping hold of her as he spoke to someone, flashing a card that she guessed showed he was a priority flyer or something.

"I'm having your things sent. Come on."

Saffron chose to believe him, and within minutes they were seated in a sleek black car, the driver taking off the moment they were buckled in.

"You can't just take me hostage," she managed, forcing the words out as they choked in her throat.

"For the next six months or however long I need to, that's exactly what I intend on doing."

She turned to face him, stared into the eyes that belonged to a stranger right now. Not the handsome, beautiful man she'd slowly fallen for since the night she'd met him. The man she'd been so scared of getting close to, of letting see how broken she was, only to find out that he was broken in just as many ways. Except right now she saw no breaks, not even a crack, just a man calmly and almost silently controlled. This was the first time she'd glimpsed what she presumed was soldier Blake—calm, cool and in control. There was a coolness that was just...*empty*.

"So you want me to have the baby?"

He looked away. "Yes. You can leave as soon as it's born if you like."

"I will not!"

He stared at her, but she wasn't backing down. Not when it came to her baby, and she sure wasn't going to be separated from her child, no matter how much money he had to throw around!

"You used me for my money," he muttered. "You got pregnant, fooled me with your stories of your career aspirations, made me believe that you couldn't ever have a baby. Fool me once, Saffron, shame on you. Fool me twice, and you'll wish you hadn't. I just can't believe I let you close, believed that you were different."

She gulped. "Blake, I'm not going to give you my baby. That's ludicrous!"

"What, you'd prefer just to take my money and raise it alone?" He glared at her. "Not going to happen. You've already done more than enough of that. We're talking about a child here."

"I didn't do this for your money, Blake! You want to investigate me, then go for it. Contact my oncologist, I still have his number in my phone. See my notes, figure out for yourself what a miracle this is that I'm even carrying a child right now," Saffron snapped at him, her confidence seeping back, not about to let him push her around, not now. "No one, not even you, Blake, can act like I haven't worked my butt off for what I've achieved. And that was supposed to be my life, my everything." She fought the tears, wanted to stay strong. "I haven't lied to you, I haven't tricked you, I haven't done anything other than try to deal with this baby on my own so you didn't have to. You've made it more than clear that you don't want a family, and I'm going to make sure my baby feels loved."

He was still just staring at her. "Are you finished?"

She turned away, not about to get into a staring competition. "You can think what you want about me, Blake. But you're wrong."

They didn't speak for the rest of the journey. Saffron wanted so desperately to cry, to just give up, but she couldn't. For the first time since she'd set her mind on being a professional dancer, she had a burning desire within her that no one could dampen. She was going to protect her baby, and no one was going to stand in the way of her being an amazing mom. She might not have wanted to get pregnant; she might not be sure how on earth she was going to do it or what the future held. Except that she had a little baby on the way who needed her more than anything else. Everybody needed a person, and she was her baby's person.

She only wished she had a person herself, someone to look out for her and love her unconditionally.

CHAPTER ELEVEN

SAFFRON HAD HIDDEN in the spare room for as long as she could, but it was starting to feel like being left in isolation in the most desolate of prison wards. Besides, if she stayed hidden any longer, she'd probably die of starvation. The little person growing inside her was demanding food all the time—she could hardly keep up.

"Morning," Saffron said as she forced herself to walk through the living space.

Blake looked up from where he was sitting at the dining table, his laptop in front of him and paperwork sprawled. He didn't say a word, just gave her an emotionless kind of stare.

She opened the fridge with a shaky hand, summoning all her strength, not about to let him bully her. She at least wanted to look strong and in control when he was watching her.

"You can't keep me here like a prisoner," she said, continuing what she was doing so she didn't have to look at him.

He ignored her. She hated the silent treatment, would rather he just yell at her and be done with it.

Saffron felt her body temperature rising, just a slow pooling of heat that started deep in her belly and rose slowly up until it flooded her face. She took a deep breath, trying not to explode.

"How dare you," she whispered, forcing her voice as loud as she could make it. "How dare you treat me like some sort of possession, as if you can tell me what to do?"

"You're not leaving, Saffron. That's all there is to it."

"You jerk," she cursed, fingers digging into the counter for support, not scared to stare at him now.

He finally showed something, let her see a flash of anger as he glared at her. "You signed the contract, remember? You were only too happy to live that life, to take my money, hang off my arm and play the doting wife." He sighed loudly. "And let's not forget about that diamond that used to live on your finger."

She swallowed, refusing to cry, to let him see that he'd hurt her. Who was this man? Where was the man she'd fallen for? Who for a moment in time she thought might have felt the same way she did. How had he disappeared so quickly?

"You told me the ring was mine," she choked out.

"And you told me that you didn't need it," he said, voice cold. "Or have you forgotten that already?"

She took her left hand off the counter, her thumb rubbing over the spot where the diamond had once sat. For months, it had been in permanent residence there, fooling her into a sense of…what? Love? She'd never once thought that he'd actually loved her, but she sure had thought she meant something to him. That it hadn't all been make-believe to him. She'd thought they'd leave their fake relationship as friends, maybe even lovers still.

"You know what? You need to leave, give me some space." She was feeling exhausted, didn't have the will or want to fight with Blake.

"And let you just walk out the door? Not a chance."

Hands on hips, she faced him. "I'm not going to run off, Blake, not now that you know. But I do need you to treat me like an actual person instead of some sort of convict."

He pushed back in his seat, eyes on her. "You expect me to believe that you won't run as soon as I turn my back?"

She glared at him. "I'm not going to run." Saffron shrugged. "You know what? Take my wallet so I don't have any money or identification. Is that enough to convince you I won't run?"

Saffron walked out, moving as fast as she could. She only just made it, not even having time to slam the bathroom door shut before she was doubled over the toilet, throwing up so violently she ended up slumped on the floor after. She wriggled down, put her cheek to the cool tiles on the floor.

"Saffron, are you okay?" Blake's deep voice echoed out from the bedroom.

He could probably see her, but she didn't care, didn't have the strength to rise or even look up. The pregnancy was taking everything from her, draining her, making her so ill she could hardly stand it, and the added stress with Blake wasn't helping.

"Go away," she muttered.

There was no other noise, no other words, and she shut her eyes, wishing for sleep but knowing that what she really needed right now was food. Something small and plain to settle her stomach, to give her the strength to face the day. To face Blake.

A door banged shut and still she didn't move, just lay there, wishing things were different, wishing he hadn't found her. Or maybe she should have just faced him, been honest in the first place.

She'd seen the laughter in their eyes, the way they'd enjoyed her pain. She'd been in love, and he'd been sleeping with more women than she could count.

Don't cry. She'd chanted those two words all day, every day. The other dancers were like hyenas, smelling out tears like a predator smelled blood, and she wouldn't give them the satisfaction. They hated her because she was too young, because she'd gotten the lead role too fast, but she didn't care.

"Sticks and stones," she'd muttered, holding her head high, pretending she just didn't care.

But the truth was that Raf's infidelity had almost killed her, because it had drained her of every bit of energy, every bit of confidence she'd had. But she'd survived it, and then she'd never trusted another man again, surrounded herself with a careful little group of friends she could count on.

Blake wasn't going to be the end of her. Blake wasn't going to take anything from her. Blake wasn't going to have the chance to make her feel the way Raf had back then, because she wouldn't let him.

The door banged again, and she forced herself to rise, one foot after another. She splashed water on her face, stared at her reflection in the mirror before braving the living room again. All she needed was something to eat, and she could go hide in bed again, take a long, never-ending shower.

"I put some things on the counter for you," Blake said, zipping his laptop into its Louis Vuitton case as she walked out. "Decaf coffee, a croissant and a bagel. I figured you'd want something."

Saffron could barely hide her surprise. "Thanks."

"Don't even think about leaving," he said, giving her a hard-to-read look. "Just don't."

And with that he was gone, disappearing into his bedroom for a moment before heading out the door.

The apartment was silent, the only noise the barely there hum of the city outside. Saffron took a look inside the bags, the smell sweet but her stomach tender still. She plucked at a piece of croissant, the delicate pastry still warm and tasting like heaven as it dissolved in her mouth.

She hated him. And she loved him.

How could he be so cool one moment then so thoughtful the next? Or maybe he just felt sorry for her. Or maybe she'd honest to God hurt him so bad he couldn't forgive her. For the sake of their unborn child, she sure hoped not.

Blake stayed at work longer than he should have, but it was easier than going home. His assistant had long since packed up and turned everything off except the two matching lamps in his office that were bathing the room in light.

He'd so far fielded calls from his mother wanting them to go out to dinner with her and postponed a business meeting that was supposed to take him out of town, and he was already exhausted with the lies. His life had once been so simple, so easy. He'd worked alongside men he could trust with his life. He'd flown Apaches and extracted teams from live danger areas. His life had been a mixture of adrenaline and fun and passion. And now he was living a life he'd never imagined, a life he'd thought he'd left behind for good. And having to lie about his fake wife who'd thrown him a curveball. He'd been stupid to think a relationship could be anything other than personal, to think he could have lived with a woman like Saffron without getting close, giving part of himself that he'd sworn never to give again. She'd hurt him just when he'd thought he couldn't be hurt by anyone ever again.

Blake poured himself a small shot of whiskey and downed it, wishing the burn of liquor did more for him rather than just temporarily stun his senses. Marrying Saffron was supposed to have made his life easier, supposed to have helped him, given him some breathing space workwise, solved his problems. After a short reprieve, now all it had done was make what was already an existence he didn't want, worse.

What he needed was to fly again, to get up into the sky and see the clouds and feel weightless. To be the rebel he wanted to be, rather than the perfect son forced to conform. His family meant so much to him;

he wanted to care for them and provide for them, but to do that he'd sacrificed his soul. Made a deal with the devil that was his father.

Blake collected his coat and flicked off the lamps. On his way home he collected takeout, choosing Italian since he knew Saffron liked it. He had no idea how he felt about her, what he wanted from her. All he knew was that she was carrying his baby, and that meant he couldn't just kick her to the curb. And he didn't want to.

Saffron had driven him crazy, made him believe in people again, and then she'd gone and betrayed him. Just like Bianca had. Just like his father had.

He steeled his jaw and let himself up to the apartment. At first it took a minute for his eyes to adjust; the lights were on low with lamps illuminating the room. Music played softly from somewhere.

Blake was about to flick the main lights back on, had his hand raised, when he saw her. Saffron had her back to him, arms raised above her head as she stretched then leaped, reaching up, doing something that looked impossible to him on pointed toes before spinning.

He was transfixed, couldn't take his eyes off her.

She dropped forward at the waist, seemed to fall effortlessly down before sweeping back up again and moving side to side. Blake never moved, didn't alert her to the fact he was standing there gaping at her. Because he'd never seen her dance before, and now all he wanted was to watch.

And then she spun in an incredible circle, and he knew he'd been spotted.

"Blake!"

She was breathing heavily, staring at him, eyes wide. It was obvious she'd had no idea he'd been standing there.

"I, ah—" He cleared his throat. "I have dinner. You looked great."

Saffron shrugged, and he noticed how her hand fled protectively to her stomach and stayed there.

"I can't move like I used to, but at least I'm not collapsing into a heap anymore."

Blake set down the food on the table and went to get some utensils and plates.

"You're still wanting to dance?" he asked, wishing he hadn't just asked outright the second the words came out of his mouth. It wasn't exactly something she could just decide to go back to with her stomach rapidly expanding.

"As opposed to having this baby?" she asked, hands on hips.

He hadn't expected her to be so defensive, so protective. She was already like a mama bear, and he admired it, even if he didn't trust her. He liked the flicker of a flame within her, was why he'd been so drawn to her from the beginning.

"You obviously want it," he said, cringing again. For a guy who didn't want to say the wrong thing, he was doing a darn fine job of it. "I just…" He didn't bother trying to finish his sentence or dig himself an even bigger hole.

Saffron blew out a breath, stretching her long limbs out. Her legs were slim but muscled in the way only a dancer's could be, and he dragged his eyes from her.

She was beautiful—that was a given even if he didn't like her anymore. Even if he didn't trust her, didn't want her in his bed, didn't... Who was he kidding? He still wanted her in his bed, only he wanted to yell at her and get everything that was weighing him down off his chest first.

"Yes, I want this baby, Blake. It's the only thing in this world I'm certain about right now." She sat down at the table, opening a container and looking in as he watched. "That and the fact that I'm guaranteed to be doubled over that toilet again at least once before morning, because what I seem to have is all-day sickness. The whole *morning* sickness thing is a lie."

Blake didn't know what to say to her, so he just sat, opening another container and waiting for her to have her first choice. She picked spaghetti Bolognese and he chose the linguine, twirling it around his fork as soon as he'd served himself, beyond hungry. Besides, eating meant he didn't have to make conversation and that he could keep his anger in check. Ever since he'd read Saffron's note it had been bubbling, always on the point of boiling over, and being around her only made it worse. He always stayed in control, was used to remaining calm in the worst situations when he'd been a soldier, but nothing had prepared him for dealing with Saffron.

"Are you worse in the mornings?" Blake asked, setting down his fork.

She looked up at him. "So long as I eat early enough I usually make it through the day. Why?"

He wasn't sure it was the best suggestion, but he was drowning here. With Saffron, without flying, with his mind such a jumble of thoughts he couldn't piece together, he was seriously starting to lose it.

"I want to take you somewhere."

She had a look on her face that told him she no longer trusted his suggestions. "What kind of somewhere?"

"Flying," he told her. "I know we've had a rough— well, whatever we've had has been difficult. But I want you to come flying with me tomorrow. In a helicopter."

If she was shocked she didn't show it. "Fine."

Blake was happy to leave it at that while it felt like a win.

"Have you told anyone?" he asked.

"About the baby?" Saffron was watching him, a forkful of spaghetti hovering in her hand.

When he nodded, she took a visibly big breath. "No. Up until you found out, it was just me and the doctor."

He was pleased to hear that she'd at least seen a doctor, that it wasn't just a home test. Although from how sick she'd been, it wasn't likely to be a mistake. And seeing her dancing, the way she'd touched her stomach… despite the fact that she still looked the same physically, she had looked so instinctively pregnant that he knew without a doubt it was true.

"Saffron, this is a difficult question, but…" He pushed back in his seat, knowing she was going to explode, that he would ruin the sense of calm they were finally experiencing. "You're certain it's mine?"

He'd expected anger, but he hadn't expected the torrent of fury that hit him like a power wave.

"Are you kidding me?" Her words were so low, so quiet, but they hit a mighty punch. She rose, palms flat to the table, leaning forward as she stood, staring him down. "How dare you ask me that?"

When he rose her eyes flashed with such a powerful anger that he should have known to back down rather than try to placate her. Blake reached for her, wanting to tell her that he'd needed to ask, to hear her say it, but the moment he approached her—

"Saffron!" He cursed as her palm made contact with his cheek. It took all his strength not to react, to steel his jaw. But he did grab her wrist; he wasn't about to let her get a swing in again.

"Don't you ever ask me that question again, Blake. Never." She yanked her arm, hard enough to make him release it, her glare like venom.

"It was a fair question," he muttered, annoyed now.

"For an idiot," she snapped.

"Come on, Saffron!" Blake laughed bitterly. "It was a legitimate question! You're asking me to be a father, to parent a child that you know is yours, and I have no idea if…"

"Stop right there," she yelled back. "I never asked you to be a father, Blake. I wanted to give you an out, to raise this child on my own without anything from you, because I knew you didn't want a baby. I wanted to give my child all the love in the world, and I didn't want to back you into a corner, to force you to be someone you didn't want to be."

He sucked in a big lungful of air, calmed down, lowered his voice. "Why? Why give me an out? Why not make me step up? Make me at least reach into my pocket? Isn't that what you wanted?" He shook his head.

"Or was that diamond ring enough money for you?" Blake knew it had been a low blow, but she'd pushed him over the edge and he wanted to hurt her the way she'd hurt him. The pain she'd caused him was real, had pushed him into behaving like someone he wasn't. He knew he was being an idiot, but he couldn't help it.

Saffron had tears swimming in her eyes now, but she didn't back down. Looked so stoic, refusing to show any weakness in front of him, and he had to admire her for that.

"You want the ring back?" she asked, staring at him as she reached into her pocket. "Here it is, Blake. Have it."

She threw it at him and it landed at his feet. He never picked it up, just looked back at her.

"You didn't sell it?"

Saffron laughed, but it was a sad, morose sound. "Maybe it meant more to me than you realized."

She left him in the room alone, with a solitaire in front of his booted feet and a table full of half-eaten Italian.

Blake fisted his hands, clenched his jaw tight and refused to react. He wasn't about to trash his apartment just because he could no longer keep his anger in check.

He bent to collect the ring and stared down at it, remembered the laughter and happiness of that day. Even though it had been a contractual agreement, not love, they'd still had fun. And Blake knew that the way he felt about Saffron wasn't...

He slipped the ring in his back pocket and sat back down at the table.

Betrayal wasn't something he was used to feeling, but he knew there was only one reason it had hit him so hard. Because he felt differently about Saffron. Because he cared about her. Because the feelings he had for her weren't anything to do with a business arrangement.

And that's why what she'd done had hurt so badly.

CHAPTER TWELVE

BLAKE HAD HALF expected Saffron to stay in her room all morning, but when he stepped out of the shower, he heard music playing and knew she was already up. He dressed and headed out, checking his watch for the time. It was a perfect, clear day, and he wanted to get up in the air as soon as they could to make the most of having the chopper for the day. It wasn't often they had one grounded unless it was waiting for maintenance, and he'd instructed his team to keep this one that way even if an urgent booking came through.

"Good morning," he called out.

Saffron was fiddling with her iPod and the music died. She was wearing the same outfit he'd found her in when he'd arrived home the night before, tight black leggings and a skintight top. He wanted to glance at her stomach, see if he could glimpse a hint of roundness there, but she gave him a frosty stare and he changed his mind.

"Are we still going up?"

Blake nodded. Living with Saffron and having so much dislike and distrust between them was like being back in his family home when his mom had been giving his dad the silent treatment. Blake had never asked, but he was certain his father had been unfaithful, knew deep down that was the reason behind why the light in his mother's eyes had slowly faded during his teenage years.

"I don't want it to be like this between us," Blake said.

"Says the man holding me hostage and treating me like a criminal," Saffron said, walking away from him.

He didn't bother answering, let her go and listened to the shower when she turned it on. A quick glance around told him she'd already had breakfast, or at least something to eat. Blake thought about ordering up something for himself but changed his mind. He'd collect some food and coffee on their way past to take up for the day.

Spending the day out with Saffron might not have been his best idea, but they were stuck together regardless of what he wanted, and he was ready to man up and deal with it. Even if catching feral cats sounded a whole lot easier than dealing with Saffron right now.

Saffron forced a smile as she stared at the helicopter in front of her. As a dancer, she was used to plastering on a smile and making herself look happy even when she wasn't. And if she was going to survive Blake, she needed to start thinking positively and acting as if she was happy—maybe one day she'd trick her own brain. She had no idea how long she was going to be stuck with him if he became intent on staying in control where their baby was concerned.

"All set?" Blake asked.

She thought about all the times they'd pretended together—that they were a happy couple, that everything was great between them. Saffron knew why that had worked, though, why it had seemed so natural and easy. She'd loved his company, liked the man he was and everything he believed in. And because they'd both entered into their arrangement with eyes wide-open, everything had seemed transparent.

"Let's do this."

She'd never been up in a helicopter, and her legs were a little wobbly at the thought of being so high in the air. Up front. With Blake as her pilot. Saffron gulped.

"You okay?"

She nodded. "Uh-huh."

"For what it's worth, I'm sorry about last night."

She brushed his apology off, not wanting to engage. The last thing she wanted was to argue with him before they went up in the air, and she wasn't ready to forgive him yet, wasn't sure when she'd ever be.

She followed his lead, keeping her head ducked down even though the rotors were still stationary. She'd been reading up about helicopter safety on her iPhone overnight, so she was fully briefed and didn't have to keep asking Blake questions.

Once they were seated, he leaned over her and helped to buckle her in. She held her breath, glanced away, but when she looked back he was still fumbling, his hand grazing her stomach.

"Sorry," he mumbled.

Saffron instinctively sat back, pulled away from him. "It's fine." Once, she'd loved any excuse to touch him and liked whenever he'd touched her. She still *wanted* to want it, but she doubted it could ever be like that again.

"I've done that a hundred times for other passengers. This is crazy." He finally snapped her safely in and sat back, doing his own safety restraints.

Saffron sat back and listened to the helicopter fire into life. He passed her a headset to wear, and when they were finally rising into the air, she clutched her seat as the ground receded below.

"How you doing, rookie?" he asked, grinning across at her.

Saffron forgot all about the ground disappearing below them when Blake flashed her his big smile. She hadn't seen a smile light up his face like that since before they'd gone out to their last cocktail party, the night she'd ended up in the restroom and found out she was pregnant.

His burst of happiness hit her like a jolt, reminding her of why she'd liked him so much, why she'd wanted to stay with him and why she'd been so afraid of hurting him. Of breaking his trust.

As he expertly maneuvered the chopper, she stared at him, unable to tear her eyes away. He was happy. Genuinely, one hundred percent happy. And it showed her a different side to him.

"You're different when you're flying," she said, still watching him.

He looked at her. "How's that?"

"Everything about you," she told him. "Even when you're just sitting, there's a bit of a smile hovering, there's a lightness in your eyes. You're just…" Saffron frowned. "Different. I can't explain it."

He was looking straight ahead now, and she admired his strong, chiseled jaw, the handsome side profile. She might not like the way he'd treated her, but deep down she got it, understood why he was so hurt by what she'd done. She only wished he'd trusted her enough after spending three months with her as his wife, instead of labeling her a gold digger without at least giving her a chance to explain properly.

"That's because this is the first time you've seen the real me," Blake said, not moving a muscle, staring straight ahead.

Saffron turned away, stared out the window, where everything started to blur a little as they moved fast through the sky. She'd been nervous about going up, but now the helicopter ride was the last thing on her mind.

"Why did you give it up?" she asked. "How could you give what you love up like that? You had a choice, didn't you?"

Blake never answered her, and she never asked again.

They'd been up in the air for what felt like forever, but Saffy still hadn't had enough time to think. She doubted she ever would, not when it came to Blake. Something about him made her crazy, made her feel things she was scared of and had thought would never happen to her.

"Descending," Blake said, loud and clear through the headset.

He hadn't spoken a word to her since just after take-off, and Saffron felt a weird kind of divide between them. There was so much she wanted to ask him, wanted to say. Only nothing felt right when she sounded it out in her head first.

They landed in a field, a ranch from what she could see, and Saffron stayed quiet as Blake did his thing. When he slipped his headset off, she did the same, watching as he exited the helicopter and then opened her door and held up his hand to help her out.

Saffron took it, letting him guide her down. She stretched, taking a look around.

"Let's go," Blake said.

"Where?"

"For a walk over there." He pointed. "We can have lunch under that tree."

Saffron didn't question him, just followed, staying a step or two behind him and looking at their surroundings.

"Where are we?" she asked when he stopped under a pretty oak tree, its branches waving down low and shielding them from the intense sunshine.

"My family used to own this ranch," Blake said. "It was somewhere we came over the summer or just for a weekend getaway. My best childhood memories were spent here."

Saffron listened as she continued to look around. She touched the trunk of the tree, ran her fingers across its gnarled bark. There were indentations in it, markings that she couldn't quite figure out.

"That's me," Blake said, standing close behind her.

She could feel his breath, the warmth of his big body as it cast a deeper shadow over her, making her own body hum even though she tried so darn hard to fight it.

"You?" she managed.

"Yeah." He leaned past her, his arm skimming hers as he traced his fingers across the same spot hers had just trailed over. "I etched my name in here a few times. I used to ride out here on a cute little pony who was always happy to go as fast as I wanted, and when I got older, I landed my first solo here."

Saffron was aware of everything, could feel his body even though he was no longer touching her, her breath loud in her own ears, heart thumping. There was nothing she could do to stop the way she reacted to him.

"My dad saw how much I loved it here, knew how much pleasure I got from flying out here, practicing everything I learned."

"He didn't want that?"

Blake made a grunting noise, and she knew he was stepping away. It gave her breathing space, but she liked having him near, wanted him to stay closer.

"It was around the time we'd started to butt heads a lot. All the time," Blake said. Saffron turned and saw him hit the ground, his big frame sprawled out. He had one leg out straight, the other bent, resting on one arm as the other plucked at a strand of grass. "I started to talk about what I wanted to do with my life, and that didn't tally up with what he wanted. He went from loving my interest in helicopters to despising it, because every time I went up in the air it made me more determined to carve my own path."

Saffron sat down, leaning against the trunk she'd been studying. "I'm sorry."

He laughed and raised an eyebrow. "What for?"

"I'm sorry that you had a dad who couldn't support your dreams. That he had a hold on you that you still haven't been able to shake."

Blake's stare hardened. "I lost that hold, Saffron. I lost it for years, but in the end it was a hidden choke hold that I'd never truly escaped. It started back then, tightened when he paid Bianca off to leave me and then again when he died."

"You need more of this. To remind yourself of what you love."

If she'd been his wife, his real wife, it would be what she'd insist on.

"Anyway, why am I telling you all that stuff?"

She wasn't buying his laugh, knew it was no joke to him. "Because you wanted me to see the real you," Saffron said quietly. "You wanted to show me who you really are."

"You sound so sure about that." Blake opened a bag and pulled out a couple of Cokes, holding one out for her.

"Can I ask you something?" Saffron said, her heart starting its rapid beat again, near thudding from her chest.

"Shoot."

"Did you ever feel anything for me? I mean, anything real?"

Blake had the Coke halfway to his mouth, but he slowly lowered it. "Did you?"

"I asked you first," she insisted, wishing she hadn't asked him but needing, *craving*, the answer.

"You mean did I want you in my bed? Did I want you at my side, on my arm?"

She sucked in a breath. "I know you wanted me in your bed—that's the only thing I'm sure about. But…" Saffron paused. "Was the way we looked at each other real? The way we…"

This time when her voice trailed off she didn't bother to finish her sentence. What was she trying to say?

"Whatever we had was just part of a deal," Blake said matter-of-factly. "Was I attracted to you? Of course. Any hot-blooded man would have been. But we didn't have anything more than sex and a contract."

Saffron had tears burning in her eyes like acid, making her want to scream in pain. But she stayed silent, swallowed them down. She'd thought the feeling had been reciprocated, that he'd felt something real for her, like she had for him, but she'd been wrong.

"Why, did you expect something else?" he asked.

Saffron bravely shook her head. "No. I was just curious." Sobs racked her body, jarred her ribs and her shoulders and every other part of her. But she kept her chin up, sucked back silent gasps to stop herself from giving in, from letting him see how much he could hurt her. *Just like dancing*, she told herself. Crying over real pain, over a real injury, was one thing, but that was the only thing any dancer would ever shed a tear over.

"Do you have anything to eat in there?" she asked instead, desperate to change the subject.

Blake nodded. "Sure. You hungry?"

Saffron nodded. She'd rather eat than talk any more.

Blake had shown her his true colors, how happy he could be in the air, what made his heart sing. Only she'd expected, *hoped*, that there would be more. That he'd say something else, tell her that he felt something, *anything*, for her.

Because even though he'd hurt her and she'd tried to run back home, what she felt for Blake was real. It always had been. She'd slowly started to fall in love with him, a man so beautiful yet damaged by a father and an ex-lover who had done him more harm than good, and a career that he'd loved yet one that had shattered parts of him emotionally, as well.

But that man wasn't hers to take, wasn't hers to love. She was having his baby, and that was it. He didn't love her back—maybe he didn't even care for her beyond what she meant to him on paper.

And that hurt so bad it made her injury seem like a cakewalk.

She touched her hand to her stomach, something she was doing instinctively all the time now. If it wasn't for the baby, she'd be long gone now, and Blake would be a distant memory. *Or would he?*

Maybe without the baby everything would have stayed the same. They'd still be living in their little faux bubble of a marriage.

"Sandwich?" Blake asked, leaning forward and passing it over.

"Sure," she murmured, not bothering to ask what was in it. She didn't care.

"You sure you're okay? You're feeling all right?" Blake asked.

Saffron forced a smile. "I'm fine. Thanks for bringing me here."

"You're the first person I've ever flown out here," he said, taking another sandwich out and holding it in his hands, watching her.

"I thought…" She didn't know what she'd thought. Did that mean something—was it supposed to mean something?

"I want our baby to start flying young," Blake said, surprising her with his smile. "It's all I ever wanted, and if I'm going to share it with anyone, who better than my child?"

Of course. It was the baby. That was the only reason he'd brought her. She'd been fooling herself that maybe he wanted to talk to her, to get away from the city with her for a reason, but now it was all about the baby.

So much for him not wanting to be a dad.

"We need to figure this out, how it's going to work," Saffron said, not seeing any point in putting it off. "You don't have to do this, playing the dad role. It was my choice to keep the baby, and I'm okay with that."

The happy lilt of Blake's mouth disappeared, replaced with a much tighter line. "Oh, yeah? So I could just write a card on birthdays or maybe just Christmas."

Saffron refused to take the bait, didn't want to end up arguing with him when she had no chance of winning.

"What I'm trying to say is that I want custody. I don't want to fight about it, but a child needs to be with its mom," she said, bravely meeting his gaze head-on and refusing to shrink away from him. "You'll always be welcome, I'm not trying to tell you to stay away, I'm just saying that..."

"Oh, I hear what you're saying," Blake muttered. "You're laying it on pretty thick."

"Blake! You don't even want this child! You don't want to be a dad!" Saffron didn't know how to keep her cool, what to say. He was driving her crazy. "We're not a real couple. There is no way for this to work."

Blake stood and stared down at her, his shadow imposing. "I wasn't under any illusion there."

He stormed off, and she didn't bother calling out. She wasn't about to follow him, either. Instead she sat there, picking at her sandwich even though the last thing she felt like was eating.

How had her life turned out like this? She was sitting here all high and mighty about how much she wanted this baby, and she did, but she wasn't *actually* ready to be a mother. All she wanted was to be back on stage, back dancing. Saying yes to performing at Pierre's retirement party. And instead she was growing a big round belly and thinking about names and genders and how on earth she was going to provide for the little future love of her life.

Saffron bit hard on her lower lip. Everything was a mess. She didn't want Blake and his money, but if he didn't let her go back home, then she'd have no other choice but to take whatever he offered. But if he even for a second wanted to take her child from her, take control... She pushed the thoughts away. It wouldn't come to that, because she wouldn't let it.

Suddenly Blake was storming back in her direction, his face like thunder. As she watched, he gathered everything up and marched it back to the helicopter. Saffron stood and reluctantly followed—it wasn't as if she had an alternate ride home.

"We're going," he said.

She shook her head. "Why can't we stay? I think you should blow off some steam before…"

He spun around, only a few feet from her, his hands clenched at his sides, his anger palpable.

"You know why I brought you here?" he asked.

Saffron stayed still, stared at the bulge in his neck where a vein was about to pop out from under his skin.

"I thought we could start fresh, put the past behind us. I brought you here because this place means something to me, and I wanted to show it to you." He ran a hand through his hair, anger still radiating from every part of him. "I wanted to see if you actually cared about me, whether we could at least agree on something to do with this child, *our* child."

"I do care about you, Blake," she said softly, telling him the truth. "You're the one who just acted like what we had meant nothing, that it wasn't real."

"Yeah? You care about *me*?" He laughed, but it sounded forced. "Well, you've got a real strange way of showing it."

"Blake…" she started. He'd just been the one saying there was nothing real between them, yet now suddenly everything was her fault!

"Get in the helicopter, Saffron," he demanded as

he spun back around. "Or find your own way back to the city."

She wanted to believe that he wouldn't actually leave her behind, but given his mood, she wasn't sure about anything right now.

"I'm sorry," she said as she followed him.

"Yeah, me, too," he muttered back.

Saffron took his hand to guide her into her seat, but she never looked at him when he settled beside her and started to flick switches, the engine humming into life. Things had gone from worse to bad to worse again, and there was nothing she could do to change it.

CHAPTER THIRTEEN

THEY'D BEEN SILENT since the ranch. Saffron had goose pimples rippling across her skin whenever she looked at him, but still they never uttered a word. They'd landed, he'd helped her out, driven her home, and now he was about to head out the door for takeout. She knew this because he'd phoned and ordered Thai, and she'd been sitting in the same room as him, snuggled under a mohair blanket while he'd been positioned at the dining table furiously banging away at his keyboard. She was half expecting him to need a new machine in the morning the way he'd been treating it.

"I'll be back soon," Blake said.

When she looked up, he was standing near the door, his eyes still shining with anger. Or at least she was guessing that's what it was.

"Okay." Saffron forced a smile, but he was still staring at her and his gaze was unnerving.

"That's it. That's all you've got to say to me?" His voice was so low, so quiet it was lethal.

Saffron gulped, wished she knew the right thing to say. But the truth was that she'd tried to run from a man with trust issues, and she had no idea what to say to make that situation better.

"I'm sorry. I'm sorry for what I did, Blake, I am," Saffron said, forcing the words out. "But I'm not sorry for what happened, because it's nothing short of a miracle, no matter how scary it is."

He went to turn and she breathed a sigh of relief, but he hadn't moved his body halfway to the door when he was staring at her again. He didn't say anything, just stared, but she could feel the unsaid words hanging between them, knew he was bottling a whole heap of something inside.

"Why can't you just accept that what happened was an innocent mistake? That I never…" She didn't bother finishing. They'd been through all this—there were only so many times she could apologize for what she'd done.

"You want to know why?"

Blake's words sent shivers through her. She was scared of the way he felt, of what he made her feel. The way she felt about him, despite everything.

"Why?" she whispered as he spun around to face her. She'd asked; it wasn't as though she could walk away from him now.

"Because I loved you." He hurled the words at her, and she instantly felt their sting. "I lied before, okay? I fell for you because I thought you were different. I was stupid enough to think that what we had meant more than…"

"Some stupid contract?" she said for him, finding her voice. "I didn't hear you ever offering to rip that up. Not once, during all the times we connected, when I felt like we were something more, did you *ever* make out like you wanted to make what we had real."

It was unfair—she'd agreed to their marriage bargain right from the start to help her stay in New York, but he was hurting her and it was all she had. Because she *had* felt the same, had thought she was falling for him, that something between them was real. That it wasn't all just about their stupid agreement.

"Why didn't you tell me," she finally said when he never spoke. "Why didn't you say something, *anything*? Why couldn't you have just done something to show me?"

"What difference would it have made?" Blake asked, his tone cold, blunt. "What would it have changed between us?"

It would have changed everything. Saffron squared her shoulders. "It would have made a difference," she said, knowing in her heart that it would have. That if she'd just known for sure that he felt about her the same way she was feeling about him…

"What, you would have felt bad about using me? About lying to me?" He laughed. "Would it have changed how guilty you're feeling right now?"

"No," she said simply, tears threatening to spill even though she was trying so hard to fight them. "Because then I would have known that my own feelings were real, that you didn't just think of me like…"

"Like what, Saffron?" he bellowed. "I've treated you with nothing but respect and kindness! I treated you like my real wife, didn't I?"

"I was in love with you, too!" she sobbed. "How could you not have realized how I felt? How could you have been so blind?" Saffron turned away then, couldn't look at him any longer. She was still in love with him, despite everything, and it broke her heart to argue the way they were. "All you had to do was say something, Blake. Instead you hid behind your daddy issues, kept acting like you could never be the man you were so good at pretending to be with me." She shook her head. "You kept saying you couldn't settle down, couldn't ever be a real husband, but in the almost four months I spent with you, I saw a man who could have had whatever he wanted. A man who could have been a darn good *real* husband if he'd wanted to be. You didn't exactly make it look hard."

He stared at her, but she was on a roll now, couldn't stop.

"You're hiding behind your past, not letting yourself live, because you're too scared of change, of what might happen, of being hurt and exposing yourself to that kind of real love. I'm not judging you—heaven knows I'm no different—but things have changed, Blake. Things changed between us long before I took a positive pregnancy test."

"Just go," he finally said, his voice hoarse, unrecognizable. "If you want to go back home to raise our baby that bad, just go."

She hated the emptiness to his tone, the hollowness. It was the same way she felt inside, like a soft toy with all the stuffing knocked from her. "After all that effort to keep me, now you're going to just give up without a fight?" Saffy knew she was being antagonistic, but it was true.

"What do you want from me, Saffron?" he whispered, eyes level with her own.

"I want you to want me, Blake!" she told him, voice shaking. "I want you to fight for me. Show me that I'm not just some asset to you."

"You want me to fight for you?" he muttered, marching toward her, stopping barely an inch away, towering over her, his body almost brushing hers, his gaze fierce. "Consider me in the ring then."

Just as she was about to reply, about to stand her ground, Blake's hand cupped the back of her head, the other snaking around her waist. He pulled her forward, dropped his mouth over hers and kissed her as if it was the final kiss of their lives.

"Stop," she protested, hands to his chest, halfheartedly pushing him away.

Blake didn't let up, kept kissing her. "This is me fighting," he said against her lips. "You want to go, you pull back."

Saffron tried—she wanted to push him away completely. She wanted to forget about him and get on with her life without him, but she couldn't. Because from the moment they'd met, something had ignited between them that she hadn't wanted to admit, and that spark was far from being extinguished. And he'd just told her that he'd loved her. Admitted that what she'd felt between them had been real.

"We can't do this," she whispered, finally parting her mouth from his, dropping her head to his chest, letting him cradle her as she absorbed the warmth from his body.

"You're my wife," he murmured, lips to the top of her head, soft against her hair. "We can do anything we like."

Saffron wanted to give in, wanted to believe him, but… "I can't. We can't." She shook her head, palms to his chest again, forcing some distance between them, needing to look up at him. "We need to talk. Actually talk. Not yell at each other, or make assumptions. I need to talk, and you need to listen. We can't just bury our heads in the sand. Not this time, Blake."

Blake took Saffron's hand and led her to the sofa, sitting down and waiting for her to do the same. He felt as if he'd just stepped off a roller coaster; his body was exhausted and his mind was a jumble. The past few days hadn't exactly been easy, had drained everything from him. And now he had to dig deep and not push his feelings away like he'd been doing for most of his adult life.

"So let's talk."

Her smile was shy as he watched her, and he sat back, glanced away, hoping to make her feel more comfortable. All he'd done since he'd hauled her back from the airport was to tell her what he thought, bully her, throw his weight around. And that wasn't him, wasn't the man he wanted to be. It was the man his father had been. The kind of cold, unfeeling, calculating man his father had shown himself to be time and time again.

Which was exactly why he'd never wanted to be in

this position, to be a dad or a husband. Blake pushed the thoughts away, focused on Saffron. Whether he wanted to be a dad or not was irrelevant now, because he was going to become one regardless. What she'd said had hit home, was true even though he didn't want to admit it. He had been hiding behind his past, living his life with a raft of excuses about what he couldn't do. And that needed to end now. If he wanted to step up and be a parent, not lose the woman who'd finally made him feel, then he needed to be a man.

"I never lied to you, Blake, and we can't move forward unless you believe that."

He nodded. "If I wasn't starting to believe that, we wouldn't be having this conversation." Blake wanted to blame her, but she didn't deserve it.

He watched as she blinked, staring down at her hands. There should be a ring on her finger, a ring to show every other man in the world that she was taken. Their relationship might have been fake to start with, but he was only kidding himself that he didn't want her as his, and he wanted it clear to every man alive that she wasn't available. Suddenly the fact that there wasn't a ring sitting against her skin made him furious.

"I'm scared of being a mom, of holding this baby when it's born and trying to figure out what to do with it, but for the first time I can remember, I want something as bad as I want to dance." She sighed. "And that scares me as much as it excites me."

Blake reached for her hand, squeezed it when he saw a trickle of tears make their way down her cheeks. If she'd wanted to show him what an idiot he'd been, she was doing a fine job. There was no way he could feel worse about his behavior if he tried.

"I'm sorry," he said, clearing his throat, wanting to do better, knowing it might be his only chance after what he'd said. "I'm sorry, Saffron. If I could take back half the things I've said to you, I would."

She nodded, eyes shut as she took a big, shuddery breath. "I want to dance so bad, but I also want this baby, Blake," she said. "I can't explain it, but it's so powerful, so instinctive."

Blake brushed the tears away with his knuckles when she opened her eyes, gentle as he touched her skin. He got how hard it was to open up and be honest, and she looked as though it was hurting her real bad to say how she felt.

"I've been an idiot," he said, finally getting the words off his chest. "I don't exactly find it easy to trust, but you didn't deserve the way I treated you. You deserve an apology."

"You're right," she said, "but I should have told you instead of running away. I made myself look guilty of the crime—you just put the pieces together. And you're not the only one who's said things they regret."

"Why?" he asked. "I still don't understand why you decided to run. I'm not going to lose the plot about it again, but you need to explain it. I need to be on the same page as you, Saffron. Why did you run?"

Her eyes filled with fresh tears as he stared into them, but this time he didn't brush them away, didn't try to comfort her. This time he just needed to listen, and she looked as if she was ready to talk.

"I was terrified you wouldn't want the baby," she whispered, no longer meeting his gaze. "That you wouldn't want anything to do with our child, and I didn't want this baby to feel unwanted."

"What?" He held her hand tighter, fought the anger as it started to bubble within him again. Blake waited a second, not wanting to overreact, needing to calm down before he spoke. He'd wanted her to be honest, and she was, which meant he couldn't judge her for her thoughts. But still, keeping a lid on the way he was feeling wasn't easy.

"I know how strongly you feel about not having a family. How determined you were *not* to be a father, to not ever be put in that position. Not to let your heart be broken by a woman, too."

He took a slow breath, not wanting to snap her head off. "I would never, ever not want my child to be born. And I'd never make a child feel unwanted. Not my own flesh and blood. *Never.*"

"But…"

"I'm terrified of the idea of being a dad, knowing that there is a baby coming into this world with half my DNA," Blake continued, needing to get it all off his chest before it strangled him. "I don't want to be a dad because I had a terrible example from my own father, and I don't want to become that kind of man. To have a child of mine feel such hatred toward me that the moment he finds out his own father has died he feels a sense of relief."

Blake stood, turned away, gulped away an emotion

that he'd never let out before. Something he always extinguished long before it threatened to surface.

"Blake?"

Saffron's hand was on his back, her touch light, her voice kind. But he didn't want her to see him lose it like this, break down when he was usually so strong, so incapable of anything getting under his skin.

"Just give me a sec," he muttered.

"You can't help the way you feel," Saffron whispered, her hand snaking around his waist, slowly, turning him toward her. "Whatever you felt when he died, it's okay. You can't keep all that bottled inside."

Blake shut his eyes, squeezed the tears away. He was not going to cry, not in front of Saffron. Not ever. Tears over anything other than an atrocity weren't for men who'd seen terrifying things, seen what he'd seen when he was serving. There was no way he was shedding tears, not now, not ever. Not over some stupid feelings he'd had for his father.

He opened his eyes and stared into dark eyes that seemed to see straight into his soul. Blake opened his mouth, wanted to tell her she was wrong, but instead a wave of guilt, of emotion and sadness and regret, hit him like a tidal wave. A gulp of tears burst out, the emotion flooring him, his knees buckling as everything he'd held back came pouring from him.

"Shh," he heard Saffron murmur as she held him, cradling his head to her stomach as he stayed on his knees, felled like an oak tree slain at the heart of its trunk in front of her. "Shh."

Her hands were warm, her touch so gentle, but Blake

couldn't stop, the sobs racking his body as the pain slowly washed over him. He didn't try to speak, couldn't get anything out except the grief he'd held so tight for so long.

"Tell me," she said. "Get it all out. You need to share it with someone. Just say the words."

Blake steadied his breathing, felt the rise and fall of Saffron's stomach against his cheek. He had no idea what had come over him, but he couldn't believe what he'd just done. And then he shut his eyes again, tears no longer engulfing him.

His baby was in there. Saffron had been holding him, comforting him, and he hadn't even realized how close he'd been to his little unborn child. It gave Blake the strength to rise and face her again, this woman who'd turned his life upside down and made him feel things, move forward instead of just treading water. If he was going to be a dad, he needed to be honest with himself. And with Saffron.

"I hated him," Blake finally said, keeping hold of her hand and drawing her back onto the sofa with him, keeping her in his arms so he could cradle her warm body against his. "I saw so much while I was serving, realized I was actually living the life I was supposed to live, making a difference in the world and flying the machines that made me feel so amazing. The only stumbling block in my life was my father. And the woman who'd hurt me, made me feel stupid and vulnerable in a way that only my dad had been able to do before."

"Did he ever accept what you did?" she asked, head

to his chest. "Ever give you praise for the career you'd made for yourself?"

Blake didn't want to look at her, just wanted to touch, to feel her there with him. It made it easier for him to say the words he'd only ever said in his head before.

"I grew up around helicopters and planes, and I loved it. I guess that's why Dad thought I was a natural fit for the company, or maybe it was just because I was his firstborn that he felt that way. Before I started to fly myself, at the ranch, I was trailing around after him at the hangars, checking out our stock and soaking up every word he or anyone else in the know said about them. It probably never crossed his mind that I wouldn't do what he wanted me to do."

"But you loved actually flying more than the company, right?"

Blake dropped a kiss into her hair, craving her, suddenly needing to stay connected after so long spent trying to push her away.

"I was addicted to flying from my first flight, and I was a natural in a helicopter, just like I told you today. After he sent my fiancée running for the hills with a pocket full of cash, I knew I had to get away. I hated him so much, and I found my place in the world. I had an amazing job in an industry that needed me, I got to fly every day and I had a new family with my army buddies."

Blake paused, thought back to how he'd felt the day his dad had passed. "He never supported my dreams or wanted to hear anything about my life, not unless I went to work for him. He didn't want to hear about the lives I'd saved, the men I'd flown into dangerous situations to help protect our country that he claimed to love so much. And he sure didn't want to hear about how bad it affected me, that half the time I couldn't sleep for weeks after I returned from a tour."

"You can't help that you hated him, Blake. We feel what we feel, and there's nothing we can do about it," she said.

"Things just got worse and worse, until I couldn't even stand being in the same room as him. Not even at Thanksgiving or Christmas, and I know it broke my mom's heart, which was something I never wanted to do."

Saffron was stroking his shoulder, her face to his chest as she listened to him.

"I have nightmares about what I saw when I was serving, dreams that will haunt me forever, but I'm the type of person who's okay with that because I want to know the realities of our world. I don't want to live in a bubble where rich people have everything and don't care about the world or real people or the next generation." He blew out a breath, amazed how fast the words were falling from his mouth now that he'd started talking, how desperate he suddenly was to share them. "When I heard his helicopter had gone down, that he was presumed dead, it was like a lead weight had been lifted from my chest, a weight I hadn't even known was there. It was a feeling I'll never forget for as long as I live."

Blake stayed silent for a moment, regretted the thoughts he was having, hated the pain he felt at what came next.

"And then I found out that my brother had been flying with him. That it wasn't just my dad, but my brother, too," he murmured. "In that one second, I wished so bad that it was all a mistake, felt so guilty that I'd been relieved about Dad disappearing off the face of the planet."

"You were close to your brother?"

Blake nodded. "My brother was my best friend growing up. We were so different and we fought like crazy sometimes, but I loved him. I'd do anything to have him back, would have traded anything and everything to change places with him and be on the chopper that day. I still would."

"You can't think like that," Saffron said, pushing back and looking up at him. "That's one thing you just can't let yourself think."

"Yeah, I can," he grumbled. "He was with my dad that day for work. If I hadn't been so pigheaded about making my own way in the world, it would have been me with him flying out to meet a new corporate client, not my brother. It would have been me missing, and he'd still be here."

Saffron didn't say anything, just kept stroking his shoulder, her fingers running lightly across his T-shirt.

"It should have been me," he whispered.

"But it wasn't, and I'm glad," Saffron said, her voice soft yet fierce at the same time. "Because then I would never have met you, and we wouldn't have a little baby on the way. This little baby that is an absolute miracle."

Blake touched her stomach, laid his hand flat there, the first time he'd done it, and it calmed him. Made him feel a crazy mix of emotions, protective over the tiny being he'd helped to create that was cradled in her belly.

"I'm scared," he admitted.

"Me, too," she whispered back. "But you're not your father, and I'll never let you turn into him. This baby is going to be whatever he or she wants to be. All we have to do is love and nurture and care for this little person. It's all he or she will need."

"You sound so sure." Blake looked down at her, realizing how stupid he'd been to have almost let her go. She'd been so close to just slipping from his life.

"Being in love and loving is the only thing I am sure about right now."

And just like that, it was Saffron with tears in her eyes and him wanting to be strong for her, and everything else fell away except the woman in his arms.

CHAPTER FOURTEEN

"So what are we going to do?" Saffron asked, closing her eyes and enjoying the sensation of Blake strumming his fingertip across her skin. She snuggled in closer to him, the sheets covering their lower halves, their uppers bare.

"Not much more of that," Blake said with a chuckle. "It can't be good for the baby."

She laughed. "It's fine for the baby. I checked with the doctor."

"I'm glad to hear you had your priorities straight when you were asking questions about our unborn child!" Blake flicked her, his touch no longer so soft and lingering.

Saffron pushed up on her elbows, looking down on Blake. "I'm serious. What *are* we going to do?"

"We're going to get married. For real this time," Blake said, pushing up and pressing a kiss to her lips, his smile serene, a peacefulness on his face that she hadn't seen before. "No registry office this time around."

She giggled when he tickled her. "I can't exactly wear white. I think the tummy will give away my virtue, or lack of."

Blake pulled her closer, rolling them over until she was pinned beneath him, his arms imprisoning her on each side.

"I can't promise that I'm going to be a good dad, but I'm going to try my hardest," Blake said, staring into her eyes. "I don't want to be my father. I don't want to ever be that kind of man, but I want this baby." She smiled, seeing the emotion on his face, the tears welling in his eyes that mirrored hers. "And I want you."

She slipped her arms out and slung them around his neck, needing to hold him, to pull him closer. "I love you, Blake," she whispered.

He dropped a soft, gentle kiss to her lips. "I love you, too."

Saffron smiled so hard, she couldn't have wiped it from her mouth if she'd tried. "I didn't think I'd ever hear you say that. Not to me, not to anyone."

He held her tighter, sighing against her skin. "Me neither, sweetheart. But then I never expected to come across a woman like you. The gloves are off, Saffron. I'm all yours."

"All mine," she murmured as he planted a full kiss to her lips. "And don't you forget it."

EPILOGUE

BLAKE COULDN'T TAKE his eyes off Saffron. *His wife.* His cheeks were sore from smiling so hard, watching as she somehow floated across the stage, twirling and leaping and…he had no idea what any of the moves she was doing were, but whatever it was, she looked incredible. Seeing her like this reminded him again of what he'd been so close to losing, how stubborn he'd been about the only woman who'd ever managed to see the real him.

"Mama."

He glanced down at the little girl sitting in his lap, clapping her pudgy little hands at least every other minute. She'd wriggled to start with, but from the moment her mom had graced the stage, she'd been transfixed, quiet as a mouse as she sat on his knee in the front row.

"Yes, Mama," Blake whispered back to her. "Isn't she amazing?"

"Mama," Isabella said again, clapping and tipping her head back so she was resting against him as she looked up.

Blake focused on Saffron again as she did something else incredible before stopping, her feet no longer moving, her pose perfect as the lights slowly went out. Within minutes the lights were rising again, flooding the theater at the same time that Saffron stood in the center of the stage, the crowd bursting into applause. Then she was joined by the other dancers, but Blake only had eyes for his wife, unable to drag his gaze away for even a second.

He couldn't believe how much she'd changed him, how different he felt from the man he'd been only a few years ago. He held Isabella tight, loving every second of having his little daughter close. She was the best thing that had ever happened to him, even if he was fiercely protective of her, so in love with her that it hurt sometimes.

"Go see Mama," Isabella demanded, wriggling so hard he could barely keep hold of her.

"Come on, let's go then," Blake said, scooping her up in one arm and holding her against his chest. She tapped his head.

"Sho-sho," she said, smiling up at him. Blake never had a chance of saying no to her, not when she looked the spitting image of her mother with her beautiful dark eyes, deepest red hair and angelic smile.

He lifted her up onto his shoulders, which was what she'd been asking for in her own little language, chuckling to himself about the fact he had a tutu all ruffled around the back of his neck. She was just like her mom when it came to ballet, too, and very opinionated about what she liked to wear. Tonight she'd wanted to look like a real ballerina, but she wasn't a pink girl, so it was a dark blue outfit with a tutu and matching shoes covered in bling and she looked impossibly cute.

"Mama!" Isabella squealed when she spotted her mother.

"Hey!" Saffron came running, her face alive as it always was when she was on a high after a performance. Blake hadn't seen her dance live in a show until Isabella was a year old, and now he hated to miss seeing her on stage. Although his daughter was very opinionated about being left home with a sitter, preferring to snuggle up in their bed.

"You were amazing," Blake said, pulling her tight into his arms for a quick kiss before he was pushed out of the way by his daughter, who now only had eyes for her mother.

"Hey, beautiful! Did you enjoy it?" Saffron asked her.

Isabella tucked her face against her mom's chest for a moment before pushing back and touching her mom's cheeks and then patting her hair. Saffron's hair was almost always down when she was home, but when she was performing, it was always pulled up tighter off her face and Isabella seemed transfixed with it.

"You know, if we were normal people, we'd have her with a sitter so we could go out for a late dinner," Blake said, laughing because he knew exactly what kind of reaction he was going to get from his wife.

"Wash your mouth out!" Saffron scolded, pulling Isabella's head tight to her chest and covering one of her ears. It was a constant joke between them, and even though Blake suggested it regularly, they both preferred to take Isabella out with them whenever they could. Especially now that Saffron was back dancing and he was so busy with the company during the day—they juggled as best they could, but after hours they liked to be a tight family unit. Unless his mother begged to have her granddaughter to stay, which usually resulted in a little girl packing her suitcase immediately and demanding to go.

"How about a quick ice cream on the way home instead?" Blake asked, reaching for his daughter and pulling her off Saffron.

"Yay!" Isabella squealed.

Saffron nodded. "Sounds good. Just let me change and say goodbye to everyone."

Blake waited for his wife, chuckling to himself how much his life had changed. Meeting Saffron had changed everything, made him realize how lucky he was in so many ways.

"You know, I took your mommy out for ice cream when I first met her."

"Mommy love ice cream," Isabella said, patting his arm, her beautiful dark eyes looking tired. Not that his daughter would admit to being sleepy for a second, though.

"Mommy was so beautiful then she took my breath away, and she still does," Blake replied without a hint of a lie. "I was a fool once, but when I found out you were in Mommy's tummy, I stopped being so stupid. I asked her to marry me."

"Tell me, story, Daddy."

"What story?" Saffron asked, slipping her arms around him from behind.

Blake grabbed her with his free hand, snaking it around her and pulling her close.

"I'm just telling Bella about when we were first together. Every time we're alone and you're dancing, I tell her how I fell in love with you when she was just a little button in your tummy."

"Oh, really?" Saffron said with a laugh, one eyebrow arched.

Blake laughed and dropped a lingering kiss to her lips when she tilted her head back to stare up at him.

"Really," he replied.

They left the building snuggled up tight, his daughter still in his arms and his wife tucked to his side. They'd never once told another soul the truth about their marriage, how they'd met and the marriage contract they'd once signed. Saffron had even managed to convince her friend Claire that they'd been secretly dating before their fake marriage. Only Blake's lawyer knew the truth, and he paid him enough not to breach attorney-client privilege.

"Our little secret, huh?" Saffron whispered in his ear.

Blake grinned and held her tighter. "Yes, Mrs. Goldsmith," he teased.

He had it all, and nothing would ever be more important to him than caring for his family, fiercely protecting them and doing everything in his power to be everything his father hadn't been.

He'd spent all his life terrified of becoming that man, and in the end nothing could be further from the truth. From the moment he'd accepted how much he loved

Saffron, to seeing his newborn daughter in his arms, he'd known there was no way he could turn into him. Not for a second.

"I love you," she murmured, head to his shoulder.

"I love 'cream," Isabella mumbled in a sleepy voice.

Blake grinned. "And I love Mama *and* ice cream."

They walked out the back exit to avoid any lingering fans, heading for their favorite ice cream parlor. The night air was cool, and he tucked Isabella closer against his chest and Saffron even snugger under his arm, loving the warmth of them.

"Surprise!"

Saffron laughed as her husband stopped midstride, eyes wide as he stared around the room. She ran over to him, throwing her arms around him. He gave her a glare that turned to a sigh and then a smile.

"You fooled me," he muttered.

She shrugged. "Yep, I did."

Saffron had told him it was a simple birthday celebration, just the three of them having dinner with his mother, and instead she'd filled their home with everyone he cared about, including some of his friends and former colleagues that she knew he'd been sorely missing.

"You're crazy," Blake said, holding her tight and kissing her hair.

"It's not only me who gets to live my dream."

He raised an eyebrow and she bit down on her lower lip, watching as his old buddies engulfed him, slapping backs and giving friendly hugs. She'd seen the pain he'd been in at giving that life up, and he'd made her dreams a reality by helping her every step of the way. Not to mention getting a whole lot of flak for re-scheduling his days when she was performing to be a stay-at-home dad. It was a role he loved, but she knew it wasn't exactly easy for a company CEO to take time off when all his peers had nannies.

"Saffron, you've got some explaining to do," Blake called out, pushing his friends away and holding out a hand to her, tugging her over.

She couldn't hide her smile, knowing what he was about to say.

"What kind of wife organizes a boys' helicopter weekend for her husband?"

Saffron winked at him, something he often did to her, and it made him chuckle.

"You might not be able to fly for the military again, but it doesn't mean you can't fly with at least some of your old team," she said, standing on tiptoes to kiss him, wanting him to have an amazing birthday. "It's only camping, but I figured it was the closest to replicating what you used to love. There's no use owning a fleet of planes and helicopters if you can't use them, right?"

His smile was impossibly charming, his eyes dancing as he gazed down at her. "You know what I do love right now?"

She tipped her head back. "What would that be?"

Blake swept her up in his arms, lifting her high-heeled feet off the ground and kissing her in front of everyone. His friends clapped and catcalled, but Saffron didn't care that they were putting on a show for them.

"You."

"Just so happens," she said, nipping his bottom lip when he tried to kiss her again, "that I feel the exact same way."

* * * * *

THE COWBOY'S
CONVENIENT BRIDE

DONNA ALWARD

To Johanna and all the editors at Mills & Boon
who have come before… I've learned so much
from you and have enjoyed every minute.
#editorappreciationsociety

Chapter One

Tanner Hudson was getting sick of the bar scene.

Unfortunately, the other option was to hanging out at home, which was nearly as bad. Particularly when his older brother, Cole, and his girlfriend, Maddy, always sat around making googly eyes at each other.

Tanner lifted his glass and took a sip of his Coke, listening to an old George Jones song on the jukebox. He scanned the room for a friendly face. The last thing he wanted this evening was a woman. His lips curved in a wry smile. He was sure that no one would believe that for a second. He knew his reputation. Cole was the steady, reliable one. Tanner was the younger brother who worked hard and played hard and liked the ladies. He set down the Coke and scowled at it. On the surface, people were right. But deep down, well, that was another story. He was pretty darn good at keeping up appearances.

Rylan Duggan walked into the Silver Dollar, dusting a few flakes of spring snow off his hat. Tanner perked up. Rylan was a friendly face, and they had a lot in common. When Ry scanned the room, Tanner lifted his chin in a quick greeting, and Rylan grinned.

Tanner got up and met his friend at the bar. Rylan

ordered a beer, and as he was waiting, Tanner put a hand on his shoulder. "Hey, buddy. Am I glad to see you."

Rylan chuckled. "Why? You want to try to win back the money you lost last time?"

When they happened to be in the same place at the same time, Tanner and Rylan would often shoot a game or two of pool. Last time, Tanner had lost a twenty.

"Sounds fine to me. Slow in here tonight."

Rylan took his beer and looked at Tanner, as if trying to puzzle him out. "Kailey's off to some potluck supper and candle party or jewelry or...well, I wasn't really paying attention. I thought I'd drop by for a burger. What brings you here? The Dollar isn't usually your speed."

Tanner shrugged, the dissatisfaction nagging at him again. "Bored, I guess. Hell, Ry, I live in a house with my parents and big brother." He shook his head. "I should get my own place or something." His own life, perhaps.

"Why don't you?"

They made their way over to the pool tables. Tanner was kind of embarrassed to answer the question, actually. It came down to two things: money and convenience. The convenience thing was understandable, so he went with that. "I'm working the place with Cole and Dad. It just makes sense to, you know, be close."

Rylan nodded. "I get it. And it can get claustrophobic, too." He started setting up the balls. "I lived in my RV until Kailey and I moved into Quinn's old place. The last thing I wanted was to be under the same roof with Quinn and Lacey, especially when they were newlyweds."

Tanner selected a stick and chalked the end. "Tell me about it. I love Maddy, I really do, but she and Cole are all in love and everything, and they're around a lot."

"I get it, bro." Rylan removed the triangle and reached for a stick, testing the feel of it in his hand. "Maybe you should settle down. Could be that's your problem. Restless feet."

Tanner laughed. "Right." Rylan's statement hit a little too close to home, though. Truth was, Tanner was pretty sure there was more to life than this.

He lined up and broke, balls scattering over the table.

"Naw, I'm telling you," Rylan said. "Married life is pretty good. I never wanted to settle down, either, until Kailey. Now I know what I was missin'." He grinned, a little sideways smile that made Tanner roll his eyes.

Tanner missed his next shot, so it was Ry's turn. As Tanner watched, he let out a dissatisfied sigh. Everywhere around him, people were in love and telling him how wonderful it was. And it wasn't that Tanner wasn't happy for his brother. He was. Maddy was a great woman, with adorable kids, and he was pretty sure wedding bells would be ringing for his brother really soon.

Tanner just wasn't sure he was built that way. Or that he was the marrying kind. He was, as his ex put it, *built for fun, but not for a lifetime.*

Fun he could do. Because he sure as hell wasn't interested in having his heart stomped on again. So he worked hard and blew off some steam now and again. As far as the living-at-home thing, he'd been young and stupid and had spent his money as fast as he'd made it. But not in the last few years. He'd saved what he would have paid on rent or a mortgage until he'd built up a nice little savings. His truck wasn't new, and other than what little he spent on going out, his expenses were few.

Maybe he wasn't a keeper in the love department, but no one would ever accuse him of being broke and worthless again. Maybe he should bite the bullet and put a down payment on a place of his own.

Trouble was, it wasn't just living at home that was making him itch. It was the ranch, too, and feeling as if his whole life was laid out in front of him. No deviation. No curve balls. It was so…predictable. He didn't hate the ranch; it wasn't that at all. But he couldn't shake the feeling that there might be something more out there waiting for him.

"Dude. It's your shot. You off in la-la land or what?"

Tanner frowned. "Sorry. I'm probably not very good company tonight."

"No kidding. At this rate, you're going to be down another twenty."

Mad at himself for being bad company, Tanner let out a breath and focused on sinking the next ball. He did, and two more, which made him feel as if he was a little more with the program.

They finished the game and Rylan asked if he wanted to play another, but Tanner just wasn't in the zone. "Sorry, man," he said. "I'm out. But I'll take that twenty."

"Come on. Double or nothing. I'm here for another two hours until Kailey's done."

Tanner thought about it, but then he shook his head. "I'm bad company anyway. You should get yourself some suicide wings and a few more beers and find another willing victim."

Rylan laughed and dug in his wallet for the twenty. It seemed like each time they met, the bill just exchanged hands, back and forth. Tanner pocketed it and shrugged back into his denim jacket. "Thanks for the game, Ry."

"Anytime. And, Tanner? I wasn't kidding. Maybe you need to find yourself a woman. You know, to relieve all that pent-up tension." Rylan winked at him and Tanner laughed dutifully, but he was far too grouchy to be amused. Women were complicated creatures. They caused any number of troubles, had the ability to stomp on your heart and strip away your confidence. And yet they remained so damned desirable. They could make a man feel like a million dollars and as if he could conquer the world. Even if it was only for one night.

"I'll see you around, Ry. Thanks for the game."

More on edge than when he'd entered the Silver Dollar, Tanner crossed the parking lot to his truck and hopped in. He started the engine and turned on the wipers, letting them brush the light dusting of snow off the windshield. Flurries in April weren't that uncommon, though he was more than ready to leave winter behind for good. Longer days and warm temperatures should improve his mood, right?

He'd driven a little ways down the street when he spotted a car with its hood up in the bank parking lot. The bank was closed this time of night; whoever it was must have stopped to use the ATM, and it was the only car in the lot. As he slowed, he saw someone bent under the hood. By the shape of the snug jeans, it was a woman. And as much as Tanner considered women trouble, he wouldn't drive away from someone with car trouble. He put on his signal and pulled into the lot.

She stood up as he drove into the spot next to her, and he recognized her immediately. Laura Jessup. Well, if that didn't complicate matters... Laura had a new baby—and the rumor was that the father was none other than Maddy's late husband. He'd seen her a handful of times since Christmas. It had been a bit awkward, considering how the families were now connected. More for her than for him, really. He liked Laura. Admired her, too. Maybe she'd made mistakes, but she was handling them.

Tanner had been the volunteer EMT on duty the day she went into labor and called for an ambulance. He knew he wasn't supposed to let things get personal while on a call, but helping the single mom deliver her baby had been a different circumstance. It was a day he wouldn't ever forget.

"Laura, hi." He called out to her as he hopped out of the truck. "Having car trouble?"

She looked relieved to see him. "Hey, Tanner. I went into the bank and when I came out, my car wouldn't start."

"Let me try. I can always give you a boost."

"You're welcome to try and I appreciate it." She ran a hand over her hair, which was in a perky ponytail with little orangey-red strands sticking out. "My phone's out of juice and the baby's in the back. Sleeping, for now, thank God."

The baby. Tanner had ridden in the back of the ambulance on the way to the hospital and had been there for everything, including the final ten minutes in the emergency room when she'd delivered. He normally would have turned everything over to the doctors and nurses in the department, but Laura had grabbed his hand and asked him to stay. Begged him, so she wouldn't be alone.

He'd stayed. Right through to the moment the first cries echoed through the room and Laura had started crying herself. Then he'd stepped back and left the room, more affected than he should have been in his professional capacity.

That had been almost four months ago. As he passed by her to get to the driver's side of her car, he noticed that she definitely had her pre-pregnancy figure back. Well, maybe a few more curves, but they looked good on her. Real good. She looked more rested than she had the last time their paths had crossed, too. She must be adjusting to mom life. From what he heard, there wasn't a lot of sleeping going on for the first few months with a new baby.

Giving his head a shake, he slid behind the wheel and turned the key. There was a whirring noise, but it got slower and slower and nothing caught. He glanced into the back seat. The car seat was rear facing, so he couldn't see the baby's face—just the edges of a white frilly hat and a pink blanket.

As quietly as he could, he got out of the car. "Looks like we'll have to try giving you a boost," he said. "And looking at your car, I'd say you're probably due for a new battery."

"Damn it." Laura let out a big sigh. "Oh well. I

guess when you drive an older vehicle you have to expect some maintenance costs."

Tanner nodded. "I know. I go through the same thing with my truck. Hang on, I'll pull up closer and get my cables."

"Thanks, Tanner." She smiled at him. "Looks like you're coming to my rescue again."

His gaze met hers, and heat crept up his neck and into his face. He was blushing, for God's sake. And all because he'd covered for another paramedic that December day when her baby was born. It didn't get much more personal than that.

Well, that wasn't the only reason. Laura Jessup was extraordinarily beautiful. Tall, with a stunning figure, thick coppery hair, arresting blue eyes and a smile that went straight to a man's gut. The rumor was that Gavin Wallace had fathered her baby while he was still married to Maddy. Looking at Laura now, with her sweet smile and gratitude shining in her eyes, Tanner figured he could understand how Gavin had been attracted to her. Particularly since she and Gavin had been high school sweethearts. She'd be a hard woman to forget.

Of course, Maddy was now in love with Tanner's brother. Which made Tanner feel as if he was somehow betraying both Maddy and Cole just by thinking about Laura this way.

He jumped into the truck and maneuvered it so it was nearly bumper to bumper with hers, and then grabbed the cables from the back and hooked up the two batteries. "Okay," he said, "hop in and try it."

It whirred for a few moments, then sputtered and caught, roaring to life. Relieved, Tanner disconnected the cables and threw them in the back of the truck. Laura got out as he closed her hood.

"Tanner, thank you so much."

"It's no big deal. Glad the boost worked. You're probably going to need a new battery, though."

"I know."

"Do you have a charger at home? In case it doesn't start again?"

She shook her head. "No, but I'll get a new battery tomorrow. Promise."

He didn't argue. The garage would be closed now anyway. Unless she drove all the way into the city, there wasn't anywhere she could get a battery today anyway.

"I'll follow you home," he said. "In case it's not your battery, but your alternator or something. You'll know because you'll see your charge dropping."

"You don't have to…"

"If your phone's dead and you've got your daughter in the back…" He frowned. "I'd like to make sure you get home all right. It's just flurrying now, but what if it starts snowing harder?"

"In April?"

He snorted. "Come on, it wouldn't be a Montana spring without a few random storms."

"Fine," she replied. "And I appreciate it, Tanner. A lot." She hesitated, then met his gaze again. "Not everyone would stop and give me a hand."

It would have been less awkward had she not alluded to her persona non grata status in town. He'd often wondered why she stayed here, but figured it had to do with her grandparents. Or maybe it had been because of Gavin and now it was logistically too hard to move.

Still, she was a tough cookie for facing the community censure day in and day out. Whatever she had or hadn't done, she'd always been friendly and polite to him—before the baby and every time they'd run into each other since. Tanner tended to judge people on what he saw, rather than what he heard.

He smiled at her. "I'd never hear the end of it if I didn't help a neighbor in need," he said. "Besides, I'm sure you want to get the baby home."

"Her name's Rowan," she said quietly.

Rowan. There was something restful about the name that he liked. "That's pretty," he said, feeling inept at this sort of thing. How did a proclaimed bachelor make small talk about babies? He had a flash of inspiration. "She's healthy and everything?" Considering her fast entrance into the world, and that he was one of the EMTs that day, it seemed a logical question.

Laura smiled again as the car idled beside them. "Yes, perfectly. She likes to keep me up at night sometimes, but we just work around it."

"That's good," he replied. "And you look good, Laura. Rested. Whatever you're doing is working."

"Thanks." She smiled shyly. And then the silence became awkward again.

"Well, you head out and I'll follow you just in case."

"Sure thing. Thanks again, Tanner."

"Anytime."

She got in her car and he backed away, letting her out so she could lead. The snow was coming down a little harder now, and would be slick before the night was out if the temperature kept dropping. She lived in a little house just west of town limits, and when she turned into her driveway and gave a wave in her rearview mirror, he thought, as he had that day in December, how lonely it must be out here all by herself, with the neighbors spread out. Her name wasn't even on the mailbox.

Tanner turned around and headed back toward town and home. It wasn't until he passed the Silver Dollar again that he thought of Rylan and his comment that Tanner should go out looking for a woman.

If he did, the last one he should set his eyes on was Laura Jessup. She might be sweet as apple pie and gorgeous to boot, but she came with way more complication than he was interested in pursuing.

"Laura, is that you?"

Laura hadn't even shut the door when her grandfather called out to her. She closed her eyes and took a deep breath, then put Rowan's car seat on the floor. "Yes, Gramps, it's me. Sorry I'm late." She took off her coat and hung it in the closet, then put her boots on the mat. For a few moments, she allowed herself to bask in the lovely warmth that came from knowing Tanner had helped her. He'd smiled as if he meant it—as if the rumors about her didn't matter. Just as he had the day Rowan was born, when he'd held her hand and assured her he wouldn't leave.

She couldn't indulge in the sentimental feeling for long, however. Rowan was just starting to wake and she'd want to be fed soon. Laura had been stuck at the bank longer than she'd anticipated thanks to her dead battery, and she didn't have any supper made. She checked her watch. Gramps liked to eat at six sharp. It was just after seven.

Before Rowan tuned up and started crying, Laura hustled to the fridge and took out leftovers from last night's roast beef dinner. Gramps loved meat and potatoes, and it was a good thing because Laura wasn't the world's greatest cook. She'd bought one of those ready-to-bake roasts, microwaved frozen vegetables and managed to boil potatoes, all without burning the house down. She checked a small plastic dish and saw there was only a little gravy left from the packet mix she'd made. Maybe she could add a bit of water to it and it would be enough for Gramps.

She was happy to have him. But trying to be Martha Stewart while he was here was proving to be a bigger challenge than she'd expected. She was sure he'd get that pinched look on his face when she presented him with a warmed-up version of last night's meal.

Rowan was awake and grumbling, so Laura took her out of the seat and held her with one arm while using the other one to take off her little pink coat and hat. Laura ventured into the living room, where she found her grandfather in his favorite chair, watching the end of the six o'clock news.

"Sorry about dinner. I'm getting it now. I had some car trouble."

Gramps was seventy-five and still sharp, but he'd never had to cook or do for himself. With Gram in the hospital for a few weeks with a lung infection, Laura had suggested he stay with her. And she wasn't sorry. She didn't have a lot of family around, and they'd been so good to her since she'd come home. But living with Gramps had its challenges all the same.

"Your car all right?"

"I need a new battery. I got a boost in town that got me home. McNulty's is closed until tomorrow."

"I was hoping to go see your grandmother tomorrow. Since we missed today."

Yes, they'd missed driving into Great Falls. Truth be told, Laura was exhausted. Between being up with Rowan, caring for Gramps, and trying to make ends meet, she was stretched to the limit. Today she'd asked to stay home because she was trying to work on a freelance project she'd taken on. The only reason she'd gone into town was because she'd realized she'd run out of diapers.

In the kitchen, the microwave beeped, indicating the first plate of food was ready. "I'll see what I can do," she promised. "Come on out to the kitchen, Gramps. Supper's on."

She went to the kitchen and swapped the heated meal for the cold one and set the timer again. "Could you put some water on for tea, please?" she asked. "I'd like to change Ro before we eat."

Gramps grunted a response, but he grabbed the kettle and started to fill it. Laura tried to be patient. Gramps had been the one to work and Gram had stayed home, raised kids and looked after her husband. Laura wasn't against that kind of existence, even though these days it was rarely practical. That had been their choice. The downside was that Charlie Jessup had never really had to do anything remotely domestic in his life, and at seventy-five he was unlikely to change. He simply didn't understand why Laura was so incompetent in the kitchen.

Once Rowan was changed, she started to fuss.

Laura made sure Gramps had his meal, but it was increasingly clear that she would not have time to eat before feeding Ro. God, she was tired. She poured water into the mugs to let the tea steep. "Sorry, Gramps," she said, trying to inject some brightness into her voice. "I've got to feed Ro. The tea's steeping, if you don't mind taking out the bag when the timer goes."

"Yeah, fine," he said. "The beef's good, by the way."

She didn't realize how badly she'd needed the compliment until it was given, and her eyes stung with unshed tears. "Thanks," she answered, scooting out of the kitchen so he wouldn't see. She went to Rowan's room. Laura slept in here, too, on one of those blow-up beds with the fold-up frame, since she'd given Gramps her bedroom for the duration of his stay. She sank into the padded rocker and settled Rowan at her breast, exhaling several times to help her relax.

She loved being a mom. And these were precious, precious moments. Laura wished she could stop being so resentful. She resented having to breast-feed in here because her grandfather found it so embarrassing. She resented having to work when she was so exhausted because her maternity benefits were long gone. And while she tried to be grateful for her blessings, it was hard when she went into town and received knowing stares from so many people. They also gave Rowan curious looks, as if expecting her to resemble Gavin.

As far as anyone knew, Laura was a home wrecker. General consensus was she'd been having an affair with Gavin Wallace and Rowan was his child. They'd been high school sweethearts, said the whispers. And the moment she'd come back to town, they'd started up again. And then the worst rumor of all: that he'd been leaving her place the night he had the accident and was killed.

One of these days, she was going to have to leave Gibson behind. Even if she could live with the rumors and whispers, it wouldn't be fair to do that to Rowan, especially as she got older. She wished she could tell everyone the truth, but she couldn't. The only person who knew was her lawyer and Maddy Wallace— Gavin's widow, who'd promised to keep Laura's secret. She had to let it go for her own safety. For Rowan's.

Gavin Wallace was not Rowan's father. And if Spence ever found out that he had a child…

It would be nothing short of a nightmare.

Chapter Two

Laura clicked the mouse one last time and sat back to look at the banner she'd created. She frowned. Something wasn't quite right. The background was beautiful, and the graphic highlighted the client's product perfectly. It was the font, she decided. It needed to be slightly slimmer, and a deeper shade of plum.

So far, the freelance work was paying her bills, but just. Still, it would take time for word of mouth to spread. At least this way she was home with her child instead of having to commute to an office, as she had done during her six-month contract that had ended in December.

Ironically enough, she was still floundering with setting up her own site. She tried to keep her personal details very, very quiet. Plastering her name all over a site made her uncomfortable, and she knew she could decide on a company name, but people still wanted the name of the person they were dealing with. It was hard to advertise and drum up business without a website. Particularly when you were a web designer.

She adjusted the font, felt better, and saved the banner before emailing it off to the client for their thoughts. Then she checked her phone. Damn. They should have left for the hospital half an hour ago. She shut down the computer, dropped the phone into her bag and went looking for Gramps.

She found him sitting on the back deck in a plastic patio chair. It really wasn't a deck, but rather an oversize landing at the top of the back stairs. There was room for one chair and that was it. She pasted on the customary smile. "Sorry I took so long. Are you ready to go?"

"Sure. Been ready an hour now," he said, putting his hands on his knees and pushing himself to standing.

There were times she knew he didn't mean what he said as criticism. It didn't mean she didn't take it that way.

Ten minutes later, they were on the road, and it seemed like no time at all and they'd arrived at the hospital. While he visited Gram, Laura sat in the family waiting room and nursed Rowan. Then she popped into Gram's room to say hello, and left again to get a couple of sandwiches from the cafeteria, as well as some cranberry juice for Gram. The nurses were very good about letting Laura use the kitchen on the floor to make Gram's favorite cold remedy—cranberry juice mixed half and half with boiling water. She always said it soothed her throat and cough and drove out the chill. Laura made a cup for Gram and a cup for herself, as she'd always liked it, too, and a cup of tea for Gramps.

By two o'clock, Laura reminded Gramps that they had to get back to Gibson, as she had an appointment at the lawyer's office. So far Rowan had been contented, so Laura dropped Gramps at the diner and said she'd be back in half an hour to pick him up. The appointment at the lawyer's office was brief. She'd wanted to check on Spence's status. The idea of him being eligible for parole after what he'd done sent a cold chill down her spine and kept her up at night. With Spence having served nearly a year of his three-year sentence, Laura wanted to make sure she kept tabs on the situation.

Like when she really needed to start worrying. She could breathe easy for another few months anyway.

She found Gramps sitting in a booth with a cup of tea and a piece of half-eaten cherry pie in front of him. She'd taken Rowan out of the car seat and held her in her arms, and when she slid into the booth, she settled the baby on her knee, curled into the curve of her arm.

"That didn't take long," he commented. "I'm only half-through my pie."

"Take your time," she said, knowing Gramps was tired from being out all day. She was, too, but rushing him wouldn't benefit either of them. Besides, the food here was better than what he got at home. Unfortunately.

He sipped his tea and took another bite of pie, and a waitress came over to see if Laura wanted anything.

"What can I get you?" she asked.

A hot bath, a glass of wine, and an hour of quiet, Laura thought, but she merely smiled. "A glass of chocolate milk, I guess," she replied. She'd forsaken caffeine months ago, with the exception of her evening cup of tea. Since she'd never been fond of plain white milk, chocolate was her way of getting her calcium.

The waitress returned quickly with her milk and Laura took a long drink, enjoying the cool, sweet taste. She licked the froth from her top lip and settled more comfortably into the vinyl seat of the booth.

"Everything okay at the lawyer's?" Gramps asked, looking up at her over his mug.

"Yes. Fine."

"Don't know why you need a lawyer anyway," he grumbled. "They're expensive."

Didn't she know it. And Gavin had helped her for free, because they were friends. His colleague was giving her a break because of Gavin, but it wasn't free.

"It's complicated," she replied, drinking again. She put down her glass. "Nothing for you to worry about, though. Promise." She smiled. Gramps was gruff, but she knew he worried and cared. He wasn't a fan of her raising her baby alone, but he'd never said a word about Gavin, or the fact that he'd been married. It was as though they'd agreed to not mention it.

He put down his fork. "Laura, are you okay? Really? I'm old and I'm not good for much, but if you need help…"

She melted a bit, her frustration of the last week ebbing away. She touched his fingers with her free hand. "I'm fine, Gramps. I've made some mistakes, but I'm working on getting my life back on track."

"You know how I feel about some of that," he murmured, keeping his voice low. "But you're a Jessup. And you're made of strong stuff. You can do whatever you set your mind to."

Except protect myself, she thought, hating the idea that she could feel so helpless, hating even more that she was scared. Still, the praise made her feel stronger. "Thank you, Gramps."

"Humph," he said, back to his gruff self. But she smiled a little to herself.

Laura didn't notice anyone approaching the table

until she heard the voice that sent shivers of pleasure rippling up her spine. "So, did you end up replacing the battery?"

She swallowed and looked up to find Tanner standing beside the booth, an easy grin on his face.

It would be easier if he weren't so darn handsome. His dark hair was slightly mussed, his blue eyes twinkled down at her and his plaid shirt was unbuttoned at the top, revealing a small V of tanned skin.

She hoped she wasn't blushing. "I did, yes. The guy from McNulty's was kind enough to bring one out and put it in for me."

Tanner frowned. "I would have done that, and saved you the labor cost."

"Thanks, but it wasn't that bad." She glanced over at her grandfather. "Gramps, have you met Tanner Hudson? Tanner, this is my grandfather, Charlie."

Tanner held out his hand. "Sir," he said, giving a nod as they shook hands.

"Tanner's the one who gave me a boost the other day," Laura explained.

"Have a seat," Gramps said. "Laura's always so bent on doing everything herself, but I'm glad there are some people who are willing to lend a hand—even when she won't admit she needs one."

Laura gaped at him. Hadn't he just said she could do anything? Of course. He still prescribed to the old school where certain things were "man's work." Auto repair clearly being one of them.

Tanner slid into the booth beside her, and she quickly scooched over so they weren't pressed together. To her annoyance, he gave Gramps his winningest smile. "Happy to do it. Though from what I've seen, Laura's pretty capable of handling herself."

Gramps gave Tanner a long look, then a quick nod and calmly cut another bite of pie with the edge of his fork.

The waitress came over with a coffee and doughnut for Tanner, and he thanked her with a wink and a smile.

"You're not working out at the ranch today?" Laura asked.

"I had to make a run in to the hardware store. I was going to grab a coffee to go, but I saw you and thought I'd see how you made out after the other day." He shrugged. "At least the weather's improved. Much more spring-like."

He looked over at her half-empty glass. "Chocolate milk?"

She grinned. "What can I say? I'm a kid at heart."

"Speaking of kids…" He peered around her shoulder at Rowan. "Wow. She's cute."

"Thanks." Laura looked down at Rowan and a familiar wave of love washed over her. "She's been an angel all day, so I'm waiting for things to go south really soon. We've been to Great Falls to the hospital to visit my grandmother, and then went to a couple of appointments. Babies have a way of letting you know when they've had enough."

"I bet. Your grandmother—is she okay?"

"She's had a lung infection, but we hope she'll be out of the hospital on the weekend. Gramp's been staying with us in the meantime."

"Laura's been taking good care of me," Gramps said, pushing his pie plate away. He patted his belly.

"That was a good piece of pie. Maybe I should have another."

Laura felt a flush infuse her cheeks. "You're just saying that because I can hardly boil water. I wouldn't let you starve, Gramps."

He grinned and picked up his tea. "Honey, I know that. You got your looks from your grandmother. But you didn't get her cooking skills. That's just a fact."

He looked so amiable that Laura couldn't be mad—though she was embarrassed. Particularly when Tanner chuckled beside her.

Rowan wriggled in her arms and Laura looked down. "We should probably get going soon," she said. "Dragging her from pillar to post today means she hasn't had her regular sleep or feeding schedule. This could get ugly." She aimed a stern look at Charlie. "She has the Jessup temper."

Tanner laughed and Gramps sent her a look of approval. But then Tanner peeked over at Rowan, and Laura suddenly felt uncomfortable. Sure, there was a lot of Jessup in Ro, but Tanner was probably looking for bits of Gavin. He was nice to her, but he probably thought the same as everyone else. Plus, he was connected to Maddy through Cole. And while Maddy and Cole knew the truth, no one else did. Besides her lawyer, they were the only people she'd trusted in all of Gibson, and that was only because her conscience couldn't take it anymore.

Tanner's face remained relaxed and pleasant, though, and she gave Ro a little bounce on her knee. The baby giggled and then shoved a fist into her mouth, sucking on her fingers. A sure sign she was getting hungry.

"Are you almost ready, Gramps?" Laura tried to urge him along. But Gramps had either forgotten the urgency of small babies or was determined not to be rushed, because he shifted in his seat and lifted his teacup. "Just a bit of tea left. I won't be long."

The noises from Ro chewing on her fist got louder and Laura smiled weakly at Tanner as he bit into his doughnut. A familiar tingling started and Laura realized it had been nearly four hours since Ro's last feeding. *No, no, no*, she chanted in her head. But Rowan started to squirm and cry, nuzzling her face towards Laura's shoulder. And when Laura looked down, she was sure her face burned with instant embarrassment.

"Damn," she whispered, staring at twin splotches on her shirt. She'd worn a light blue cotton blouse, and there was no mistaking the wet spots. Sometimes breast-feeding was not completely convenient.

It would be the better part of twenty minutes by the time they paid the bill, she got everyone in the car and they drove home. And if she were alone, she'd discreetly slide to the corner of the booth, drape a flannel receiving blanket over her shoulder and do what was necessary. But Gramps wasn't comfortable with it at home, and she was certain he'd make a big fuss about it in public.

"What's the… Oh." Tanner's voice was soft beside her. Rowan started crying in earnest and people started looking over. To her frustration, Gramps poured more tea into his cup from the small silver pot.

"I can go. If you…that is…"

She shook her head and motioned toward Gramps. Thankfully, Tanner understood.

"I see. Give me two minutes."

He scooted out of the booth and went to the counter. A moment later, he returned with a young, pretty waitress behind him.

"Tanner says you could use some privacy for a few minutes." The words were said kindly. "Come with me."

"You're sure? I don't want to inconvenience you…"

"Don't be silly." She raised an eyebrow and her gaze dropped to Laura's shirt. "The sooner the better from the looks of it."

Laura was pretty practical when it came to nursing, but she had to admit that this moment was pretty humiliating. She grabbed the diaper bag and slid out of the booth. "Thanks," she whispered to Tanner as she passed by him, and he flashed her a smile.

The waitress led her to an office in the back. "This is Joe's office," she said. "But he's not in today, so you won't be interrupted."

"Thank you so much, Miss…"

"Shoot. Just call me Chelsea." She grinned. "My big sister has two kids and believe me, I understand."

She closed the door behind her with a quiet click. Rowan was frantically rubbing against Laura's shirt, and with a sigh, Laura sat on a saggy sofa and got Ro settled.

Several minutes later, she tucked everything back into place. Ro had eaten, burped, and was now sleeping peacefully in the crook of Laura's arm. But Laura was anything but peaceful. Her grandfather was still out in the diner, probably irritated beyond belief at being kept waiting. She really should pack up and get him home.

She was putting the flannel cloth back into the diaper bag when a soft tap sounded on the door. "Come in," she called quietly. She expected it to be Chelsea, so she was surprised to see Tanner poke his head inside.

"Is everything okay in here?"

She laughed. "I'm put back together, if that's what you're asking."

He stepped inside, and she laughed again at the relief that relaxed his facial muscles. "Chelsea mentioned that…" His cheeks colored. "Well. That you might want a different shirt. I went to the department store and bought you something," he said, and she thought he looked rather bashful admitting it. He handed her a small bag.

She reached inside and took out a black T-shirt in what appeared to be the right size. "Chelsea said that?"

He nodded. "Yeah. She's a nice girl. She…well, never mind. She said a medium would probably fit you."

"You bought me a shirt?"

"Well, your other one was… You know."

"Stained with breast milk?"

He blushed deeper.

She sighed. "Tanner, that was really sweet of you. I'm sorry if I was too blunt. I honestly think that once you have a baby you kind of give up on maintaining any sense of dignity. Stuff just happens." The wonder of being a mom was sometimes tempered with a direct hit to a woman's vanity.

He smiled. "Hell, Laura, I was in the ambulance that day. I think that ship sailed a long time ago."

Yes, he had been. He'd held her hand, breathed with her, checked on her progress. Just as any ambulance attendant would have. Except…she vaguely remembered pleading with him to stay with her. She'd felt so alone, so afraid, so…adrift. Without an anchor to keep her steady and hold her fast. And he'd stayed, she remembered. He'd held her hand and encouraged her to push and told her how great she was doing.

Then he'd disappeared. He'd done his job and gone above and beyond, but that was all it was. His job.

Buying her a T-shirt was not his job. And neither was boosting her car or finding her a private spot to nurse her baby. Tanner wasn't just a good EMT. He was a good man, too.

"This really was very thoughtful." She met his gaze. "And I should get out there. My grandfather is probably having a canary by now."

"I actually looked after that, too. He was grumbling, so I told him to head home. I told him I'd bring you along when you were ready." He wiggled his eyebrows. "I hope he didn't lie when he said he still has his license."

"He does. But he only drives in Gibson. Ever since his accident last year, he doesn't like going on the highways or driving in the city."

"Which is why you went to the hospital today."

"Exactly. He's aged a lot since the accident. And he relies so much on my gram that I thought it would just be easier having him at my place for a few weeks."

He must have sensed some hesitation in her voice, because he raised his eyebrows. "And has it been? Easier?"

She sighed. "I wish. I feel pretty inadequate most of the time. Suzie Homemaker I'm not."

"Charlie's old school. Hell, you're supporting yourself and your kid. You can't do everything."

She knew he meant the words to be encouraging, but instead she ended up feeling a familiar dissatisfaction. This wasn't what she'd wanted her life to look like. How had she gotten so off track?

"Anyway, if you're ready to go, I'll drive the two of you home."

Laura swallowed. Gramps was probably put out by the whole thing and now she'd ended up inconveniencing Tanner, too, who probably had things to do. "I'll be right out. I just need to change." She pushed herself up off the couch, but the busted springs meant it took her three tries. By the end of it, she was trying not to laugh, because Rowan was peaceful in her arms and Laura didn't want to disturb her.

"Here," he said gently, and reached for Rowan. "I'll hold her. And I'll turn around."

As carefully as if he were holding glass, he took Rowan and tucked her into his arms. She looked so small there. Small and safe.

Just as he'd promised, he turned his back to her. Laura quickly unbuttoned her blouse, took the tag off the T-shirt and pulled it over her head. It was a little too big, but she was okay with that. The soft cotton was comfortable, and the black wouldn't show any lingering moisture. She wondered if he'd thought of that when he picked it out. She doubted it. Guys weren't generally that astute.

But then, Tanner was different. She'd known that for a long time.

"Thanks," she said, putting a hand on his shoulder. "The shirt's great. Where's the receipt? I'd like to pay you back."

Tanner turned back around, his eyebrows puckered

in the middle. "Pay me back? Don't be ridiculous. It's just a cheap shirt. An emergency shirt." Again the impish gleam lit his eyes. "Come on. My truck's out front."

"Can I ask one more favor?" It was late in the afternoon. Laura had planned to be home earlier, and was tired from the running around. She really needed to put in a couple of hours on the computer tonight. "Could we make a quick stop at the grocery store? I think I'll grab one of those rotisserie chickens from the deli section."

He chuckled, and she sent him a dark look. "Not one word about my cooking."

She took Rowan from him and then swung the diaper bag over her shoulder.

"You're really good to him, you know. He loves you a lot. I could tell."

Laura knew it was true, and sometimes it was the only thing that kept her in Gibson. "He and Gram have been very good to me, too." She wanted to say how grateful she was that they'd never thrown the rumors in her face, but she didn't want to open that can of worms with Tanner. "It's the least I can do. That's not to say I won't try to save my sanity where I can." She grinned. "And save him from an ulcer."

He laughed again and she realized she liked the sound of it. It was happy and carefree, two things she hadn't been in quite some time.

"The grocery store it is."

They were walking through the diner when she realized the car seat had been in her car. "Tanner? I forgot her car seat. Oh no…"

Tanner walked ahead and opened the door. "I put

it in my truck. I don't have a clue how to fasten it in, but it's there."

Relief rushed through her. Gramps fussed and went on about how in his day people simply carried babies on their laps, but she would never do that with Rowan. She needed to be buckled in securely. Safe. Protected.

Laura swallowed against a lump in her throat. Everything she did these days was for Rowan's protection.

At the grocery store, Tanner offered to stay in the car with Rowan while she ran inside. Her daughter was sound asleep, so she left her in the backseat, knowing she'd be perfectly safe with Tanner. In less than ten minutes, she was back in the truck and they were on their way to her place, the interior of his vehicle smelling like roasted chicken.

She and Tanner chatted about the ranch a bit, and she mentioned her graphic design work, which led to explaining what she'd been doing since leaving Gibson after high school. She left a lot of blank spaces, but then, so did he. He didn't mention Cole or Maddy at all, and she knew why.

She wished she could tell him the truth about Rowan's father. But the more people who knew, the more likely it was to get around, and right now that secret was her biggest form of protection.

He carried the grocery bags to the door while she managed Rowan and the diaper bag. When they walked in, Laura discovered her grandfather emptying the dishwasher. She nearly fell down from the shock.

"Gramps!" she said, slipping off her shoes. "You don't have to do that."

He gave his customary harrumph. "Don't know

why everyone thinks I'm helpless. I can put some dishes away now and then."

"I guess I'll get a start on supper, then. You'll be relieved to know I stopped and picked up a chicken."

"Are you staying, young man?"

Laura's mouth dropped open. Had Gramps just asked Tanner for supper? Oh, she hoped he wasn't getting any ideas. Tanner Hudson was the last person she should get involved with. Talk about complicated!

Besides, she was hardly looking for romance. She had her hands full right now.

"Thank you, but I should probably get home."

Laura was surprised to feel disappointment at his refusal, but the last thing she wanted was for him to feel obligated. "You're welcome to, Tanner," she offered weakly, knowing Gramps would expect it. "It's the least I can do for all your help. But if you need to get back to the ranch, I understand."

He rubbed his chin. "I don't need to hurry back. I guess it would be all right."

Oh Lord. Oh Lord, oh Lord. She was actually nervous. Tanner Hudson was going to eat supper at her house. With her grandfather. After seeing her in a mess this afternoon. What on earth? He didn't seem to care a bit about her reputation, either. And there was no way he could have remained oblivious. He had to know about the gossip. About what kind of woman she was… And that had nothing to do with Gavin Wallace and everything to do with her decisions before coming home to Gibson.

Gramps patted Tanner on the shoulder. "Come on in the living room. It's been a while since I've had another man to talk to."

Tanner looked over at her. "Do you need anything?" he asked. "I'm not a complete idiot in the kitchen."

She shook her head. "Thanks, but no. You go. Entertain each other." She gave a self-deprecating grin, glanced down at the chicken and then back at him. "It's not like it'll take long."

He flashed her a smile that felt very intimate, as if they shared a joke. She liked, too, that he'd offered to help, and wondered if he'd said something to Gramps earlier that had prompted the dishwasher emptying, because that was an unprecedented event.

As the men sat in the living room and talked about community goings-on, Laura buckled Rowan into her bouncy seat and began putting together a green salad. She then took out a pretty bowl and transferred potato salad into it rather than simply putting the tub on the table, and placed a paper napkin in a little basket and filled it with buns from the market bakery.

Maybe she hadn't cooked it, but she could at least make the meal look a bit homey.

Just before everything was ready, the baby woke and Laura made a quick trip to the nursery for a change and tidy-up, and then, by some miracle, it all came together.

The table was set, Rowan was playing with the activity bar on her bouncy chair and Laura called the men to supper as she put the carved chicken on the table, along with the salad bowls and butter for the buns.

There was chatter, and the clinking of silverware on plates, and the odd laugh. A lump formed in Laura's throat as she realized this was the nicest meal she'd spent in her house. It had been so long since she'd experienced a relaxed, pleasant atmosphere that she'd nearly forgotten what it was like.

But as Tanner laughed at a story Gramps told, it all came rushing back to her. And it made her both a little bit happy and a little bit sad. She had been lonely for so long.

And that was why, despite the grumbling and inconvenience, she'd offered Gramps a place to stay, she realized. She was *so* tired of being alone.

After dinner, Tanner insisted on helping with the dishes, which didn't take long at all. When they were done, he said goodbye to Gramps and then pulled on his boots and prepared to go.

"Supper was good," he said, standing in the doorway. "Thanks for having me."

"You're welcome. And thanks for being so kind to Gramps. I think he's been a little lost the last few days. It was good for him to have someone besides me to talk to."

"He's a good old dude," Tanner said. "He's pretty proud of you, you know. Says you have gumption."

She blinked back sudden tears. "He's not crazy about me being unmarried with a baby."

"Being a single mom is hard. He knows it. He just wishes you didn't have to do it alone."

"He wishes I'd been smarter."

Tanner studied her for a minute. "Maybe. But I think that's you putting words in his mouth."

He was right. She was pretty hard on herself, and she knew it. And yet Tanner didn't seem to judge. She wondered why.

"Doesn't it bother you?" she asked bluntly. "What they say about me?"

His eyes darkened. "You mean about Rowan's father?"

She nodded, nerves jumping around in her stomach. He was the first person she'd broached the topic with, and she realized that for whatever reason, she trusted him. Oh, maybe not with the truth, but he'd already proved he wasn't about to shun her because of the grapevine.

"It's none of my business," he stated, not unkindly. "And believe me, Laura, after all these years, I know what it's like to have to live with mistakes. And live them down."

"You?" Granted, she'd heard he was a bit of a player, but if that was the worst anyone said about him...

"Right. You were gone for a while, so maybe you don't know. I was married once. For three whole days. In Vegas. The entire town knows about it. My best man at the time wasn't discreet with the details."

She blinked. "You were married for three days?"

"Yeah. Until we both sobered up and she came to her senses. You don't have the corner on mistakes, Laura, and I certainly have no right to judge anyone. So no, what they say doesn't bother me."

He leaned forward and placed a chaste, but soft, kiss on her cheek. "Take care and thanks again for dinner."

"You're welcome. And thank you for everything today." She smiled. "You're starting to become my knight in shining armor."

He laughed. "Oh, hardly. Just being neighborly. Anyone else would have done the same." He raised his hand in farewell and stepped outside. "See you around."

He fired up his truck and drove away, leaving Laura

back in reality again. But it was a softer kind of reality, because for the first time in a long while, it felt as if someone might be in her corner.

And she truly hadn't realized how lonely she'd become until someone walked in and brought sunshine with him. Tanner had said that anyone would have done the same, but she knew that was a lie. She'd been in that parking lot for a good half hour with the hood up before he came along to help. Others had passed right on by.

It was just too bad that Tanner Hudson was the last person she should get involved with. Even if Maddy was gracious enough to understand, she knew the town of Gibson never would.

Chapter Three

Tanner threw a bale of hay down the chute and followed it with two more. The physical exertion today was his form of therapy. If he had to hear one more time about how much his parents loved Maddy and how happy they were that Cole was dating her and how adorable her twin boys were, he was going to lose it.

He got that the whole family was happy that Cole had fallen in love. Hell, he expected there'd be an engagement announcement any day now, and he was truly happy for his brother.

But this whole love-fest thing just made Tanner feel more like a loser every day. The last thing his ex Brittany had said to him was that he'd be a joke for a husband. And seeing Cole and Maddy and his mom and dad so thrilled only seemed to highlight the fact all the more.

Tanner was good for a good time. Girls loved him for that. And that was it. The problem was, it wasn't enough for him. Not anymore.

His bad mood persisted through the chores, over breakfast, and late into the morning. He decided to saddle up Bingo and go for a ride, using the excuse of checking on the calves in the east pasture. Maybe the fresh air and open space would help put him in a better frame of mind.

He loved the scent of the young grass, the spears yellow-y green in their newness and the buds that were getting plump on the trees, nearly ready to leaf. Spring was a relief after a particularly harsh winter, and since that last snowfall earlier in the month, the weather had turned mild. Even if they did get a late season storm, there was a sense that the weather had truly turned a corner and there were warmer, greener days ahead. Spring was a time of year Tanner usually loved.

But this year he was filled with a nagging dissatisfaction. As he walked Bingo along the fence line, he sighed. It was only partly to do with Cole. He found himself thinking about Laura quite often, too.

Maddy had seemed to mellow out where Laura was concerned. Maybe that was because she was happy with Cole. But Tanner had noticed the sideways looks aimed in Laura's direction the other day at the diner. If he noticed, he was certain she did, too. People looked at her and saw a woman who'd had an affair with a married man. But where was the blame on Gavin? Just because he was dead, it was as if he was blameless.

Sometimes people put their faith and emotions in the wrong people. He knew that as well as anyone. They shouldn't have to pay for it their entire lives.

Dinner at Laura's house a few weeks ago had made one thing clear to him. Laura Jessup was in sad need of a friend, and no one would go near her. It was as if they were afraid they'd catch something. He hadn't seen such a lonely person in a very long time. Talking to her grandfather, Charlie, had enlightened him a fair bit. She never had friends over. Rarely went out anywhere other than errands. No wonder she'd clung to his hand the day Rowan was born. How afraid she must have been, facing that alone. When he'd given her that cheap T-shirt at the diner, she looked so surprised, so touched, that he wondered how long it had been since anyone had done anything remotely thoughtful for her. Her grandfather had also been concerned, but reserved. It wasn't hard to see he disapproved of the situation, even though he loved her.

Tanner turned Bingo around and returned to the ranch a little less on edge, but still unsettled about the whole situation. It wasn't just Laura. His life seemed stuck in place. What was he going to do, live with his parents forever? Satisfy himself with short-term hook-ups now and again? That whole scene was getting old. Maybe having a place of his own would be a start.

When Tanner returned to the house, he found Maddy there, helping his mom paint the back deck while the boys napped. Cole and Dad had driven down to Butte to look at some stock. Tanner was at loose ends, so once he grabbed a sandwich for lunch, he hopped in his truck and drove into town. And through town, and west. There was no sense kidding himself. He was going to see Laura. Just to see how she was making out. If there was anything she needed.

He pulled into the driveway and noticed things he'd missed the last time he was here. Like how the paint was peeling on the railing of the front step. A piece of soffit was missing from the roof overhang, and one corner of her eaves trough needed to be repaired, too. Nothing major, but little things that needed fixing that she probably couldn't do herself. Or could, but because of her situation, didn't have the time or money.

She came outside the moment he got out of the truck. He lifted a hand. "Hi," he greeted, and a lot of the restlessness he'd felt all day dissipated at the sight of her. She wore a pair of faded jeans and a cute white top, and Rowan was on her hip, dressed in a pink flowery outfit. They made a sweet picture.

"Hi, yourself. This is a surprise."

"Yeah. I'm not here at a bad time, am I?"

She shook her head. "Come on in. Rowan's up as you can see, so I'm spending some time with her and I'll go back to work when she's napping again."

"Work? What are you doing?"

He climbed the steps and she opened the door, leading the way in. "I'm working on a web design for a new client. I only had a six-month contract at the last place, and with Ro being so little, day care's not an option. This gives me some freedom and some income."

"That's smart." He followed her inside. Just like the other night, the place was spotless. His respect for her grew. She might not have much, but she took pride in what she did have. "What about Charlie?"

She laughed. "Oh, he's been back home for about a week. And thrilled about it. Gram's still taking things slowly, but at least he's eating better. Do you want some coffee or tea? I have both."

"Naw, I'm good."

"Then what are you doing here, Tanner?"

He floundered for a moment, and then decided he might as well tell her the truth. "I guess I found myself thinking about you a lot, and wondering how you are. Wondered if you, uh, needed anything."

Her gaze turned sharp. "You feel sorry for me, is that it?"

"No!"

She sat at the kitchen table, so it only made sense for him to do the same. "Not sorry, per se," he continued. "Well, crap. I have no idea how to say this in a tactful way. I'm a guy. And this is kind of like navigating a minefield."

She put Rowan on her lap and handed her a plastic ring with big, colorful keys on it. The baby shook the keys and a little giggle bubbled out of her mouth. Tanner couldn't help the smile that tugged on his lips. The kid was so darn cute. A few short months ago she'd been tiny, all arms and legs and thin cries. He couldn't help feeling a strange sort of attachment, knowing he'd helped bring her into the world.

"You want to ask me about Gavin."

He met her gaze. She was looking at him evenly, but as though she was bracing for whatever he was going to say or ask. "Not exactly. I just noticed the other day that…" He hesitated.

"Just say it, Tanner. I've heard it all."

He sighed. "That's what I mean. I noticed you're kind of, I don't know, set apart. People treat you differently. Not mean, just…"

"Polite. And look at me sideways like they're trying to figure something out."

"Yeah. And I wanted to say I'm sorry about that. And if you need anything, you can give me a shout. I don't judge. If Rowan is Gavin's…well, it took two of you, and until someone walks in your shoes, they really don't know about a situation."

She smiled softly. "That sounds very insightful. Is this about you or me?"

"Maybe a little of both," he admitted. "You didn't

know me when we were all kids. I'm a few years younger than Cole, and you were gone when I ran off to Vegas with Brittany. I screwed up, but people have long memories around here. It's like they've never made a mistake in their lives."

"So what is this? Are you championing an underdog? Or maybe throwing things back in their faces? Proving they're right about you, that you're a screw-up by hanging around with the wrong kind of woman?"

"Ouch."

A wrinkle formed between her eyebrows. "Sorry. That was me being superblunt again. I'm the first one to admit I have a bit of a chip on my shoulder."

Despite the harshness of her words, he could tell she'd asked an honest question, and he thought hard about how he would answer. Was he doing this to prove a point? Because if he was befriending her in a way that was anything less than genuine, that made him no better than anyone else.

"No," he said softly. "That's not what I'm doing. But that was a really good question to ask, Laura." Rowan dropped the keys on the floor. He leaned down, picked them up and handed them to her. He received a toothless grin as his reward. "It's more that I know how it feels, and it's wrong. I'm not afraid to be your friend if you need one. You *and* Rowan. I was there when she was born. It was a big moment."

He didn't expect tears to gather in her eyes. It made the blue depths even bluer, and his heart stuttered a little. He wondered what the heck he should do now.

"Sorry," she murmured, and reached for a paper napkin to wipe her eyes. She took a few deep breaths.

"Honestly, you're the first person to say that since Gavin. That you're my friend, that is."

"I'm sorry," he said, and he meant it.

She cuddled Rowan closer. "Tanner, I can trust you, right?"

A little ripple of warning slid through him. No one asked that sort of question unless they were planning on revealing something personal. But then, he'd just said he wasn't afraid to be her friend. So he nodded, holding her gaze. "Yeah, you can trust me."

"Because there are only two people in Gibson who know the truth besides my lawyer. One is your brother. The other is Maddy Wallace."

Gavin's widow.

"This has to do with Gavin?"

She nodded. "Okay, here goes. The baby's not his, Tanner. Gavin was a good friend, but nothing more. He was married. I would never get involved with a married man. I've made a lot of bad decisions, but that's not one of them."

Tanner sat back in his chair. On one hand, he felt a surge of relief knowing she'd never slept with Gavin. But on the other, he was completely perplexed. If their relationship had been nothing more than friendship, then why didn't she set the record straight?"

"I don't understand," he said.

"You want to know why I let everyone think otherwise."

"Well, yes!" He frowned, leaning forward again and resting his elbows on the table. "Laura, you know that people think you two had an affair. That Rowan is his. You're deliberately letting that happen, and letting them make you an outcast. Why would you do that?"

"Because the truth is worse than the lie," she said quietly. "And as difficult as it is for me, it's in Rowan's best interest, and I have to put her first."

Which really didn't explain anything.

Rowan started fussing, so Laura got up and put her on her shoulder. Tanner noticed again the difference in coloring. Laura's hair was wavy and a gorgeous auburn shade of red that he knew most women coveted and few came by naturally. Her skin was creamy white with a few light freckles, her eyes a clear summer blue. Rowan, while having the same pale skin tone, had perfectly straight dark brown hair, and her eyes were blue, but not the same vibrant shade as her mother's. Gavin's hair had been brown like that, too, but he couldn't remember the man's features well enough to know if there was any imagined resemblance.

To the townspeople, the implication was enough. He knew that people often saw what they wanted to. Such was the power of suggestion.

So if Gavin wasn't the father, who was? And why was that truth so much worse than letting the world think Rowan was Gavin Wallace's?

"Tanner? Let's go into the living room. She's got a bouncy seat in there that she loves. It's almost nap time anyway, and I can explain a little better."

He followed her into the living room and sat on the sofa while she settled Rowan in the little chair and gave it a bounce. The girl's face lit up and she smacked at the toys on the activity bar in front of her.

"Best thing I bought for her," Laura said, smiling. "She loves it and it's saved my sanity more than once. Now that she's awake longer through the day, she gets bored." She sat in the chair to the right of him and let out a big breath. "I suppose I need to elaborate a bit, don't I?"

Did she? Was it really any of his business? He thought about what it meant to be a good friend. He had friends, but Cole was really the guy he was closest to. And even then, there were things his brother didn't know. Tanner totally understood how it felt to want to keep the darkest parts hidden away. Curious as he was, he knew how he had to answer. "Tell me only if you want to," he said. "You don't owe me any sort of an explanation at all."

"And that's very generous of you. And surprising."

"Like I told you before, I've had a few moments that are not my finest. I don't judge."

She smiled at him then, a soft curving of her lips that reached in and grabbed him right by the heart. It was sweet, and perhaps a bit vulnerable—something he hadn't seen in her up to this point. Except for one moment, last December. When she'd had a particularly nasty contraction and she'd reached out for his hand in the ambulance. She'd looked so scared and yet so trusting.

"You know, I'm starting to believe that's true," she whispered.

There was a long pause, and then she put her hands on her knees. "You've been nothing but kind to me, and I trust you. So here's the truth, leaving out some names if that's okay with you."

"You can tell me as much or as little as you like."

She looked relieved. "The truth is, up until last spring I lived in Nevada, in Reno. I was working for a small graphic design company and my roommate tended bar. Through her, I met this guy and we went out a few times. He was really handsome and charming, and he said he was in sales." She laughed bitterly. "Pharmaceutical sales. God, I was so dumb, so naive," she said, giving a bitter laugh. "Anyway, it was a bit of a whirlwind thing. But then he said he was being transferred to a new territory for a few months and he ended it. A few months later, he came back, and he was still handsome, still charming…but something felt off. I couldn't put my finger on it, but there was an edginess to him that hadn't been there before. A… hardness. I think I knew I should end things, but I told myself I was imagining it. I ignored all my instincts."

Tanner didn't like where this was going. At all. "Did he hurt you?" he asked gently.

Her eyes clashed with his, but she shook her head a little. "No, not like that. He never laid a hand on me. He came into my work and wanted to start up where we left off, and I fell for his charms all over again. I let him stay with me at my apartment until he found a new job. But after a few weeks back together, I knew it wasn't what I wanted. I didn't feel safe, though I couldn't explain why. A few times, some guys showed up at my door, and I knew he wasn't honest about who they were. All my internal alarms were ringing and so I decided I needed to break it off."

Tanner hadn't realized he'd been holding his breath until she paused and he let it out. "And then what happened?"

"The day before I was going to do it, the cops came and arrested him. He totally lost it when they showed up, and God, it was so ugly. He was charged with violating his parole, assault and battery and possession of a controlled substance. I had no idea about the drugs.

Turns out that transfer? He wasn't working. He was in prison." Her normally sparkly eyes had dimmed, her lips thinned to a straight, disapproving line. "He wasn't a pharmaceutical rep at all. He was dealing. To kids. And I was too blind to see the signs. By then it was too late."

Tanner didn't say anything; he simply sat quietly while she composed herself. He knew what it was like when you found out the person you thought you loved turned out to be totally different. Though at least Brit hadn't been a felon. Just...not who he thought she was.

"The baby's his?" he finally asked.

She nodded miserably. "When they left with him, he looked right at me and said he'd be back, just like last time. Not to worry, he'd come find me when he got out. The way he said it...it made my blood run cold. It wasn't reassuring. It was a threat. If he knew about Rowan..."

Tanner looked from her to the sweet baby bobbing in the bouncy chair. The two of them weren't his, but damned if he didn't feel protective of them just the same. "He'd come after you both."

She nodded again. "Yeah. I had to give a statement to the police and I found out a lot about his past. I was so stupid, Tanner. So blind. I believed every lie he fed me. How many kinds of idiot could I be? And then to get pregnant..."

The agony in her voice was real. "I'm pretty sure you didn't mean for that to happen," he said quietly. He got up and moved to the end of the sofa so he was closer to her, and he reached out and put his hand on her knee. "Listen. Remember that marriage I mentioned? I was totally in love with this girl Brittany from Lincoln. She and a couple of girlfriends moved to Vegas, and I thought I'd surprise her one weekend. It was crazy." He decided to leave out some of the more sordid details about the weekend activities. "By the end of it, we'd gotten married at a chapel on the Strip."

"Oh."

"Yeah. Oh. And when I asked how long it would take her to pack up and come home with me, she laughed. She had no plans to leave. She loved it there. She loved the lights and the excitement and the party. She certainly didn't love me. It was all a crazy, fun adventure to her."

"And you were dead serious."

"You betcha." He smiled wryly, trying not to think of the moment when Brittany had all but fallen over laughing at him. "We all make mistakes. And I guess now I understand why you haven't set the record straight. Because you'll take the gossip if it means keeping your daughter safe."

A tear slid down her cheek. "Oh, damn. I spent enough time crying. You'd think I'd be over it by now." She rubbed the tear away. "It's such a relief to actually tell someone, and I think it's made me super-emotional. Maddy only knows the bare minimum and no details. I couldn't stand the thought of her thinking Gavin had cheated on her any longer. He loved her so much."

"But it's rough on you."

"It's worth it if Rowan stays safe."

"Damn, Laura. Why not move somewhere else, where no one knows?"

Once more she looked into his eyes, and he saw shadows there.

"The only way I could get this house was if Gramps and Gram cosigned the loan, and that was before all the rumors. There's no way I'll get financing for another place, not with the little bit of freelancing I'm doing. And I'm having a hard time building the business because I don't want to put my full name on anything. It'll make it too easy to find me, you know?"

"So you're stuck."

"Yep. I mean, I grew up here, but it doesn't mean it's not awkward."

Awkward was putting it lightly. "Gavin was helping you, wasn't he?"

"Yeah, with some of the legalities. And he did the legal fees for the house pro bono. His partner's been keeping me updated on Spen…on my ex's sentence."

She sighed, looked down at Rowan. The bouncing had stopped, and Tanner saw that each blink of Rowan's eyes was slower than the last.

"I feel like I'm spinning my wheels." Her shoulders were slumped a bit as she rested her elbows on her knees. "I want to start over, but it's hard to do when you want to remain invisible. At least with the contract work, my name was kept out of it. But if I'm going to freelance, I can't stay anonymous. Even if I'm careful, it's not hard to find the trail."

"Too bad you can't change your name," he replied, half joking. "Then he'd be looking for Laura Jessup and not Laura someone else."

A crazy, ridiculous, ludicrous idea flitted through his brain.

No. She'd never agree and besides, it was a dumb idea. He kept hearing Brit laugh and say how he wasn't husband material. Maybe not, but perhaps he could be friend material. No one else was stepping up to give Laura a hand. The only one who had was gone, and she had no one to be on her side.

Plus, he was tired of living at home. This could be beneficial to both of them.

"Laura, how open are you to harebrained schemes?"

She lifted her head, chuckled softly. "Why? Do you have one?"

Something twisted in his gut, in an oh-my-God-are-you-really-going-to-ask way. His palms started to sweat and his breath caught. He'd said the words once before in his life, but this time it was different. This time it wasn't for love. So why was he so tied up in knots?

"I just might. And you're going to be tempted to say no, but hear me out."

Her eyebrows pulled together in a puzzled look.

"Laura," he said, not quite believing what he was about to say. "I think we should get married."

Chapter Four

Laura started laughing. Marry Tanner? That was the most ridiculous thing she'd ever heard. "Oh God," she said, between breaths of mirth. "You shouldn't even joke about that."

He was chuckling, too, which was why his next words surprised her even more. "I'm actually perfectly serious. I've wanted to move out of the house for a while now. And if you married me, you could be Laura Hudson. Laura Hudson could set up her own business in that name and not be so easy for this guy to find."

Her laughter died in her throat. She was starting to think he meant it. Her face went hot. Sure, Tanner was good-looking. Extraordinarily so, but she hadn't really thought of him in a romantic kind of way. For a moment, an image flashed through her mind—of her and Tanner doing things that married couples do. Her face burned hotter.

"Tanner, I… I mean, you and me…"

He seemed to understand what she was getting at. "Laura, I'm not talking about a *real* marriage. It would be in name only, of course. We hardly know each other."

"My point exactly." She exhaled a relieved breath.

They were, at best, friends. Their contact had been limited to the ambulance ride to the hospital, running into each other and chatting on a few occasions in town, and the events of the last few weeks. Sure, she liked him well enough, but she wouldn't be roommates with someone she knew so little of, let alone husband and wife.

Husband and wife.

He leaned forward, put his elbows on his knees and peered into her face. "You said you were hesitant to put out your shingle online because it made you too visible. Even if you use a company name, your contact info is going to be listed somewhere. When you register your website, or fill out business forms for taxes and stuff."

All true, but it wasn't as simple as a different last name. "Tanner, it's not like it would be impossible to figure it out, even if I did change my name. There'd be marriage records to show that I was once Laura Jessup."

"Maybe," he conceded, "but it would make it more difficult. And if you're married, chances are that even if this guy did find you, he'd probably think that the baby was, well, your husband's."

"Yours," she said, the word echoing in the strangely quiet room.

"Yes."

Silence fell. He'd hit her squarely where it hurt— her daughter. Her top priority was protecting Rowan. It was why, after all, she let the town of Gibson collectively assume that the baby was Gavin's…even though that made her an adulteress and a home wrecker. But this was different. This was marriage. A wedding. And she wasn't sure what Tanner wanted to get out of it. There must be something. There was no way it was a purely altruistic move.

Good gracious, was she actually considering it?

Of course she wasn't. Harebrained was a great way to characterize the idea. She'd made enough mistakes over the last few years; she wasn't too keen to compound them by marrying a stranger just so she could change her name.

She got up and walked to the window, looking out over the backyard. The grass was greening up, but there were dry, bare patches where the ground was hard and unyielding. Laura sighed. Yes, she had her own place, but it wasn't much. She kept it clean, but it was hardly better than the lousy apartments in Reno. Rundown and unloved. Funny, she was starting to think of herself in those terms, too.

Marrying Tanner was a stupid idea. She'd just keep on doing what she was doing and figure it out somehow. She always did.

"Tanner, I appreciate the offer, but I don't need to be rescued. It's a crazy idea and I think it would be a disaster."

"Why? I like you. And I think you like me." He smiled at her. "We'd be roommates, that's all. No funny business, I promise."

She frowned. "If you want to move away from the ranch, do it. There's nothing stopping you. You don't need to live with me to do that. You're a grown man."

He paused, and then nodded. "That's true." He frowned a little. "Can you sit down, please? You're making me nervous standing up there."

His voice actually sounded as though he wanted to

have a serious conversation, which at this point seemed so surreal it was laughable. No one did marriages of convenience anymore. She certainly didn't. When she eventually said her "I do's," she wanted to mean them.

An ache settled in her heart. That day might never come. She didn't have a whole lot of faith when it came to romance. Now she was a single mom, which made relationships even more complicated.

Laura sat on the sofa, crossing her hands primly on her knees.

"Laura," Tanner began, "I have my own reputation to live down in this town. My three-day wedding in Vegas is still talked about. There's always been speculation about it and I have never said anything because…well, my mom always taught me that a gentleman doesn't talk about a lady. So the consensus seems to be that I'm not serious about matrimony. The truth is, I was the serious one. She wasn't. I didn't come to my senses and want the marriage annulled. She did." He hesitated. "I asked her to come back here with me and she laughed in my face and told me I was the kind of guy girls wanted a fling with, but not marriage."

"If this is your sales pitch, it needs work," she replied dryly.

He gave a little huff that might have been amusement at her witty response. "The point I'm trying to make is that this would be purely an arrangement to get you out of a bind and to get me out of a house where I'm surrounded by—" he made a face, as if tasting something bad "—people who are in love and *show it all the time.*"

"If you're looking for a roommate, why even bring

marriage into it? This isn't my grandparents' generation. People actually live together. Even boys and girls." She rolled her eyes. At least she could still find a little humor in the situation.

She'd lived with Spence, because she'd been a dumb idiot who'd had her socks charmed off. As well as various other articles of clothing.

"Because the marriage part is what gives you the freedom to put your business out there. We could do it quietly, at the courthouse, and down the road, when we both think it's time, we divorce. Nice and quiet and friendly."

He did have a point. And she was longing to get a site built and start taking on more clients. Still, marriage was incredibly drastic. "You're crazy."

"You'd be saving my reputation, too. I'm starting to get tired of the Good Time Charlie label."

"Don't you think your rep would be resurrected when we divorced? I mean, if I were nuts enough to go along with this stupid idea." She shook her head. "Tanner, do you even want to be marriage material? Or care what the town thinks of you? Your reasons are flimsy at best, so it makes me think there's something more to your offer."

TANNER WAS QUIET for a few beats, and then he pushed his hands against his knees and straightened. She was right. It was a crazy idea and if he wanted to move out, he could. He didn't need to get married to do it.

It was something else. It was the fear in her eyes when she mentioned this "Spence" guy. She was afraid of him and Tanner suspected she had a real reason to be, if the creep was serving jail time. He liked Laura, and she was struggling after having made some bad decisions. The simple truth was, he wanted to help. Even if it was temporary, if standing in front of the justice of the peace or a judge meant she could have some measure of protection, he was willing to do it. If he helped her, he'd feel that he was doing something important. Meaningful. He couldn't deny that he felt a strange responsibility toward her and her daughter.

"Laura," he said softly, "I'm not looking for love, and I'm not looking for a real marriage. I was burned once before. Is it so wrong that I feel terrible that you have to deal with this? I know what it's like to have everyone look at you sideways."

"So you're doing this entirely out of the goodness of your heart? Out of charity?"

"Are you too proud to take it? Not everyone likes to accept help." He expected she'd had to swallow a lot of her pride over the last year. Maybe she was tired of it. "If not for me, do it for Rowan."

"You realize that the idea of offering me the protection of your name seems very...well, it's straight out of one of those historical novels my gram likes to read."

He grinned. "Some would call it chivalry."

She raised an eyebrow. "Some would call it antiquated. And an affront to feminism."

He went to her and put his hand on her shoulder. "Sweetheart, my mama always taught me that feminism means the right to choose whatever path you want. You can choose what you want to do now. And there is no shame in choosing something that makes your life a little bit easier and safer for your child. I can't think of a better reason, actually."

Laura blinked. "That's what my mom used to say to

me, too. That it was about owning your choices. I've made some horrible ones, and I don't want to leap into another, you know?"

"Then let me leave it with you. Just think about it. Yes, it's unorthodox. And it's for sure not what you planned, but it could be a solution."

He got up to go. There was no sense banging on about it. Either she'd take him up on it or she wouldn't. And perhaps he was completely crazy to even offer. It seemed like a no-brainer, that's all. When someone was in trouble, you stepped in to help. Sure, this was kind of extreme, but it was also really simple. Never mind that the thought of her ex made his gut clench. Whatever he'd done had to be pretty significant for her to want to be invisible and let everyone think the worst of her.

She walked him to the door. He was on the front step when her soft voice stopped him. "Tanner?"

He turned and looked at her, standing there in the doorway. Her hair curled around her shoulders in dark red waves, and her eyes were clear and soft, perhaps a little sad. She didn't smile. She looked resigned.

"Thank you," she said quietly. "For offering to rescue me. First Gav, now you…well, even if it's a dumb idea, the fact that you offered shows me there are still good men in the world. It means a lot."

"Hell, Laura, you don't need to be rescued. You've got a spine of steel. You couldn't have dealt with the last few months if you didn't. Either way, the offer's still open."

"It's too much." He started to protest, but she raised her hand. "I know, it's only temporary. But it's too extreme."

A cry sounded through the open door; Rowan was awake and complaining. "I'd better go," she said, taking a step back. "See you around, Tanner."

"Bye."

He waited until she shut the door before he went to his truck. He thought about her all through the drive home. Thought about how pretty and sad she looked—except for when she looked at her daughter. Then her face was contented, happy and beautiful. He thought about the tiny house and the little things in need of repair, and wondered how she'd manage on her own. Thought about the man she spoke of and wondered how dangerous he really was. And Tanner thought about his own life, and how long he'd been holding back his real feelings of discontent because there was nothing to be done about them.

The ranch was a family operation and he was needed there. He knew it and it wasn't even that he resented it. It was more of a general feeling that he wanted something more. Something meaningful. Opportunities for that were slim in a town the size of Gibson. Particularly for a rancher with no formal education beyond his EMT certification. Maybe he couldn't make a difference to a lot of people, but maybe he could to one. Well, two. He smiled, thinking of Rowan's soft, dark hair.

When he arrived back at the ranch, he saw Maddy's car out front. She'd be there with her twin boys and she and Ellen, Tanner's mom, would be talking about recipes and all sorts of other domestic things. He thought again of Laura and how she'd admitted she wasn't much of a cook. Maddy was a town darling, and Laura was a pariah, even though she hadn't done what everyone thought she had.

He cut the engine but stayed in the truck, frowning as he surveyed the front yard, everything neatly trimmed around the front porch and a velvety carpet of grass surrounding the property. It wasn't that he begrudged Maddy any happiness. God knew she'd had a rough time, losing her husband. But her life was coming up roses, and Laura was scared...and alone.

It didn't seem fair.

Instead of going inside, he walked to the pasture just west of the barn where the newest calves frolicked about on long, gangly legs. There was something about them that he gravitated toward. They were so cute and unencumbered and playful.

Carefree.

Tanner rested his arms along the top of the fence and watched for a long time, trying to remember the last time he'd felt such youthful exuberance. He suspected it was probably before that fateful trip to Vegas when he'd had his heart stomped on and then handed back to him with a smile. Yes, that had made him grow up in a hurry.

Now he was just tired. Tired of the bar scene, tired of the label that had stuck to him, tired of spinning his wheels.

Laura had asked him what he would get out of such an arrangement. The truth was, marrying her would take a lot of the pressure off him. Pressure to live up to the single man reputation, the opposing pressure to settle down and the pressing need to get away from home and find his own place to live. And if marrying Laura—even for a short while—accomplished that, and kept her and her baby safe, as well? It seemed like a win-win in his book. Love didn't need to enter the equation.

A couple of calves approached the fence to investigate, and he put out his hand, wondering if they'd venture close enough for him to touch. One did, and he scratched the spot between his ears and rubbed his hand along the soft jaw. There was just one problem, of course. Laura thought his plan was nuts. Probably because it was. He was also pretty sure he had no idea how to change her mind.

He'd need to think of something else. With a sigh, he turned away from the fence and toward the house. He couldn't stay away from his family forever.

Chapter Five

As the evening meal ended, Tanner cleared his throat.

"Uh, I wanted to bring something up with you guys and see what you think."

Cole sat back in his chair and folded his arms. "Are you still thinking of buying that bull from Wyoming?"

"This isn't to do with the ranch. At least, not directly." His mom, Ellen, was clearing the table, but Tanner reached out and put a hand on her wrist. "Mom, sit for a minute, okay?"

Their father, John, hadn't said anything up to this point, but Tanner saw one thick eyebrow go up, just a tick. His opinion mattered most of all. John had had the least to say after the Vegas debacle. And he rarely said much at all, which meant that when he did speak you knew it was important. He'd built his whole life around the ranch and had a certain outlook on life. Including what a man did and didn't do.

Tanner was sure his father would have something to say if he knew his son had proposed to Laura Jessup.

Ellen sat back in her chair. "What is it, Tanner?"

He glanced around the table.

"I think it's time I found a place of my own."

Cole frowned. "You do?"

Tanner nodded. "Hell yes. Come on, Cole. You and Maddy are a big deal, and I bet it won't be long before those boys'll be here all the time. You're the real head of this place now and that's how it should be. And I'm a big boy. I probably should have moved out a long time ago. It's just been convenient to stay."

Ellen patted his arm. "Honey, I'm sure no one wants you to feel pushed out."

"I don't," he assured her, though he wouldn't say that he often felt like the odd man out. He knew she—and Cole—would feel badly about that. "I'm a grown man, Mom. Living at home. I kind of want my own place."

"Good," John said.

"Good?" Tanner met his father's gaze. Maybe Ellen hadn't been speaking for everyone.

"A man has to make his own way. You need to figure out what you want, Tanner. And I'm not sure you're going to do that living at home. A little independence can be a very good thing."

That wasn't what he'd expected from his father at all. "Thanks, Dad."

"Of course I'll still expect you bright and early in the morning. We still have a ranch to run."

Of course. Figuring out what he wanted was all well and good, as long as the work got done first. But then, it wasn't any different from what he'd expected, was it?

"Any idea where you'll go?" Cole asked, putting his empty coffee cup on his dessert plate.

Tanner knew where he'd like to go. Despite the poor cooking skills, the little house that Laura had bought was perfect. Maybe he should have suggested roommates first. What an idiot he'd been to propose. He could have helped her with expenses, at least. Instead he'd come up with the cockamamie idea about marriage. He'd laugh, but then he figured his folks would want to know why he was laughing, and there was no way he wanted to explain his impulsive proposal.

"I don't know yet," he replied honestly. "I'll have to look for a place in town, I guess. Or buy a place."

"Wouldn't you need some savings for a down payment?" Cole asked, chuckling a little.

It annoyed Tanner that his brother assumed he had no money. "I've got enough put aside. But I don't want to buy right away. Not until I'm sure where I want to be."

The silence around the table told him he'd surprised them all.

"I've been saving for a few years," he said, shrugging. "You've been paying me ranch hand wages, Dad, and giving me room and board. I haven't spent it all."

There was a glint of respect in his father's eyes, and Tanner welcomed it.

"You really want to do this?" his mom asked.

Unless he was mistaken, there was a sadness in her voice. He'd be the first of them to leave home, though most parents would be thrilled that one of their grown sons was getting out. He nodded. "I really do. I know the ranch is a family operation, but at some point we have to grow up and do our own thing, don't you agree?"

Ellen laughed. "You say that, but I bet you'll still eat most of your meals here and bring your laundry home."

Warmth flooded him at the affection in her tone. He felt a bit guilty for his dissatisfaction, because there was no doubt in his mind that he was loved. "I'd be an idiot for choosing my own cooking over yours," he said, pushing away from the table and standing. He leaned down and gave her a peck on the cheek. "Thanks, Mom. And Dad."

Cole stood, too, and grabbed the coffee cups from the table. "Face it, little bro. You're just looking for some privacy."

Tanner frowned, his eyebrows pulling together. "You know, Cole, I'm not getting anywhere near as much action as you think I am."

The kitchen fell oddly silent. "Gee, Tan," Cole said into the quiet. "I was just teasing."

Tanner shoved his hands into his pockets. "I know that ever since Vegas you've found it hard to take me seriously. And I played in to that, because I didn't want everyone to know the truth about what happened." He shook his head a little. "Oh, the wedding details are about right. But it wasn't all a lark. I was in love with Brit and I didn't want anyone to see how badly she'd hurt me. So I pretended to be a bit of a rebel and a ladies' man until the label stuck. The last thing I wanted was pity. This was just easier. But it's not who I really am. I thought that at least my family understood that."

Ellen's face creased with concern and even his dad's eyes widened with surprise. "Tanner," he said, his voice deep and sure, "you're a damn fine worker and a good man. You've never given us any reason for embarrassment, so if this is what you want, we're behind you."

He wondered if his dad would say the same thing if he knew about the proposal to Laura.

"Yeah, sorry, bro," Cole added, contrite. "I was just teasing, but I guess I hit a nerve."

"Sometimes people aren't what they seem on the surface," Tanner answered, watching his brother. According to Laura, Cole and Maddy knew that Gavin wasn't Rowan's father. "Sometimes people try to protect themselves by deflecting the truth."

Something flickered in Cole's eyes. Tanner was tempted to let Cole know that he also understood Laura's situation. In fact, he probably knew more about it now than either Cole or Maddy. But it had been told to him in confidence, and he would keep it to himself.

"I'm going out for a while," he said, knowing the alternative was sticking around here and getting stuck in front of the television. Right now he wanted some fresh air and room to breathe.

SEVERAL DAYS LATER, Laura couldn't stop thinking about Tanner's ludicrous suggestion.

She sat back in her desk chair, the casters rolling along the floor. The chair was comfortable enough, though hardly ergonomic. Still, the corner of her bedroom that she used as a home office was cozy. Particularly with a soothing cup of mint tea and an almond cookie from the pack she'd bought at the market. Only one—she was making them last.

As proposals went, Tanner's was hardly romantic. He'd been kind and, well, sexy, though she was pretty sure that was unintended. Tanner Hudson would sound sexy reading the darn phone book. No, his proposal had been just shy of a business proposition.

That had to be the only reason why she couldn't get it out of her head. Because from a purely business standpoint it actually kind of made sense.

Work was slowing down. She was building a website right now, but it was basic, and in another day or so it'd be finished. She should be spending this time building her own site. Drumming up her own business. But every time she thought about registering her domain, or filling out the proper tax and registration forms, she got a horrible twisting sensation in the pit of her stomach.

It was fear. In principle, hiding behind Tanner's name would make her a coward, and she didn't want to be that person. In practical terms…hell, she'd often thought that if she could just change her name she could breathe a lot easier.

Could they do it? It would be in name only; he'd said so. She'd become Laura Hudson. Not, she determined, Mrs. Tanner Hudson. The only thing that would change was her last name. And the fact that she'd have a roommate.

A roommate who she knew would also kick in with the expenses. There was that to consider, too. Even if she shouldered the mortgage on her own, someone to help with groceries and the light bill would be a huge help.

Of course, maybe Tanner wasn't interested anymore. It had been totally impulsive. And if he was, they'd have to lay out some ground rules right off the bat. Including how long they intended for the fake marriage to last.

She'd done a lot of crazy things in her life, but this one might just take the cake.

Before she could think better of it, Laura picked up her cell, and then realized she didn't even know his phone number. She was contemplating marrying the guy and she didn't even have his number in her darn phone. She laughed to herself, a soft sound of disbelief, and shook her head. When the best solution she could come up with was a wedding to a virtual stranger, things had really gotten out of hand.

Later, after Rowan was up from her nap, Laura dressed her in a cute little sweater and bonnet and made the drive into town. She was trying to cook for herself more, finding it cheaper than grabbing a meal at the diner or something prepackaged. Her efforts were dismal at best; she'd burned the stir-fry and discovered charred broccoli smelled horrible, and she'd undercooked the breaded chicken breast she'd attempted, leaving it crispy on the outside and gelatinous in the middle. But she wasn't giving up yet. She'd found a few recipes that looked simple, and she had a list of ingredients to buy. Laura hoped keeping the recipes simple translated to being easy on the wallet, too.

She had Rowan in a Snugli carrier and wheeled the grocery cart in front of her, adding a few packages of ground beef, a small tray of chicken thighs and a couple of pork chops from the meat department. Some people watched her curiously while others didn't seem to know she existed. It wasn't until she'd made it all the way through the store and was finishing up at the bakery section that she crossed paths with Tanner.

Something rushed through her, something that put her on alert. It was pleasure, she realized. She was happy to see him. And from the way his smile lit up his face, he was glad to see her, too.

"Well, hello." Tanner grinned and gave a polite nod. "Oh my gosh, Laura. I think Rowan gets bigger every time I see her."

Bonus points for complimenting the baby right off the bat.

"She certainly does," Laura replied, disgusted with herself for being so elated. She really didn't get out much, did she?

"How've you been?" Tanner asked. He leaned a little closer. "Any progress on the business?"

She shook her head. "I'm still trying to figure that one out." He didn't need to know how little work she was bringing in now.

She noticed the plastic container in his hand and smiled. "Glazed doughnuts?"

He chuckled. "I have a real thing for doughnuts. I love the cakey sugared ones at the diner, and my mom makes awesome chocolate ones. But then there are these kind, too, the puffy, yeasty ones with the sticky glaze. I swear I can eat six before I realize what's happening. They just melt in your mouth."

She thought back and remembered him getting a doughnut that day at the diner when she'd been there with Gramps. "So you have a doughnut addiction," she mused, grinning. "That's a pretty big vice you've got there, Hudson."

He raised one eyebrow. "I know. I've tried to find a Doughnuts Anonymous meeting, but they're scarce."

She laughed outright. When was the last time someone had teased and made her laugh like that?

"What about you?" He looked at her expectantly. "Any vices?"

"French fries," she said without hesitation. "Crispy, hot, salty French fries."

"Yum."

"Right?"

Tanner looked down at Rowan once more and unless Laura was mistaken, a look of tenderness passed over his face. The more she came to know him, the more she was sure that Tanner Hudson was a good man. Her experiences hadn't jaded her to the concept that there were a few of them still out there.

"I'd better not keep you from your shopping," he said, taking a step back. "I just came in for a midday pick-me-up. I'm apartment-hunting this afternoon."

He truly was determined to move out. A momentary flash of panic darted through her body. Maybe she'd lost her chance. It seemed he was serious about getting out on his own and it wasn't something he'd simply made up so his proposal would hold water. That was reassuring.

Laura quickly took things into account. He liked doughnuts. He was a handsome, hardworking guy, low maintenance, practical, but fun. Maybe she'd be stupid to let him slip through her fingers, even if it wasn't a "real" relationship. If she left it any longer, he'd find himself a place and the window of opportunity would close.

"I'm almost done," she found herself saying. "Do you want to grab a coffee to go with those doughnuts?"

"Sure, why not?"

He said it so easily. As though it didn't matter a bit that he was being seen with her. Even if he knew the truth, no one else did. Yet Tanner didn't seem to care. She doubted he knew how much she appreciated that.

It was a beautiful day, so instead of coffee Laura added a bottle of lemonade for herself to her grocery order and checked out. "Why don't we meet by the library?" she asked, digging out her wallet. "We can sit on one of the benches and enjoy the fresh air."

"Sounds good to me," Tanner replied. "I'll go grab a coffee to go with my doughnuts."

Laura sighed in relief as she wheeled the groceries to the car and put them in the trunk. Tanner was generally so solicitous that she'd half expected him to offer to help carry her groceries and then she'd have to refuse. But he hadn't, and she liked him more for it. Chivalry was nice, but it was also good to feel independent and capable and perhaps respected for it. Humming softly, she fastened in Rowan's car seat and drove the block and a bit to the library. When she pulled in, Tanner was already there, holding a brown paper cup in one hand and the doughnuts in the other. She chuckled a little and wondered how many of the sweets he'd eat with his beverage.

It took a minute to get the diaper bag and the lemonade and then put Rowan on her shoulder, but she did it. Rowan perked up, pushing one pudgy hand against Laura's shoulder and looking around with bright, inquisitive eyes.

"You always have your arms full," Tanner commented. "Maddy says she has huge biceps from lugging the twins around." It was no sooner out of his mouth than he looked stricken. "Oh, heck. I shouldn't have said that."

"Why not?" Laura led the way to the crushed gravel path. "I don't harbor any hard feelings toward her. We've made our peace, Tanner. Plus she's going out with your brother. You can talk about her. It doesn't bother me in the least."

"It's just, well, a little awkward."

She shrugged. "The perception of it is for sure, but it's not so bad. She knows that Gavin and I were just friends." She smiled a little. "It's everyone else who is all weird about it."

"Don't you ever wish you could set the record straight?" he asked, falling into step beside her.

"Of course. But then I look at Rowan, and I think that the longer I can keep assumptions where they are, the better."

They found a bench and sat down. Tanner stretched out his legs and sighed. "The sun feels good."

It really did. The warmth of it bathed Laura's face, while a light breeze whispered over the skin of her arms. Both of them wore simple T-shirts—Tanner's brown with a crew neck and hers a navy V-neck. She settled Rowan on her lap, then opened the lemonade bottle.

"Cheers," he said, tipping his coffee cup.

She laughed again, loving how being with him was so fun and easy. "Cheers." She tipped the neck of her bottle and then took a refreshing, tart drink. "Ahhh. That's good."

She bounced her right knee a little, keeping Rowan occupied, but the baby was so happy to be in the sun and fresh air, with all the bright colors of grass and sky and trees and flowers, that she sat perfectly contented.

"She likes it outside," Tanner said, putting his coffee down carefully and reaching for the doughnuts.

"She does. I wish our backyard was in better shape. We've gone out a few times, but it's not like this. Not with the nice grass and the flower gardens."

"You should put out some planters. Maybe a bird feeder or two. I bet she'd like that."

Laura nodded but looked down. She'd love to, but it always came down to money. And the fact that she wasn't making any. And that she needed to get her business officially up and running. Put out some proposals. She clenched her teeth, knowing what she had to ask. Feeling stupid. Feeling…desperate. And yes, even a little cliché. Screw that. A lot cliché. *Ugh, ugh, ugh.*

He held out a doughnut.

She took it, the sugary glaze clinging to her fingers. "Thanks," she murmured, and dutifully took a bite. Light, sweet, melt-in-your-mouth delicious. She licked the extra glaze off her lips and swallowed.

"Looks like Rowan wants some, too," he said, giving a small nod.

Rowan was leaning toward Laura's hand, her eyes focused on the doughnut and her little lips smacking. Laura laughed, put a tiny bit of the sweet on her finger, and placed it on Rowan's lips.

The happy smacking that followed made them both laugh. And that was when Laura knew what she had to do. She'd started a new life for herself and her daughter, but she needed to disappear better. And to do that, she needed Tanner.

"Tanner, about your suggestion the other day…"

He crammed the rest of his doughnut into his mouth and her confidence faltered.

It took several seconds for him to chew and swallow. "What suggestion? Do you mean…"

Her heart pounded ridiculously. "About us getting, you know…married. In name only, of course."

The smile slid from his face, and she was certain he'd changed his mind.

He licked off his thumb, turned a little on the bench so he faced her. "You've reconsidered?"

"When you mentioned apartment-hunting, I realized you must have been serious about wanting to get a place of your own. I actually considered asking you to move in as a roommate. That in itself would be a help…"

"Financially," he finished. "But not with the other problem. Of wanting to stay unfindable."

After a pause, she replied. "Yeah. So maybe we could be roommates who share a last name? It's not exactly ordinary, but it could work." Lord help her, did she actually sound a little hopeful?

His gaze held hers for a long minute. She noticed the deep blue of his irises, the black pupil, the little darker ring of blue that seemed to outline the color. This was riskier than she'd admit to him, because he was incredibly attractive and kind to boot. She'd have to be very careful not to let herself get personally involved. Stay friends. Ignore any inconvenient attraction that cropped up.

"You're sure? I mean, I'm still game if you are."

She glanced down at Rowan and a familiar wave of love washed over her. "For Rowan," she said softly, then looked up at Tanner. "I would do anything to protect her. You didn't see his face when he said he'd find me. I believe him. And whether or not it makes me weak…well, I'm scared, Tanner. If this means I can provide for my daughter and stay out of his way, I'll do it."

There was one thing that nagged at her. To be honest, there were several things they needed to talk about if they went through with it, but the one that she'd wondered about most was the reaction of the town. "You do realize you'll be the subject of gossip. That people will think you're crazy. I'm used to it by now, but you're not."

"After the Vegas incident, they'll probably say we deserve each other." He gave a self-deprecating huff, but then took her hand in his. "It'll be okay."

"Remind me again why you're doing this? Because marrying someone is a pretty big favor, you know? It's not like boosting a car or picking up a loaf of bread, or—"

"Shh," he said, giving her fingers a squeeze. "Maybe I don't like how you've been treated. And it's not like marriage holds a whole lot of meaning for me anymore, you know? I'm not going into this with any illusions. It's a contract between friends."

It sounded so cold. And yet there was relief, too. Why couldn't marriage be a simple contract for them? They didn't need to go into it with a lot of emotion and sentimentality. They could define it however they wanted.

"So we're going to get married?"

He nodded. "Let's do it." Then he rubbed his hand over his hair and laughed.

"What?"

"I just realized I have no idea where to start."

"Me, either," she replied. "I suppose we have to apply for a marriage license. Book a judge or justice of the peace or something. Tell our families."

Tanner's eyes caught hers. "Yes, we should do that. Are you up for it?"

The very idea made her stomach feel weightless. Somehow she dreaded telling her grandparents more than facing down Maddy and Cole, and Mr. and Mrs. Hudson.

She swallowed tightly, then nodded. "Let's iron out some details first, though, okay?"

"Good idea." Tanner closed the lid on the last remaining doughnuts, the plastic snapping together and getting Rowan's attention. Her hands waved up and down at the sound. "I have to get home and help Cole finish up for the day. But maybe later? I'll clean up and come over to your place, after Rowan goes to bed. We can work out the finer points then. How does that sound?"

Scary as hell.

"That's fine. We'd better get home, too. I have groceries in the car and I should get some of them in the fridge."

They got up from the bench and walked the short distance to the library parking lot. They were nearly to her car when Tanner slowed, and she looked back to see what the hold-up was.

His brows was knitted a little. "Laura, do you... I mean...hell. Do you want an engagement ring?"

That he asked made her heart hurt. Tanner Hudson was a genuinely nice guy. And despite the very platonic nature of their relationship, he was standing there looking like an unsure schoolboy asking if she wanted an engagement ring.

Maybe this was a mistake. But then again, Laura had accepted long ago that she would probably never have a real wedding and husband. Things didn't tend to work out that way for her. That didn't mean she didn't believe in them, though. To wear a ring when it wasn't real seemed almost sacrilegious.

"It's okay, Tanner. I don't need a ring." She smiled at him, wishing she could be happy and not feel this sadness weighing her down. "I'll see you later tonight, okay?"

"Okay."

He looked relieved. And not for the first time, Laura berated herself for the choices she'd made that put her in this position.

Chapter Six

By the time Tanner turned into Laura's driveway, the sun was almost down and his bad mood had moderated slightly.

Granted, he'd been edgy ever since he'd gotten back to the ranch. Laura had taken him by surprise today. He'd already decided that proposing had been foolish and silly, and of course she wouldn't say yes, which was why he'd started looking for his own place. But once she'd started talking he couldn't possibly tell her he'd changed his mind. Besides, it didn't have to be a huge deal. Like he'd said—it was nothing more than a contract between friends. The problem came with the realization that they'd probably have to keep that part quiet, which complicated things a fair bit. Were they going to have to pretend to be in love? He thought of her thick, coppery hair and blue eyes and the way she smiled, and knew pretending wouldn't be that difficult. A blessing and a curse.

Laura had turned on her porch light and he looked at it for a few seconds after he killed the engine.

He'd had had a few moments of panic since leaving her this afternoon. And then, after dinner, Cole had started in on the "going out yet again" thing and how

Tanner was never home. His parents said nothing, but he'd felt their agreement with Cole, real or imagined. In response, he'd snapped back that this was why he wanted his own place, and he'd gone out the door with his sour attitude leaving a bad taste in his mouth.

He was going to get married.

He blew out a breath, wishing he felt the same sort of happiness that Cole experienced with Maddy. Tanner had, once. It had been his biggest mistake. He shouldn't expect happiness now. He *didn't* expect it. He was looking to help someone who needed a hand. To do something that mattered more than shoveling cow shit and fixing fences. That was all this was.

If they married, a woman in a tough situation would be better able to provide for her daughter. As reasons went, it was good enough for him. And everyone else could take their opinions and shove them. He was sick to death of them.

Tanner got out of the truck and shut the door. It really was peaceful out this way, he realized. The air still held that spring-like scent, and he could hear peepers nearby, from either a little brook or some resting water. The sky was a peachy-lilac color, striated by wisps of pearly clouds. He took a moment and breathed deeply, trying to stop the merry-go-round in his head. He and Laura would figure this out, one detail at a time.

He climbed the steps slowly, lifted his hand and knocked on the door.

When Laura opened it, all the practiced words flew out of Tanner's head. She looked…wow. She'd dressed up. Nothing fancy, but she wore a pretty dress with little flowers on it that fell to just above her knees.

The gravity of what they were going to discuss struck him again.

"Hi," she said, and her cheeks flushed as she stood back and held open the door. "Come on in. Rowan's already asleep."

"Thanks." He entered and took a few moments to pull off his boots and put them by the door. She walked over to the fridge and the skirt of her dress swayed with each step. Tanner's mouth went dry.

"I made some iced tea. Do you want some?"

"Sure." His voice came out on a croak and he cleared his throat. "That'd be nice."

She turned back from the fridge with a glass pitcher in her hand. "I can't cook, but I can manage tea, hot or cold." She put it down and reached for a glass. "I guess you should know that right away if you haven't figured it out already. I'm not much of a cook. Sweet or plain?"

"Plain's fine," he said, and she poured and handed him the glass. Their fingers brushed and he got that nervous swirling in his gut again. Which was stupid. It hadn't been this way this afternoon in the park.

Laura poured her own glass of tea, added sugar and stirred it. Then she looked up at Tanner and took a shaky breath. "Are you having second thoughts?" she asked.

"Are you?"

She shook her head. "No fair. I asked you first."

He was, but he didn't want to admit it. It wasn't about wanting to or not, but more to do with the seriousness of the situation. He was glad of that, actually. That neither of them was being flippant about it.

"No," he replied.

"Okay. Let's go in and talk, then."

He followed her into the living room. A lamp was already lit in the corner, chasing away the twilight and making it cozy and welcoming. Laura sat in a chair, leaving him the sofa. It told him a lot that she didn't sit with him, but chose to put some distance between them. Keeping it businesslike. Which might have worked except for that dress. He'd never seen her in one before. When she crossed her left knee over her right, he caught a glimpse of a small tattoo just below her ankle bone. From where he sat, it looked like a hummingbird.

There was a lot he didn't know about Laura Jessup.

She picked up a pad of paper and a pen from the end table and clicked the top, preparing to write.

He got the feeling he was about to fill in a lot of the blanks.

LAURA FIGURED THE only way to get through the evening was to treat it like a business meeting. Otherwise she'd be liable to lose her focus and get all sentimental or weaken and not go through with it.

A contract. That was all this was. They needed to discuss terms and plans and timelines, and to keep it straight, she needed to write it all down.

"So," she began, forcing her voice to come out calm and even. "The first thing we should do is pick a date and work from there."

"The sooner the better, I suppose." Tanner sipped his tea and smiled encouragingly.

"It's May. We're headed right into prime wedding season, and most officiants are probably booked.

Would you like me to check into it and find the first available date?"

He looked shocked for a moment, and then the pleasant expression returned to his face. "Yes, that would be great."

"Surely we can find something in the next month. Why don't we work with that presumption, and then we'll shift if we need to? Does it matter if it's on a weekend?"

He was quiet, so she looked up from her paper. His expression was slightly blank, so she nudged, "Tanner?"

"It doesn't matter. One day is as good as the next."

"Good." She made a note on her paper and looked up again. "I'm assuming you'd like to tell our families before we go to the county office for a license. I was thinking this weekend we could get it over with and then Monday go fill out the paperwork. Do you think your parents will be around for that? I can call my grandparents tomorrow and set something up. Gram's still slow getting around, so they'll probably be home most of the weekend."

"I suppose telling them should be first on our list." He frowned.

"And probably the hardest part," she said. "And we should talk about how we're going to present it. Are we going to be honest about why we're doing it? Or are we going to, you know, act like it's real?"

Tanner stared at her for a long moment. "I don't know," he answered cautiously. "What do you want to do?"

She sighed and her shoulders slumped as she sat back in her chair. "I honestly don't know. I keep thinking how disapproving my grandparents will be if we tell them it's in name only. They're old-fashioned. They already think our generation doesn't take marriage seriously enough."

"They'll still be disappointed down the road, when we divorce." Tanner ran his finger along his lower lip. "The question is, which would be worse for them? Or harder for you? Now or later?"

She didn't answer. "What about your folks? What do you want to tell them?"

He pursed his lips. "I don't know. I don't know if we could sell it to them, you know? Your grandfather has at least seen us together, and we could let him draw conclusions. But I'm not sure that'd work with my family. I'm not sure they'd believe we fell in love."

He almost stumbled over the words, and she realized the idea had him scared to death. It was probably just as well.

"Plus, Maddy and Cole will ask questions," she said.

"And Mom and Dad…well, they know the rumors, Laura." His eyes were wide and honest as he looked at her. "Maybe it would be better to tell them the truth."

Laura shook her head as her chest tightened. "No, Tanner. Too many people know already. I know your parents are good people, but the more who know, the greater the chance of something slipping. Maybe we can tell them we've been seeing each other in private. With the baby, we might be able to sell that notion."

Tanner nodded slowly. "That might work. I go out a lot, just to get out of the house. And I mentioned wanting to move out recently. But, Laura…" His gaze touched hers. He was so serious right now. It was strange seeing him this way, and not the happy, smiling guy she normally encountered. There was something incredibly alluring about Tanner Hudson when he was being responsible and somber.

He sighed. "With my family, I think you're going to have to be prepared for some push back. Because of my history, because of yours. It shouldn't matter, but there'll be questions."

"Like if we want to rush into this. If you're ready to be a father. If I'm the kind of girl you want to be saddled to for life." It hurt to say the words, even though she knew it was true.

"Possibly. And for you, too. I have a terrible track record with marriage. They'll want to know if you're sure you know what you're getting into."

"So we shouldn't count on them for unqualified support."

"They'll come around. But probably not right away. I don't want to see you get your hopes up."

She chuckled, a dry, humorless sort of laugh. "Hopes, Tanner? I gave up on high hopes a long time ago."

The sad truth of that settled around them. "I'm sorry," he said, and he sounded as though he absolutely meant it. It was an odd moment to feel so incredibly close to him, but she did. What a pair they made. Romantic failures, both of them. Poor judges of character. And yet this time, in this one instance, she felt she was one hundred percent right to trust in him.

"So," he said quietly, "that just leaves deciding what to do about, uh, living arrangements."

She swallowed. "Well," she said, lifting her eyes to his, "you might as well move in here. You can have the bedroom and I'll sleep in with Rowan, like I did when Gramps was here."

Tanner frowned and shook his head. "Laura, you're not sleeping on a blow-up mattress. You should have the bedroom. Maybe we can move Rowan's crib in there and I'll sleep in her room."

Laura thought of the pastel-painted walls, the frilly curtains and the decals of flowers and hearts she'd stuck on the wall in lieu of more expensive decorating. "Really? It's not quite your style."

"Then we'll get you a new bed. Put it in that room so you have a decent place to sleep."

"It should be a single bed. It's cheaper and that way Rowan can move into it when she's older and we're—"

She stopped abruptly.

"Divorced," he finished.

"This is the strangest conversation," she admitted. "Tanner, are we crazy?"

"Probably," he agreed. "But it's our business. No one else's."

"You can move in as soon as you like," she said. "Either before or after the...the wedding."

"Okay." He tapped his foot lightly, and she realized he was nervous. It made her feel better somehow, and made her like him even more. Tanner was a good man. But he was also human, and she didn't feel like a complete failure around him. That was something very different from other relationships, including the one between her and Gavin, which had been friendly. Still, there'd been a superiority there that neither had spoken of, but existed nonetheless. Gavin had been married, with twin babies, and a career as a lawyer. What had Laura achieved since high school beyond screwing up? Sure, she had a career, but it barely paid her bills and her personal life was a disaster.

"If we've covered the basics, I guess I should go," he said, putting his hands on his knees. "You probably want to get to bed soon."

It was barely past eight-thirty. "You could stay a while if you wanted," she suggested. "If we're going to live together, we'll have to get used to being in the same room from time to time."

"Of course. We're friends. That doesn't have to change at all." The words were the right ones, but there was a strain around them, too. As if he was trying to convince her—or himself.

"Do you want to stay and watch TV for a while? I usually watch one of those procedural dramas from nine until ten. Or we could watch something else if you want."

"That sounds fine to me." He patted the cushion beside him. "You can sit over here if you like. I don't bite."

The sofa did afford a better view of the television. She got up from her chair and picked up the remote, then sat carefully on the cushion, leaning against the padded back and crossing one leg over her knee. There was no sense pretending this was easy. Maybe it would be better if they just got everything out in the open. "This is kind of awkward, isn't it?" she asked.

Tanner grinned. "Aw, it'll just take some practice. If we're going to be convincing, we should get used to spending some time together. It'll be expected."

"I suppose you're right. I hadn't thought of that."

He turned to face her as she clicked the button

on the remote to turn on the TV. "You can trust me, Laura. You know that, right?"

Did he realize he'd said those words to her before? She found herself locked in his gaze, his earnest eyes searching hers. It had been in the ambulance on the way to the hospital, and she'd started to panic. The pain had been getting intense and she was scared and feeling alone and as though everything was out of control. Tanner had been there beside her, focused on her face as the contraction seized her body, reassuring her that her baby was fine and everything was going to be okay. "You can trust me, Laura," he'd said, holding her hand. "Everything is going to be just fine. Breathe."

It was hard to breathe again, but for a very different reason.

"I want to believe that," she said. "You've been the first person to really be a friend since…"

"Since Gavin died."

She nodded.

"Do you miss him?"

The sound from the television provided some background noise, but she heard only Tanner's voice, saw only his face. There was no judgment or condemnation written on it. It was the strangest thing.

"Is it wrong to say no?" she asked, feeling her cheeks heat. "I mean, not in the way you mean. We dated in high school, and he was a good man, but we were truly just friends. I felt terrible when the accident happened, of course. He was far too young and with such a nice family. But I wasn't in love with him, Tanner. Our past gave us a connection and I knew he was a good man. That was why I asked for his help. Not because I was still…no."

She squeezed Tanner's fingers. "Thank you for asking, though. You're the first. Because of the rumors, I haven't felt entitled to any grief, you know?"

He squeezed her hand back.

"Tanner?"

"Yeah?"

She licked her lips nervously. "There's something else I want you to know."

"Okay."

"Even if I'd had feelings for Gavin, I wouldn't have acted on them. I've made a lot of mistakes, but I'm not the kind of person who would cheat, or be The Other Woman."

"I know that," he said easily. Just like that. As if there was no question at all of her integrity.

And then he smiled at her, and her heart gave a definitive thump in response.

She slid over on the sofa and turned to face the TV. Roommates. That was all they were going to be. Maybe they'd have to pretend otherwise for a while, but she'd simply keep reminding herself that it was fantasy. That it was all for Rowan and her future.

The opening theme of her show began and she pretended to concentrate on it while Tanner relaxed and hummed along a little with the music.

They were going to do this. It was the craziest thing she'd ever done. And if it worked out, the smartest. Just as soon as they got to the county office and got the license.

Chapter Seven

Tanner's palms were sweating as he and Laura made their way from the truck to the front steps of her grandparents' small bungalow. The yard was plain, but it was well kept, with the grass freshly mowed and a few pots of red flowers sitting on the gray-painted wooden stairs. Charlie and Patricia Jessup were in their seventies, but it looked as though they were still more than able to care for the property.

Laura was dressed in neat pants and a flowery spring top. Very casual, but pretty and feminine, too. She'd dressed Rowan in a romper that was red and white and ruffled beyond reason. Right now Rowan was perched on Laura's arm as they neared the door. Laura looked as nervous as he felt. But they'd agreed that telling her grandparents first would be easiest.

Patricia came to the door and opened it in welcome. "Laura, dear!" Tanner noticed the older woman's skin was pale, but her eyes twinkled out a welcome. "Goodness, Charlie told me you'd been spending time with a young man." Her smile widened. The knot in Tanner's stomach tightened.

"Gram, this is Tanner Hudson. Tanner, my grandma Patricia."

"Ma'am," Tanner said, taking off his hat.

"Oh, no need for ma'am." She flapped her hand at him and opened the door wider as they ascended the steps. "Come in, you two. I baked some cinnamon rolls this morning and I put on a pot of coffee."

"You didn't need to do that," Laura chided. "You should still be resting."

Patricia chuckled. "I'm not dead yet. Besides, those cinnamon rolls aren't a speck of trouble. And they're your grandpa's favorite."

The inside of the house was so clean Tanner was sure they could have eaten their rolls off the shiny floor. The décor was old-fashioned, but welcoming, and Patricia led them straight through to the kitchen. Patio doors led to a small back deck, and the door was open and the screen pulled across so the warm breeze wafted in, bringing with it the scent of grass and the sweet aroma of some sort of flowering shrub.

Charlie came around the corner. "Well, now. I knew there had to be some occasion for cinnamon rolls. Hello, sweetheart." He grinned and went right to Laura, planting a kiss on her cheek. Then he touched an arthritic finger to Rowan's nose before holding his hand out to Tanner. "Nice to see you again, Tanner."

"Thank you, sir."

"Sit down, you two. Tanner, what do you take in your coffee?"

"Just a little cream, thanks."

"Are you having coffee, Laura?"

"Maybe just half a cup," she said, and Tanner glanced over at her. He knew for a fact that she wasn't drinking much caffeine because she was still breast-feeding. The idea itself made a warm blush crawl up his chest, thinking about the way her full breasts filled out her top. He needed to stop that sort of thinking. Truth was, he was sure that she only agreed to the coffee because she was anxious about this afternoon and wanted to be as accommodating as possible.

When everyone had a cup of coffee and a plate with a warm roll, Laura settled Rowan on her knee and smiled weakly at Tanner. She wanted to get it over with. As the moment stretched out, her eyes seemed to plead with his. She wanted him to be the one to speak up.

His heart pounded in double time and he took a deep breath. He put his mug on the table. "Mr. and Mrs. Jessup, we asked if we could visit today because we wanted to tell you some news."

Charlie's gaze narrowed slightly, but an easy smile remained on Patricia's lips.

Different phrases rushed through his head, all jumbling together as he struggled with what to say next. "We, uh…that is, since Christmas…" He coughed and started again. "You probably know that I was one of the EMTs in the ambulance the day Rowan was born."

"Yes, of course," Patricia said, smiling encouragingly. "And she's so precious, isn't she?"

"She is," Tanner agreed. "The thing is, since then, well, Laura and I have been seeing a lot of each other. The other night I asked her to marry me and she said yes."

Charlie's keen eyes darted from Tanner to Laura and back again. Tanner noticed that Laura's cheeks held twin red spots and that she was focused on something on Rowan's collar instead of looking up.

"Laura?" Charlie said her name gently, and Tanner saw her steel herself, then lift her head and smile at her grandfather.

"Tanner's been so good to me," she said, her voice sweet and soft. "He's kind, and considerate, and gentle. And he doesn't mind that I'm not a very good cook." She laughed lightly, and Tanner admired how she was able to make a small joke. It somehow made her explanation seem more authentic. The compliments already made him feel a little awkward. He also felt guilty for lying, and imagined her guilt was far worse. After all, Charlie and Patricia were her family, not his.

Though his was up next.

"Oh, sweetie," Patricia said. "I'm so happy for you, if this is what you want. That sweet little girl should have a daddy."

Ouch. He knew that would hit Laura right where it hurt, but she only smiled at her grandmother and ran a hand over Rowan's dark cap of hair.

"You're sure this is what you want?" Charlie asked, his gaze sharp and assessing. The blush on Laura's cheeks brightened, and Tanner stepped in.

"Laura's a strong, capable, kind woman. I'm a very lucky man, Mr. Jessup."

"I seem to recall telling you not to hurt my girl," Charlie said, his lips a thin line as he stared at Tanner.

"Grandpa! When did you do that?"

"The day I was at your place for dinner and we were in the living room," Tanner replied, holding the old man's gaze. "And I have no intention of hurting her, sir. Just the opposite. I want to take care of her."

"I can take care of myself," Laura said acidly.

He looked at her and raised his eyebrows. "Of course you can. That's obviously not what I meant."

Of course she could look after herself. But he figured the couple they were trying to convince would appreciate the sentiment.

Patricia did for sure. "Will you stay at the family ranch, then? And does this mean you're not going back to work, Laura?"

He let Laura field the questions. "We'll live at my house, and Tanner will drive to the ranch each day. And I most certainly am going back to work. I'm going to increase my business and work from home. That way, I can help support the family and still be with Rowan."

Her grandma smiled. "I've always felt a girl needed a skill. You just never know when you might be on your own. Good for you, honey." She turned to Tanner. "Tanner, this girl's going to keep you on your toes."

"I'm counting on it," he replied, picking up his fork.

"One more thing," Laura said. "Neither one of us wants anything big. We've booked a justice of the peace for three weeks from today."

"That's the third week of June. Oh, what a lovely time for a wedding. But can you be ready that soon?"

"It'll be a small civil ceremony, Gram. It's what we want."

Tanner wished he could take Laura's hand. He wondered if she was thinking about a big church wedding with a white dress, flowers and all the trappings women seemed to like. Maybe he should have asked if she wanted that. It just seemed more expedient this way. Besides, he'd have a hard time making his vows in a church knowing they weren't for real.

"Are we not to be invited, then?"

There was disappointment in Patricia's voice, and

he gave Laura a short nod. Surely, they could each have a few people present. He'd want Cole to be his best man, or at least his witness for the official documents.

"Of course you're invited," Laura replied, her voice light with what he thought sounded like relief. "You're my closest family."

"It'll just be you, and a few from my side," Tanner said. "We haven't picked a location yet, but we'll let you know as soon as we do."

The conversation relaxed for a while then, and they ate cinnamon buns and sipped coffee and talked about Rowan's latest milestones and Patricia's recovery from her illness. After they'd been there an hour, Rowan started to fuss and Tanner knew they should get on to the ranch and get the rest of the day over with. Laura disappeared to change Rowan's diaper and Tanner thanked the Jessup's for the hospitality, trying not to feel like a fraudster. It wasn't until they were outside on the step that Charlie put his hand on Laura's arm.

"Girly, are you sure you know what you're doing?" He said it in a low voice, but Tanner heard. He knew Laura had to answer this one herself, and wished she could be spared having to. However, they'd decided to do this and it had been with the full knowledge that difficult conversations were part of the package.

"Gramps," she said softly, patting his hand, "it's about time I started making some smart decisions in my life. I have Ro to think of now, too. Tanner's a good man and I'm happy when I'm with him. I know I'm doing the right thing."

Charlie's sharp eyes softened somewhat. "You take care of our girl, you hear?" He aimed this command at Tanner. "She's one in a million."

"Yessir, she is," Tanner agreed. "Thank you for the coffee and rolls, Mrs. Jessup."

She held out a plastic container. "I packed some for you to take home," she said, pressing them into his hand. "Let us know the details, now."

"We will."

They walked back to the truck, and Tanner felt both a rush of relief that it was over and another wave of anxiety since they still had to face the Hudson family. Laura buckled Rowan into her car seat and then got in the passenger side, letting out a deep breath as Tanner started the engine.

"One down, one to go," he said encouragingly, while inside he felt like a man about to start the long walk to the gallows. Maybe he should tell them alone, but then they'd wonder why Laura wasn't there.

And to be honest, it felt right that they face their families together. It was what real married couples did and they needed to give the impression of being a real couple, didn't they? Unless...

"You're sure you don't want to tell them the truth?" he asked, half hoping she'd changed her mind.

"I keep asking myself the same question," Laura answered as they turned out of the drive onto the road. "But the fewer people who know about Spencer the better, Tanner. I keep coming back to that."

"You can trust my parents, you know. And Maddie and Cole already know."

She sighed. "Can we talk about this later? Maybe someday down the road? But not today."

He heard the stress in her voice and felt badly that he'd added to it. "Okay," he replied, heading east toward the Hudson ranch.

They were halfway there when Rowan started crying.

"Is it nap time or something?" he asked, his nerves starting to fray. He was edgy enough without adding the shrill cry to the mix.

"Yes, probably. And she's hungry. I knew I should have fed her earlier, but my grandfather is so uncomfortable with me nursing...."

Tanner's jaw clenched. "And you probably don't want it to be the first thing you do at my parents' place, either, huh?"

"I should have, you know, expressed enough for a bottle." Her cheeks were bright red.

Tanner tried a smile. "The practicalities of having a small baby," he offered. "As a paramedic, I've heard a lot of moms say that once you've had a baby, modesty kind of goes out the window."

She gave a relieved laugh. "Yeah, that's about right. Modesty is sometimes a real luxury. Moms do what needs to be done."

"And sacrifice themselves."

Tanner turned off the highway down a side road and pulled into a little lane that led into someone's field. "Okay, Mom. There's not a soul around but me. Your baby's hungry. I can take a walk if you like."

"Only if you're uncomfortable," she said, blushing again. He thought she looked really pretty when her cheeks pinked up like that. "I mean, I'm going to be doing it at home for a while yet. And I'd rather not hide in the bedroom."

He stared at her. "Hide in the bedroom? Don't be ridiculous. If it's privacy you want, say the word and I'll be the one to leave."

Rowan was still crying. Laura looked as if she

wanted to say something but instead she got out and opened the back door, took Rowan out of the seat and brought her up front. Tanner made sure he focused on whatever was outside his window and not the rustling sounds happening beside him.

"Tanner," she said softly. "It's okay. See?"

He looked over. She'd spread a soft flannel blanket over her shoulder, creating a discreet drape over Rowan's head. But he saw the little feet resting on the curve of Laura's belly, heard the quiet suckling sounds and realized something incredibly new, strange and disconcerting.

The natural act of a woman feeding her child was an intimate and profound thing, filling him with awe and respect and affection and...

He swallowed against a lump in his throat and turned away. And love. There was something so feminine and powerful about it. Rowan must have pulled back and he heard her cough a little bit, and Laura's attention was diverted as she adjusted things. When Tanner glanced over, he caught a glimpse of creamy white breast, and Rowan's soft little head tucked securely against her, obscuring any view of Laura's nipple.

He shifted in his seat and stared, unseeing, out the windshield as minutes ticked by. He was marrying this woman and she was asking him to be her friend. Entertaining thoughts that ran deeper than friendship would only complicate things. But how did you stop thoughts?

"She's asleep, Tanner. I'm going to put her back in her seat and we can be on our way."

He looked over. Laura had adjusted her blouse and it was as if nothing had happened. He pasted on a smile. "No problem. Kid's gotta eat." But when Laura carefully got out to fasten Rowan in her seat, Tanner let out a huge sigh. There was no sense fooling himself. He'd felt something unexpected when he saw the curve of her breast, pictured more. It had been desire, pure and simple. She was a pretty woman, and she was kind and generous, too. A man would be crazy not to fall for that.

He'd have to be careful if they went through with this marriage. She wasn't interested in him that way and he didn't want to make things weird. It was just the stress of the day, he reasoned, and the intimacy of the moment that had gotten to him.

When Laura got back inside the truck, she treated him to a wide smile. "Thank you for stopping," she said. "It'll save me from an embarrassing moment or ten later on."

"No problem," he replied, and put the truck in reverse.

He needed to get them to the ranch. Because if they sat here in the middle of nowhere for much longer, he was going to do something stupid. Like kiss her. And that would throw a monkey wrench into all their plans.

LAURA FOLDED HER hands in her lap, but inside, her stomach was flip-flopping like one of the trout that Gramps used to catch on their Saturday morning fishing trips. It had been totally considerate of Tanner to stop, and a relief, too. But she'd thought he'd hop out of the truck, take a walk. Instead he'd stayed, and she'd tried to be discreet.

Until Rowan had coughed and pulled back, and Laura had had to adjust the baby and blanket. The flannel slipped and for a few moments her breast had been exposed.

It's just a breast, she reminded herself. She was pretty sure Tanner had seen one before. The preposterous idea nearly made her laugh. The difference was he hadn't seen *her* breast before, and he probably hadn't been in a situation where he was on his way to tell his parents he was marrying a woman he didn't love, and on a temporary basis.

And then there was the fact that the idea of him seeing her sent a strange tingling to her core. It wasn't much of a stretch to imagine what it would be like to be loved by a man like Tanner. He was handsome, charming, sexy as hell. Chivalrous and kind. He'd be a gentle lover, she suspected. Gentle and yet intense…

Snap out of it, Laura, she thought, and forced herself to look out the truck window instead of stealing glances at him. Those were her feelings, but they weren't real, she was sure of it. Besides, she was pretty sure there was nothing sexy about watching a woman breast-feed. What had he called it? Oh yes. Practicalities. Not a thing romantic about that, was there?

There was no danger of Tanner having similar feelings, so she might as well push them aside and stop worrying about it.

Her heart rate was nearly back to normal when he finally reached the front gate to the lane leading to the Hudson house. It was probably three times the size of her little bungalow, well-kept and homey looking with balcony planters on the front railing and a pair of wooden rocking chairs out front. A car and a truck already sat in the drive, and she looked over at Tanner, silently questioning.

"My mom's car and my dad's truck," he explained, but she noticed a new tightness to his jaw. This wasn't going to be an easy hour. They were expected for dinner, but as Tanner's obvious nerves proved contagious, Laura wondered if they'd even stay that long.

Might as well get it over with. Cole and Maddy and the boys weren't there at least. Smaller numbers were easier to manage in her limited experience.

"You ready?" she asked, trying to lighten her tone.

"Are you?"

"Tanner, they can't say anything worse than what I've heard whispered around town. But they're your folks. Your relationship with them is important. I'll be fine. It's you I'm worried about."

He reached over and took her hand. "You're a strong woman, you know that?"

"I don't know. I don't think I'm that strong. Maybe I just know what I can't change so I deal with it."

Her fatalistic point of view wasn't as cheering as she'd hoped, but Tanner gave her fingers a final squeeze. "So we're sticking to the seeing-each-other-since-December story?"

She nodded. "I still think it's best."

"Okay. If that's what you want."

She retrieved Rowan from the back and cradled the sleeping baby against her shoulder. Tanner solicitously carried the diaper bag and they walked up to the front door. Laura's insides truly trembled this time. Her grandparents were one thing, but this... this was quite another. She'd probably be judged. Be found lacking. Be asked intrusive questions and she'd be lying, something she was getting used to and didn't like about herself at all.

Tanner must have sensed her anxiety because he'd been about to knock on the door, but instead dropped his hand and turned to face her. His eyes were troubled as he stared down at her, his lips a thin line. "We don't have to do this."

"Meet your parents? Or get married?"

"Either," he confirmed. "I'll help you find another way."

"Why?" she asked, keeping her voice low. Rowan's warm breath made a damp patch on her collar. "Why are you doing this? Why do you even care?"

He lifted his hand and put it gently along her cheek. "Because five months ago I sat in an ambulance with one of the bravest women I'd ever met. That's the only birth I've ever attended, do you know that? Something happened to me that day, and it made me look at things differently. Then when I got to know you better, and you trusted me with the truth... Laura, no one should have to go through that alone. I'd like to think we're friends. And friends help each other."

"This is a pretty big favor. It goes well above and beyond friendship, Tanner."

His charming grin was back. "I don't see anyone else beating down my door looking for happily ever after," he said lightly, chuckling. "This isn't a sacrifice for me, Laura. But somehow I don't think I'll be able to convince you of that."

"I don't deserve this," she murmured, and the hand on her cheek slid down to cup her chin.

"I don't want to hear you say that again, you hear? Everyone deserves a second chance." And he leaned forward and kissed the tip of her nose. Just as the front door opened and Ellen stood in the doorway.

Chapter Eight

Laura stepped back quickly, holding Rowan tight in her arms. Her cheeks flared; she could feel the heat rush into them as Tanner turned to his mother and offered a wide smile. "Hi, Mom."

"Sweetheart," she said, moving forward. "And, Laura. Welcome. Come on in."

Ellen said nothing about the tender moment she'd interrupted, but it had certainly set the tone. Laura could feel Ellen's assessing gaze as they went inside, and Tanner put the diaper bag down on a chair just inside the living room. If he'd wanted to give the impression of romance right off the bat, he'd done a fine job.

"Your dad should be up from the barn any moment," Ellen said. "Would either of you care for a drink or something?"

Tanner looked at her, questioning, and Laura forced a smile. "Maybe some water. That would be great."

"I'll get it," he said, and went to the cupboard for a glass. "Have a seat, Laura. We can sit and relax for a while. Right, Mom?"

"Of course."

And still there was that guarded, questioning look.

"So," Ellen said, her tone deceptively smooth. "You're the one Tanner's been so secretive about."

Laura opened her mouth and closed it again, unsure of how to reply. Tanner handed her a glass of water and smiled. "A man my age doesn't want his mother to know everything," he teased. He looked back at Ellen and sent her an outrageous wink. "We wanted some privacy until we sorted a few things out."

"I see."

Laura doubted that his mom did see, but Tanner was doing a wonderful job of deflecting and she went to his side. They walked into the living room and sat on the sofa while Ellen sank into a plush wing chair. "Thank you for having us over, Mrs. Hudson." This was the woman who, for a short while anyway, would be her mother-in-law. She'd rather have her as an ally than an adversary.

Rowan shifted on her shoulder and Laura made a small adjustment, then saw a softening of Ellen's expression as she looked at the baby. Rowan might just be the ticket here, she realized. From everything Tanner had said, Ellen doted on Maddy's twin boys.

"This is Rowan," Laura said softly, the smile coming naturally as it always did with regards to her daughter. "She's five months old."

"She's beautiful," Ellen acknowledged, a little of the strain leaving her voice. "She's got such a lovely head of dark hair."

Ellen looked up at Laura. Laura's hair, of course, was like waves of copper. Clearly, Rowan didn't get her hair from her mother.

"It was a little lighter when she was first born," Laura offered, touching the soft cap of hair.

"You and Tanner. You're involved?"

"Mom..." Tanner began, but Laura shook her head at him.

"It's okay, Tanner. She's your mom. And while Rowan is still so very tiny, I can imagine that moms always look out for their kids, no matter how old they are." She met Ellen's gaze. "Tanner has been so kind to me ever since the day Rowan was born. He's a rare thing these days, I think. A gentleman through and through." She grinned now, remembering. "He even passed muster with my grandfather, and he's a tough nut to crack."

"You've spent time with Charlie and Patricia?" There was a note of censure in Ellen's tone, as though she was annoyed at being left out.

"Charlie mostly," Tanner said, jumping into the conversation. "He stayed with Laura when Patricia was in the hospital a while back. I ran into Laura and Charlie at the diner one day, and then had dinner with the both of them. He's a real character."

"Always was," Ellen said affectionately. "I'm sorry, Laura. This is just a bit awkward. Considering Maddy and everything. No sense dancing around it."

"I know." Her throat felt tight and her chest small as she faced yet another person's censure. "Maddy and I have made peace, Mrs. Hudson. We talked just before Christmas. Not that we're BFFs or anything, but we're good."

"How can that be?"

Laura pursed her lips. "Honestly, that's between Maddy and me. You'll have to ask her." And Laura hoped if she did she'd keep her secret as she'd promised.

"Laura," Tanner said quietly beside her. She knew

what he wanted. He wanted her to tell the truth. And oh, she was tempted. Just as she had been for months, with the words to vindicate herself sitting on her tongue, ready to be spoken. And then she thought of Spence, and Rowan, and the reason for doing all this in the first place, and she swallowed them down like a bitter pill.

"Mrs. Hudson, there are things you don't know, and things I can't tell you. But if Maddy can forgive me, maybe you can, too?"

The back door opened and shut and Laura realized that Tanner's dad had arrived. The sudden noise of the door stirred Rowan, who nuzzled against Laura's shirt and then lifted her head, rubbing one chubby fist over her nose as she blinked, coming awake. John came in from a back room—Laura assumed it was a back door to a mudroom or some such—and halted at the scene before him. She and Tanner were on one side of the living room, sitting stiffly on the sofa. Ellen was across from them, ensconced in the chair. And they were clearly on different sides of the conversation.

"Hope I'm not too late," he said cautiously.

"Of course not, Dad." Tanner stood and stepped forward to shake his father's hand, causing a look of confusion to pass over John's face. "Have you met Laura?"

"Mr. Hudson," she said, smiling and offering a small nod. She held Rowan with her right arm, which made shaking hands cumbersome, so she decided a smile would have to do.

"Hello," he said, then looked at Tanner, glanced at his wife, and back to Laura again. "Who have we here?"

"This is my daughter, Rowan. Tanner helped deliver her last December."

It was easy to tell when John understood. His eyes widened slightly and his gaze darted to Tanner again. "Oh," he said, and that was all for a few moments. Then his eyebrows lifted again and he peered at her shoulder. "She's a sweet one." He smiled and his whole face softened. John Hudson liked babies. That might work in their favor, too.

"Yes, she is. Sleeping through the night most of the time, which is a great relief to me." Laura felt herself relax just a little. Tanner's father felt like an ally. Mothers were bound to be the overprotective ones, weren't they? Particularly with their sons?

There was a momentary distraction as Ellen asked John about a cup of coffee and gave him a phone message, so Laura turned to Tanner and let out a breath.

"Your mom isn't happy."

"She'll come around."

"But we haven't even mentioned the wedding yet." That troubled her. And she'd brought Maddy into it without intending to. "Right now she just thinks we're dating." Laura bit down on her lip.

She needed to compose herself if they were going to get through this visit. "Could you show me where the bathroom is? I need to excuse myself for a moment."

"Of course."

Tanner led her down a short hall, but once there he reached for Rowan. "Let me take her for a few minutes."

"Are you sure?" She realized he hadn't held her much, except for that brief time at the café when she'd turned her back and changed her shirt.

"Of course I'm sure. I've held her before. And it's only for a few minutes."

She eased Rowan into his arms, seeing his biceps curl in his shirt sleeve as he bent his arm to cradle her close.

She sighed, getting a swirly, silly feeling at seeing her baby daughter in his strong arms. What was it about tough men and babies and puppies that turned women into mush anyway?

She turned around and resolutely went into the bathroom and shut the door behind her.

When she returned to the living room, Tanner sat on one end of the sofa, with Rowan sitting on his thigh and leaning back against the wall of his chest, patting her hands together happily. His parents were seated in matching chairs across from him, smiling at Rowan and something Tanner was saying.

He looked up when she approached. "Hey. I was just telling Mom and Dad about you and your battery and then Ro had a big burp. Cracked us up." He grinned at her, as if her daughter's gas was the most amusing thing in the world. God, he could be sweet.

"Classy," she replied, trying to keep the mood light for as long as they could. She sat down beside him, not too close, but close enough. Rowan seemed content, so Laura left her where she was. It was strange, knowing she and Tanner weren't an actual couple, and yet feeling a certain intimacy with him that suggested they were.

"So you've been seeing each other awhile now, I take it?" This came from John.

Tanner met Laura's gaze. His eyes were warm on hers—he was a better actor than she expected. Then he took her hand. "For a while," he agreed, looking back at his parents. "We came over today to tell you we're getting married."

The warm vibe shattered as Ellen's mouth fell open and John's mouth pursed and a furrow appeared on his brow.

"Married?" There was no way to describe his mother's tone other than shocked and dismayed.

He nodded, the same relaxed smile on his face, but his fingers had tightened over hers.

"Yes, married." He faced them squarely. "Considering the circumstances, we're going to have a small civil ceremony and I'll be moving into her place."

"Circumstances? You're not… I mean, Rowan's so small."

It took a few moments for Laura to comprehend what Ellen was asking, and as soon as she understood, heat rushed to her face. "Oh, gosh no! I'm not pregnant, if that's what you mean." She was so flustered she said the only thing that popped into her head. "Goodness, I just started getting a full night's sleep."

Tanner chuckled, down low. She closed her eyes momentarily, completely embarrassed. She'd made it sound as if she was too tired for sex. Which she usually was, although when Tanner looked at her a certain way she didn't suppose she'd be too hard to convince. And it wasn't that she actually wanted his parents to think they were sleeping together. She couldn't think of a graceful out to save herself.

Not for the first time since arriving, she wished she could become invisible.

It was a blessed relief when Ellen shifted the subject slightly. "But, Tanner, I thought you were apartment-hunting."

Laura hadn't expected a warm reception to their news, but somehow Ellen's response made her feel small and unwanted. Her fingers tightened on Tanner's, too, like holding on to a lifeline. They didn't have to do this—he'd said so. And here he was, facing his parents head-on. She felt like she should be the one to give him the out—only he'd been the one to do the asking in the first place. What a jumble.

"I was, but then I realized it was stupid to sign a lease, when…" He looked at Laura. She couldn't help the moisture that gathered in her eyes at his warm expression. What had she done to deserve such a champion? When Tanner smiled reassuringly, she gathered strength and faced his parents.

"Mr. and Mrs. Hudson, I know this is a surprise. And I know I'm probably your last choice for a daughter-in-law. I also know what people say about me here in Gibson."

"Laura," Tanner said in a low voice, but she shook her head.

"It's okay, Tanner. People think Rowan is Gavin Wallace's baby. I know that. I've always known that."

"Are you saying she's not? If Gavin's not the father, who is?" Ellen leaned forward, her gaze intent on Laura.

Laura hesitated, and then looked at Ellen evenly. "Frankly, it's nobody's business."

"Tanner?" Ellen stared at him next. "Are you saying you don't know and you don't care?"

"I do know," he said quietly. "And it doesn't matter to me, truly. It's Laura's business, and hers to share if she wishes. She's shared the truth with me, and I respect her for that."

Laura peered at Tanner's father. Mercy, the two of them looked alike. Thick dark hair, though the elder Hudson's was sprinkled with gray. Deep blue eyes, strong jaw. Tanner's expressions were more roguish than his dad's, but now, when the discussion was serious, she could see so much of his father in him. John Hudson was the kind of man who, when he spoke, people listened. Not so much with Tanner, and she wondered if that was behind his need to break away and do his own thing. He was the younger son and Cole was popular in Gibson. Maybe Tanner was tired of always being in the shadows and wanted to get out and be his own man.

"Are you ready to be a father, son? Because when you marry a woman with a child, that's what you are. A father. In all but blood."

Laura held her breath. They hadn't really talked about his role with Rowan.

"Yes, sir," he replied, still holding her child close in his arms. Rowan's little fingers wrapped around his index one. "I'm going to be there, for Laura and for Rowan, and whatever they need."

Oh God, she wasn't sure she could do this. It was all such a big lie. And Tanner was making it sound like undeniable, unimpeachable truth. Guilt and fear crowded in on her. How had she ever agreed to go through with this? So much could go wrong!

Remorse stuck in her throat and she swallowed around the lump of it. Maybe she should just come clean. But then she looked at Tanner and couldn't say anything. The words wouldn't come. The truth of it hit her then. Deep down, she wanted this. Even if he never felt anything romantic for her, even if they ended up divorcing after a year or two, she wanted this now. She wanted him not for his protection, but for his companionship. She wanted to feel she wasn't so alone in the world, as though she mattered to someone, as though someone mattered to her. Oh sure, there was Rowan, and having her had made her experience a love far deeper than she'd ever known. But this was different.

She wanted a kind of fairy tale—even if it was all pretend. For however long, there'd be someone there with her at the end of the day, across the table, someone to share a morning coffee with or laugh at a movie or TV show.

It wasn't as if there was a lineup of candidates anxious to fill the position. Tanner would also give her the protection of his name. Ironically, it was binding herself in marriage that would free her.

She looked first at his father, then his mother, and this time there was no hesitation in her voice when she spoke.

"Tanner is the kindest, gentlest, most generous person I've ever known. I'm aware that the honor of this is entirely mine, and I'm crazy lucky that he asked me to marry him. I'll try every day to make sure he doesn't regret it. He's a good man and he's…he's my best friend."

Tanner was looking at her now with something like admiration and surprise. "Best friends, huh?" he asked, and her heart gave a solid whump at the tender look in his eyes.

She knew how pathetic it probably sounded. She didn't really have friends here. The few she'd met with after she'd moved home quickly distanced themselves from her when the rumors started.

She nodded a little, and stared down at her lap. And was surprised when he scooched over and slid his free arm around her, so they made a unit: her, Tanner and Rowan, who had turned on his lap and now played with one of the buttons on his shirt.

Ellen's expression had softened, but Laura still sensed a certain amount of reserve. "Tanner, what about Maddy? You know she and Cole are probably going to announce their engagement any time. I don't mean to be crass, Laura, but it could make for some tense situations in the family."

This one Laura could field with a little confidence. "As I said, we've made our peace. Cole, too. We'll probably never be close friends, but we have an understanding. That's not to say it won't be awkward, I guess. Which is another reason to keep the wedding small."

"You don't want a regular wedding? In a church with the dress and flowers and so on?"

Oh, she had wanted that, once upon a time. But her choices had led her to this moment, and a big wedding would be highly inappropriate. Even if it had been the real McCoy, based on love and everything…making a wedding a big production would be tactless given the situation, and a bigger expense than either of them could justify.

"I'd like something small. Just the two of us…" She looked at Rowan and corrected herself. "…the three of us, and a few witnesses, and maybe a few little flowers. A bride should have flowers."

The words came out and it was all she could do to

keep her emotions in check. She wouldn't cry. Not here, not in front of Tanner's parents...not ever.

Quiet fell over the room for several long moments. Finally, Ellen sighed. "I don't mean to be a Negative Nelly. It's just a shock. We didn't even know you were involved. And now marriage... What's the rush? Surely, you can wait. Plan a proper wedding, say six months from now or so. It just seems so fast."

How could Laura possibly explain the necessity for expediency? In six months Spence would be eligible to apply for parole. Not to mention her employment situation. While she fumbled with words, Tanner once again stepped in.

"Because this is what we want, Mom. We've talked it over."

"But, Tanner—"

"Ellen, leave the boy alone," his father said firmly. "He's a grown man, able to make his own decisions and learn from his own mistakes."

Laura's already low spirits plummeted. That was all she was—a mistake. A bad decision. It could be the sweetness from the cinnamon buns at her grandparents' or the coffee she hadn't had for months, but she doubted that was behind the sick feeling in the pit of her stomach.

"Maybe we should go," she suggested on a whisper, avoiding Tanner's gaze. "And give them a chance to get used to the news."

"That's probably a good idea," Tanner agreed, and the smile he'd kept on his face for the last hour had faded. "Plus, Rowan didn't have much of a nap." The baby was rubbing a fist against her eyes, a sure sign she was tired and ready for sleep. Laura knew Rowan could sleep like an angel in her arms, but it was as good an excuse to leave as any.

"You're not staying for dinner?"

"I don't think so, Mom. Thanks anyway. We'd better get Rowan home."

It only took a few seconds for them to gather their things, but it was long enough for Laura to understand that Tanner had made a stand today. He'd stood for her and for her daughter. It still befuzzled her why he'd do that, but he had his reasons.

"Tanner, are you... Will you be home tonight?" They'd stopped at the door, preparing to say their goodbyes, when Ellen's hesitant question halted them.

"Yes, I'll be home," he said, patting her shoulder. "Besides, I want to talk to Cole."

"Of course you do."

They didn't say anything to Laura. She tried not to be hurt by it, but she was just the same. After months of suffering sidelong looks and whispers, she thought she'd have a tougher skin by now. Not so, it seemed. She'd felt small and, well, a bit like someone's dirty laundry. Worst of all, she'd wanted it to go well for Tanner's sake. Now he was caught in the middle.

He didn't say anything the whole way back to her place. But when they arrived, he hopped out of the truck and rushed around to open her door for her, then reached in for the car seat and carried Rowan to the front door.

Once inside, Laura released the breath she'd been holding. This was her house. It wasn't much, but it was hers, and it was a little oasis where she didn't feel she had to prove anything. It was such a relief to be under her own roof again.

Tanner shut the door, put down the car seat with a slumbering Rowan inside and placed his hands on Laura's shoulders.

"Are you okay?" he asked.

Despite her earlier determination, she took one look at him and started to cry.

Chapter Nine

Tanner was not used to dealing with crying women.

He made it a policy to keep things light and non-committal. A few dates and he moved on before any serious attachments could be made. But this was different. For one thing, he and Laura weren't in love. And for another, she was about to become his wife and she'd called him her best friend.

It had been a hard afternoon and she'd borne the brunt of it. So he gathered her against his chest, put his arms around her and let her cry it out.

"I'm sorry," she wailed softly after a few minutes of gulping and sobbing. "I don't usually cry. I just…" She stopped midsentence and sniffed again.

"You just what?" he asked gently, stroking her back with his hand.

After a few moments, he heard the words muffled against his shirt. "I felt so small. So…dirty."

"Oh, honey." His heart went out to her. Letting everyone think Gavin was the father of her baby had cost her plenty. Telling them the truth wouldn't help, either—this was a small town where a baby fathered by a felon was pretty much on par with an extramarital affair.

"I should never have come back here. I should have gone to a city somewhere. Gotten lost in the crowds, been anonymous."

"Except you wanted to come home," he supplied, still rubbing her back.

She nodded and snuffled. "I did. I needed somewhere familiar. I needed what little family I have. I know I'm undesirable. *I know it.* But it still hurts when it's pointed out."

He was treading on treacherous ground. How much did he want to tell her about his feelings? About how he felt this unexplainable need to make sure that Rowan—and Laura—were cared for? Getting to know her better only proved he was right. She was a kind, sweet person who was scared and misunderstood.

"You're not undesirable," he said gently, pressing his lips against her hair. "I promise you, Laura. People see the mistakes, but they don't see the wonderful things about you. Human nature is always that way, though it shouldn't be."

"Look at me," she contradicted. "I'm a single mom who…well, I'm living in fear, aren't I?" She pushed against his chest and peered up at him, and his heart ached at the sight of her red eyes and tear-streaked cheeks. "I've made so many mistakes, and now all I know how to do is run. Do you know how much I hate that about myself? That instead of standing up and fighting, I'm making decisions on how to hide better?"

He raised his hand and ran his thumb over her cheek. "You're a mom. Moms do what they need to do to protect their children. No one can blame you for being mama bear."

She shook her head. "Tanner, you're wasting your

time with me. Why tie yourself down for a year or two when you could be out looking for Miss Right? Someone far more suitable than me? Someone your family will approve of and welcome with open arms?" To his dismay, her tears welled again and she dropped her chin. "Someone worthy of the kind of man you are."

"I don't ever want to hear you say that again." Tanner's heart pounded painfully, hating how negative she was about herself. "You are not unworthy. You are definitely not undesirable, Laura. If you could see you the way I see you…"

She bit down on her lip.

He sighed, lifted her chin with his finger. "You are a tigress. I watched you bring that sweet baby girl into the world with a ferocity that was mind-blowing. You have endured the looks and the gossip for months in order to protect yourself and your baby, even though it cost you a lot personally. You are one of the strongest women I've ever met, and if people can't see that, then that's their problem."

He knew he shouldn't, but he ran his hand through her hair, the thick coppery strands slipping over his fingers like silk. She had a few pale freckles on her cheeks, just on either side of her nose, and they made her look young and artless. Her bottom lip was swollen and plump from where she'd bitten down on it. She was so damn beautiful.

"Tanner?" she whispered, her voice unsure. And it was that question that moved him forward, so close that their bodies brushed as his hand cradled her head and he kissed her.

He meant for it to be a kiss of reassurance, something gentle and affirming, to let her know that she was, indeed, desirable. He failed utterly, because the moment his mouth was on hers, there was nothing gentle or reassuring about it. Her breath caught deliciously as her lips opened beneath his, as instinctive as a flower turning toward the sun. His body felt super-charged and he pulled her closer, losing himself in the sweet taste of her. When she made a little sound in her throat, he nearly lost his mind. He threaded his other hand through her hair and tilted her head back, sliding his lips from hers and trailing them down the soft skin of her neck.

She cried out, a thin impassioned sound that only fired him up further. When her hips rubbed against his, he ground back, loving the feel of her. She fit against him just right, and he licked a path from the hollow of her throat up to her earlobe, and she spread her hands on his back, holding him close.

He disentangled one hand and slid it down to cup her full breast. The tip was hard and pebbled against his hand, but that was when Laura suddenly backed off, pressing her fingers on his wrist, pushing him away. He let her; he wasn't into coercion or force. Instead he listened to their breathing echoing through the kitchen, marveling that a few minutes ago she'd been crying against him and now his brain was a complete fog, filled with the haze of wanting her.

"Oh God," she said, leaning back against the wall and resting her head against the firm surface. "That was…oh, dammit."

"Dammit? Was it that bad?" He tried a little joke, anything to lighten the tension. She wanted to stop. He needed to stop thinking what it would be like to carry her into her bedroom and finish this properly.

"We can't… We shouldn't… This would complicate everything." Her wary eyes watched him, but he could only see her lips, so obviously freshly kissed.

"We have an agreement," she reminded him. "Platonic. In name only. Tanner, if we do this—get married, I mean—you can't be kissing me in the kitchen."

He didn't realize that he'd rubbed his hand over his zipper until he saw her eyes widen and her cheeks turn hot pink. "Can I kiss you in the living room, then? In your bedroom?" He smiled at her, teasing, but deep down he was just as confused as she was. That wasn't supposed to happen. Not that fast. Not that hot and demanding.

"Be serious," she said. And then she looked down at herself and cursed softly, not quite under her breath.

It took a moment, but he saw what caused her consternation when he dropped his gaze to her chest.

"Sexy, isn't it?" At least it was a distraction and a good "deflating" change of topic. "Gotta love oxytocin."

Tanner was a rancher. He knew enough about animals to know what happened when females nursed. What he hadn't realized was that arousal caused the same chemical reaction. He wasn't sure if he was horrified or terribly intrigued.

"It's probably for the best," she continued, sliding away from him and rolling her shoulders. "We needed to stop."

He wasn't so sure of that, but he could tell she was, and that was all that mattered. "I didn't expect it to be so…well. Explosive."

She was a good five, six feet away now, a safe distance. It didn't feel very safe, though, when she looked up and met his gaze. The fire was still there, just waiting for a puff of oxygen to fan the flames. "I guess it's been a big dry spell for me," she countered.

For him, too. Longer than most people would believe, given his reputation. But that wasn't it. Dry spells were mere convenient excuses. It was probably better to agree with her, though, than to point out that they had incendiary chemistry.

"Now do you believe you're desirable?" he asked, taking a small step backward and trying hard to relax his tense muscles.

"Is that what that was? Trying to prove a point?"

He swallowed against the lump in his throat. "At first. You were so sad and pretty and I wanted to kiss you and make you feel better, but as soon as I did…"

There she was, biting on that lip again. He really wished she wouldn't. It was sexy as hell.

"It got away from us," she said.

"It sure did."

She turned away and he smiled a little as she tossed her hair over her shoulder. She had spunk and she didn't even realize it.

"Getting married is probably a mistake," she said.

"You've changed your mind?" He knew she was simply reacting to what had happened. It had thrown them both.

She shrugged. He saw her inhale, then exhale slowly before turning around. "I don't know. This complicates things a lot."

"It doesn't have to happen again," he assured her. He could control himself, after all.

"It doesn't have to, but it doesn't mean it won't."

Tanner went to her then. He saw her eyes widen at

his approach, wondering if he was going to kiss her again. But he didn't. He put his hands lightly on her shoulders and looked down at her. "Nothing will happen that you don't want," he said firmly. "I'm not into persuasion or forcing my hand."

Laura gazed up at him for so long he thought he might drown in them. "You mean that," she whispered.

"You have my word." As much as he hated to give it, he would. Because it was what she needed right now.

"Maybe…" She started to speak and then stopped, frowning. "Hmm."

"Maybe what?"

"Maybe what we need to do is give this a trial run. You know, before the ceremony. It's three weeks away. You could move your stuff in here in the meantime and we could see how we get along. If it doesn't work, we cancel the wedding and that's it. I figure out something else and you can resume your apartment-hunting. We'd only be out the marriage license and the fee for the officiant."

He considered for a moment. It was actually a very practical, very sound plan.

"Then tomorrow we have some things to do, don't we?"

"We do?"

He nodded. "We're supposed to go for the marriage license. Then we'll shop for a bed afterward, and I'll bring what I need over tomorrow night after work and dinner."

"You're sure?"

He nodded. "I think it's a smart idea. It gives us a chance to get used to each other. Settle in. Besides, then we won't be worried about it for the next three weeks. We'll have all that adjustment stuff down pat."

It sounded great, except for just one thing. While he could promise he wouldn't touch her or make any moves, he couldn't promise not to think about it. He knew from experience that thinking too much could just about do a man in.

"And no more funny business." She pointed a finger at him and then dropped it, giving a small, slightly crooked smile. "Isn't that what you said that first night?"

It was, and he found it telling that she remembered. Had it been on her mind?

"Laura, I find you incredibly attractive and I like you a lot. But I made a promise. So if anything happens between us, it'll be because you come to me. Okay?"

She gave a tiny nod. "Okay. So no worries there, then."

"No worries there."

It was only one kiss. They'd get over it.

"Now, are you okay? I should get back home. I told Mom I would. Plus I need to break the news that I'm moving out *and* talk to Cole."

"Sounds like a fun evening."

"It could be a lot worse." He laughed a little. In fact, despite tonight's confusing events, he was looking forward to it. A guy could only live with his parents for so long before wanting to get out on his own. Even if the arrangement was slightly unorthodox. "I'll see you tomorrow, then? I'll come by and pick you up late morning, is that okay? We'll get the license thing looked after and whatever else needs doing."

"Okay," she answered, smiling back.

There was a moment before he left that they both hesitated and the kitchen was quiet. It was a moment in which a regular couple would come together for a goodbye kiss, or a hug, or their hands would twine together and then drift apart—or all three. Instead Tanner stepped forward and kissed the crest of her cheek, keeping his hands to himself. "See you in the morning. Get a good night's sleep."

It wasn't until he was seated in his truck with the engine running that he completely relaxed his shoulders and allowed his real thoughts permission to run freely.

The truth was he was starting to really care for Laura, far beyond friendship or responsibility or to serve his own purposes. He'd explained those feelings away for weeks now, but he couldn't explain away the reaction he had to her kisses or the feel of her body against his.

That kind of passion didn't happen every day. And when it did happen, and with someone he also liked and wanted to care for…

This marriage wasn't going to be as platonic as he had thought. At least not for him. For his own sake, they'd best keep it short, then.

LAURA GATHERED THE sheets from the dryer and took them into the bedroom, making up the bed fresh. Tonight Tanner would be sleeping in it. It would be his long body beneath the covers; his head on the pillow.

The day had passed in a blur. First, they'd gone to the county office for their marriage license, which had been nothing more than official paperwork and certainly nothing romantic about it. They'd gone from there to a furniture store in Great Falls—one of those discount chain places—and Tanner had bought her a single bed, complete with mattress. Laura hadn't liked that too much, but she didn't have the cash pay for such a purchase. And then Tanner pointed out he was taking her bed, and if he moved into an apartment he'd have to buy furniture anyway and also pay first and last month's rent. When he put it that way, she didn't feel quite so bad. When they stopped at the department store in Gibson, she made sure she paid for the new sheets, comforter, and extra pillow.

It was as if the previous evening hadn't happened. Nothing improper, no long, lingering looks or touches. Nothing to suggest that less than twenty-four hours earlier she'd been twined around him like a vine on a fence post, clinging to his lips like a blossom reaching for the sun.

When they'd finally arrived home again, she helped him carry in the heavy boxes containing the bed parts. He'd be over later to put it together, bringing his things with him. All very practical and businesslike.

In the meantime, she'd put Rowan down for a nap and was working on making her room into Tanner's. This job seemed far more personal, because she was making room for him in her house. In her life.

She sorted through Rowan's things and packed away anything she'd outgrown, and then took the bottom two dresser drawers for herself. The rest of her clothes she stored in Rowan's small closet, hanging up what she could and putting some on the top shelf. Her "good" clothes she left in her bedroom closet, pushed over to one side to make room for Tanner's.

The computer she left where it was, at least for now. During the day, Tanner would be at the ranch, so she could come in here and work. If it became a problem, they could look at moving her desk somewhere else, though the living room was pretty small for more furniture.

Rowan woke and Laura fed her. Lately, Ro had been fussing more and more, and Laura figured it was probably past time to start feeding her some solids. Particularly since she'd started waking in the night again. After taking forty-five minutes to change and feed her, she put Rowan on a blanket in the living room and threw the new bedding in the washing machine. She heated up a can of soup and made a peanut butter sandwich to go with it, and by the time Tanner arrived at seven, she had Rowan in the bathtub, splashing happily.

"Hello?" he called, and Laura's stomach filled with butterflies. *He's here.*

"We're in the bathroom," she called. Even though the baby was in a type of ring that kept her from sliding in the tub, Laura wouldn't leave her alone. She soaped up the washcloth, preparing to cut bath playtime short since Tanner had already arrived.

He peeked into the bathroom and leaned on the door frame. "Well. Someone likes her bath."

Rowan splashed with both hands, slapping the water and giggling at the sound and the droplets that were flung in and out of the tub.

"Always," Laura agreed. "I'll be a few minutes here. I made room for your things in the bedroom and put fresh bedding on the bed. You can bring your stuff in if you want."

"Sounds good."

She was dying to know how it had all gone at his parents' place. If they weren't thrilled about the wedding, they probably had their noses out of joint about him moving in with her so quickly.

While she finished with Rowan, she heard him making trips back and forth from his truck to the bedroom. When Rowan was finally snapped into her pajamas, Laura hung up the towel and put the baby on her shoulder, then went out to investigate.

Tanner didn't have suitcases. Instead, two large duffel bags sat on the floor in her room, as well as a couple of cardboard boxes. "That's it?" she asked. "It sounded like you made more trips than that."

"I did. I brought some tools and stuff and put them in the basement. I figure it wouldn't hurt for me to take on some odd jobs around here, right?"

She rubbed Rowan's back absently. "Odd jobs?"

He nodded, wiping his hands on his jeans. "You know, like maybe painting the front railing and trim. I noticed one of the steps could use replacing, too, and the soffit needs tending." He grinned at her. "Might as well earn my keep."

She wasn't sure what to say. It would be nice to have those things done, but it wasn't because she couldn't do them. Deciding it would be best to simply be honest, she met his gaze squarely. "Tanner, I can paint and even fix the step. The reason I haven't is that I prioritized my spending and fresh paint was more of a want than a need."

"I figured that. But it's June and I bet you've paid your mortgage for the month already, haven't you?"

"Yes."

"Then I'll pick up some supplies and putter away in the evenings in lieu of rent for this month."

"But you bought the bed. That was instead of first and last month's…"

"And you have all the rest of the furniture. Trust me, Laura, I'm the one getting a bargain here. Besides, maybe you can help me."

His smile was so big that she couldn't argue with him. It would be nice to spruce up the place a bit. Hadn't she been lamenting the fact not long ago?

Through it all, Rowan was just looked around, wide-eyed. Tanner laughed. "Wow. I'm not sure the kid approves. Look at that face." Indeed, Rowan seemed very sober.

"She's getting tired," Laura said. "I was thinking, maybe we can put off putting the bed together until tomorrow. I'll just sleep on the mattress tonight."

"You're sure?"

She nodded. "By the time we unpack the pieces and get them put together, she'll be beyond ready for bed. I've got the bedding. We can flop down the mattress. It'll be just as comfortable."

They were still standing in between the living room and kitchen. Belatedly, Laura stepped back. "You'd probably like to unpack, though. What time do you get up in the morning?"

He stuck his hands in his pockets. "I should be out the door by seven or so. I'll try not to wake you both."

"Okay. There's bread and jam for toast, or cereal for your breakfast. And eggs in the fridge. Just help yourself. This is your place now, too." It felt so weird to say it. This wasn't just her place anymore. It was theirs. And would be theirs until they decided otherwise.

"Sounds fine. I'll go put my stuff away, I guess."

"The chest of drawers is empty," she said, calling after him as he walked down the hall.

For a good half hour, she heard sounds coming from the bedroom; drawers opened and shut and the odd zipper rasped through the silence. Rowan started fussing and it was close to bedtime, so while Tanner finished up, Laura settled back in the corner of the sofa and nursed. For the first time in months, she longed for a glass of wine to steady her nerves. It was weird. So real, now that he was here in the house, larger than life and with his sunny smile. She'd just tucked everything back into place when Tanner came out, his hair mussed as if he'd run his hands through it several times.

"There. I think I'm mostly set. I feel like a heel, kicking you out of your room, though."

They were going to be married. If they were like a normal married couple, no one would be kicked out of anywhere because they would be sharing a room. But not here, no, sir.

"Don't think anything of it. I'll be snug as a bug in there." She smiled. "Besides, the new bed is far more comfortable than the blow-up mattress."

He perched on the edge of a chair, looked at Rowan's sleeping face for a moment, and then back at her. "This feels weird, doesn't it?"

She let out a relieved breath. "A little. We'll adjust. It's a crazy thing we're doing, after all."

"Yep." He slapped his knee lightly with his hand. "I brought a six-pack over and I feel like a beer. Do you mind?"

"Of course not."

"You want one?"

She glanced at Rowan. "I probably shouldn't."

"Okay." He got up and went to the kitchen. She heard him open the beer and a minute later he was back. He carried a small glass with him, a scant few inches of beer in it. He handed it to her with a wink.

"Maybe just a bit to toast?" he asked.

He was too cute to resist when he looked at her that way, all devilment and sexiness and with his silly hair sticking up on one side. She took the glass and grinned. "Oh, what the heck?" she said.

He lifted his bottle. "To you and Rowan and me. New beginnings, unorthodox arrangements and a bright future ahead for all of us."

Laura lifted her glass and swallowed it all in one gulp, the creamy, fizzy beer sliding down her throat easily. She handed it back to him. "That was quite a speech."

He poured a little more in the glass and handed it back. "It's true, though. We might not be doing things the normal way, but it's for all the right reasons, don't you think?"

This time she didn't answer, but she drank the sip he'd added to her glass. All the right reasons? In her whole life, she'd never considered marrying for anything but love. And that was conspicuously absent.

The thought made her more than a little sad.

Chapter Ten

Laura slept fitfully that night. It wasn't the bed or being in the same room as Rowan; she'd done that when her grandfather came to stay and was used to it. It was knowing Tanner was down the hall, sleeping in her old room. It was remembering the banal, ordinary sounds of another person in the house getting ready for bed. A door shutting, the tap running as he brushed his teeth, the gentle creak of the mattress as he got into bed.

Tonight he'd acted as if their kiss had never happened. As if he'd never licked the sensitive skin of her neck or run his hand over her breast. She swallowed in the darkness, staring at the ceiling. She didn't want a real marriage. She didn't want to care for him or feel this inconvenient attraction, but she couldn't always control it. She remembered something her grandma had told her when she was a teenager and everything with friends and boys seemed so dramatic. "Nothin' you can do about other people, sweetie," she'd said. "The only thing you can control is how you react. You're in charge."

She was in charge. So while she might get a fluttery feeling when Tanner walked into a room, while she already liked the way the house felt with someone else in it, she was still in charge of her actions. Tanner need never know any of how she was feeling. As far as he was concerned, they would strictly be roommates.

She finally drifted off to sleep, only to be wakened early by the sound of Tanner rising and getting ready to leave for work. She stayed curled under her blankets, waiting for him to leave for the day. Rowan slept on, the soft sound of her deep breathing barely audible in the room. Laura checked her watch. It was only six-thirty. When Tanner closed the front door behind him ten minutes later, she let out a deep sigh and went back to sleep.

Her day progressed fairly normally after that. There was laundry, tidying, and caring for Rowan. Now that plans were in place, she booted up her computer and tried to ignore the signs that Tanner now occupied the bedroom, focusing instead on sending out emails to former clients to try to drum up business, then working on her own website design now that she had a launch date of right after the wedding. She threw together a quick sandwich for lunch and had just changed Rowan's wet diaper when she heard a car pull into the driveway.

When she looked out, her heart did an awkward skip. It was Maddy, the last person she'd expected.

Maddy. Gavin's widow. And probably soon to be Tanner's sister-in-law—and hers, as well. Maddy, who up until Christmas thought that Rowan was her husband's daughter. To say things were awkward between them was an understatement. What on earth did she want? It had to be something to do with Tanner. Laura twisted her fingers together. Damn.

It didn't help that Maddy was so pretty. Laura had dated Gavin once upon a time, sure, but the woman he'd married made Laura feel hokey and, well, inadequate. Maddy wasn't just beautiful. She was a kind, generous human being, a wonderful mother, the town sweetheart who could do no wrong. It wasn't a competition by any means, but Laura felt that she fell shy of the mark when standing next to Maddy.

Maddy knocked on the door. Laura counted to three, and then opened it, putting on a polite smile at the same time.

"Maddy. This is a surprise." She injected as much warmth as she could into the words. She didn't dislike Maddy at all; she was simply nervous.

"Hi, Laura. May I come in?"

"Please do." She stood aside and opened the door wider. "Can I get you anything? Something to drink?"

"No, thanks." Maddy smiled at her and Laura felt marginally better. Nothing about the woman sent an adversarial message. "I was wondering if we could talk for a few minutes."

"Of course." Laura led the way through to the living room. "Do you mind if we sit in here? I've got Rowan in her Exersaucer. It keeps her occupied. She likes spinning around." True enough, when they entered the room Rowan gave a little bounce with her feet as she sat in the middle of the contraption, and then spun a quarter turn to bat at a bar holding a colorful wheel.

Maddy grinned. "Oh, we had those for the boys. Gosh, they loved them. When they got older, they jumped so much we thought they would bounce themselves right across the floor." She laughed. "Now I wish I could stick them in it again. They're mobile and holy terrors."

It seemed motherhood was a great shared topic. It also helped that Maddy was one of the few who knew that Rowan wasn't Gavin's child.

"So," Laura said, as they sat.

"I'm here about Tanner. But you probably knew that already." Maddy's lips were slightly pursed, a small frown marring her perfect eyebrows.

"I didn't, but thanks for getting right to the point." Laura folded her hands and regarded Maddy evenly. "I didn't have a chance to speak to Tanner about what happened with you and Cole. He brought his stuff over last night and was gone early this morning, before we got up."

"He didn't waste any time moving out."

Laura hesitated, not wanting to rush her words. "I guess you guys don't approve, huh."

"It's so fast." Maddy's eyes searched hers. "Laura, I'm not trying to judge you. But I do find it hard to believe that you and Tanner are ready for marriage. You can't have been seeing each other very long."

"How long were you with Cole when you knew?" Laura asked the question, knowing fully it was a deliberate diversion, and that it was playing into the lie that this was a love match.

Maddy's cheeks turned pink and she smiled softly. "Not long. A month? But we're not rushing to the altar, either."

Laura shrugged. "That's between you and Cole, Maddy. Tanner asked me, and I said yes. It's only a few weeks until the wedding, so he decided he might as well move in now. It's no big deal."

"No big deal?" Maddy's voice rose and she stood for a moment, turning away briefly before turning back again. "Laura. Please. I know how hard it is to be a single mom. I know what you told me about Rowan's father, too. Tanner told us that you've told him everything. Have you?"

Unease settled heavily in Laura's stomach. "More than I've told either of you," she admitted. "I wouldn't go into this hiding things from him."

Maddy's shoulders relaxed a little. "I'm glad. He deserves honesty."

"You're protecting him, and I get that. But he's a big boy. He knows his own mind. You don't understand. He's kind and gentle and funny and easy to be around and…" She ran out of descriptors but was shocked to see a warmth in Maddy's eyes now.

"You really do love him."

The words seemed to suck all the wind out of her sails. Laura was speechless for a second, knowing Maddy was wrong, but unable to protest without giving herself away, knowing if she did it wouldn't be completely truthful. She did like Tanner. In love with him? No. But neither was she completely immune. Maybe he could pretend their searing kiss hadn't happened, but she couldn't. She didn't want to.

It had been nothing short of splendid.

"Maddy, I'm not exactly comfortable talking about this with you," she said, hoping to dodge the bullet. "Because of the circumstances and because we're not exactly friends. Not that I dislike you in any way. Please don't think that!" she hastened to add. "It's just that I don't have many friends left here in Gibson, and I'm not used to talking about my personal life."

Maddy laughed. "Good Lord. Ask me how many friends I've lost since Gavin died. When the gossip started, it was like I'd somehow changed. People gave me their sympathy but kept their distance. I don't talk about my personal life, either."

Guilt bore its weight on Laura. "God. I hadn't considered that. Oh, Maddy, I'm sorry. That's my fault. I should have made it clear from the start… I just didn't know what to do."

"It's water under the bridge," Maddy assured her. "I'm happy now, and that's the main thing. But I don't want to see you and Tanner leap into anything that's not going to make you both happy. Cole told me to leave it alone, but…" She shrugged helplessly. "Tanner's a great guy. And despite the situation, you haven't exactly got it easy in this town. I don't want either one of you to get hurt."

It was a magnanimous gesture, and knowing Maddy's reputation as she did, Laura had no doubt it was sincere. There wasn't a false bone in her body. It was a little intimidating being faced with all that perfection.

Laura looked at Maddy, trying to envision a world where the two of them might be friends. If it weren't for the history, it would be easy. Maddy was extremely likable. Perhaps a little too perfect, but she didn't throw it in anyone's face or act superior. "Maddy," she asked cautiously, "is Tanner's family really that upset?"

"Bah, bah, bah!" babbled Rowan, an abrupt sound in the stillness as Maddy considered her answer.

"Upset? I don't know about that. Concerned? Sure. Have you really been seeing each other since Christmas?"

"He helped deliver Rowan." She had to expect these sorts of questions and how to answer them. "It's a pretty intimate experience, you know. And he was so strong and kind and steady. Do you know that one day my car wouldn't start and people drove by for a long, long time, but it was Tanner who stopped to help? He's never treated me like a pariah. And there was this time at the diner when Rowan was fussing and he just stepped in and smoothed everything over. No one's ever done things like that for me, Maddy." She smiled, feeling a silly sentimentality. "He has this thing for doughnuts, did you know that? And he won't admit it, but I catch him looking at Rowan or holding her and he's not awkward or intimidated. I'd be crazy not to want a man like that in my life."

She was really laying it on thick, wasn't she? And yet every single word of it was true.

"You're sure you don't want to wait to get married?" Maddy asked. "I think it's the rush that is really throwing Ellen and John."

Laura shook her head. "I'm not popular here, and it's not like we'd have a big guest list. Something small and quiet is what we both want. We just want to get on with our lives, you know?"

"Still, it's a wedding. Surely, you want some romance to it. A month or two to plan things properly."

And give Tanner time to change his mind? Or for her to get cold feet? Or worst of all, for Spencer to get out of jail? "The wedding's set for just under three weeks," Laura replied, sitting a little straighter. "I've got lots of time to plan what I need. We already picked up the license and booked the JP."

"You need a dress. Rings. Flowers."

At this point, Laura's heart hurt. She didn't want this to be real. She felt guilty enough as it was, without the trappings of a real wedding, no matter how simple. "Really, Maddy. I'm just going to wear something in my closet. Or something I can wear again."

Maddy sat down and considered Laura for a long time. Rowan was playing happily, thanks to a full belly, dry diaper, and another hour before nap time. Maddy's face softened as she looked at the little girl, then back to Laura again.

"She's beautiful. She's got your nose and eyes. Even if the color isn't the same, the shape of them is."

"Thank you."

Maddy sighed. "Laura, you shouldn't feel like you have to sneak away like you've done something wrong. Why not have a new dress? A pretty bouquet?"

It's an extravagance for a farce, she wanted to reply, but held her tongue.

"Surely your parents, your grandparents…"

"My parents are in California now, and won't be coming up. Gram and Gramps, though…"

"Will expect you to look like a bride. Where are you having the ceremony?"

Once again Laura shrugged. "We haven't decided yet."

"Maybe you can have it at the ranch."

Laura was stricken by the suggestion. A guilty conscience was a terrible thing.

"Or below the library, at the gazebo, you know the place?" Maddy's smile widened. "Think about it. If there are only a few people, everyone can be beneath the roof if the weather isn't ideal. And if it's sunny, you've got a beautiful setting for pictures at no charge. You just have to reserve it with the town office."

Laura's throat tightened, touched by Maddy's acceptance and enthusiasm. "Why are you doing this? Everyone in Gibson thinks you have a big reason to hate me. And we've never been friends. Even without the affair, I was Gavin's high school girlfriend. It should still be awkward as hell."

"I'm doing it because you've had a rough time and you told me the truth when you didn't have to. And because we're probably going to be sisters-in-law and I'd like it to be so that family gatherings are fun."

Laura shook her head. "You have a very forgiving nature."

"I have a wonderful man who loves me and makes me see the world a little bit brighter than I did a few months ago. Please, Laura. If you love Tanner, give him a real wedding day to remember. His last one was such a farce and hurt him so badly."

Her words had the opposite effect than she'd intended. For the second time, Tanner's wedding was going to be a farce. He'd given up, hadn't he? He didn't believe in happy ever after and all that stuff. When he'd said he wasn't giving up anything to marry her, he'd meant it.

The thought made her sad, because deep down, she still believed in love. She still had a flicker of hope despite all that had happened. Tanner didn't. He was prepared to be completely pragmatic about the whole thing.

Briefly, she considered a wedding with a few more frills, but then what would be the point? It wouldn't change anything.

"I'll talk to Tanner," she promised. "It's his wedding, too, and he should have a say."

"Just consider it," Maddy said, folding her hands in her lap. "You can still have something quiet and small with very little fuss. It's just a few little touches. I think it would reassure John and Ellen, too."

"I'll think about it." She already was. The suggestion of the gazebo was a good one. They had to have it somewhere, after all. It wasn't as if they would get married here in her living room.

There was a long pause where the atmosphere became slightly uncomfortable again. Maddy looked as though she wanted to say something, and her hands fidgeted in her lap, but she was holding her tongue. Laura knew she should probably let it go, or change the subject, but curiosity got the best of her. "Maddy, if you've got something more to say, please say it."

Rowan spun in her saucer, the whirring sound of it occupying the silence for a few seconds.

"You had Rowan less than six months ago. It's not a long time from courtship to wedding. And no one knew you were seeing each other. It's so rushed. Are you absolutely sure this is what you want, Laura? That it's what's best for you and Rowan and for Tanner? Marriage is for a lifetime."

Except when it's not, Laura thought. She was tempted to explain, but held back. Maddy wouldn't be the last to question their motives. And it wasn't as if Laura had ever done anything to really earn their trust. She'd let everyone believe she'd had an extramarital affair for months. Even the reason for the secret was enough to wreck her credibility. What kind of person got pregnant with a drug pusher's baby?

And that line of thinking did absolutely nothing to prop up her already fragile confidence.

Except Tanner knew. And he was still beside her. Maybe not at this exact minute, but he was willing to help her when she needed it most. Despite her mistakes.

"I'm sure," she whispered. And with those words she silently promised herself that she'd never give Tanner a reason to regret his decision.

TANNER SIGHED HEAVILY as he climbed the front steps. He hadn't had time to change and there was blood on his uniform shirt. He was dog-tired and couldn't get the image of Carson Baxter out of his head.

What he really wanted right now was some peace and quiet, a hot shower, and a stiff drink. The last few days had been an adjustment, living at Laura's place, but they were managing all right. She was quieter than he expected, and he caught her looking at him sometimes with a strange expression on her face, but then she'd smile and go on doing something else.

If the worst thing about the move was missing his mom's cooking, he figured they were doing okay.

He wrinkled his nose. The windows were open and a strange, acrid smell wafted outside. It wasn't a scent he could place, but it sure didn't smell good. His already sensitive stomach turned over as he opened the door and the aroma grew stronger.

The kitchen was definitely not peaceful or orderly. A rolling pin and dirty mixing bowls sat on the table, some sort of strange batter stuck to the sides. Flour was everywhere, and on the stove was a still-smoking roaster. He did a quick check to make sure it wasn't still on the burner. It wasn't.

Beside the stove, he spotted the cause of the smell. It was a pile of what he thought must be doughnuts, but they were unlike any that he'd ever seen in his life. Dark brown, lumpy bits of dough that…well. His stomach turned again.

And where were Laura and the baby? The car was out front so they had to be here somewhere. A horrible thought popped into his head. Had something happened to Rowan that had caused Laura to forget the hot fat in the roaster? He hurried from the kitchen, calling out for her.

"Laura? Laura, are you okay?"

He rushed right past the living room to the bedrooms, but her soft voice came from behind him. "In here."

She was in the rocker next to the TV, tucked away in a corner of the living room. Rowan wasn't in her lap. It was just her, sitting there with tears streaking down her face.

"What is it? What's happened? Is Rowan okay?" He rushed to her and knelt before the chair. "Is it Spence? Laura honey, what's going on?"

Her lower lip wobbled. "She's napping. I—I tried t-t-to make you doughnuts b-because I know they're your favorites." She took a breath. "Nothing went right. The b-batter was weird and didn't hold together and then I burned them, but when I took them out the i-inside was still ruuuunnny…" The last word was drawn out with despair, but finally ended when she punctuated the sentence with a sniff. "I—I'm so sorry, Tanner. I wanted to surprise you."

"So nothing's wrong? This is just about dough-nuts?" God, he was so relieved. With the mess in the kitchen, the silence and everything that had already happened today…not to mention the situation with Laura and how worried she was about her ex. He'd never experienced his heart freezing before, but that was what it had been like. As if it had stopped and everything had turned cold.

Another sniff. "I wanted to do something nice for you."

He dropped his head, unsure how much more of a roller coaster he could take today. "Goddammit, don't scare me like that again, okay?"

She flinched. "I didn't mean to scare you. I—I was just in here feeling sorry for myself. I'll go clean up the mess. I didn't mean to upset you. I'm really sorry."

It occurred to him how much she was apologiz-ing and it made him feel like a heel. He softened his voice. "Stop saying you're sorry. It's fine, really. I've just had a hell of a day, that's all. I'm all wound up and nowhere to put it."

She placed her hand on the side of his face, and he looked up abruptly. Her face was still streaked and her eyes red, but there was concern in them, too.

"What is it?" She looked at his shirt, and the color drained from her face. "You've got blood on your shirt."

"We got a call midmorning." He closed his eyes, wishing he could unsee the scene. "It was a bad one."

"Do you want to talk about it?"

He shook his head quickly. "No."

Her thumb rubbed against his cheek. "Okay. Then

let's get you out of your uniform. Unless you're still on call."

"No." His throat felt raw. "Not… I mean, someone else is covering for us." It had been Sean McEachern on call with him today. They'd been debriefed and then relieved.

"Come on, then." The color had returned to Laura's face and erased the weakness he'd seen only moments before. She grasped his hands and stood, urging him to his feet. *Damn, he was wobbly.*

Laura got up from the rocker and held his hand as she led him down the hall. Tanner felt an unfamiliar tightening in his chest, which was at odds with the numb sensation in his legs and arms. It was like an out-of-body experience, following her, and that was when he realized why he'd been sent home for the rest of the day. He'd functioned through it all. The call, the debriefing at the hospital, everything…but now it was setting in and his body started to shake.

"Sit down, Tanner."

Her soft voice commanded him and he obeyed, not knowing what else to do. He sat at the foot of the bed, staring at her as she went to a couple of drawers, looking for a T-shirt. She took one out and then stood before him, reached for the buttons on his shirt and began undoing them, one by one.

"Let's get your shirt changed first. I'll call my grandma and see what she suggests for getting the stains out."

Blood. It was blood. And that was only a small part of it.

Her soft, cool fingers pushed the shirt off his shoulders and she tossed it onto the bed behind her. As gently as if she were dressing Rowan, she helped him put on the soft cotton T-shirt.

"Can you stand up, Tanner?"

"Huh? Oh. Yes."

"Do you have a pair of sweats anywhere?"

He nodded numbly. "Shelf in the closet."

It was the oddest sensation, having a woman unbuckle his pants without there being any sexual overtones. She was simply gentle and efficient, helping him take them off, putting his feet through the legs of the sweats and pulling them up to rest on his hips.

"Better?"

He nodded, though he knew it wasn't. He was trying so hard not to shake right now. He didn't want to be that weak in front of her. This was all so stupid. He'd been working as an EMT for some time. He'd been on calls for vehicle accidents, heart attacks, strokes and yes, even Laura's baby. But today...

He shivered all over.

She urged him back on the bed, and he let her, which surprised him. "I'm fine," he protested. "I'm just coming down from the adrenaline. Give me a minute."

"Okay," she agreed. "And I think you should come down from the adrenaline by being horizontal. You're a lot bigger than me, Tanner." She smiled at him. "If you tip over on me I'll be squashed."

"Just for a minute, though."

"Fair enough. Would you like some water or something? I can't burn that."

He tried to smile. "Water's great. Thanks."

She disappeared for a moment and he forced himself to take deep breaths. He'd been running on autopilot for the last few hours, and then his adrenaline had spiked again when he thought something might be wrong with Laura and Rowan. Truth was, he was all over the map and he was smart enough to know his body—and his fiancée—was telling him to hold up for a bit and find his feet again.

Finding his feet was something that Carson Baxter would never do again.

Tanner closed his eyes, but nothing erased the image of that kid.

Laura came back and sat on the edge of the bed, holding the glass of water. "Here," she said quietly. "Drink slowly."

He took a sip, but then put the glass on the table beside the bed. "I'm okay."

"It must have been really horrible, huh?"

He nodded. "Yuh. Worst I've been on. It's just catching up with me, is all."

She waited a few seconds and then asked hesitantly, "Was anyone killed, Tanner?"

This time he couldn't get his voice to work. He nodded.

"Oh," she said, a quiet lament. "I'm sorry."

He might have been able to reply. Might have found his voice and said something strong and restorative, except Laura leaned forward and slid her arms around his middle and put her head against his chest. He was leaning against the headboard, and the scroll of the wood dug into the back of his head. He welcomed the sensation, let it anchor him, let the feel of her embrace anchor him, too. He put his hand along her back and felt the warmth of her skin through her thin top. And then the next thing he knew, he'd reached out and gathered her close and pulled her on to his lap, holding her tight.

She didn't fight. She simply let him hold her as if she knew that was exactly what he needed. And he absorbed her warmth and strength until he began to feel whole again.

"Do you want to talk about it now?" she finally asked.

He sighed. "No. But it'll be on the news, in the paper. You'll hear about it anyway."

"It was an accident?" she prodded gently, her hand still rubbing reassuringly on his back.

"Yeah. Out at Baxter's place. Do you know where that is?"

He couldn't tell for sure, since she was still snuggled up against him, but he thought her head movement indicated no.

"It's a ranch south of town. The call came in just after ten." He took a deep breath and just said it. "A tractor rolled over and killed the driver."

"Oh God," she said, squeezing him tight.

"He was fifteen."

Those three words settled in the room, heavy with sorrow and the loss of all the possibilities that would have been ahead for that young life. "Oh, Tanner," she said, and for a moment or two he just held on.

"Sean and I…we worked on him for a long time. He wasn't dead when we got there, but he was…" Tanner halted when his voice broke a bit. He cleared his throat. "He was hurt real bad. And his dad and a couple of the hands were standing there crying and we had to just focus and not see the kid, just the job."

"Which is impossible, of course."

He nodded. "We were almost to the hospital when we lost him. They worked on him awhile there, but the internal bleeding was too much. And now I can't get that kid's face out of my head."

She pulled back out of his arms a bit, and he drank in the sight of her face, so beautiful and alive. He'd needed her today, he realized. He'd thought about going home to the place he'd lived all his life, but instead he'd come here. To her. He wasn't sure he was comfortable with that, but he'd think about it later. Right now he was just grateful he was where he needed to be.

"I shouldn't be dumping all this on you," he said.

"We're friends, and I'm glad you did." She slid her fingers down to his hands and squeezed. "I've been feeling like this arrangement is so one-sided. You being there to help me out of trouble, but me offering little in return. If I can help you with this, it makes me feel useful. Like... I'm giving you something back." She sighed. "Like I actually have something to offer."

"You have more than you realize," he murmured, tightening his hands on hers. "Talking has helped, actually." He paused. "And letting me hold you. I think I needed a nice, warm human being this afternoon."

When her lips turned up in a sweet smile, the ugliness of the day seemed to melt away. "Maybe we should get you a dog," she joked.

"I said human being," he replied, but he smiled in return, feeling some of his muscles relax.

He hadn't realized how tightly he'd been holding himself until he started to let go.

Chapter Eleven

As Tanner relaxed, he started to notice other things, too. Like how her coppery hair set off her creamy skin; her eyes were a deep shade of blue that seemed bottomless, her bottom lip was fuller than the top and she had a habit of nibbling on it when she was nervous.

It would be the easiest thing in the world to reach for her right now. To sink his hands into that gorgeous waterfall of hair, to kiss her soft lips and pull her body close against his. Her thumb rubbed against the top of his hand, and his body responded to the simple touch, fueling a desire so profound it shocked him. He didn't just want to have sex. He thought of how guileless she was, how unaware of her own attractiveness, and wanted to show her the way he saw her.

Tanner wanted to make love to her. It was very different from scratching an itch or fulfilling a fantasy. He wanted to worship her body with his.

But he wouldn't. The unexpected emotions that prompted these thoughts were the same ones that reminded him of the fragility of their situation, of the need for care and caution. After their last kiss, he'd agreed they wouldn't complicate things by becoming physically involved.

She needed to be able to trust him to keep his word.

So he pushed his libido aside—with difficulty—and focused instead on the unique practicality of the situation.

"Let's change the subject to something happier," he suggested, sliding back a little and stretching out his legs so their pose wasn't so intimate. "Anything new with plans?"

She took his cue, thankfully, and slid her fingers away from his. "Actually, yes. I looked into a site for the ceremony. We can have it at the gazebo on the riverbank, you know the one? Just beyond the library. I checked with the town hall and apparently we can book it for an hour that Sunday afternoon."

He nodded. "That sounds nice."

"Maddy made a point that we shouldn't just have it in the living room. That we should do something at least modestly matrimonial."

His eyebrows shot up. "Maddy?"

"She stopped by a few days ago. After you'd talked to her and Cole."

Ah yes. The conversation that had been strained at best, though they'd put on a good face the moment he'd brought up that he knew they knew the truth. Their concerns had been the same as his parents', and he been on the brink of telling them the truth. It bothered him to lie to his brother, in particular.

While it had been difficult to keep up the pretense of a real marriage, it hadn't been hard at all to stand up for Laura. His defense of her probably went a long way to his family reconciling themselves to the wedding.

Maybe they weren't in love. But neither was Laura opportunistic or callous. He was unexpectedly touched by her words today about feeling helpful and needed. She'd made room for him in her house. In her life. That was far bigger than a piece of paper.

"I suppose people are going to expect a certain, I don't know, sense of occasion." He floundered over the words. He wasn't good at this sort of thing. "The park sounds really nice. You should have a new dress, and one for Rowan, too. Order a few flowers. Get your hair done. When was the last time you pampered yourself a little?"

She wasn't looking at him now and he got the sense he'd said something wrong. "Laura? What is it? Did I say something wrong? You don't have to do those things if you don't want to. I just thought… Never mind. I'm probably an idiot."

When she looked at him, he swore her eyes were damp, though no tears glistened on her lashes or touched her cheeks. "It's not that. It's a lovely idea. Except, well, we're at the point where we're honest with each other, right?"

"You did my laundry yesterday." He smiled at her. "You've officially folded my underwear. We're living together. I think honesty might be a good idea."

He was gratified to see her smile a bit.

"It's two things, really," she admitted, and he noticed she picked at a cuticle with her fingernail. "I don't really have the money to go do all those things. And even if I did…" She swallowed. "A bride should have a sister or girlfriends or someone to go on a shopping trip like that. The thought of going alone is gross."

A reminder of her outcast status in the community. He got it. It was that way because of the sacrifice she'd made thinking it would be best for her daughter. "None of your old school friends have stayed in touch?" After all, Laura had grown up here. Surely she'd stayed friends with someone.

"A few did at first, until it was obvious I was pregnant. When everyone thought it was Gavin's, they stopped calling."

"I'm sorry."

She made a "what can you do?" face. "Even if I'd said Rowan wasn't his, I doubt anyone would have believed me. So I kept my head down and my mouth shut."

The thought of dress-shopping was not a happy one, but neither was the idea of her feeling so incredibly lonely. The people in this town needed a kick in the rear.

"I'll go with you. And I'll pick up the tab. I'm pretty sure I can afford a dress and a few flowers or something."

"Tanner, that's generous of you, but I can't let you do that."

Pride. He was starting to understand that she seemed to be keeping a running tab in her head. "Listen, keep the receipts if you like. When your business is up and going, you can pay me back, if you feel that strongly about it."

He didn't have any intention of taking her money, but she didn't need to know that.

"You really want to go shopping?" She raised an eyebrow at him.

"Why not?" He had a suit, so he shrugged. "Maybe I'll get a new tie."

Her face lit up. Just a bit, but he knew he'd done the right thing by suggesting it.

"Let me know what day is good for you. I'll work around your schedule."

"If I tell Cole I'm taking a day for wedding plans, he won't think anything of it. We'll go into the city. Have lunch. Make a day of it. Maybe Monday? I'm on call again this weekend." And he'd deal with that when the time came. He loved his EMT work. He wasn't about to abandon it because of one horrible call.

"Okay," she said, nodding. "But nothing fancy. I'd like something nice that I can wear again."

He wasn't sure if that was a practical streak or if she really thought she didn't deserve any better. He hoped it was the first.

She touched his knee. "Thank you, Tanner. Are you feeling any better now?"

He was. There was a lingering heaviness when he thought about the day's events, but the shock and shakes had worn off from the distraction she'd provided. He suspected she'd done it deliberately, clever woman.

"I am. Now that the adrenaline's worn off, I'm kind of crashing, though. Man, I'm so tired."

"Have a sleep, then. Rowan will be up soon and I should go clean up the disaster that was the doughnuts." She crawled off the bed and stretched.

"Laura?" He looked up at her, felt helplessly as though he was starting to care far too much. "About the doughnuts. Really, you don't have to try so hard. I appreciate the effort." He sent her a crooked smile, because they both knew what a mess it had turned out to be. "But seriously, you don't have to be anything other than who you are. That's enough. I want you to remember that, okay?"

Her gaze touched his, and he felt the strange thump in his chest that seemed to happen whenever she looked at him with her eyes all soft and her lips slightly parted.

"You're a good man," she murmured. "Thank you for saying that, Tanner."

She slipped out of the room before he could say anything more, and he closed his eyes and sank back against the pillows. She'd thanked him for saying it, but he got the impression she didn't believe it.

Dammit. He was only supposed to like her. What the hell was he doing falling for her anyway?

LAURA KNEW SHE had no right to be so excited.

It wasn't a real wedding. She wasn't shopping for a real wedding dress. And yet the idea of going shopping, of buying something new and pretty was so exhilarating. And something for Rowan, too, she determined. She could afford to buy her daughter a little frilly dress for the ceremony.

By nine o'clock Monday morning, they were ready to go. Tanner had gone to the ranch early to help with morning chores and catch up on some other odd jobs, but he'd promised to be back by nine-thirty.

Rowan was fed, bathed, and dressed in cute leggings and a ruffled top with a bonnet on her head that she kept picking at in boredom. Laura had dressed up, too, in the same dress she'd worn the night Tanner made his crazy proposal. On her feet were little sandals with kitten heels that she thought might work while trying on dresses. She had everything in the diaper bag, including a small dish containing some dry cereal that she'd recently started feeding to

Rowan. Now she was pacing, waiting for Tanner to come home, stopping in the hall mirror to check her lip gloss one more time.

It felt real. It had felt real ever since he came home last week, his shirt spattered with blood and heartbreak in his eyes. Something had changed that day, when he looked at her before going to sleep. He hadn't kissed her, hadn't done anything inappropriate. But there was a different closeness between them now. An awareness. Maybe it was wrong, maybe it was ill-advised, but it was there all the same. It would take a stronger woman than her to resist Tanner's gallantry.

He'd worked two more shifts on ambulance duty on the weekend, and she'd worried about him. He'd come home quiet and somewhat subdued, but on Saturday night, Rowan had been fussing a bit and he'd sat on the floor with her and played and seemed to come around. Lord help her, for a few minutes they'd actually felt like a little family.

Would it be so bad to pretend it was a tiny bit real?

A growl in the front yard announced the return of Tanner and his truck. They'd agreed to take her car today, since it was easier on gas and the car seat was already inside.

"You ready, darlin'?" she said to Rowan. "Gonna get you a new dress today. Mama, too."

Tanner bounded in, his face relaxed and smiling. "You're all ready to go. Excellent."

"Ro always has me up early. Plus, I think she's excited for shopping."

"Oh, she is, is she? I think her mama's the one who's excited."

"Maybe just a little."

"I thought we'd hit the mall in Great Falls, unless you want a specialty shop or something. I don't know much about dresses and stuff."

"The mall is fine. There's a JCPenney there." She was more than happy to go to the department store. Just having the day away from Gibson was enough.

"Let's go, then. I've got a hot chocolate for you in the car, and coffee for me. Thought we could use it for the drive."

Hot chocolate, and a shopping trip. Wasn't he full of surprises?

She smiled at him. He was all sexiness today, in dark jeans, boots and a clean shirt—had he changed at the ranch? And he was wearing a hat, his good one, clean and dust-free. The quintessential cowboy heading into the city to buy his girl a dress. If that wasn't swoon-worthy, what was?

It only took a minute to fasten Rowan in the back and head down the driveway. Laura waited to open her hot chocolate until they were on the highway, heading away from Gibson. To her amusement, Tanner took a sip of coffee and then reached down beside him for a paper sack.

She laughed. "Let me guess. Honey glazed?"

"You know me too well," he said, grinning and shoving half a doughnut into his mouth.

She was starting to, she realized.

When he'd swallowed the enormous bite, he glanced over at her. "Thanks for getting my uniform shirt clean, by the way. I don't think I thanked you before."

She smiled. "It wasn't me. I took it over to Gram's. She showed me how to get the stain out."

"Some home remedy or trick, I suppose," he commented, focusing on the road again.

She laughed lightly. "Actually, she had a stain stick. It worked great."

Tanner laughed.

It seemed like no time at all before they were at the mall. She removed Rowan from her seat and put her in a little stroller, small enough to be convenient for the aisles of the department store. They headed straight for the women's clothing, and Laura noticed some of the sidelong looks that followed them. It was so different from Gibson. The looks were warm and approving, rather than judgmental. As though they were looking at the three of them as a family. It was nice, and she wondered again at the wisdom of staying in Gibson. Maybe in another few years, she'd be able to afford to move outside the town.

This marriage would give her freedom she couldn't otherwise afford. Not just from the name change, but the sharing of expenses.

It was a sobering thought.

They made their way through women's wear to the fancy dresses. Laura stared at the clothing on the hangers and her heart sank. There were actual wedding dresses here. Oh, nothing over the top, but long white dresses appropriate for weddings. Once upon a time she'd dreamt of such things.

"Do you see anything you like?"

She swallowed, her throat working against the emotion lodged there. "Tanner, I don't think I can wear a long white dress."

"It's up to you, but I got the impression that the

whole 'white' thing doesn't really matter much anymore." He smiled at her. "Get something you like."

The gowns were beautiful, but not right. "Maybe there's something over here, in the cocktail dress section," she said, leading him away. Rowan peered around curiously, intrigued by the lights and colors.

It wasn't long before she saw a few dresses that she considered appropriate. There was a white one, short and strapless yet modest. She let go of her "no white" idea because the dress was so cute. Then she found a periwinkle satin-y number and a blush-pink lace dress with a ribbon sash, which she adored but wondered how it would look with her red hair.

"Will you watch Ro while I try these on?" she asked, her stomach curling with excited nerves. The dresses were all so pretty. Not cheap, but not overly expensive, either. Maybe she'd even have occasion to wear it again, though she didn't know where. Maybe if Cole and Maddy got married…

She slipped into the dressing room.

First up was the white dress. She liked it a lot, but the bust was a bit tight, and with it being strapless, she wasn't sure what would happen with her breasts, since she was still nursing.

The periwinkle one had a nice style, but the coloring was all wrong with her hair and complexion. She looked completely washed out. She took it off as quickly as she'd put it on.

"Everything okay in there?" came Tanner's voice.

"Just a little longer. Is that okay?"

He chuckled warmly. "Take your time. Ro's chewing on her giraffe."

She slipped into the pink dress and zipped it up. The

moment she turned to the mirror she knew. The pale pink was subtle enough that it didn't clash with her hair, and the lace overskirt was incredibly feminine. Plus, she didn't feel as if her bust was on display. The satin ribbon at the waist added a touch of class and formality that would suit a wedding just fine.

She wouldn't feel as guilty wearing pink.

"I think I've found it," she called out.

"Let's see," Tanner suggested.

"No." She clung to at least a little bit of wedding protocol. "It's bad luck."

His voice was close to the change room door. "Laura, we're not exactly conventional here."

She pressed her head against the door. "Tanner, please. I'd like to keep *something* a surprise. Okay?"

"Of course it's okay." His voice was soft. "You're sure you don't want to look at something else?"

She was sure. It fit perfectly and she felt pretty in it. "I'm sure. You'll learn me fairly quickly, Tanner. I'm kind of low maintenance."

He laughed. "Okay, then. We'll disappear for a minute while you come out."

She changed back into her regular clothes and reluctantly hung the dress on the hanger again. She took all three out, gave two to the saleslady to hang back up and then handed her the pink one to hold on to until they were ready to go. "I'm going to look for shoes and a dress for my daughter," she explained, looking longingly after the dress. She hadn't wanted to take it off.

She found Tanner and Rowan in the children's section. Tanner was staring at the ruffled items, and she hesitated for a moment, committing the image to memory. The lean, rugged cowboy surrounded by tiny lace and eyelet dresses and bloomers.

"Hi," she said, smiling and stepping forward. "Find anything you like?"

"I wouldn't know where to start." He had his hands on the handles of the stroller and Laura got all squishy inside.

"Well, babies are fun to buy for. Especially baby girls. Ruffles, cotton lace, frills and all that stuff." She ran her fingers over racks of adorable sets, but then found one rack with little pastel dresses. Her heart melted.

"Oh, look," she said. She picked up a white cotton lace dress with a pink sash. "Isn't this cute?"

"Look at this kid." He pointed at Rowan, who drooled over her plastic Sophie the Giraffe. "I challenge you to find anything that wouldn't be cute."

Laura browsed for longer than she'd taken with her own dress, but then she spotted a beautiful pink dress with a two-tiered pleated skirt and a little shrug that resembled rosebuds. It was perfect. With Rowan's dark hair and heavily lashed blue eyes, the pink would be amazing. And Laura already had the perfect pair of white soft shoes to put on her feet.

"This is the one," she said, holding it up.

Tanner looked down at her and her she went all mushy. "You went with the pink one for your dress, didn't you?"

She didn't want him to know for sure. "Well, it's not the periwinkle."

"You mean the purple-y one?"

She grinned. "Yeah. I did try on a white one, though."

He shook his head, his gaze steady on hers. "Nope. It's the pink one."

"What makes you say that?" she challenged, though she was loving every minute of the exchange.

"Because of the way your face looked when you took it off the rack. It got all… I don't know. Soft-looking. And now with the pink dress for Rowan…"

She couldn't remember the last time she'd been this happy.

"Do you think I could look at shoes?"

"A new dress needs new shoes. Or so Maddy told me."

Maddy. An unexpected ally.

The day was like a fairy tale. They went to the shoe department and she found a pair of simple blush-colored pumps. When they were done, they headed back to the first saleslady and Tanner pulled out his bank card and paid for the three items.

"Tanner, thank you. I promise I'll pay you back."

"It's my pleasure," he assured her.

She had a sudden idea. "Hey, you know how you said you might get a new tie?"

He nodded.

"Will you let me get that for you? As a wedding present? I know it's not exactly equal—"

"But it would make you feel better," he finished for her.

"Well, yeah."

"I'd be honored, Laura." He let go of the stroller for a moment and reached for her hand. "I don't want us to have to keep track of every penny, you know. We're both getting something out of this arrangement. For what it's worth, I'm happy being out of the house. It was past time for me to do it."

"So, a tie. What color is your suit?"

He shrugged. "Black."

She laughed. "Of course it is. Black suit, white shirt, right? Okay."

They detoured over to men's wear and stopped at a table with an assortment of silk ties. Laura considered dove gray, black, white, but in the end she chose the light pink one. She picked it up and held it to his shirt front. "What do you say? Are you man enough to wear pink?"

He laughed. "It's a tie. It's not like you're going to dress me in a tutu. I think I can handle it."

He was so easygoing. Did he realize how amazing that made him? Tanner worried about the big stuff and didn't sweat the small stuff. Laura admired him for that. More than he knew. "Then I will buy it for you. A proper wedding tie."

It was a little thing, but she took pride in taking it to the sales counter and paying for it herself. She tucked the little bag into the larger one containing their dresses and her shoes. "Well," she said, "it's hardly noon, and we're done already. What's next?"

He patted his belly. "I'm out of doughnuts. I was thinking we could grab some lunch somewhere before heading back." He chuckled. "You're an efficient shopper, Laura. I was prepared to spend the day in lots of stores and a lot of time outside change rooms."

"You learn to be economical with your time when you have a baby," she replied, gazing at Rowan in the stroller.

"She's been so good today."

"Sleeping better lately, too. It might be because I've started her on some solids." Thank God for rice cereal.

"So, what do you feel like? Mexican? Asian? Sandwiches? Greek?"

It was all fast food choices yet it felt extravagant just the same. "Asian? Is that okay with you?"

He laughed. "I'll eat anything."

"Even my cooking?" she teased.

He grinned. "Well, maybe not your doughnuts, but you haven't poisoned me yet."

At the small restaurant, Laura scanned the menu. When was the last time she'd had takeout like this? She decided on a small order of chicken lo mein and a bottle of water; Tanner ordered a bigger combination meal. Seating was limited, but he snagged them a spot in the corner, and while Tanner waited for their order, Laura put Rowan on her lap and opened a jar of pureed bananas. She'd expressed enough milk for a bottle as well, so she'd be spared any awkward moments during their shopping trip. By the time Tanner returned to the table with the tray, Rowan had gobbled up almost a third of the jar of bananas and was settled happily with the bottle.

"Wow, you didn't waste any time." Tanner divvied up napkins and forks, and then considerately opened her water, since her hands were fairly occupied.

"I figured I'd feed her before she started screaming about it," Laura said. "I guess I should have started her on some solids earlier. She loves her cereal, and bananas and applesauce."

"It's not like you've ever done this before," he noted, digging his fork into a mound of fried rice. "She looks pretty happy to me."

Indeed, Rowan was drinking away happily, and Laura was having a great time. No one knew them here. They were simply a couple out shopping, enjoying lunch and relaxing. There was nothing to worry about in this moment, and it was a glorious feeling. "You look happy, too," Tanner said. He speared a piece of saucy chicken and popped it into his mouth.

"I am. It's been a lovely morning."

"It's just shopping." He chuckled a little, but she shook her head. How could she possibly explain that it was far more than a little shopping? What it meant that he'd taken his time and hard-earned money to make this possible? She felt as though she didn't deserve any of it.

And she was starting to wish that it were real, that Tanner did care for her and her for him. The last part wasn't much of a stretch; any woman would be lucky to have such a man on her side.

"Here," Tanner said, putting down his fork. "Let me take her for a few minutes. You've hardly managed to eat anything."

"Are you sure?"

He nodded. "I've held her a few times now and we're getting used to each other." He held out his arms and she shifted, taking the empty bottle from Rowan's lips and wiping a dribble of milk from her chin.

Laura put Rowan in his arms and watched as he cradled her daughter close, as gently as if she were spun glass. Her pulse thumped as she handed him the flannel blanket. "She might have some gas," she said.

"We got it covered, don't we, short stuff?" he asked the baby. Rowan stared up at him with wide and trusting eyes. Then she burped, dribbling some milk over her chin, which Tanner deftly wiped up with the flannel.

Laura took the precious opportunity to have two free hands. She forked up some lo mein and the flavors exploded in her mouth. "Mmm, this is so good," she mumbled, swallowing.

"Really? It's not gourmet, you know." Tanner's eyebrow was raised in amusement.

"Doesn't matter. One, I didn't cook it." She scooped more on her fork and met his gaze. "Two, it's been so long since I had Chinese food. This is a real treat, Tanner. Thanks."

She shoveled more into her mouth, chewing happily.

"I'm glad." Tanner bounced his knee a bit, keeping Rowan happy. "You deserve to get out now and again."

"And the dresses and stuff, too. I promise I'll pay you back. Do you know I have my website nearly ready to go? I'm putting the finishing touches on my submit-for-quote forms to make them as straightforward as possible. Once I do that, I can start doing up proposal packages and really going after some business."

"That's great." He was smiling and it was so nice to feel someone's approval. She hadn't realized how terribly she'd missed such a simple thing, but clearly she had. Her work at her last job had been satisfactory and her boss had always been pleased, but it wasn't that this time. She respected Tanner's opinion, and having him support her choices meant more than he knew.

She scraped the bottom of the carton and sat back in her chair. "I'm stuffed. What should we do now?"

"I took the whole day off. Is there anything else you need to do for the wedding?

There was one thing in particular, but as much as

they'd shopped together today and were treating the wedding as a simple event, she found she couldn't bring it up. It was a sensitive topic and she wasn't sure how to broach without feeling terrible about disregarding the sanctity of marriage or having it seem that she was making more of it than there was.

But someday soon, they would need to talk about what they were going to do for wedding rings.

Chapter Twelve

In the end, Laura lost the nerve to bring up the subject of rings. Instead, she took a day and went to the city herself, and picked out what she hoped would be the right size for Tanner in a plain gold band. There was no way she was going to ask him to buy his own wedding ring.

The weather was nearly summer-like, and when she got returned from town she found him on the front step in a T-shirt and jeans, a tool belt slung low over his hips. "You're home early," she called out, realizing how very domestic it sounded.

"I wanted to fix the front step, and in another few days we'll be ready for our first cut of hay. I'll be working longer days at the ranch and probably won't have time."

"Oh." She'd miss him being home in the evenings, but she was guessing it would be close to dark when he got home. Maybe he was regretting leaving the ranch. If he lived there, he wouldn't have any travel time.

But she didn't say that because she didn't want it to sound as if she didn't want him at her house when she did—so very much.

He stood and she saw the way his muscles filled out

the light cotton of his T-shirt, how his jeans sat on his hips, the waistband just above the leather of the tool belt. The wedding ring she'd bought was cushioned in a little ring box in her purse, and Rowan sat on her arm, her small bonneted head looking all around. Laura noticed Rowan following the progress of a butterfly and she smiled. Lord, she was precious. For all of life's troubles, she wouldn't trade her little one for anything in the world.

"She's looking cute today." Laura hadn't realized that Tanner had come down the few steps to meet her, and she started when she realized how close he was.

"I have to say, I love shopping for the cute little clothes. Sometimes we just go to the secondhand store in town. Babies outgrow things so quickly that they're hardly ever worn out. Stained a little sometimes, but still in good shape."

"My mom always said the best bleach in the world was sunlight."

Laura nodded. "Gram said that, too, the day I took your shirt over to wash. We hung it on her line."

"Let me help you up the steps. I still have a tread to replace. But it should be much sturdier for you."

The third step, the one just before the small landing, was missing, but Laura could see the fresh yellow-y brown boards on the other steps and noted how solid they were beneath her feet, with no creaks or tilts. When she got to the second to-the-top step, Tanner put his hands on her waist and simply lifted her—and Rowan—the eighteen inches to the top.

"Oh!" She couldn't stop the light exclamation. Goodness, he'd done that as if she weighed nothing at all, when she knew very well she was still carrying a good portion of her baby weight, as well as her baby.

"There you go. I shouldn't be long here. What's for supper?" He winked. He asked that almost every night, always teasing. Her lack of cooking skills had become a bit of a running joke.

"Spaghetti," she replied. This was something she could manage halfway decently by using canned goods for the sauce. There was a salad kit in the fridge, which only required her to dump everything into a bowl. She'd picked up sugar cookies as a treat for him to have for dessert.

She put Rowan to play in a playpen she'd found at a garage sale the past weekend. Her daughter was now starting to scooch herself along in a prequel to proper crawling. Humming softly to herself, Laura browned a little hamburger in a pan and then added a couple of jars of sauce. A quick taste proved the sauce to be somewhat bland, so she added seasonings to spice it up a bit. Then she put water on to boil for the pasta, dug out a salad bowl and listened to Tanner's random sounds of sawing and hammering.

When the pasta was cooked, she drained it and poured it into a big bowl, poured the sauce over top and put it on the table along with the salad. She went to the door and stuck her head outside. "Tanner? Dinner's ready."

"Great. I got the last step fixed and I'm starving."

He unbuckled the tool belt and Laura tried not to follow the movement of his hands with her eyes. She failed. When she glanced up, he was watching her with an amused expression.

Her cheeks flared. "It's getting cold."

"Certainly. Just let me wash up."

When he'd come back from the bathroom, she was seated at the table, scooping a big helping of pasta onto his plate. "So," she said, determined to start a normal conversation. "You're starting haying. Does that mean the wedding is bad timing?"

"Not really." He picked up his fork, took his plate from her fingers. "Thanks. Anyway, my mom and dad never work on Sunday. Well, I shouldn't say never. If the weather forecast is bad, we might work right through. But other than daily chores? Mom and Dad always believed in a day of rest. During our busiest times, that was always our day for family."

"That sounds nice," Laura said, loving the way his family sounded more and more.

"When I was younger, it was a pain in the ass. Now I appreciate it, though. Everyone needs some down-time."

"I officially invited my grandparents," she said, taking the salad utensils and putting some lettuce on her plate. "With your folks and Cole and Maddy, that makes six. Is there anyone else you want to tell?"

He shrugged. "I've got friends, but we're keeping this small, right? Cole will be our witness. How about you?"

She thought of a few friends she'd reconnected with when she came back to town, and who'd then awkwardly found excuses to back out of plans when the rumors about Gavin started spreading. "No," she said, quite definite. "Let's just have the eight of us. Nine, including Ro." She smiled. "Perfect number for in-side the gazebo."

"Hey," he said, "this spaghetti isn't half-bad."

"A rousing endorsement."

He laughed. "I mean it. You're getting better."

From anyone else it would sound patronizing. From Tanner, though—she knew it was a genuine compliment, and she took it as such.

After dinner, she offered him a couple of cookies and a fresh cup of coffee. While she cleaned up the mess, Tanner headed back outside, and to her surprise, she saw him wielding a paintbrush. He was painting the railings a lovely, brilliant white. It was going to look amazing. It warmed her heart in ways she couldn't explain. While Tanner hadn't given her actual rent for this month, he'd taken her shopping for wedding stuff and picked up the tab. He'd bought groceries, changed the oil in her car and filled it up and now fixed the steps. That was worth far more than rent.

He kept up his work and she finished the dishes, fed Rowan pureed sweet potato and peas, then gave her a bath and dressed her in clean, fuzzy pajamas. The evening was turning soft, the light muted through the windows, when she finally sat in the rocker in the living room to nurse Rowan before bed.

Tanner came in and called out, "Laura, I'm going to clean the paintbrush and stuff down in the basement, okay?"

"Sure."

She'd started to fall asleep in the chair, and only roused when she heard Tanner's steps coming up from the basement. Rowan was sound asleep in her arms; Laura awkwardly set her clothing straight as best she could before he came into the room.

He stopped in the doorway and rested his shoulder on the frame. "Out like a light."

Laura nodded.

"Looks like her mama's about ready, as well. Did you fall asleep again?"

It was the *again* that got her. It spoke of habit, of intimacy. She already knew she would miss him when they went their separate ways. How hard would it be months from now when they lived together for so long?

"I might have dozed off for a few minutes," she confessed. "You painted the railings."

"A first coat. It needs a second because the wood soaks up the paint so much. But it's a start."

"Thank you so much."

He pushed away from the frame, pulled up a foot stool and sat in front of her. He touched a single, rough finger to the soft hair above Rowan's ear, the ghost of a smile flickering over his face. "Laura, I wasn't sure what to expect when I moved in. I know we said it would be like a trial period. The wedding's a little over a week away now. I know we've made the plans and everything, but I wanted to make sure this is still what you want."

"Is it what you want?"

His gaze held hers. "Yes. Very much. I like coming home to you. To you both."

Her heart leaped. "I like having you here, too. It feels... I don't know. More like a home somehow."

"I'm glad."

"I know you're busy, and I want to thank you again for everything you've been doing around here."

He put his hand on hers. "It's something I can contribute, and I like doing it. Otherwise I might feel like I was merely a boarder. Know what I mean?"

She nodded, understanding completely.

"Besides, you make a man want to do things for you. When you smile at me and say thanks, it's good for my ego." His grin widened, and his fingers tightened on hers. Before she knew what was happening, they'd twined with hers so they weren't just touching, but holding hands. Really holding hands.

She was no innocent girl. And he certainly wasn't an innocent man. He'd been married and she'd borne another man's child. But in that moment, when their fingers meshed and their eyes met, something changed. Something pure, and yes, even innocent. Something big and important. For the first time, she let her feelings flood her heart. She didn't just like Tanner. She loved him.

It was so not part of the plan. She wasn't supposed to fall in love with him. And if she told him? Everything would be ruined. They couldn't get married if he knew the truth, so she determined to keep it buried deep inside. For as long as it took.

He leaned forward and kissed her, lightly, a whisper of a kiss that was far more devastating in its tenderness than the most passionate of embraces. She was in real danger here, torn between wanting to follow her heart and doing what she knew she must.

When the kiss ended, she sat back and smiled. "Well, we should be fine on the day. No awkwardness."

His gaze cooled a little, and understanding flickered in his eyes. But she saw something else, too. She saw that she wasn't fooling anyone.

Rowan shifted in her arms, perhaps uncomfortable from the slight squeeze of moments before.

"You're tired. You should put Rowan to bed and head there yourself."

And away from him. It wasn't a bad idea. She'd read. Or stare at the ceiling and marvel at how she was incredibly talented at getting herself into impossible situations.

He was far enough away that she could get up, holding Rowan close in her arms. But she needed to slide past him to go toward the hall and the bedrooms, and he didn't stand or move aside, either.

She brushed by him and ducked into the bedroom, exhaling a breath. She then turned back and leaned out a little. "Good night, Tanner."

"Good night, Laura."

Maybe one of these days she'd get up the courage to bring up what was happening between them. Today definitely wasn't that day, she thought with a rueful laugh as she lay down on top of her bed.

She hadn't brushed her teeth or done any of her bedtime rituals, but she was such a chicken that she couldn't bear sneaking out of the room to do them now. So she lay there, listening to Rowan's soft breaths, listening for Tanner's footsteps past the door, listening to the beating of her heart until she fell into a restless sleep.

THE WEEKEND CAME and went. Tanner finished painting the railings and then he was home late several nights because of haying. It didn't stop him from doing his odd jobs, though. Sunday, he installed a clothesline, and on Monday, Laura used it for the first time, hanging out Rowan's frilly dresses instead of putting them in the dryer. Then she did the sheets, and loved the smell of them fresh off the line and on the bed.

Another night he unloaded planters from his truck and set them on her step. "Mom had extra bedding plants," he explained. "These ones I can hang as soon as I install some hooks." There were two other large pots with petunias and geraniums. Laura took them and placed them on either side of the door and became ridiculously excited.

"Oh, that's just what we needed around here!"

"She said she's going to do some clippings and if you want some for your yard, to let her know."

"She said that?"

He nodded. "I think she's coming around a little, to be honest."

"I'm glad."

"Me, too. I think it goes a long way for her to know I'm happy."

He was happy. Happy living with *her*. She shouldn't feel so elated about it, but she was. It was a nice feeling, knowing she contributed to someone else's happiness.

"I'm happy, too, Tanner." She smiled. "And it looks so good around here now. With the paint and the flowers and everything."

"Let's show Ro the flowers."

He'd shortened Rowan's name. And he stepped around Laura, went inside and scooped Rowan out of her playpen without any hesitation at all.

Just as a dad would.

No. She wouldn't think like that.

He walked from planter to planter, showing Rowan the brightly colored flowers, letting her gently touch the petals. She heard his deep laugh, and Rowan's higher squeal of excitement. "Do you mind if I take her for a walk around the yard?" he asked. "She seems to like it out here."

"That's fine. Just don't stay out if the bugs are bad. I get the feeling insect bites would be a real pain, you know?"

"Of course."

He gave Rowan a bounce so that she was settled on his arm perfectly, and the two of them set off down the driveway. He'd mowed the lawn, but the ditch had grown and some wildflowers grew there. Laura watched them, Tanner's lips moving as he talked away to Rowan, pointing at things Laura was sure her daughter didn't understand. They stopped at the corner of the property, where a wild rosebush bloomed, the perfume sweet and strong from the pink blossoms. They moved along the edge to the poplar and birch trees, then the circle of spruces. He waved a hand at his face and they turned around to come back.

If she could have handpicked a father for her child, it would be someone like Tanner. Hardworking, honest, caring, fun. Did he even realize how much of a family man he was deep down?

"The bugs were worse toward the backyard. There's a bit of a dip there that holds water."

"It's nearly her bedtime anyway," Laura answered. "I can take her."

When he put Rowan in her arms, their hands brushed. That simple touch was enough to send her stomach into whorls of excitement.

Four more days. Four days from now she'd stand in front of a justice of the peace, his parents and her grandparents to falsely pledge to love and honor him forever. The problem was, it didn't feel so false, and to mean it would only break her heart in the end.

Chapter Thirteen

The phone call came on Thursday, at precisely nine forty-two.

Laura answered it, expecting a final call from the florist in town about the simple bouquet and bouton-niere she'd ordered. Instead it was Gavin's partner at the law firm, the lawyer who'd taken on her affairs after Gavin's death.

"Laura, could you come to the office for a meet-ing this morning?"

Unease rippled through her stomach. "I guess I can get away. Is it important?"

"Nothing to worry about, but I do need to give you an update as soon as possible. My schedule's open this morning. Just tell the receptionist when you get here."

In her experience, *nothing to worry about* was often something to worry about. She hung up the phone feeling slightly sick. The only reason he'd call was if there was news about Spence. The fact that it had hap-pened just three days before her wedding—something she was already nervous enough about—only added to her anxiety.

She didn't often ask her grandmother to watch Rowan, but this morning she did. She had the feeling she needed to be alone at this meeting. She made a quick call, ensuring that Gram was okay to watch Ro for a few hours, and then put together a well-stocked diaper bag, scraped her hair up in a ponytail and swiped a little lip gloss on her lips. That was all she was going to make time for today.

Gram was ready and waiting when she arrived, perked up considerably since her illness and looking like her old self. She took Rowan from Laura's arms and gave her loud kisses in her neck, prompting a belly laugh. "Are you all right, sweetie?" Gram asked. "You sounded upset on the phone."

"It's fine. Just an unexpected appointment that'll be easier without Rowan. I shouldn't be too long. Thanks a million."

"Anytime. We haven't seen her for a while now and she's growing like crazy."

Laura smiled. "I know. Love you, Gram." She kissed her grandmother's cheek. "See you soon."

"Wave bye to your mama," Gram said, lifting Ro's pudgy arm.

Ten minutes later, Laura arrived at the law office; a minute after that the receptionist ushered her into the lawyer's office. To say the quick service made her nervous was an understatement.

"Laura, hello." Richard was middle-aged, with steel-rimmed glasses and salt-and-pepper hair, which gave him an air of both authority and competence. "Have a seat. Can we get you a coffee or anything?"

She swallowed tightly. "With all due respect, you do charge by the hour." She smiled at him, hoping the quip might lighten things for her.

He smiled. "Okay, I know I was kind of cryptic on the phone. You haven't seen the news today, I take it?"

"The news?" She looked at him with some confusion. "No, I don't usually watch in the morning and I hadn't logged on to my computer yet."

"Good. I wanted you to hear it from me, first."

"Hear what?" God, had Spence been paroled? And yet that was hardly something that would make the news. Her blood turned to ice. Escape? Was he coming here? Oh no. She'd left Rowan at Gram's...

Richard reached across the desk. "Forgive me, Laura. I haven't gone about this the right way. You have nothing to fear, all right? Spencer is dead."

The room started to spin. She heard a chair scrape on the floor and a warm, gentle voice beside her. "Okay, now," he said, gently but firmly. "Head between the knees. Try to take deep, slow breaths."

She was hyperventilating. Her heart pounded, her body felt cold and distant, and her head was spinning. She did as she was ordered and dropped her head between her knees, the lawyer's warm hand on her back. It gave her something to focus on until the panic and shock passed and she could breathe again.

"I'm so sorry," she whispered, putting her elbows on her knees and holding her head in her hands. "I wasn't expecting that."

"It's fine. You okay now?"

"Yes, thanks. Though I might like a glass of water."

He disappeared for a moment and then returned with a glass, tinkling with ice cubes. "Here, drink this and I'll fill you in."

The water was cold and refreshing and Laura took a big breath, sitting back in the chair and regaining her composure bit by bit. When Richard was sure of her, he took off his glasses and put them on his desk, then folded his hands and looked at her evenly.

"I'll cut right to the chase, Laura. There was a fight at the prison and Spencer was killed. It's on the news today. I've made a few calls on your behalf, and early reports say he got on the wrong side of someone inside, something gang related. I'm guessing, from what I know of his background and what you and Gavin told me, he probably got a little bit vocal and cocky and someone decided to shut him up."

"He's really dead? Not just injured or something?"

"Really dead. There'll be a full investigation, of course, and I can keep you up to date with that if you like, but mainly my job here today is to tell you that you no longer have to worry about Spencer being a threat. He can't come after you. He can't frighten you anymore, Laura."

She set down the glass, unsure of her feelings. Relief, certainly. This had hung over her head for months, causing so much worry and fear. To know that Spence could never touch her or their child was indeed a relief. But there was sadness, too. Sadness that someone had to die for her to feel safe. She might have wished for a lot of things, and she might even had had the thought that if Spencer were dead, her worries would be over. But she hadn't *truly* wished him dead. She had cared for him once. Sitting in her lawyer's office, she realized that deep down she'd hoped he'd find a way back to being the kind, sweet man she'd first met.

If that man had ever existed.

"It seems so dramatic. Like something out of the movies or cable TV."

"I know." He smiled ruefully. "Laura, Gavin told me what a strong woman you are. I know you've done everything in order to protect your daughter, but don't you think you can let down your guard now? Exonerate yourself—and Gavin?"

"I know." She nodded, a lump forming in her throat. "It wasn't fair to him, or Maddy."

"Or you," Richard added gently. "Now you can set the record straight."

It was too much to process. "First, I need to let this soak in. To see how I feel. To think about what's next."

Next. In three days she was supposed to be marrying Tanner. *Oh my God.* The very reason for their marriage no longer existed. What was she going to do?

She stood and held out her hand. "Richard, I really appreciate you telling me in person. I hope you're not offended when I say I'm glad I won't require your services for a while. At least not in this matter."

He stood, too, and shook her hand. "Not offended at all."

"If your assistant could send me the final bill, that'd be great."

"I'll see to it. Good luck, Laura."

"Thank you, Richard."

She left the office, feeling as if she were walking through a dream.

Outside, the early-summer sun instantly soaked through her light shirt, intense heat in contrast to the air-conditioned comfort of the legal office. She'd gone cold inside, too, so the temperature change was drastic and very welcome. Instead of going to her car, she wandered through town until she arrived at the library. She strolled through the grass, to the bench where she and Tanner had shared doughnuts and coffee, and where she'd decided she could marry him after all.

She couldn't marry him now. And as relieved as she was that Spence could no longer hurt her, she felt incredibly empty when she thought about Tanner not standing beside her at the gazebo on Sunday, or coming in the door at night with a smile, teasing her about her cooking or making faces at Rowan.

She had to tell him. And she needed to do it as soon as possible.

People came and went along the path; the sun moved directly overhead, then passed to her left as time slid by. A dozen possibilities and roadblocks passed through her mind, none of them clear. All she knew—*all she knew*—was that she must be honest with Tanner. She needed to release him from his promise. She'd lied enough over the past year and a half. It was time for truth. Only truth from now on.

Still in a relative daze, she walked back to her car and drove to pick up Rowan. She couldn't leave her at her grandparents' place indefinitely. Laura smiled brightly and told her grandmother everything was absolutely fine, went home and, once Rowan went down for her afternoon nap, called the ranch. Ellen informed her that the boys were out in the fields and wouldn't be back until evening, though she could call out if there was an emergency.

Laura told Ellen it was not an emergency and she'd talk to Tanner in the evening, and then set about trying to keep busy for the rest of the afternoon.

She made dinner, which consisted of pre-breaded chicken breasts, instant rice and frozen vegetables. She certainly didn't trust herself to make anything more involved in her state of mind. She ate alone around seven, tired of waiting and getting hungry since she'd forgotten to eat lunch. She cleaned up the mess, got Rowan ready for bed, saw daylight soften and twilight begin to move in as she tucked her daughter into bed.

The house was cloying, somehow, so she went out on the back landing. Now the space for the chair was shared with a little bucket full of clothespins, as well as a small pot of lavender, the soft scent winding its way around her as she breathed deeply of the night air.

It was nearly dark when she spotted the headlights coming down the road. They disappeared around the front of the house and then swept up the driveway. Tears sprouted in her eyes. She'd only just realized she loved him. Now she had to let him go. Perhaps it was better this way. It would hurt less in the end. Her confusion of this morning had waned and now she saw things clearly. She couldn't go through with the wedding. It wouldn't be fair to either of them.

Laura waited until she heard his voice calling her softly from inside, and then she called back, "Out here."

The patio door slid in its track, strangely loud in the quiet of the night. "What are you doing sitting out here in the dark?" he asked.

"Just thinking. Long day for you, huh?"

"Yeah. Rain forecast for tomorrow, so we wanted to get what we'd cut baled. We worked until we practically couldn't see anymore. Mom said you called the house looking for me."

"I did, yeah. But I didn't want to pull you away when they needed you."

"What's wrong?" He knelt beside her, put his hand on her knee. "You sound down."

"I don't know what I feel. Grab a chair, Tanner. We need to talk."

"That doesn't sound good."

"Actually, it's good news, sort of." She tried to smile. "It's kind of momentous."

He went inside and grabbed a kitchen chair and brought it out on the small landing. She was glad they were outside, where it was dark and he couldn't see her face completely. Her expression was liable to give away her feelings and she needed him to believe her when she told him the truth about Spence.

"Okay," he said, sitting down. "Fire away and tell me what's got you tied up in knots."

"I got a call from my lawyer today."

"This is about Spencer."

"Spence… Yes. He's dead, Tanner. There was some sort of fight and he was stabbed." She'd gone online to read the news and had found out that much. "I don't have to be afraid of him anymore."

Tanner leaned back and blew out a surprised breath. "Wow. You weren't kidding when you said it was big news. It must be wonderful to feel safe again."

Her smile was genuine. "Yes, yes, it does." She sighed. "And sad, too, and a bit guilty. He made his choices, but he could have made different ones. It didn't have to be this way, you know?" She hesitated. "And with him gone, it leaves us with having to make some choices of our own."

There was a beat of silence. "Right. I suppose it does."

"Tanner, the whole reason for us to get married was

so I could change my name, so I could run my business and Spencer couldn't find me when he got out. He's not an issue now, so there's really no reason for us to get married."

"Are you sure?" he asked, the low, silky tone sliding over her.

No, she wasn't damn well sure, but he didn't love her. Like her, yes. She looked at him and her heart swelled.

"Tanner, be serious. You only wanted to get out on your own, and it was a mutually beneficial agreement."

"Right."

"And it's easier to call it off now than if this had happened a week from now. Crazy timing, actually."

Quiet descended. The only sound was the breeze through the leaves on the cottonwoods. Usually, their rustling and tinkling calmed Laura. Tonight, they made her restless.

"You're not saying anything," she noted softly.

He sighed heavily. "I don't know what you want me to say."

"I know the timing is strange, but really, you don't need to feel obligated anymore. Not that you were in the first place. It was incredibly generous of you to help me out of a scrape and I'll never forget it, Tanner. I'll make sure the dresses and everything are returned and you're refunded every penny." She realized she was borderline babbling, but the more she talked, the more nervous she became.

Tanner pushed back his chair with an abrasive scrape and got to his feet. "Shit, do you think I care about the damn dress?" He turned around and rested his elbows on the short railing.

"Then what do you care about, Tanner?"

In the shadows, she saw a muscle tighten in his jaw. "Is it so inconceivable that I might care about you?" he asked, but his voice was grim, not tender.

Had she actually hurt him? She'd only wanted to release him from the arrangement, to convince him that she was okay with it.

"I care about you, too, but this is marriage we're talking about. And if we're not doing it for… What did they used to call them? A marriage of convenience? Then why?" She placed her hand on his shoulder. "Tanner, you married for the wrong reasons before. Do you really want to do that again?"

She saw the hurt on his face, the way his lips turned down, and a rather haunted look appeared in his eyes. "You're not Britt," he said quietly. "You're nothing like her."

"Maybe not," she whispered, "but jumping into marriage would be a mistake, don't you think? We'd set out the rules and reasons before, but now everything's changed. It would be wrong to go ahead with it without…love."

There, she'd said it. Maybe if he said it to her now, she'd be able to tell him how she felt. How the last month together had made her fall in love with him, with the man he was, with the man she could see he wanted to be. How sharing in a laugh and also sharing in his pain had made her feel closer to him than she'd ever felt to another human being.

But instead, he stepped back. "You're right, of course," he murmured. "We started this to give you some anonymity that you don't need anymore. It was a solution to a problem that no longer exists."

It hurt to hear him say it, even though she'd led him to it. "Listen," she said, "I know it's not as cut-and-dried as it might have been. We've…shared things. It's just that marriage is so huge."

"No, I get it. It has to be for the right reasons. Before it was for the greater good. That's all."

She nodded, her heart hurting.

"I can move my stuff out Saturday. I was planning on taking the day before the wedding off anyway."

Alarm shuddered through her. Right. The other benefit to their marriage was him living in her house. She would miss him so much. In just a few weeks, he'd made this place into a home. She looked forward to seeing him at the end of each day. He was someone to talk to and laugh with. Forget her deeper feelings; the basis of their relationship was friendship, and right now that seemed strained at best.

"You don't have to go, Tanner. You could stay. We could be roommates." It wasn't what she wanted from him, but neither would she kick him out. Not when he'd done so much for her.

"I don't think so, Laura. You have the ability to tell the truth about Rowan and Gavin and restore your reputation. You'll never be able to do that if you're living with a guy. No one will believe it's platonic. And Gibson's small, you know that, and old-fashioned. The whole living-together thing, it wouldn't help your situation at all."

"I don't care what people think."

"Yes," he said, "you do."

He didn't say anything more, but then he didn't have to. She did care. The only reason she hadn't spoken up before was because she'd wanted to protect Rowan.

"You have a second chance," Tanner finally said, in a voice that was quiet and sure in the darkness. "You can set the record straight. You can start over. No games, no lies, no fear. A lot of people would give anything to have that. Your decisions can be about what you want for the future, and not about reacting to what's happened in the past. A fresh start, Laura. Reach out and take it."

He was right. He was absolutely right, so why did she feel so awful?

Because she loved him. And because while he proclaimed he cared about her, he didn't love her back.

"You don't need to rush," she responded, trying to keep her voice from shaking. "You can get your things whenever."

"Thanks."

"Where will you go?"

He gave a humorless huff. "Oh, back home at first, I suppose. And then I'll start the apartment search again." He straightened and shoved his hands in his back pockets. "Well, I suppose I'd better get going."

"What?" She blinked in surprise. "You're not going to leave now, are you?"

"Under the circumstances, I think I'll spend the night at the ranch."

"Tanner…"

"Don't sweat it. I have to be there early anyway. This'll cut down on my commute."

Had it really only been days ago he'd said he was happy?

"Don't you want any supper?"

The longer the conversation continued, the firmer his voice became. "I ate at Mom and Dad's."

That was it, then. Somehow there wasn't anything more to say. Nothing to postpone his leaving; no more chances to be honest. It was just *done*.

"I'll be around for my things," he said, squeezing her arm briefly. "I'll let you know when."

All she could do was nod. She found she couldn't speak while her heart was breaking.

He wasn't even all the way out the front door when she began to cry.

Chapter Fourteen

A tap on the window had Tanner stirring from sleep.

Tap. Tap, tap. "Tanner. Get up."

It was Cole. Tanner squinted against the early morning sun and tried to stretch. Oh, right. He'd spent the night in his truck because he'd been too much of a coward to go inside.

"Keep your pants on," he grumbled, knowing Cole probably couldn't hear him. He rubbed his hand over his face and felt the night's growth, rough against his hand. Still groggy, he turned the key in the ignition, just enough to turn on the battery and push the button to lower the window.

"Mornin', sunshine. Trouble in paradise before the wedding?"

He must have looked terrible, because Cole's teasing look fled. "Oh, shit. What happened?"

"I don't wanna talk about it."

"Is there even still a wedding?"

"Cole, please." Dammit, even hours later he could still hear Laura crying. He'd gone out the front door, but she'd been on the back deck and he'd heard it. Faint, but unmistakable.

Stupid thing was, she was the one who'd made

damn sure they didn't go through with this thing. She'd said in no uncertain terms that the reason for their wedding didn't exist anymore.

And then she'd cried about it. He would never, ever understand women.

With a scowl marring his face, Cole went around the front of the truck and got in the passenger side. "You been drinking? You shouldn't be operating machinery if you're hungover."

"God no." Tanner shook his head. "I came here last night, and I just couldn't go inside. I knew you'd ask questions, that Mom would ask, and I just didn't want to talk. So I sat here for a long time. Thinking. And I guess I fell asleep."

Cole smiled a little. "Wouldn't be the first time you slept in your truck."

"Nossir."

They shared a low chuckle, and then Cole said, "What's going on?"

There wasn't much point in hiding the truth now, and besides, Cole already knew bits and pieces. "The guy—Rowan's real father? He was in jail. He was the one killed in the prison fight that was on the news yesterday."

"Holy shit."

"I know. The thing is, Cole, you guys were right in the beginning. This wedding? I was doing it so she could be Laura Hudson. No one would come looking for Laura Hudson, and she could start her own business and be safe. And free."

"Wow. Mighty nice of you, bro."

"Shut up." Tanner knew that knowing tone. Sometimes having a big brother was a pain.

"So the whole thing was for appearances? What was in it for you?"

Tanner sighed. "A place of my own, I guess. And I liked it, too. She's a good roommate. A good friend."

Cole considered for a minute. "More than a friend, Tan?"

"No." The answer came easily enough. "But…"

"Ah," Cole said, leaning back against the seat. "The world-famous 'but.'"

"But she could have been. I really care about her, Cole. And if people knew her the way I know her…and that kid. She's so damn cute. And she likes to cuddle. I wondered before how you could get so attached to Maddy's boys, but it really isn't hard, is it?"

Cole shook his head. "You know what? I think there's more to it than wanting a place of your own. What's going on with you, Tanner? You've been restless for months. I know you like your EMT volunteering, and you're a good rancher, but sometimes it feels like your heart isn't in it."

It wasn't an easy question to answer. It was true. He loved the ranch, but he wasn't as passionate about it as Cole. And he did love his work as a paramedic, even if the town was so small it only warranted a volunteer service. At least he felt that he was helping people. That he was doing something meaningful.

That he had a purpose. He swallowed. There was more to him than a hick cowboy who knew how to two-step and do tequila shots. He'd spent a lot of years enjoying the single life, but once those days were done—right around the time Britt had asked for a divorce—he'd found he didn't have much left.

Tanner glanced at his brother. "If I'm being completely honest, the ranch is your thing. I love it, and I don't mind the work, but it's not really what I want. I want to feel like I'm doing something to help people. To do something important to make someone else's life better. I know that ranching's important, and we provide work and food and preserve the land, but it's not the same."

"Do you want to leave?"

"Tough questions this morning."

"Ones that maybe needed to be asked a while ago." Cole crossed an ankle over his knee and tapped his fingers against his thigh. "Because somewhere in all this, Laura fits in, and you need to figure out where."

Did Tanner want to leave the ranch? Funny thing—the past month or so he'd been far happier at work. He'd caught himself whistling, or humming the tune of a recent song on the radio. There'd been that horrible day when he'd responded to the tractor rollover, but he knew that bad calls were part of the territory. Still, the good had outweighed the bad. And at night he'd gone home to Laura and Rowan.

A lump swelled in his throat. Ever since they'd made their agreement and he'd moved into her house, life had changed. It had become richer, fuller. Maybe being there, with her, was what gave him something to work for.

Her face when she'd seen him fixing the steps, or smiling at him across the table at night had filled him with a simple joy that lifted his heart. Her gentle, understanding touch had helped him get through one of the worst days of his life. She'd tried, too, to do nice things for him. Like when he'd gotten into bed after she hung sheets on the line, and he'd chuckled at the strangely placed puckers where she'd put the clothes-pins, or how she'd attempted to make doughnuts because she knew they were his favorite.

They'd been far more than roommates. And it had been far more than a legal name change on the line.

Cole's voice was uncharacteristically gentle as he asked, "Do you love her, Tanner?"

Tanner's response was ragged with emotion. "Yes, I think I do."

Cole slapped Tanner's leg. "Well. Hell of a thing, isn't it? Turns a man inside out and scares him to death."

Tanner frowned. "Don't be so smug."

"The way I see it, you have two choices. You can be miserable forever, or you can tell her how you really feel. Maybe she'll send you on your way, but you won't know until you try."

The fact that Laura was crying last night gave him a sliver of hope. "I've had love kick me in the teeth before, you know. I'm not too crazy about taking a chance on a repeat, but if this is the real thing, I think I need to find out."

"Yep. And since the wedding day is almost here, time's a-wastin'. I'm gonna get to work, since it looks like we'll be a man short today. My advice to you is to go inside, let Ma cook you a big breakfast, take a long shower and for God's sake, shave. Then go make your case."

"You always were the bossy one."

"And you, little bro, were the softhearted one who hid behind charm and humor. But I know you. No one can love a woman better than you. You're the kind that goes all in, heart and soul."

"Go on, you're getting all mushy on me. Gross." Tanner shoved Cole's shoulder. "And you're right. I'm hungry and need a shower and a shave."

They both hopped out of the truck, Tanner turning toward the house and Cole to the barns. But then Tanner called back, "Hey, Cole?"

"Yuh."

"Thanks. I needed that."

Cole grinned. "Wasn't that long ago I was in your shoes. Anytime, Tan."

LAURA SLEPT POORLY. Instead of going into Rowan's room, she'd gone to her old room—Tanner's room—and crawled beneath the covers. She didn't want to wake the baby with her crying. But once in there she'd been surrounded by his things, by his scent still in the sheets, and she'd felt a loneliness so profound it was as if someone had bored a hole clear through her, leaving an empty, painful place behind.

Letting him go had been the right thing to do. He didn't need to be obligated to her in any way, nor had he ever been. But oh, she was going to miss him.

In the harsh light of morning, things were no better. Laura took one look at her face and grimaced. She forced herself to take a shower and put on a little makeup so she didn't look as ragged as she felt. Rowan was up and all smiles, which boosted Laura's spirits in some moments and made her sad in others. All she kept thinking was *I love him. And he left.*

But you pushed him away, she reminded herself. *You made sure he wouldn't come back.*

After a good hour and a half of moping, dealing with Rowan's morning routine and using up tissues, she took a deep breath. This was stupid. She'd said that it was only going to be truth from now on, but she hadn't been honest, had she? She'd hidden her true feelings. She'd told him to go and had used their original plan as a shield against being hurt or humiliated. And she'd sent him away, when he was the best thing to happen to her since giving birth to Rowan.

What did she want? She paced the kitchen, stopping to occasionally watch Rowan playing happily in her playpen. She wanted Tanner. She wanted him back in this house. She wanted to kiss him without feeling as if she were breaking a rule, and she wanted to see him holding Rowan in his arms and showing her the flowers and leaves and buzzing insects. He didn't think so, but she knew he'd make a wonderful father. He was patient, kind and loving. She, simply put, wanted Tanner Hudson in her life. For good.

And if that was what she wanted, what was she going to do about it? Tell him the truth? Tell him that she wanted this marriage to go ahead anyway? Tell him that she loved him?

The very idea scared her to death. And yet she knew if she didn't try, she'd regret it forever. The wedding was scheduled for Sunday. She hadn't phoned her grandparents and she had no idea what he'd told his family last night. But she hadn't cancelled the justice of the peace or the flowers or anything. Why?

Maybe because she didn't want to believe it was really over.

For months now, she'd let herself be urged along. All her talk about being strong and independent was a farce. She'd fallen for Spence's charms—that was mistake one. Then she'd accepted Gavin's help, and because of her fear, she'd damaged his reputation along with her own. She had let Tanner come to her rescue… Ugh.

For so long, she'd told herself it was for Rowan's protection, but when it came down to it, she was a coward. And she didn't like herself very much for it. She was better than this. She could be better than this.

If she wanted Tanner back, she needed to make a stand. She would have to conquer the things she'd shied away from. A new hope filled her breast, warm and expansive. She knew the perfect first step. Just as soon as she made a few phone calls.

Chapter Fifteen

Tanner smoothed his already smooth hair and lowered his hand, holding it out in front of him, hoping it was steady. It was not.

Ever since Laura had called the house, asking if they could talk, he'd been a wreck. He was terrified that she wanted to discuss details of canceling everything. Meanwhile, he was trying to work up the nerve to tell her he loved her. And Rowan, too. God, that little girl had him wrapped around her finger.

He looked at the little house that—as recently as yesterday—he'd called home. Plain, but cute. A little paint here, some flowers there. He was proud of the changes he'd made in a few short weeks, knowing they'd made Laura's life a little sunnier. He could do more of that for her. He'd work every day to make it better if that was what he needed to do for them to be together.

Taking a shaky breath, he got out of the truck. He'd put on what he considered dressy clothes—khaki cotton pants and a pale blue button-down shirt, one button open at the neck.

The windows were open, and a delicious smell wafted out of the kitchen. It filled his nostrils as he climbed the steps. Man, he was as nervous as a teenager on his first date. The smell was vanilla and cinnamon and nutmeg... Oh Lord, had Laura been baking again? He grinned, loving her even more for her ineptitude in the kitchen, not in spite of it. He couldn't give a good damn if she could cook or not. He'd eat mac and cheese every day if she'd just say they had a chance. That she felt the same way about him.

He knocked on the door, slightly sick to his stomach.

The last time he'd shown up with the intent to propose, she'd worn a pretty spring dress. Today she was wearing jeans and a slate-blue T-shirt, her hair gathered up in a ponytail. With it pulled back from her face, he noticed how her skin glowed and her eyes twinkled, big and blue. "Hi," he said, and when she smiled, it felt as if his tongue thickened and he couldn't say anything else.

"Come on in, Tanner." She stepped back.

As he entered the kitchen, the first thing he noticed was the platter of doughnuts.

The kitchen itself was spotless, but a deep fryer sat on the counter, the only evidence she'd made them herself. Unlike the last burnt offering, these sweets were perfectly round, with little holes in the middle, and rolled in plain sugar. They looked—and smelled—incredible.

"It's a peace offering," she said. "I had some help, of course. Gram came over and helped so I didn't screw anything up. Including bringing her deep fryer so I could regulate the temperature of the grease."

She'd made his favorite thing. Laura, who burned

nearly everything she set her hand to, had made beautiful, golden-brown, delicious-smelling doughnuts.

She picked up the platter and held it out. "Try one," she said, and because she looked so hopeful, he took one, even though eating was the last thing he wanted to do.

The sweet was still warm. The sugar clung to his fingers the moment he picked up the doughnut, and he obligingly took a bite. It was pure heaven. Cakey, not too moist, not dry, rich with cinnamon and nutmeg. He chewed and swallowed, then smiled at her. "Delicious. So good."

Her face relaxed, pleased with his verdict. "God, I'm so relieved," she said, putting the plate down on the table.

"You didn't try one?" He took another bite. Half-wished for a glass of cold milk to wash it down with, but he wasn't going to ask.

She shook her head, her ponytail bobbing. "I couldn't eat," she admitted. "I was too nervous."

He finished the doughnut and brushed the sugar off his hands. "Nervous? About what?"

She bit her lip. "About seeing you. About the things I need to say that I didn't say last night."

"Me, too," he admitted.

The color drained from her face. "Can I go first, Tanner? I think I really need to get this off my chest."

Maybe he wouldn't have to tell her at all. A peace offering might only mean she wanted to preserve their friendship, when what he wanted was so much more. If she shut him down, what point would there be in telling her how he felt?

"Do I need to sit down for this?"

She shook her head. "Rowan's asleep. Let's take a walk outside for a few minutes. It's about time I enjoyed my yard, I think."

She slid on a pair of sandals and they headed outside, walking across the grass towards the trees where it was cooler. The early-afternoon sun was hot and welcome, and Tanner briefly thought of his brother and father out haying today. He felt a little guilty, not being with them, but also as though this day was an important one for his future.

They stopped by the rosebush. Laura tentatively reached out, being careful of thorns, and plucked a delicate pink blossom from the shrub.

"I love wild roses, don't you?" she asked. "They're so soft and pretty and smell so nice, and yet they're hardy and grow just about anywhere. Even in this yard, where the ground is hard and the drainage isn't great, here they are."

Tanner peered down at her, more sure than ever that he was in love with her. "Is this some sort of metaphor, Laura?"

She looked up at him, squinting a little against the sunlight. "Yes, it is. I'd like to think that I've become stronger the last few months."

"You've always been strong," Tanner began, but Laura shook her head and cut him off.

"No, I haven't. I've hidden behind my situation. I've used my fear as a crutch. I've hurt people telling myself it was for the greater good. But it was selfish of me, Tanner. Last night, I lied to you. I had promised myself after I saw the lawyer that I would only tell the truth from now on. And then, only hours later when you were in front of me, I lied." She turned the flower around and around in her fingers. "I need to tell you the truth now."

"Which is?"

The flower stopped spinning. "I love you, Tanner. I know that wasn't the plan. I know I wasn't supposed to. But I do anyway. I love your kindness, and your sense of humor, your duty, and honor. I love your big heart and the way you make me feel like I'm some-body. I love the way you hold my daughter in your arms, and the way you look at her when you think I'm not looking. This was supposed to be a mutually beneficial arrangement, but I broke the rules. I fell in love with you."

The rose trembled in her hand. "I don't expect you to feel the same way. And Lord knows it's fast and I come with a crap ton of baggage. But I promised to tell the truth and that's it. I love you."

It was so unexpected, so heartfelt and...for God's sake, she'd given him an itemized list of what she liked about him. It was almost too much to comprehend. But the one phrase that stuck in his brain, keeping it all together, was "I love you."

He took the nearly wilted flower from her nervous fingers and tucked it gently behind her ear. "I slept in my truck last night," he confessed, unsure of where to begin, but knowing he'd somehow get to the right point eventually. "I couldn't stand the idea of going inside and answering questions. I was so confused, you see. Taking Spencer out of the equation changed everything, and made me look long and hard at us and what we might look like without him pushing us together."

He brushed his thumb over the crest of her cheek.

"It forced me to look at why I was marrying you. And I figured out it wasn't so I could have a place of my own, or even so you could change your name. Those were just excuses. The reasons I told myself. But deep down it was something more. It was me searching for meaning in my life."

She pulled his hand down from her face. "Tanner, I know you're not a hundred percent happy on the ranch. I know you volunteer as a paramedic because you like helping people. But I can't be some pet project to make you feel better. Not now. Last night, I said that marriage had to be for the right reasons, and I still believe that."

"No, no, you don't understand." Instead of letting her drop his hand, he linked his fingers with hers, holding them tightly. "What I mean is, my thinking that there had to be something more was true, but it doesn't have to do with the ranch or a job or anything like that. The something more I needed was for in here." He lifted their joined hands and pressed them to his heart. "When everything went wrong a few years ago, I told myself I was not the marrying kind. After all, that's what I'd been told. That I was good for a good time, but not forever. But she was wrong, Laura. *She* was built that way, not me. I believed what she said for far too long until you showed me something different. Turns out, I'm not a party guy. I'm a family man. The weeks spent here, with you…that's the happiest I ever remember being. Fixing the little things around here was a joy because it felt, well, it felt like I was doing it to my home, too. The thing is, Laura, we've been playing house. And I don't want to play. I want it to be real."

"By real, you mean?"

"I mean," he said, his heart clubbing against his ribs, "that I fell in love with you, too. With your sweetness, and the way you love your daughter, and the compassion you have deep inside. That day when I came home and you'd burned those silly doughnuts…" He squeezed her fingers, gazed into her eyes. "That was such a horrible day. But you sat with me, and held me, and made everything better. You cared for me in a way no one has ever done before. You treated me…" His voice broke a little. "Honey, you treated me like the man I wanted to become, rather than the man I thought I was."

Tears gathered in her eyes. "You really love me?"

He nodded. "I do. And you are stronger than you think, you know. I knew that the day I sat in the back of the ambulance and held your hand as you brought Rowan into the world. You were fierce, and gorgeous, and beautiful. I think both our lives changed that day. You became a mom, and I caught a glimpse of what my life was meant to be." He drew her close and looped his arms low around her back. "With you. If you'll still have me."

She didn't answer. But she didn't have to, either, because she jumped up on tiptoe and wrapped her arms around his neck, hugging him close. He closed his eyes and tightened his embrace, feeling all the pieces of his life that had been flung far and wide last night click back into place.

They held each other for a few minutes, enjoying the sensation of giving their feelings liberty at last. When Laura pulled back, Tanner kept one hand on the curve of her back and put the other beneath her chin, cupping it gently in his fingers. Then he finally kissed her the way he'd wanted to for weeks. With nothing between them—no arrangement, no worry about what was appropriate, no secrets. Just love, and the simmering attraction they'd been denying for too long.

"Mmm," she murmured against his lips. "It feels good to finally do that."

"I know," he said, kissing the tip of her ear. "Know what's better? We can do that anytime we want now."

"But I might not get anything done, because I'll want to do it all the time."

He chuckled, down low. "It?" When she blushed, he wanted to wrap her in his arms and hold her close forever. "Sweetheart, this might seem stupid and traditional of me, but I kind of like the idea of waiting for the wedding night."

Blushing or not, she lifted her chin defiantly. "Well, I can wait a little longer if you can."

"You still want to go through with the wedding?"

She nodded. "I'm sure, Tanner. We have the place, and the justice of the peace, and I have the dress. It feels right. I want you here with me, and with Rowan." She touched his face. "I want you to be her daddy, and show her flowers, and teach her to ride a horse and read her stories at bedtime."

He was so honored, so humbled. Every decision Laura had made in the last year and a half had been for Rowan. For her to choose him, to trust him... "I want that, too," he said. "And someday, maybe a few more."

She grinned. "Holy cats. We're going to do this, aren't we?"

He nodded, then lifted her up by the waist and held

her tightly. "Yes, we are. And we're going to do it for the right reasons."

"For love," she said.

"For love."

Chapter Sixteen

Every bride wanted a sunny day for her wedding, and
at dawn Laura wasn't sure that was what she'd get. But
then around 9:00 a.m., the showers stopped, the clouds
drifted away and the sky turned a brilliant blue with a
few white puffs gliding along for contrast.

She was getting married today. Today!

The ceremony was at two, with a small tea and
sweets reception to follow at her grandparents' house.
They'd insisted on hosting, as Laura's only family
present, and she'd been touched. Now the day would
be even more special because she and Tanner didn't
have to pretend to be in love. They were truly in love,
and it was marvelous.

After she'd fed Rowan lunch, Laura put her down
for an early nap. Then she went to work dressing, putting on her makeup and twisting her hair into a low,
classy chignon at the base of her skull. She teased
loose a few pieces of hair at the side of her face to give
herself more of a romantic look. Inspired, she put on
some old shoes and walked through the wet grass to
the rosebush. She clipped a couple of blossoms and
put the stems in a damp paper towel.

Once Rowan woke, Laura changed her and put her

in the pink ruffled dress she and Tanner had bought, and slipped tiny white shoes on her feet. With excitement drumming through her veins, Laura tucked the ring she'd bought for Tanner into her purse, made sure the diaper bag was stocked and rushed out the door to make the last stop before the park: the florist.

By the time she got to the parking area near the gazebo, she saw her grandparents' car and Tanner's truck already there. Cole and Maddy had arrived, too. Cole was dressed in a suit, but with the customary black boots and hat. She smiled, and then she saw Tanner. He was dressed exactly the same as Cole, and her heart thumped in approval. No matter what he said, he was her cowboy. Everyone was milling about together when Tanner finally noticed their arrival. 3Laura's new pumps made clicking sounds on the asphalt of the parking lot.

He came forward, all long strides and big smiles. "Hello, bride."

"Hello, groom." She had Rowan on one arm and her bouquet in her other hand. Without missing a beat, Tanner reached for Rowan and Rowan put out her arms for him.

"Hello, sweetheart," he said, dropping a kiss on her head. "You look so pretty."

He looked down at Laura. "After today, I get to be her daddy."

"Yes, you do," she said. "Isn't she lucky?"

Tanner planted a firm kiss on Laura's lips.

"Hey, now, you two. None of that until the end of the ceremony. Sheesh. Don't you know anything?"

Cole was teasing. Maddy smiled beside him, and

even Tanner's parents looked happier about the wedding than they had the last time Laura saw them.

And Gramps—well, he was grinning from ear to ear and held Gram's hand as if they were twenty again.

They all walked to the gazebo, where the justice of the peace waited. Just before they got there though, Laura paused. "Maybe Gram could hold Rowan during the ceremony? Besides, you're missing something."

As Tanner handed off the baby, Laura plucked the wild rose from her bouquet. She'd had the florist bind the stem and substitute it for the white rose boutonniere she'd ordered. The other rose was tucked into Laura's hair. "Let me pin this on you," she said, smiling up at him.

The pink was a few shades darker than her dress, but it didn't matter. They both knew the flowers had meaning, and Tanner held her simple bouquet of roses and alstromeria while she pinned the blossom on his lapel.

"Now I think we're ready." She put her hand briefly on his chest.

"I know I'm ready," he said.

He took her hand and they climbed the gazebo steps together. Made promises, gave each other rings, sealed it with a kiss. It was remarkably short, but Laura committed every moment to her memory. She couldn't take her eyes off Tanner, and sniffled when he whispered, "I love you" after he kissed her.

But the best part was when they were announced as Tanner and Laura Hudson. That, she decided, felt like victory.

SHE DIDN'T GET a chance to speak to Maddy until they were drinking champagne at her grandparents' place.

The bubbly had been a surprise, and meant all the more because it came from Tanner's mom and dad. Laura knew more than one truth needed to be set right, so she found Maddy and offered her a piece of wedding cake.

Laura put down the plate and touched the woman's arm. "Maddy, there's something I need to say to you."

"Sure." Her response was much more relaxed than it had been in the past. Laura wondered if one day they might be friends, as well as sisters-in-law. It went without saying that Cole would pop the question one of these days.

"Letting people think Gavin was the father of my baby was wrong. I don't know why I ever thought it was a good idea, other than I was scared. But I could have found another way. I made you promise not to say anything before, but I release you from that now. If you want to set the record straight about Gavin at any point, you're free to do so. And I'll do the same."

"Thank you, Laura. Though it really doesn't matter now, does it?"

Laura shrugged. "Someday Rowan will be going to school with your boys. They don't need to deal with that kind of thing. I'm not planning on taking a page out in the paper or anything, but I'll do what I can to restore his reputation. He was too good a man."

Maddy smiled wistfully. "Yes, he was. And now we've both ended up with good men."

Laura laughed and glanced over at Tanner, talking with his brother. "I don't know what I did to deserve Tanner, but I'm feeling pretty blessed."

"You truly do love him."

"I didn't plan to. Tried not to." She winked at Maddy. "I hear you know what that's like."

They laughed a little, but then Laura sobered. "Thank you, Maddy. For being here today. For being so forgiving."

Maddy smiled. "I got that from Cole. And I'm glad to see Tanner happy. The rest we'll figure out as we go along."

Cole looked over and touched his watch. Maddy sighed. "I'm sorry. I've left the boys at my mom's, but they have plans tonight. We have to dash out."

"Of course. I'm just glad you and Cole came. It meant a lot to both of us."

To her surprise, Maddy gave her a quick hug. "Congratulations."

When Maddy had darted away, Tanner came over. "Mrs. Hudson, did Maddy just hug you?"

She smiled. "Yes, she did. And please, call me Mrs. Hudson some more. I like it."

"Mrs. Hudson." His smile was lopsided and he dropped a kiss on her lips. Then he slid behind her and put his arms around her, so her back was pressed against his chest. She felt safe and secure in his arms. She looked around the room. The people they cared about most were here. Cole and Maddy were just making their way out to pick up the twins. Laura's grandmother and grandfather were ensconced on the sofa, still holding hands. Tanner's mom, Ellen, held a very sleepy Rowan in her arms, while John sat in an armchair and talked to Charlie about the ongoing issue of installing a traffic light in town.

"Happy?" he asked.

Laura put her hands over his forearms and held him close. "The happiest," she said.

And she was.

* * * * *

LET'S TALK
Romance

For exclusive extracts, competitions
and special offers, find us online:

f facebook.com/millsandboon

◎ @millsandboonuk

𝕏 @millsandboon

Or get in touch on 0844 844 1351*

For all the latest titles coming soon, visit
millsandboon.co.uk/nextmonth